I0788161

MAGICK TRILOGY

by

J.E. Taylor

Magick Trilogy© January 2024 by J.E. Taylor
3rd Edition

Magick Trilogy

Accused of overdosing her fiancé, Paige Turner must clear her name. But with all the evidence pointing in her direction, proving her innocence may be an impossible feat, especially since she's locked up in a sanitarium.

To make matters worse, her dead fiancé doesn't want to move on. He is happy to haunt her until Austin, an orderly at the hospital, takes notice of Paige, and she responds to his attention.

Then her fiancé's ghost becomes enraged. And there is nothing simple about dealing with an angry spirit in an insane asylum.

When the ghost takes possession of Austin, Paige must figure out a way to free him before her fiancé takes over for good. But banishing a ghost is tricky, especially when her magick skills are rusty.

Will her spell save Austin?

Or will it just transplant the furious ghost into a different body, one primed for revenge, and doom them both?

This trilogy includes the following books:

Magick

Black Magick

Practical Magick

If you have any triggers, or issues with dark situations, group action, coercion, and violence, then *Magic Trilogy* is not for you. But if you like a little kink in your style and aren't afraid of a dark undertone in your stories, then, by all means, pick up the book... if you dare.

Magick
Chapter 1

"ARE YOU READY YET?"

Paige turned away from the mirror at her desk; the liner paused in the space where her lips had just been. She smiled at April, her best friend and sorority sister. "Give me a couple of more minutes and I'll be done," she said, and went back to outline her full lips with the berry liner. Once she was satisfied, she dabbed a brush in the bright gloss, painting the space between the lines with a blood red shine.

When she finished, she rubbed her lips together and leaned back, studying the effects. A smile spread, making her teeth seem unnaturally white against the red, and she glanced at April in the mirror.

"I wish I could do that with my eyes," April said with a sigh. Paige glanced at her reflection and the sexy upturn she had outlined at the edges of her eyes. That, along with the thick mascara, really highlighted her blue eyes, and she shifted her gaze to April's dark brown eyes devoid of make-up.

April was never big on make-up, but she really didn't need to be. Her face could have represented the natural beauty of a mid-western farm girl and the only thing she seemed to splurge on was a dab of blush and the highlight of a clear gloss on her pouty lips.

"I can hook you up if you want me to." Paige stood and waved her hand at the seat she just vacated.

April sent a soft smile and a shake of her head before her gaze dropped to her watch. "We're already late. Besides, Hunter and Max are downstairs, and I'm sure they're getting antsy."

Paige let out a little laugh. "Hunter is always impatient." She turned and picked up the black dress, pouring herself into the Elvira costume. With a few tugs here and there, she smoothed out the front and turned toward April with her arms out and eyebrows raised.

"Damn, girl, you just might turn me tonight." April pressed her lips together against a smile.

Paige rolled her eyes. "Seriously?"

"Hell, yeah." She pounded her staff on the ground to punctuate her statement, and Paige laughed.

"I wish the party was here," she said and collected her ID badge, dropping it in the little black clutch, and headed towards the door.

"Me, too," April agreed.

"You trying to clean up your reputation?" Paige waved at the Bo-Peep outfit, a smile toying with her glossy lips.

April sent a smirk in her direction.

"Max agreed to be a sheep?" Paige asked as she stopped at the doorway to close and lock her bedroom door.

"No," April said with a laugh. "He's actually a wolf."

"That makes perfect sense."

Max always had this hungry leer whenever April was around. It was almost as bad as taking a peek at an X-rated movie. His intentions were clearly displayed on every inch of his expressive face.

They reached the stairs and paused, giving each other the nod. It was time to descend the famous Delta house stairwell. Delta was the grandest sorority house on campus with all the charm of a Georgia mansion, complete with a heart-shaped stairway. Southern charm transplanted into the cool northern woods, out of place in the small New England town, but perfect for the elite girls of Dartmouth.

Hunter's green eyes widened as they stepped onto the landing, and Paige grinned at the flash of heat that colored his cheeks under the pale makeup. The slow drizzle of fake blood cascading from his neck created a stain on his shirt that caught her attention, and she followed the latest drop, licking her lips at the thought of trailing her tongue along the path of the sugary substance. He did a fantastic job with the vampire victim costume they'd discussed, especially the wound with dripping blood.

"Wow," he mouthed, scanning her as she descended.

Paige traded a smile with April as they reached the bottom step. Max was in a full werewolf costume, complete with a wolf-head mask, so his reaction to April was hidden behind a mass of hair and teeth.

When Hunter's gaze drifted to the display of pure innocence next to Paige, he smirked and raised an eyebrow. They all knew what a farce April's feigned innocence was. After all, she had a legendary reputation for bedding whomever, whenever she felt the need strike. It wasn't until Max snagged her attention that her run-around days had fizzled, and now all of her focus was on him.

Hunter had never sampled the goods, not even at the out-of-control frat parties she frequented. At least that's what he professed, but Paige was never sure. Hell, if April came onto her in earnest, she was sure it would be a tempting thought, but Hunter had her heart, along with every fiber of her body.

He held out his elbow and escorted her to Max's car, idling at the curb. Hunter's hand was warm and inviting on the small of her back, and as always, his touch sent tingles of pleasure through her. When she slid into the car, the slit in her dress exposed her milky thigh and Hunter's gaze locked on it. His hunger magnified, turning his eyes that bright, horny green she was accustomed to. The minute he sat in the adjoining seat, his hand found her skin, and he grinned as he slid it higher than the slit allowed.

"Hunter!" Breathless, she scolded him before either April or Max stepped into the vehicle.

He gave her a squeeze and removed his hand just as Max opened the passenger door for April.

Hunter flashed a playful smile in Paige's direction with the silent promise he was going to investigate her further as soon as he got her alone. Paige's insides turned to a slow simmer as her mind wandered to the same place. Hunter was a stunning lover. His touch was like magic, and she couldn't wait to wrap her legs around him.

The moment the engine cut, the music from the party reached into the space of the car.

"Catch you inside?" Max said. His gaze met Hunter's for a minute and before Paige could ask, both Max and April got out.

Hunter lingered, taking his time stepping out, and then he reached his hand inside, taking hers and helping her out. As soon as she was on her feet, he closed the door and took her hand, leading her around the side of the house, instead of into the belly of the party.

"Where are you taking me?" Paige asked when they crossed the yard, heading toward the massive cemetery bordering fraternity row.

"Somewhere quiet," he said, leading her through the broken links of the fence.

"Um, these heels aren't suited for walking across the grass," Paige said after a couple of slow steps with her stilettos stabbing the earth.

Hunter paused and looked down at her feet. When his eyes met hers, he smiled and scooped her up in his arms. "Better?" he asked as he continued heading toward the heart of the cemetery. His voice was soft and sensual against her ear.

A small pond sat at the very center of the cemetery, lined with cattails and mums.

Benches dotted the circular path and the moonlight reflecting off the water painted the surrounding cemetery stones with an eerie glow.

It was the perfect atmosphere for a Halloween scare, but when Hunter took a knee in front of her, Paige's heart began its frantic pump. She stared at his iridescent eyes, stunned into silence as he reached into his pocket. The refracting light caught the stone as he held out the ring.

"Paige, we've been together for as long as I can remember and I can't remember a time I didn't love you. I can't imagine a future without you standing by my side and I figured tonight..." He paused and looked up at the full moon and around at the cemetery and back at her. "With a full moon on your favorite holiday, was the perfect night to ask. Will you marry me?"

Paige's gaze bounced between his bright eyes, his lips and the ring, and her hand fluttered to her mouth with a gasp. The shock of the moment blew as her eyes dropped back to the shining diamond. It was as if a lightning bolt hit her and jumpstarted her heart again and Paige flew into his arms, voicing one word in a husky whisper before her lips crushed his. The 'yes' echoed over the pond and they hit the ground.

"Baby, the ring," he said underneath her kiss.

Paige pulled away and steadied herself on him, letting him slide the diamond onto her left hand before his lips were back on hers. He rolled, pinning her on the damp grass, and Paige squealed, arching away from the cold.

His chuckle met hers as he climbed to his feet and extended his hand to help her up. His grin was infectious and she couldn't help matching it.

"I think I messed your lipstick up," he said, trying to minimize the damage with his thumb, but all it did was smear the lipstick on her face even more.

"I don't care." She pushed him onto the bench and straddled him, resuming the kiss. Each swipe of their tongues sent a line of heat right to her pussy, and he knew it. His hands yanked at her skirt, hiking it up, adjusting until there was nothing between them but the thin fabric of her underwear.

When the quiet whisper of his zipper intruded on the dark, she pulled away and stared down into his bright eyes. "In a cemetery?" she asked as he moved the line of her panties aside, plunging his hard cock into her with a smile and a nod.

"That is so kinky. And to think, I didn't even have to cast a spell for this," she chuckled, moving with the slow cadence of his hips.

"I bet you never dreamed of fucking your fiancé on all Hallows eve in a cemetery," he whispered against the skin of her neck. His nibbles sent shivers through her.

"Dreamed? Yes, I've dreamed of it, but it was never this perfect," she said, tilting back to take a look at the moon as he buried his face between her breasts. "This is pure magic." Her breathy exhale turned into more of a moan and the spark in his eyes lit, igniting the passion, matching their hip thrusts and yanking an eerie howl from her.

"Do you believe in magic?" he whispered, his husky voice laden with the drive controlling his hips. He winked just before his eyes rolled back and a groan surfaced.

He pulled her into a kiss, drowning out his groan of ecstasy.

Every muscle tightened and then shuddered before they both slouched from the post-release relaxation. Paige rested her forehead on his before straightening and inspecting the ring on her finger. Moonlight danced on the finely cut stone and she grinned.

"I love you," Hunter whispered.

Paige gave him a gentle kiss. "Thank you for making this so perfect," she said when their lips parted. "There is no other way you could have outdone this." She waved her hand at the surroundings. However macabre they seemed to the normal soul, this was the perfect spot to claim their future.

"Max thought I was nuts when I told him I was going to ask you to marry me here."

Her laughter rang out, and in the distance, a door opened in the back of the fraternity house, letting the music flow over the dark and quiet landscape.

Magick
Chapter 2

THE PARTY WAS IN full swing when they walked in. April danced in the center of a half-dozen guys, all of whom had a hand on her somewhere. Paige knew the wasted look in April's eyes, and she glanced at Hunter.

"How long were we out there?" She hooked her thumb over her shoulder.

Hunter scanned the room and then glanced at his watch. "Apparently, too long," he said.

"It couldn't have been more than an hour," Paige said.

He slid his gaze to hers. "You don't think I could do an hour?"

A smile played on Paige's lips and Max made his way through the crowd, gave Hunter a pat on the back, and handed him the two beers in one of his hands before heading toward where April was entertaining the boys. He glanced over his shoulder just before the crowd swallowed him and Paige swore there was a glare in the mask she hadn't noticed before. It was an eerie illusion that disappeared as quickly as he did, but it left the impression that Max was angry.

At her.

She blinked the unease away and focused on Hunter, taking the beer he offered.

"You might want to fix your make-up," he whispered in her ear, and she pulled away.

"Why?" She scanned the smear of red on his face. "If I look anything like you, it looks like we've both been doing some ravishing." She clinked the neck of her bottle against his and took a sip. The beer wasn't cold, and she forced the swallow down with a grimace.

Hunter didn't seem to mind his, and guzzled it down. When she offered hers, he traded the empty and Paige decided to take a look at just how off her make-up really was. She made her way through the tight crowd, ignoring the hands that grabbed at her and the bodies that bumped against her. That was the status quo for the annual Halloween bash; so was some tantalizing show, like the one April seemed to put on for the crowd.

Paige finally squeezed herself into the vacant bathroom and closed the door on the thriving music and the increasingly raunchy crowd. The reflection in the mirror pulled a laugh from her. The Elvira in the mirror looked as if she had been through a zombie war. The ruined make-up wasn't just focused on her lips. Even her mascara had fallen subject to arbitrary smears. Combined with Hunter's white base. She really looked awful.

A small stack of the rough industrial bathroom hand towels sat on the edge of the sink, and Paige grabbed a handful and soaked them in warm water. The removal of make-up was as painstaking as the application and when she was done, she stepped back, satisfied with the clean skin. With her fingers as a comb, she reduced her hair to a sleeker flow and smiled at the change. The door opened, pulling her attention away from the mirror.

Max stood in the entry without the mask.

"I thought you may have gotten lost," he said. He crossed his arms and leaned his back against the door, blocking her way out. His less than conspicuous study of her made her shift.

"I'll get out of your way." She tried gracefully to get around him to the door, but he remained in place like a solid sentinel.

"You don't really want to go out there yet," he said.

"Why not?"

The way he raised his eyebrows set her on edge, and when he stepped closer and stared down at her with his piercing blue eyes, she swallowed hard.

"What is happening out there?" She meant it to come out much stronger, but it sounded meek and a little unsteady. His slow smile sent a shiver down her spine.

"It's an impromptu bachelor party." His eyes rose to the ceiling, away from hers.

"Move." This time her voice carried authority, but the command didn't garnish the results she expected. Max moved, but he pushed her into the corner of the bathroom against the wall, pinning her in place with his body. "That's not what I meant!"

"You didn't drink your beer, did you?" It wasn't a question, and she narrowed her eyes.

A pinch pulled her attention away from Max's face and she looked down as he pulled an empty syringe from her exposed thigh. "You ass," she whispered and glared at him until the muscles in her face slackened with the introduction of the drugs.

"If it's any consolation, Hunter was just as difficult to persuade, and he drank his beer," he whispered as her world spun into a dizzy swirl. "But the minute April unbuckled his pants; he succumbed to the inevitable display."

The bang at the bathroom door made both of them jump. Max dumped the syringe in the garbage and wrapped his arm around Paige's waist, leading her to the locked door. With a quick twist of his wrist on the knob, the wood swung open, and Paige stared into one of the other fraternity brother's faces. The ruckus beyond pulled her slow gaze.

It seemed the party had become clothing optional, and those dancing had taken on a lewd quality that her mind couldn't quite wrap around. A few blinks and she understood. The Halloween bash had morphed into a giant orgy and right in the middle of the action lay Hunter with women trading places between his cock, his hands, and his mouth. April looked straight at Paige as she climbed onto the table and straddled his face. To her shock, Hunter's mouth found the offered pussy and April smiled, spreading her legs wider for him before she leaned forward. Her gaze found Paige's and kept eye contact while she opened her mouth, swallowing Hunter's hard cock.

The fire of rage at someone else benefiting from Hunter's touch bloomed strength into Paige's lax muscles and she struggled in Max's grip. He navigated her through the mass of fornication, marching her right into Hunter's field of vision. But Hunter's eyes were closed, so any recognition of what was truly happening was masked by whatever fantasies played behind his eyelids.

"Hunter," Paige said, her voice nothing but a drugged slur and her legs wobbled. Max lowered her to her knees, pulling her legs wide before stripping the dress.

"I have dreamed of this," he whispered in her ear, and the rip of fabric preceded the feel of his fingers twirling her clit.

Max pressed against her back, but she couldn't argue, couldn't say no to this bizarre ritual. Not with Hunter in full compliance mode, his hands now joining the same plunge as his tongue, and Paige felt her own heat as she watched his fingers slowly fucking her roommate with as much seductive care as he usually showed her.

Despite the aggravation, Paige also felt the first seeds of lust as she watched the spectacle. The knowledge she was now a participant as opposed to an onlooker pushed her farther into the land of decadence and she moaned, accepting the stimulation, almost welcoming it as much as Hunter.

More hands joined in the exploration of her flesh, but it was Max's seductive finger twirl that pushed her over the edge. April's moan increased and Hunter's wet sucking sound filled Paige's ears. Her friend's cum spouted like a geyser, covering Hunter's face with her juices. His groan followed and April's moan drowned into the cum sucking sound Paige was familiar with and then April rolled off Hunter, leaving him out of breath and twitching.

Hunter's eyes blinked open, and he lifted his head, scanning the room before his head fell back. When his stoned gaze passed over hers, Max whispered in her ear.

"Come for me, Paige. Come for me like April did for Hunter. Drench my fingers, baby."

Hunter's gaze bounced back to hers. Max wasn't the only one caressing her, and his eyes widened. Max played her until her entire body seized with the orgasm, ripping a moan from her throat.

"Fuck, yeah," Max said, sliding his fingers into her pussy while Hunter watched.

Hunter's eyelids fluttered with confusion and then his eyes rolled back as another sorority sister took him in her mouth, stroking him back to life. His head tilted farther back at the pure sensation.

They had both heard about the drunken escapades of these parties, but neither Hunter nor Paige had ever stayed long enough to witness the decadence. Now they were the main attraction.

"Ever been so full of cock you thought you'd split?" Max whispered. His voice tickled her ear and her pussy clenched around his fingers, dripping at the thought.

Hunter's green eyes found hers again, and she moaned, thinking of the dreams she had with him and other men. She was loath to admit it, but Max often played a co-starring role. But even in those dreams, his touch paled compared to the real thing. It rivaled Hunter's, and for the first time in her life, she wondered what April's touch would be like. In her dreams, she made a cameo appearance from time to time, and those seemed to be the ones she woke from with a healthy dose of cream in her underwear.

She let out a breathy sigh as more hands drew into the mix. Hunter's eyes lowered, taking in the fact his best friend's fingers were inside her pussy and she was moving with his easy stroke. When his eyes moved back to hers, something wrapped in anguish crossed his irises, but it soon flashed over into that horny passion she recognized.

Beyond Hunter sat April, and her chocolate eyes locked on Paige. The color in her cheeks heightened as her fingers worked her clit and her lewd display brought Paige to another edge. Her pussy tingled, becoming slicker with each finger flick.

Max used the tip of his cock to play a game of eenie-meenie-miney-mo between her pussy and her ass. Each syllable whispered in her ear between nibbles.

Hunter's breath became that ragged quality announcing his own buildup, but he didn't groan, and his gaze stayed on the exhibition she was entwined in. The room was full of the grunts and moans of sex, but all Paige heard was

Hunter's breathing, along with the sound of a deep throat blowjob in progress.

His slow blink and the jump of his jaw muscle, followed by the flush that encompassed his face, broadcast his release; but this time there was no groan or satiated sigh. His gaze hardened just as Max breached the ring of Paige's anus, pulling a gasp from her lips. When Max lifted her by her thighs, plunging his full length inside her, he spread her legs, offering her wet pussy as an open invitation to the room. Hunter stared at the cum coating her lips and his cheeks turned that horny rose color. Before he could turn and take Max up on the offer, a horde of girls pulled him onto his back, busying him with their favor.

Paige had never had anal sex and the raw burn of it drew another groan from her, but Max was slick and each time he lifted her away, the anticipation of the plunge gripped her. Every time he rammed his cock deep, it hit her g-spot, and she cried out, spewing more wetness from her pussy than she thought possible.

Max settled back onto the coffee table, using his legs to push deep with each plunge, speeding up his hip grind as his fingers continued to strum her clit. Another frat brother stepped in between her legs, blocking her view of Hunter, and Paige blinked, her gaze falling to the monster cock lining up to her pussy. The thick black rod slid inside her in one brutal plunge. and she wailed, writhing between the two men.

A third man stepped over her and slid his cock into her mouth mid-gasp. The room erupted into cheers as the three of them fucked in unison, as if one supreme being controlled their every move. Paige's eyes rolled back in her head as the next orgasm ripped through her, pulling groans from her patrons as her pussy clenched and unclenched, juicing up the way for more.

Being triple-teamed made her nipples harder than they had ever been and hands kneaded her flesh as the three worked her with a brutal pounding, stretching her ass, her pussy and her mouth beyond what she thought possible.

A second cock pressed against her ass, and she gasped, trying to shake her head, but the man using his cock as a battering ram in her mouth wouldn't let go of her hair. The pressure of another hard penis sliding into her ass pulled a moaning scream from her that was promptly drowned by a river of semen.

As the mouth fucker stepped away, Paige stared into two pairs of eyes, one as dark as the face it peered out of and the second pair—she locked her gaze with. Hunter's green eyes pierced hers as his cock joined in, stretching her to her limits.

"You didn't think I'd let them have all the fun," he said, his voice slow, but his horny raspy quality heightened her excitement.

Paige arched, the scream building as much as the pressure of three men inside her, and a leg swung over her face. Paige blinked at the clean-shaven pussy inches above her mouth and her eyes moved higher to the perky breasts and the innocent pigtails of Bo-peep beyond.

April grinned. "Fuck me with your tongue," she said, her voice as clear as Max's grunting breath in her ear, and April lowered onto Paige's mouth.

Paige dipped her tongue in her roommate's snatch, French kissing her pussy, twirling her tongue inside the dripping passage before moving higher to find the nub of her clit. She sucked it between her teeth before swiping her tongue over the sensitive flesh. April moaned.

The five of them moved like the tide, sinuous and languid and then borderline frantic until a rush of hot liquid escaped, dousing Paige inside and out. One by one, the mass of arms and legs unraveled until it was only Hunter.

Hunter wrapped his arms around her in the afterglow as both their chests heaved in exertion.

Magick
Chapter 3

PAIGE SAT UP GASPING, and her eyes darted in the blackness surrounding her. The complete darkness sent a wave of fear through her tired limbs, but she was still too ensnared in her dreams to recognize where she was. The sheets were wet with her sweat and both her nightgown and her underwear clung with a tacky stickiness that made her shiver.

Before she could shift into a more comfortable position, the light switched on. She squinted, blinking, and slid a glare in what should have been April's direction. Except it wasn't April. It was Max.

Fully clothed and in an unfamiliar chair, Max leaned his elbows on his knees and cradled his head like the light was just as painful for him as it was for her. She hadn't noticed any stubble on his cheeks at the party, but he sported bristles that looked as if they were a few days old.

The last thing she remembered was being wrapped in Hunter's arms, and she blinked, scanning her surroundings. A plume of panic surfaced, creating an icy shiver. The sheer sterile quality of the room sent heated alarm through her, and she went to reach for the covers, to pull them closer, but her wrists stopped a couple of inches from the mattress.

Her gaze snapped to the bed. Focusing on the padded wrist restraints holding her hands in place, shifting her legs was equally difficult and she could only surmise her ankles were in the same condition as her wrists.

"What the fuck, Max?" Paige said, but the words sounded harsh, as if she had been screaming at a concert for four days straight.

"You tried to kill me," Max snarled. When he sat up, it afforded her a view of his neck and chest. Raw scratch marks cascaded down his skin and some cuts penetrated deeper, leaving bloody clots dabbled along each gash.

Paige's gaze dropped to her fingers and the raw skin coupled with the jagged and broken nails confirmed his words. But for the life of her, she couldn't figure out why. The last active memory she had was being the center of the wild orgy and she didn't recall scratching the hell out of Max, especially since he was behind her.

"I…I don't understand. Where's Hunter?"

His gaze dropped to the floor, and he shook his head, cradling it after a moment. When his shoulders shook, her throat constricted, making it nearly impossible to draw a breath. Fear crawled into her skin, leaving her shaking and feeling exposed in the light nightgown she wore. Everything about this was wrong and when Max looked up with tears staining his cheeks, her fear turned to a silent panic that made her eyes dart around the room looking for a logical explanation or an equally welcomed escape.

Max opened his mouth to answer her, but nothing came out and his gaze lowered again. The slow shake of his head sent her heart slamming against her ribs.

"What does that mean?" Her voice broadcast panic, pulling a hitch and a huff of a laugh from Max.

"It means you finally succeeded in killing him."

His words stunned her to non-reaction, and she stared into his glare. Her last foggy memory of Halloween was Hunter whispering he loved her in her ear. Then a dark curtain dragged her under. "What are you talking about?"

"Whatever the hell you took before you came inside made you two insane and that's what killed him."

A slow understanding scraped her skin and her muscles tensed against the onslaught of fury burning holes in her stomach. "You son of a bitch! You drugged us."

He sighed, dropping his gaze to the ground for a moment before he shook his head in denial.

"You gave me a shot of something in the bathroom," Paige said, her voice rising in disbelief. Max was hanging her out to dry.

He laughed and moved his gaze to hers. "I gave myself a shot of insulin," he said. "My blood sugar was off the charts, and I couldn't wait for you to finish whatever the hell you were doing in the bathroom."

His diabetes was something that was well known, and her jaw tightened at the lie. Max couldn't keep eye contact and dropped his gaze.

"You fucked me," she whispered and again, he laughed, this one a little more bitter than she expected, but at least he didn't deny it.

"You gave us all quite the show."

"That's not what happened, and you know it."

"You nearly killed *me* when Hunter collapsed."

Paige narrowed her eyes when Max avoided her gaze.

"Are you serious? You're the one who drugged us. You're the one who had us at the center of your freak show orgy. You're the one who called it an impromptu bachelor party. And you're the one who fucked me up the ass."

He huffed and met her gaze. "I most certainly did not."

"You are such a liar," she whispered, her gaze dropping to her barren and bound hand. "Where's my ring?"

"What ring?"

The snap in his voice matched the fiery anger in his eyes.

"The ring Hunter gave me in the cemetery before we came back to the party."

"There was no ring. You crazy bitch," he snarled. "You killed my best friend!"

Paige glared at him. "You orchestrated an orgy." The ache in her body was testament to the activities she recalled as vividly as sitting in this room.

"That's not what happened at all." He leaned toward her, speaking through clenched teeth.

"You and Hunter fucked like rabbits until a group of drunker guys joined in."

"You and April started it."

"No, Paige. We didn't. You fucked Hunter until his heart seized. You continued to fuck him after his heart stopped. I pulled you off him and that's when you realized he was dead and freaked out."

"Liar," she whispered. "If I ask them to do a rape kit on me, they'll find your semen up my ass."

The sarcastic smile did her in and she struggled against the bindings, growling her discontent.

"They already tested you and the only DNA they found inside your nasty little cunt matched Hunter's and one of the other fraternity brothers."

"You little shit," she spat. The reality of the situation sank in. "Hunter asked me to marry him, and you killed him," she whispered, her eyes filling with unwilling tears.

"He dumped you," Max said with such conviction that her head whipped in his direction. "He broke up with you and you drugged him or did something else that made him just as much of a freak as you."

"You're only doing this to cover your own ass," she said, sending a glare in his direction.

"I didn't have to be here when you woke up." He stood and matched her glared. "As a matter of fact, they told me it wasn't a good idea. They said there is no reasoning with someone who has had a psychotic break. I guess they were right." He turned and marched to the door, knocking and waiting a few moments before the door opened.

"You bastard!" She thrashed in the bindings holding her in place and the orderly who let Max out stared at her a moment too long before he closed the door.

Magick
Chapter 4

THE LIGHTS FLICKED OFF and Paige stared into the darkness. Hot tears pooled in her ears as she tried to pry her memory open. The black curtain remained firmly in place, and she could not reconcile the lies Max rained on her with what her mind showered her prior to blacking out.

She shifted, gritting her teeth against the flare of pain in her groin. The muscles had been stretched to the ripping point, and she certainly was paying for having her legs tied in place. A sliver of light crossed the room, accompanied by the creak of the door.

Paige didn't have time to glimpse who had entered, but the light shuffle of feet and whisper of fabric pressed dread into her chest, making her breath wheeze. The sheet covering her was dragged off in slow motion, like a macabre seduction, and the bed creaked as the intruder settled between her spread legs.

No words passed, but rough hands pushed the flimsy hospital gown up and pushed her thighs wider before fingers spread her. A hot, wet tongue passed over her and she tried to pull away.

"No," she whined.

"Yes," his voice rang in her ears, shocking her.

"Hunter?"

Another slow lick was punctuated with a twirl around her clit. His signature move, and she sighed.

"Max said you were dead." The words were lost in the motion of his mouth and hands. It wasn't until more than one finger spread her that she moaned his name. His soft chuckle tickled against her wet pussy.

Slow pressure built, reminding her of being filled by three cocks at one time and she moaned louder, writhing under his expert tongue fuck. The creak of the door pulled her eyes open and the light from the hallway illuminated her bare lower torso, and even though she couldn't see him, she certainly felt his caress.

The orderly from earlier stared at her. Lust filled his features and his cock snapped to attention, creating a tent in the front of his scrubs.

"You really are a freak," the orderly whispered, and glanced over his shoulder.

Hunter's touch ignited her, and she let out another moan, pulling the orderly's attention back in her direction. His gaze dropped to her pussy, and he licked his lips, his eyes darting between her and the hallway, as indecision shadowed his features.

Paige was too far-gone, and she whispered, "Oh, God!" Her back arched as the orgasm took hold. The room was illuminated enough for her brain to realize Hunter wasn't physically there, but his hands and mouth were doing things to her body that she couldn't deny.

Max hadn't been lying about him being dead and the truth pressed on her chest as surely as his ghostly fingers pulled her to another plateau.

"Tell him you'll let him fuck you if he lets me in." Hunter's words caressed her ear, even as his fingers still plucked her like he was playing a complex guitar solo.

Paige's lungs filled with another moan. "Just say yes, and you can fuck me," she whispered, her voice breathy and on edge as she met the orderly's wide-eyed stare. He blinked and took a quick glance over his shoulder before stepping into the room.

The light faded as the door closed and it wasn't until the bed creaked that her heart thundered against her ribcage at the thought of the strange man's hands on her.

"Say yes!" Paige's panicked voice filled the room as the orderly's fingers slid up her thighs.

"Fine. Whatever," he said. "Yes."

The moment the word slipped out, the air swirled, and a radiant light filled the orderly. His eyes blinked and in the dull illumination, Paige saw the glow of Hunter's green eyes in the foreign face. He didn't hesitate. The moment the light settled over them, his cock slid inside her.

"I waited for you to wake," he whispered, his smooth voice layering over that of the orderly he had momentarily possessed. His hips started that slow grind and her eyes rolled back in her head.

Questions kept popping into her head, interrupting her bliss. "Hunter?"

"Mhm?" He stilled his hips and met her gaze. The green shimmered over the orderly's gray eyes and he started the slow motions again as she got lost in his gaze.

"I didn't kill you, did I?" Her voice cracked as the question blanketed them.

The rhythmic motion stopped, and he slowly shook his head. "No."

"Am I crazy?" The question popped out, and she dreaded the answer. His soft chuckle didn't encourage any sort of calmness; in fact, it just sent her heart into overdrive.

"No, baby, you aren't crazy," he finally said, and his breath caressed her lips before he crushed them under his. The kiss was as authentic as she remembered, and she sighed, wishing she could wrap her arms around him.

When his lips parted from hers, she opened her eyes again and could almost see the smoke of his form wrapped inside the orderly. There were no other words needed, and his ghostly form crushed into her with the same bravado he'd possessed when he was alive.

Paige arched into the orgasm at the same moment Hunter's possessed form reached his peak. They groaned in unison and his body shuddered onto hers.

Hunter lost the connection, leaving only the orderly panting on top of her.

His ragged breath tickled her ear. "What. The. Fuck?" Each word came out in an exerted huff and Paige shivered under his weight.

"Get off me," she hissed, trying to shift her weight from under him.

"But," he started and stopped, uncoupling from her. The bed creaked as his weight shifted. The silence unnerved her. "Did we just?"

His confusion was almost laughable, but she was bound to the bed in a compromising position.

"What the fuck did you do to me?" The menace in his tone sent a dose of fear through her bloodstream.

Instead of answering his question, she said, "I'll scream." Her attempts to roll him off her were futile, with the bindings holding her in place and vulnerable.

"You won't be able to scream if your mouth is full of cock," he said, crawling his way up her body until his knees pressed against the sides of her head. "Suck me to life and I'll forgive whatever the hell that was."

Hunter, where are you?

The thought barreled through her mind as the orderly rubbed his slick and flaccid cock against her lips. She couldn't move her head with the way he held her, and she pressed her lips together. Hunter's silence crushed her, pressing on her chest with the force of an elephant.

"Come on, suck me," he whispered, moving the tender flesh across her lips.

When she wouldn't open her mouth, he slapped her pussy; the sting drew a gasp from her, and his cock slid between her teeth. She entertained the thought of biting him, but his fingers had already started on her clit, manipulating her pleasure centers into submission.

He grew thick in her mouth, prompted by her sucking. He wasn't hung the way Hunter had been, but what he lacked in length, he certainly made up in girth. He was wide enough to stretch her lips and the way he rode her mouth wasn't brutal, like the guy at the party. It was more controlled.

More seasoned.

He pulled away from her, leaving both her mouth and pussy unattended for a moment, and the emptiness filled her, almost pulling a moan of anguish from her. His weight shifted and the brush of his knees on her shoulders told her he turned around. When the wet tip of his cock swiped her lips, she didn't argue. She just opened her mouth, accepting him inside.

This time when he plunged into her mouth, it was with more of a vengeance and he pushed far enough in that his balls bounced off her forehead.

"That's it, swallow me whole," he said, forcing every inch of himself into her wide mouth. The bed creaked and the orderly's lips clamped onto her clit, sucking with purpose.

Tilting her head back with the moan gave him a chance to thrust his cock deeper into her throat and she gagged, moaning around his hard cock. The orderly spread her wider, alternating between sucking and licking her. His hips started the more frantic pace, plunging his hard cock in and out of her mouth as she sucked.

He plunged his fingers inside her, coating them with her slickness before he moved on to her ass. Two fingers slid into her anus as he twirled his tongue on her clit. The effect was immediate, and Paige arched, her body reacting, spurting a small stream of hot cum from her core.

The pace of his fingers and tongue matched that of his hips, and it wasn't much longer before he filled her mouth with cum. He didn't mess around either, just pulled out of her and got dressed in the dark before flipping the overhead light on.

"Do you need a bedpan?" he asked with a gruff voice, his questioning gray eyes scanned her.

"I'd like to use the bathroom," Paige said, trying not to gag on the taste in her mouth. She prayed the orderly would unclasp her wrists and ankles and let her do her business. Instead, cold steel slid underneath her, and hot tears burned her eyes.

"I'm not allowed to let you out of these." He flicked one of the wrist straps and gave her a one-shoulder shrug. "You seem to get off on being tied up," he said, and a slow, salacious grin surfaced.

Mortified, she accepted her situation and closed her eyes from his less than courteous stare, willing her body to relax and purge. He gently wiped her and pulled her nightgown over her before tucking her in.

"If you say anything about tonight..."

"You'll what?" she snarled in his direction, and his features hardened. The orderly wasn't ugly by any means, and given any other situation, she might have thought he was cute, but he wasn't in Hunter's league, either.

"I'll make sure you remain locked up in these things for the foreseeable future." He flicked the straps again. "And next time, you won't be able to walk for a week when I'm done with you."

"There won't be a next time," she said, trying to level a glare, but in her vulnerable state, there really wasn't a thing she could do if he came back for more, and his 'wanna-bet' smile just sent a cold chill right down to the center of her lost soul.

Magick
Chapter 5

PAIGE SOBBED IN THE silent darkness. The bed rattled with the force of it.

"Paige?" His voice sounded weak and groggy, and her breath hitched.

"You left me alone with him," the words came out wrapped in anguish.

"I'm sorry, baby. They warned me possession was dangerous." His cool palm cupped her cheek, and his lips brushed hers before his head settled on her chest. "It drained me."

"He said he would be back for more." She sniffled.

"No one will touch you again but me," he whispered and planted a kiss on her stomach. "Okay?"

"Yes." She stared into the absolute blackness surrounding her. "Max told me you broke up with me." The sensation of Hunter's head lifting from her skin pulled her focus to where he would be. She swore she saw a green flash at the edges of her blink.

"He's lying. He lied to the police and the rest of the fraternity backed him because they know how much trouble they'd get into for drugging us." His head pressed against her again.

"Can you untie my bindings?"

"No. The buckles are made of steel coated iron," he muttered.

Futility squeezed, drawing a quiet wail from her lips. Being bound by iron meant she couldn't cast a spell, either. She was trapped in this bed and at the mercy of whoever came through the door.

"We'll figure it out," Hunter said, his ghostly voice wrapping her tight, but it didn't help the despair creeping into her bones.

She wanted to ask how, but exhaustion pulled her into a deep restless sleep filled with nightmares of a legion of men doing unspeakable things to her.

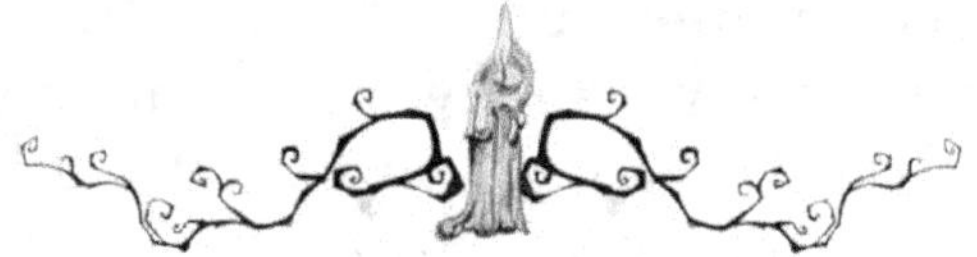

THE CREAK OF THE door drew her out of the dark and she blinked her eyes open to the bright rays of daylight blanketing the room. She turned her head toward the door and the bespectacled doctor entered, his attention focused on the chart in his hand. When his gaze finally moved from the paper to hers, she shivered at the cold inspection.

"Looks like you're with us today," he said, and she nodded.

"Can I take a shower?" Paige asked, her voice small and quiet. She needed to feel clean. "You can lock me back up after if you have to, but I feel gross."

The doctor glanced at his clipboard and flipped through a couple of papers, reading some comments before he looked back at her.

"I think we can arrange for that." He took a seat and adjusted his glasses. "I'm Dr. Schaeffer. Do you understand where you are?"

"I'm in some sort of hospital."

"You are in a sanitarium." He jotted a note on the paper. "Do you know why you are here?"

All the lies Max had said tumbled through her head along with the truth, and she sighed. "My fiancé died, and everyone thinks I killed him."

"But you don't?" He adjusted his glasses again.

Paige shook her head.

"What do you think happened?"

"We were drugged and whatever they slipped into us killed him."

Dr. Schaeffer nodded. "Hunter Garrett died of a drug overdose." His eyes locked on her, but his expression was not agreeable. "But witnesses say you were the one who drugged him."

"I did not drug him," Paige said through clenched teeth.

"They found a deadly amount of GHB in his system."

"GHB? Isn't that the date rape drug?"

"And the police found a syringe full of GHB in your pocketbook."

Her head whipped in his direction.

"With only your fingerprints. And an empty syringe was found in the bathroom of the fraternity house, again, with only your fingerprints."

Paige just stared at him, her mind firing over the facts and the complete misalignment of her memory.

"And they found the source vial in your desk at the sorority house," he added, adjusting his glasses.

Her heart dropped, and she closed her eyes against the burn. She swallowed, pressing her lips together against the sob. Even April had turned on her, and her entire form shook.

"Did you want to explain to me how you were not involved in drugging Mr. Garrett?"

"What about me? What did I have in my system?"

Silence layered the room, and she opened her eyes, turning her head to him. Dr. Schaeffer glanced at the chart and slowly shook his head. "There was no trace of GHB or any other synthetic drug in your system when you were brought in."

Tears flooded her eyes, and she closed them again. Hot paths traced her face, pooling in her ears as she cried silently. "I didn't kill him."

The shuffle of fabric was her response, and she turned, watching as he left.

"What about my shower?"

"You are still suffering from delusions. I can't let you out of those restraints until I am sure you will not attempt to hurt yourself or anyone else," he said and left the room.

Paige let out a heartbreaking scream as he closed the door, leaving her tied to the bed and writhing as the magnitude of Max and April's subterfuge settled into her bones.

A nurse came into the room with a bedpan and slid it underneath her. Paige stared at the ceiling, willing her body to purge its waste. Afterwards, the nurse returned with a sponge and a small pan of warm water. She cleaned Paige from neck to toe before she called for an orderly.

When her nightly visitor stepped into the room, she tensed, but he was all business, unclasping her ankle from one side of the bed and attaching it to the same space her other foot was. He did the same with her arm. Back and forth, until the bed sheets were changed. The nurse took her leave as he repositioned her the way she had been.

With a quick glance at the door, he slid his hand gently over the sheet, tracing her thigh through the fabric before straightening the sheet and folding it over on her chest. The sly smile he sent her was more than she could deal with at the moment. All Paige wanted was a shower, and she didn't care what the cost would be.

"If you let me take a shower, I'll do anything you want me to," Paige whispered before he turned away.

"That's quite a complicated request," he said, meeting her gaze.

"I'll do anything," she whispered, begging him with her eyes. She needed to feel clean, even if that meant letting him fuck her.

His eyes sparkled as he scanned her form. "I'm not working tonight," he said and met her gaze. "And even if I was, I wouldn't risk my job for your crazy ass."

"Please," she whispered, trying not to cry.

He gathered up the soiled laundry and stopped at the door. "Anything?" he asked without turning.

"Yes," she said, even though everything inside her screamed no.

He glanced over his shoulder with a salacious grin. "I'll see what I can do."

The moment the door closed, Paige let the hot tears take over. Hunter was dead and Max had made it nearly impossible for anyone to believe her. Even her best friend had rolled over on her. The only way the drugs could have ended up in her desk was if April had been a part of the plot against her.

The memory of her roommate sitting on her face surfaced, and she shuddered.

AFTER AN EXCRUCIATINGLY LONG day of scheduled feedings and bedpan relief, the lights went out. The darkness wrapped around her, and Paige stared at the ceiling, wondering just what she would have to do in exchange for a shower.

"Hunter," she whispered, cold without his touch. No response came, and she squeezed her eyes shut against the doubts creeping in. Her heart thundered in her chest as she wondered if the prior night had been part of her supposed delusion.

It wasn't until the door cracked and closed just as quickly that she realized she was truly in hell and Hunter wasn't coming to the rescue.

"Anything, right?" his whisper cut through the dark.

"For a shower... yes."

A rag covered her mouth, and she inhaled in shock, not expecting the fabric or the medicinal smell. She struggled against his grip until he overwhelmed her, and she succumbed to the sleep-aid.

A foul stench assaulted her, and she snapped her head away from the source, clamping her eyes and scrunching her nose to avoid inhaling. Her eyes burned, and she blinked against the bright light.

"Wake up, my little sex freak," his voice broke through the haze.

Paige blinked the blur from her eyes and her heart leaped into her throat at the sight of the camera pointed at her, along with the orderly's naked body beyond the lens.

Fine mist rained down on her and she looked up in confusion. Her wrists were fastened to a bar above her, and her eyes focused on what was beyond the bar.

A showerhead. One that must have been set to mist, and she closed her eyes, focusing on the feeling of it wrapping around her in a warm hug. It wasn't until the slap of a palm on her ass that she tilted her head back towards the orderly.

"What the hell?" she whispered in a raw voice.

The orderly looked around the eyepiece and grinned with a wink. "You said anything."

Paige's mouth opened as her gaze dropped to the metal table behind him and the array of sex toys spread out over the surface.

"I've always wanted to make a porn video," he grinned and glanced at his toys. His free hand caressed her breast and then trailed down to her pussy. "You don't mind toys, do you?"

Her eyes drifted to the vibrators and rubber cocks of all sizes and whether or not she wanted to, the thought of being fucked by any of the toys turned her on. She moved her gaze back to his.

"When I'm done, I'll clean every inch of you."

She swallowed and glanced up at the soft, warm mist raining from the showerhead before she nodded. "I did say anything for a shower," she whispered and wondered where Hunter was.

As if her thoughts called him to life, his form shimmered, and her heart sped up as he grinned at the display. When he sent a raised eyebrow in her direction, she felt the heat paint her cheeks.

"If you're going to film yourself fucking me, you can at least tell me your name," Paige said to the orderly, and he lowered the camera a little, focusing his gray eyes on her.

"Austin."

A smile toyed with her lips. "I've always wanted to visit Austin." Hunter rolled his eyes in the background and pointed from his chest to Austin, and her gaze moved back to the grinning orderly. "I think Hunter wants his turn with me first. Be a dear and say yes?"

A crease formed between his eyes, and he pressed his lips together. "I don't think so. The last time I said yes to you, I lost a half hour, and

I felt like I missed something hotter than hell." He set the camera on the table and wrapped a heavy strap around her thigh before attaching the ends of the strap to a hook. With a yank on the chain, the strap pulled her leg up, fully exposing her pussy. He did the same to her other leg and then took a step back, reaching for the camera.

Austin stepped close and took her breast in his mouth. Hunter crossed his arms and took a seat on the edge of the table, watching as Austin played with her breasts. Something about the way he was watching the display was as much of a turn on as being filmed, and when he looked at the toys and ran his fingers over some of the larger dildos, Paige couldn't help but smile at the suggestive cock of his eyebrow.

Austin's mouth trailed down her body, and he lowered himself to his knees. With the camera angled towards her exposed pussy, he leaned in and flicked her clit with his tongue. "Come for me," he whispered between flicks.

"Do you want me to show him how it's done?" Hunter asked with a smile playing on his lips.

"I want you," Paige whispered and Austin sucked her harder, his tongue alternating between playing with her clit and licking her folds. Hunter just smiled.

"I want to see you come for him first," he said in a low whisper that caressed her skin with a chill, sending a wave of gooseflesh over her.

Paige let out a small moan and Austin glanced up at her, following her gaze to the table. He smiled and pulled the metal across the distance before reaching for the closest toy, a massive dildo that looked like it belonged on a Norse god. Instead of just plunging it into her, he set the camera on the floor, aiming it up at her pussy while he played with her clit between his fingers and rubbed the end of the dildo against her lips.

"Suck on this, baby," he said, and Paige opened her mouth. Austin slid the tip of the giant cock into her mouth, stretching her lips as he slowly slid it as far into her mouth as possible without splitting her lips or choking her to death.

The slow progression in and out of her mouth, along with his finger plucking, formed a pool of heat in her belly and she moaned just thinking of this dildo stretching her pussy.

Austin pulled it from her mouth and dropped to his knees again. His fingers continued to play with her until his mouth took over. When he spread her ass and pressed the pliant rubber against her anus, she moaned and tried to squirm away.

"It's not going to fit," she gasped.

Austin ignored her and her gaze jumped to Hunter as the pressure increased until the tip breeched her anus. The slow pressure progressed as the dildo filled her ass, pulling a moan from her. Hunter stood and crossed the distance, disappearing behind her. His hands covered her breasts, and his cool breath tickled her neck.

"It will fit," he whispered. "So will I," he added and pressed his cock against her, using the smooth skin of the dildo to slide inside her.

"Oh, God!" Paige moaned and Austin's tongue sped up. He continued to slowly push the dildo farther into her, stretching her as Hunter moved just as slowly, but his in and out motion heightened her sensitivity, and his fingers rolled her nipples as his mouth traveled the line of her neck.

"Come for me, Paige," he whispered and nibbled her ear.

The buildup started in her core, spiraling outward like a tsunami, and her moan filled the shower, echoing off the walls. "Faster," she gasped, and both Hunter and Austin complied, banging her until cum squirted from her pussy, coating Austin's chin and chest.

He pushed the dildo as far as it would go and then retreated to the table, grabbing another rubber toy. Returning, he slid it inside her soaking pussy and she cried out at the pressure. When he flipped the switch and the tool started vibrating, her cry turned to a moan.

Austin's cock joined the vibrating dildo, and he grabbed her ass, plunging inside her and stretching her pussy, making her come again. The fucking she received from both Austin and Hunter's ghost, along with the dildos, ripped orgasm after orgasm from her until her entire form trembled.

Her ghostly lover and the orderly groaned at the same moment, and Paige felt the hot flood from both men fill her pussy and her ass.

Hunter's ghost disappeared like he had before, as if an orgasm made it so he couldn't reach her. Austin pulled away from her neck, trembling as he pulled out. The absence of their cocks was tempered by being filled with the dildos.

Austin slowly pulled each of the rubber toys out of her, and she whined at the emptiness. His fingers replaced the dildos. The slow strokes in both her pussy and her ass brought another throaty cry from her lips, and he glanced up at her with a smile.

Austin's smile reminded Paige that it wasn't Hunter making her body sing with ecstasy, and she shuddered, wishing her ghostly lover was still present.

"You are so fucking hot," he whispered and pulled his fingers out of her before taking up the rear. His wide cock slid easily into her ass, and he took her earlobe between his teeth as he slowly fucked her. "So, fucking hot."

His hand found her clit, and between the beat of his hips and the plucking of his fingers, she felt the wave satiate her. He squeezed her breast tight as he moaned in her ear. Hot semen flooded her ass, and he pulled out of her, pressing his forehead to the center of her back as he tried to catch his breath.

After what seemed like forever, his breathing evened out and Austin unclasped her legs, lowering them gently to the floor before setting the camera on the table and stepping away from her. Something in the way he gazed at her made her shiver, like the episode had endeared her to him in some way. He crossed to the wall of controls and flipped a couple of the switches. After a moment, the mist turned into a flood of warm water and she leaned her head back, letting it fall into her mouth and bathe her face before she looked back at him. He crossed the distance, and her gaze took him in for the first time. His physique was a lot like Hunter's. Lean and muscular, and with his wet hair falling over his forehead, he looked much sexier than he did with it slicked back away from his face.

He gave her a shy smile and his cheeks bloomed red as he opened the bottle in his hand and stepped behind her. A sweet scent filled the steam, and she closed her eyes as he lathered her hair with shampoo. The slow way he cleaned her hardened her nipples, and she cursed herself for this odd attraction.

Austin rinsed her long locks, running his hands from root to tip until they squeaked clean.

"I've never done this before," he whispered in her ear as his hands caressed her body with suds.

"You could have fooled me," Paige said and turned her head to meet his gaze.

"I mean fuck a patient," he said.

"You've fucked girls with those toys?"

A smile played on his lips and the heightened color in his cheeks made her bite down on a comment.

"No, not exactly." His gaze dropped to the floor.

"You fucked guys with those toys?" she asked, and his eyes snapped to hers. His head shook, denying the question.

"I, um, borrowed these from my roommate." He shifted in front of her and continued to clean her body. His tender touch sent a rash of shivers through her. "I've watched her use them," he muttered under his breath and met her gaze. "I guess I'm as much of a freak as you."

"I'm not a freak."

He laughed, and the sparkle in his eyes caught her off guard. "You can make yourself cum with no one touching you. That's kind of freakish."

Paige bit her lip and met his gaze. "What if I told you I had a visit from my dead fiancé?"

He laughed, but it faded as she kept his gaze and offered an awkward shrug.

"That night when you said yes, he possessed you."

His smile dropped and his eyebrows rose. Austin's hands stilled, landing on her waist. "Now you're just messing with me." His hands resumed cleaning her, but this time, they were all business as he chewed on his lower lip. He cleaned each leg all the way to her toes and glanced up at her from his position on the floor. "You are messing with me, right?"

His eyes filled with such worry that she took a deep breath before she shook her head and then his gaze hardened. "You are crazy," he muttered and stepped away, slamming the soap down on the table before shooting a glare in her direction. His intense study of her left her shaking despite the warm water cascading over her.

"Was it worth it?" he asked after a few moments of silence.

Despite the ache in her pussy, the feeling of clean skin was worth every decadent act, and sharing the event with Hunter made it all worthwhile.

He stepped closer and took her chin in his hand. "Was it?"

"Was what worth it?" she asked. "The shower?"

His half smile and sigh took her by surprise. "Okay, was the shower worth it?"

She couldn't help but smile. "Yeah," she whispered. "But it would have been better if my arms weren't tied to a metal rod."

His soft laugh filled the space. "If I didn't have you tied up, you would have tried to escape."

He wasn't as dumb as Paige gave him credit for, and each minute spent in his presence worried her, because his gaze softened. And she didn't need this type of complication. All she wanted was Hunter.

She sighed and dropped her eyes to the floor.

Austin turned away, crossing to the controls, and the water shut off, leaving her dripping as the chill of the room wrapped around her. He leaned over and grabbed a towel off the pile in the corner, and she couldn't help but stare at his perfectly formed ass.

He wiped the water from his body and pulled on his clothing before turning back to her. Paige stared at him as he crossed the tiles and disappeared behind her with a fresh towel. He dried her body and then rubbed the moisture from her hair before dropping the towel to the floor. The same comb that had slicked his hair back ran through her hair, snagging on knot after knot until it ran clean through her damp hair.

He stopped combing her hair and stepped closer, his dry hands snaking over her breasts from behind. "It was worth every second for me," he whispered in her ear, and gently squeezed her breasts. His lips found her neck, nibbling as his thumbs gently rubbed her nipples. "Even if you are as crazy as they say."

Paige turned toward him again and met his gaze. "I'm not crazy. I was set up."

His lips pressed together, and he sighed. "I know you believe that, but the sooner you face the truth, the sooner they'll let you out of the restraints."

"Can you please let me out of these, even if it is for a minute? My arms are killing me." Paige whispered, sending her pleading puppy dog gaze that always melted Hunter. It seemed to have the same effect on Austin.

He closed his eyes, grumbling under his breath for a minute, before he reached up and unhooked her right wrist. Her arm fell to her side like a lead weight and when he unlatched her second wrist, gravity came crashing down on her. Before she could crumple to the floor, Austin swept her up in his arms.

He smiled at her. "I have a wheelchair over there all set for you," he said and headed toward the annex room, "and I'll leave you unchained if you promise not to run away."

"I'm naked. Where the hell would I go?"

He chuckled. "Being naked never seems to stop crazy people."

"I'm not crazy."

"Then prove it and stay put." Austin gently dumped her in the chair and grabbed an empty backpack from the floor before disappearing into the shower room. He came back a few minutes later, zipping the bag. He hung it from one of the chair handles and crossed to a bank of lockers. Punching numbers in the control, the locker clicked open, and he pulled out standard hospital scrubs and brought them to Paige.

"I figured you might want something other than that sweat soaked night gown. I couldn't do anything in the way of underwear, but I found these warm socks."

Paige scanned the offerings and slowly reached out, taking them from him, humbled by the sincerity in his eyes. "Thank you," she whispered.

"I could get into a lot of trouble for this."

A smirk crossed her lips, and she looked up at him after covering herself with the shirt. The pants required a little help standing, and he offered her his hand. When she sat down, he kneeled and slipped on her socks for her before meeting her gaze.

"You think?" she asked.

"Well, for that I could get arrested," he waved toward the shower. "But I could get fired for just letting you take a shower and giving you clean clothing." He stood.

"Why did you risk it?"

His easy smile faded as he stared down at her. "I don't know." Austin ran a hand through his hair and sighed. "I've never done anything like what I've done with you. It's stupid and irresponsible and just plain insane for me to take these risks."

He disappeared behind the chair and started slowly pushing her down the hall.

"Do you believe me?" Paige asked before they entered the main hallway.

Austin remained quiet until he closed the door to her room. He stopped and stared at the messy bed. They had changed the sheets before his shift was over, but he stepped to the pantry and pulled out another set of sheets and a clean pillowcase, handing everything but the fitted sheet to Paige.

She watched as he stripped and changed the bed and then he helped her onto the mattress. With a sigh, he stared at the restraints and then moved his gaze to hers.

"Do I believe you were set up?"

Paige thought he had forgotten she asked, and the conflict in his eyes told her more than the simple way he sucked in his lower lip. She nodded, waiting for the inevitable no.

"I don't know what I believe. You didn't run, and you didn't try to hurt me." His gaze dropped to the restraints on the bed and then back to hers, the apology in his eyes as clear as the conflict. "You're acting... normal." His casual shrug punctuated his statement. "I don't know."

Paige closed her eyes and hung her head. Austin stepped closer, took a seat on the edge of the mattress, and hooked his finger under her chin. She opened her eyes and met his gaze. His expression was a far cry from that first night. It was softer and more caring, and she swallowed the lump in her throat.

"Did you kill that guy?"

Paige blinked away the sudden mist that formed over her vision and slowly shook her head. "No. He had asked me to marry him earlier that night, and Max drugged both of us when we got back. I don't remember much, but I know I didn't kill my fiancé. Max did."

Austin picked up Paige's left hand and met her gaze. "There wasn't a ring when you came in," he said and gently fastened the restraint around her wrist. It was loose enough, so it didn't chafe like it had before. He reached over her and fastened her other hand in the same fashion before he stood and covered her with the sheet.

"No ankle restraints?"

He glanced at her. "Do you think I need to put them on?"

Paige shook her head and Austin turned toward the wheelchair. He grabbed the backpack and slung it over his shoulder before folding the chair up and storing it in the closet.

"Austin?"

He stopped at the door and glanced over his shoulder.

"Thanks for the shower," she said and felt the heat caress her cheeks.

He smiled. "I'm the one who should thank you," he said and sent a wink in her direction before disappearing.

Paige stared at the ceiling, and just before sleep pulled her down, the bed creaked, and the exhausted ghost wrapped his arms around her.

"Goodnight, Paige," Hunter's cool voice whispered, and Paige nuzzled the top of his head

with her cheek before falling into a restless
slumber.

Magick
Chapter 6

AUSTIN STEPPED INTO HIS apartment and unzipped the bag, pulling out the camera before he stowed the backpack in his roommate's closet. He had filmed her fucking herself a few times and despite how much it turned him on, she never let him touch her. Hell, Heather let no man touch her.

He sighed, stepped into his bedroom, and turned on the light over his desk, powering up his computer. He caught sight of himself on the monitor just before the Windows logo appeared.

"What the hell are you doing?" he asked his reflection. He still had no answer to the question he'd been asking himself ever since he first caught her with the sheets down and her legs wide. The wetness dripping from her pussy had pulled him into the dark room and he hadn't been able to shake her since.

Even worse, when she sent those sincere blue eyes in his direction, he seemed to lose his mind completely and had no doubt that if she asked him to get her out of that hospital; he would be compelled to do her bidding.

He shook the thoughts from his head and stripped to his underwear, debating between sleep or transferring the video. The thought of seeing her naked again made his cock twitch, and he opted for transferring the video before getting some rest.

Austin plugged in the camera and found the beginning of today's recording. With a few keystrokes, the screen filled with the video as it transferred real-time. Just the sight of her naked, with her legs spread wide, made his cock hard and his hand dropped into his underwear, stroking slowly as he watched. The fact he was near blowing his load within a few strokes gave testament to the power she held over him, and when her lips wrapped around the tip of the giant dildo he let out a quiet groan, remembering just how good she was at blowing him.

"Oh, fuck," he whispered when the giant dildo slid into her ass, and he sped up his hand job. The buildup tightened the muscles in his legs and heat pulled from the tips of his fingers, rocketing toward the center of his body. Just before he blew his load, a form stepped behind Paige on the screen and his hand stilled. A chill encompassed his entire body as the stranger's cock joined the dildo in her ass. He blinked at the picture of him sucking her clit and the cock slowly fucking her at the same pace he was moving the giant dildo.

He reached over and turned up the audio. Her soft pant and Austin's sucking sounds filled the room along with the wet sounds of fucking.

No one was in the shower with them tonight. He was the only one fucking Paige, but the video before him said otherwise.

A voice he had never heard before whispered, "Come for me, Paige."

Her moan followed along with her demand of "Faster!"

Austin shivered and slid away from the screen when his form stood and joined the vibrator in her pussy.

The camera clearly showed two men fucking her, and she was moaning with each plunge. Despite his fear, Austin's cock demanded release and his hand stroke picked up along with the pace of the two of them double teaming Paige on the screen.

A hot stream of cum covered his hand at the same moment both men grunted on the video. Austin kept stroking, even as the man fucking her ass just dissipated like a drift of fog. "Fuck," he muttered as another thin spurt covered his flesh. He slumped in the chair, letting the cum just drip off his hand onto the carpet as the remainder of the evening played across the screen. When the video ended, he grabbed a towel and cleaned his hand and lap, still staring at the blank screen.

"I must be fucking exhausted," he muttered, unable to trust what he thought he saw. It took him two more viewings, one on the computer and the other on the camera, to believe that he wasn't the only one in that shower.

Instead of following the instinct that something supernatural had occurred, he shoved those thoughts away and tried to grasp at any explanation that could exist. Nothing logical could wipe away the chill forming in the center of his being, and sleep was just as elusive as a reasonable answer.

When his alarm went off the next morning, Austin dragged his ass out of bed and into the shower. The fog of no sleep wrapped around him as he washed and rinsed his body. His eyes flew open at the memory of her telling him a ghost had possessed him the other night.

"Holy fuck," he whispered.

She was telling the truth.

A bang at the door made him jump. "Don't take all the hot water!" Heather's voice bled through the door, reminding him he had been zoning out.

Austin shut off the water and rushed through his morning routine, anxious to get to work and see Paige. He had a million questions circling around in his head and, for the first time since he peeked at her file, he thought perhaps she might be the one telling the truth.

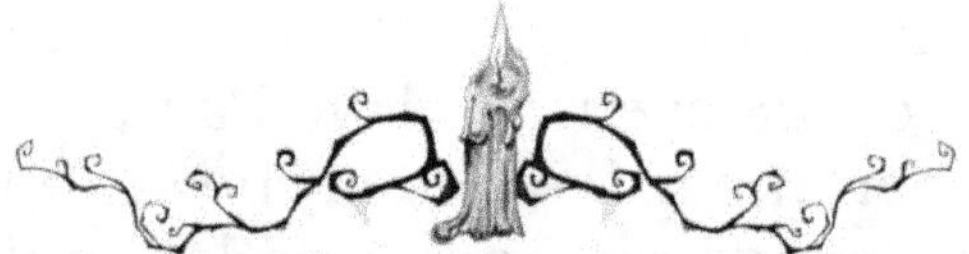

THE MINUTE HE CLOCKED in, he headed straight for her room, opening the door without a second thought.

Dr. Schaeffer shot his gaze from the paper on his clipboard to Austin's face. His features hardened.

"Did you let her take a shower?"

"I told you it was someone I had never seen before," Paige said before he could speak.

Austin's gaze bounced to hers for a moment and then back to the doctor's. "I wasn't working last night."

His face pinched in aggravation. "Well, if you find out who let her shower, let me know. I want to have a word with them."

"Okay," Austin said and traded a glance with Paige before taking his leave. He stepped out of the room and closed the door. The fact she didn't give him up to Dr. Schaeffer confused him. With everything that had gone down, she could have hung him out to dry and he wouldn't really blame her. Not with his less than professional behavior.

He kept an eye on her room and the moment the doctor left; he crossed to the door and stepped inside.

Her gaze met his, and she offered a strained smile before returning her eyes to the small window frame.

"Um, I have a question," Austin said, pulling her gaze back to him.

"What?"

The lack of enthusiasm in her voice yanked at his heart, like she had all but given up hope. "What you said about me being... possessed..." He trailed off when her eyes rolled back in his direction.

"I'm delusional," she said. "Or hadn't you heard?"

"Why did you cover for me?" he asked, starting with the easier of the questions floating in his head.

A rose hue filled her cheeks, and she offered a one-shoulder shrug. "You let me have a shower and some clean clothes."

Austin glanced at the door and then took a seat next to her. "You earned it," he mumbled and looked at his hands. "And I'm feeling like shit for everything I've done."

"I hated you after that first night," she whispered, and he moved his gaze to hers. The blue of her irises shimmered under a layer of tears. "But last night," she started and trailed off, blinking. A tear slipped out of the corner of her eye.

Every detestable act made him shrink inside his skin and he dropped his head into his hands. "I'm sorry," Austin said.

"Don't be. Last night was incredible. Maybe I am more of a sex freak than I care to admit," she said, pulling his gaze back to hers.

He huffed a laugh. "Would that be because I wasn't the only one in the room with you?"

Her eyes snapped wide, and the rapid blink made him smile.

"You saw him?"

Austin laughed. "Not while we were... you know. But he's on the video in living color. Who is he?"

"Hunter."

A chill settled into his bones. "Your fiancé?"

She nodded.

Austin dropped his gaze to the floor, studying the pattern before he stood. His tired brain couldn't wrap around everything. Until he saw that video, he hadn't believed in ghosts. Hell, he didn't believe in Heaven or Hell, or angels or any supernatural shit.

"Where are you going?" Paige asked when he stepped toward the door.

"I need some air," Austin whispered. His chest tightened when he glanced at her. He stopped with his hand on the door handle. "He possessed me the other night, didn't he?"

"You said yes," she shrugged. "You're the one who let him in."

His hand clamped on the metal as his jaw clenched. "You begged me to say yes." The hint of a smile that appeared on her lips burned the lining of his stomach. "So last night was all for him?"

Her smile faltered as she met his glare. She opened her mouth to speak and then dropped her eyes to the floor. When she pressed her lips together, sucking the lower one between her teeth, Austin thought he was going to punch something.

All that electricity he felt the night before was all because of a fucking ghost. He turned the doorknob.

"No."

Austin blinked, staring at the door, wondering if her soft answer had been a figment of his imagination.

"At first it was, and then..."

He inhaled and glanced over his shoulder before letting the air out of his lungs.

"And then you let me out of the restraints."

Her gaze met his and damn it, a zap of electricity sent a shock wave through him.

"And it bothered me that you didn't believe me."

"I'm not sure what I believe anymore," he said. She hadn't conceded that any of the mind-blowing sex had been for him, but the admission that it wasn't all for a ghost fanned that spark. He offered her a smile and left her with those words.

The rest of the day crawled by, and Austin's exhausted brain just kept skipping forward to when his next rounds would bring him back to her room. It wasn't until late in the evening when he glanced through the glass. His hand stopped on the doorknob.

Another girl was in the room, standing at her bedside with her back to the door. The anger etched on Paige's face was enough to burn the paint off the walls. He stepped away and pulled up the visitor register on the computer at the nearest nurse's station. No one was listed as visiting, and Austin headed back to the room.

This time he didn't hesitate, and when he stepped inside, Paige's fiery gaze moved to his.

The girl's back stiffened, but she didn't turn.

"I'm sorry, but Miss. Turner isn't allowed to have guests."

The girl turned, leveling a green-eyed glare in Austin's direction before exchanging a glance with Paige. "Fine," she said under her breath before spinning on her heel and storming out of the room.

Paige's gaze bounced between the door and Austin.

"Why did you do that?"

"You aren't supposed to have visitors," he answered, taken aback by the panic in her voice. He crossed to the side of the bed. "And you looked upset."

She pressed her lips together and her blue eyes shined in the low light. "You have to stop him."

Austin tilted his head to the side and looked at the door before bringing his gaze back to Paige. "Who?"

"Hunter. He possessed April, and he's going after Max," Paige whispered, but her eyes were wild with worry.

"Paige," Austin started.

"Please. I don't want him to hurt anyone. They didn't mean to kill him, they just... I don't know, but he's got murder in his heart. He wants them to pay for what they did," she said, and tears spilled down her cheeks.

"Is that what you were arguing about?"

Paige's eyelids fluttered in confusion.

"I saw you through the window." He hooked his thumb towards the door. "Your... friend never signed in."

Paige pressed her lips together. "She isn't really my friend. She is convinced Max gave her the ring."

Austin glanced at her left hand and raised an eyebrow at her. "I'm guessing Hunter?" He nodded toward the engagement ring glistening on her left hand.

Her eyes followed his, and she nodded. "It has an inscription." She straightened her finger. "Go ahead. Then you won't have any doubts."

Austin hesitated. Until this moment, everything was still conjecture. Except, of course, the second person on the video. When his hand touched hers, he almost drew back. He didn't want to know, but knowing she wasn't as crazy as a bat would be comforting.

The ring slid off easily, and he held it at an angle. The inscription read: P... my forever love... H.

Austin closed his eyes and curled the ring into his fist. While not absolute, it was enough to confirm part of her story. She hadn't been lying when she told the doctor the guy proposed. But the leap to possession. Could he really make that? The stone bit into his palm and he opened his eyes with a sigh.

He slid the ring back on her finger and met her gaze. "Where?" he asked before he lost all nerve.

Paige didn't answer right away, and her gaze dropped to the spot between her bound feet. "I don't know. Maybe the fraternity house, but I'm not sure if he'll do anything with other people around," she answered, and bit her lower lip.

When she met his gaze, he offered a nod for her to continue, and when she didn't, he raised his eyebrow. "Which fraternity house?"

"Beta. Beta Theta Pi."

Austin looked at his watch and bit his lip. "I can't leave until my shift is over." Her eyes flashed in that panicked way that made him stiffen.

"Please..."

He held up his hand, stopping whatever plea she was gearing up for. "I only have a half hour,

and then I'll go to the fraternity house and see if
I can find them. Okay?"

Paige pressed her lips together and dropped
her eyes. Her nod was slow and when her gaze
returned to his, Austin sighed. Tears laced her
eyelashes.

"I can't just leave, Paige," he said, his voice
soft, and she nodded, but didn't speak.

"I know, it's just... I don't want him to do
anything as horrendous as he was ranting
about," she finally said.

"You told him how you felt about hurting
Max, right?"

She nodded.

"If he loves you, it will eventually sink in."

"And if it doesn't?"

Austin held her stare and shrugged.

AUSTIN SAT IN HIS car, staring at the fraternity
house, wondering what the hell he was doing.
With a sigh, he slipped out and crossed the front
of the house, stopping in his tracks at the scene
unfolding within the house beyond the large bay
windows. Shock dropped his jaw and after a
moment, he closed his mouth, recovering some
of his bearings.

The girl Paige insisted had been possessed by
Hunter, was engaged in a lewd orgy with a group
of fraternity brothers and as he stared at her
naked form fucking with abandon, heat stirred
in him. Watching had always been a turn on and
Austin knew it was sick and twisted to just

stand there, but he couldn't tear his eyes away and his feet wouldn't budge from the spot.

Green eyes flashed in his direction as if she knew he was watching through the window and he stepped into the shadow of the trees, hiding his presence and keeping the spectacle within sight. He curled his hands into fists to keep himself in check. He didn't need to be caught jerking off on the front lawn.

The scene seemed familiar, and his brain flashed back to Paige's recount of that night in the doctor's immaculate scrawling script. As four men took on the blonde bombshell in the window, Austin kept envisioning Paige being ravaged in the same way and her cries for mercy drowned by the number of cocks flooding her mouth with semen.

"Shit," Austin whispered, and stepped farther into the shadows, shaking the visions from his head. Just the thought of her in the same situation burned, and raw anger bit into him, cooling the heat of his voyeuristic tendencies. His heart clamored against his ribs, jumping to a frantic beat, and his breath whistled from his chest as he gained control. Lifting his eyes again, he studied the unfolding orgy through the eyes of a clinician.

She kept going. When one man gave out and stumbled away, another took his place and she seemed to revel in each depraved act. Austin huffed a laugh. If the tables were turned, he might be just as tempted to know what a woman's orgasm felt like. From the look on the slut's face, she was enjoying every sensation.

A flash of lights drew across the window, interrupting Austin's train of thought and he ducked behind the closest tree trunk. As the rumble of a car cut off, Austin glanced around the oak, his eyes trailing a very distracted Max as he stepped inside the house.

Austin stepped back to the spot that afforded him the greatest viewing. He had a moment to wonder what Max's reaction would be to seeing his girlfriend fucking the entire frat house, before all hell broke loose.

To say Max was unhappy was an understatement, and for some unknown reason, his blind tirade pleased Austin. If he had pulled all the shit Paige said he did, this is exactly what the bastard had coming.

His girlfriend laughed at him and continued fucking the fraternity members she had already been coupled with, but based on the shock and fear in their eyes, if they hadn't already been inside the vixen, Austin didn't think they would have touched her, even if their lives depended upon it.

The telltale shudder of orgasm gripped both of them and they pulled away from her. She stood, opening her arms wide and egging Max on in some fashion. The profile of his red cheek gave Austin a hint of the level of his fury.

Max backhanded her, and even at this distance, Austin heard the smack. Her head snapped to the side and her hair obscured Austin's view of her face, but when she looked back at Max, Austin swallowed a gulp of air and took a step backwards, right into the solid wall of the tree.

Her swing was coupled with a flash of steel that sliced across Max's throat. Red splattered her and it took Austin a moment to understand what was happening inside. Max wasn't the only one who was on the receiving end of her wrath. By the time she was done with her rampage, she looked like the character in the movie Carrie, soaked in the blood of the dead.

The lights went out in the living room and Austin blinked, frozen to the spot where he stood, shaded by the tree, and hidden from view by the bushes. Fear kept him in place, and it took her a while to appear in the doorway. When she stepped onto the stoop, he slid behind the tree, unnerved by how clean she was.

After the girl drove off, Austin slowly lowered himself to the ground and held his head in his hands. The massacre he witnessed still burned on his eyelids and his throat closed around the stream of bile that rose, but he couldn't stop it. He rolled onto his hands and knees and vomited before climbing to his feet and crossing to his car, spitting the vile taste from his mouth.

Austin drove without purpose, his mind unable to wrap around what he had witnessed. His tired brain turned over every outcome, from him stepping inside when he first arrived, to interceding during the rampage, and each scenario left him just as dead as the rest of the men in that house. He shivered, justifying his inaction as best he could, but the guilt still clung to him, like the taste of vomit in his mouth.

Magick
Chapter 7

PAIGE BIT HER LIP and stared at the ceiling in the dark. Her foot tapped against the footboard, expressing her nervous energy in a constant rhythm that matched her elevated heartbeat. It had been over an hour since Austin left, and neither he nor Hunter had returned. She kept imagining Hunter's fury unleashed on Austin, and the thought terrified her more than having him unleash it on Max.

The night nurse stopped in her room for one last round, letting Paige relieve herself before giving her the prescribed night medicine. The sleep aid didn't take long to kick in and Paige had a bear of a time keeping her eyes open.

The creak of the door and sliver of light on her eyelids computed in her muddled brain, but she just assumed it was the nurse giving her one last check, especially with the quiet click of the door closing.

She turned her head toward the shuffle of feet, but her eyes were too heavy to open, and her voice failed her. The drugs numbed her ability to react, even when the soft hand ran down her arm. The warmth told her that whoever was in the room was human, not a ghost, but the touch was too light, too soft and when it slid under the covers cupping her breast, she knew just by the size of the palm that it wasn't Austin, which only meant one other person.

"Hunter?" Her voice came out in a whisper of a sigh and a light, quiet laugh met her.

"Who else would it be?" he said, but his voice was wrapped in April's soft purr.

The covers disappeared, leaving her exposed. Earlier in the day, the hospital pants Austin had given her had been removed, and all she had on was the thin shirt.

"What are you doing?" Paige asked, her question coming out in a groggy slur, but when a tongue parted her pussy, she knew he had no intention of talking, except to demand she come or do the same things to him he was now doing to her. Her sudden swell of irritation faded with each pass of the insistent tongue fuck, and Paige got lost in the sensations.

Hunter's cunnilingus execution was beyond amazing, especially using April's mouth and hands to achieve his goal. Paige clamped her lips together, preventing the moan from escaping as her body complied with his every whim.

Trembling, she lay on the wet sheets as he continued to bring her to the brink and beyond, each hurdle coming faster and faster in time with the swipes of his tongue.

"I wish I had your friend's toys," he mumbled and shifted until April's pussy ground against her lips.

She smelled of sex, and Paige turned her head away.

"You let Max fuck you?" It was the only logical explanation.

His dark chuckle gave her shivers. "I want to feel your tongue on this body," he whispered against her pussy and then sucked her clit between her teeth, pulling a gasp from Paige's lips.

"Hunter," Paige said in disgust, and his motion stopped. He shifted April's pussy away from her face and sat between her legs, fondling her gently with soft fingers.

"Max didn't touch this body," he finally said, but before he could say anything else, the door cracked open, pulling both their gazes to the door.

Austin stood framed by the light from the hallway. Paige couldn't make out his features, but he just froze in place with the door open wide enough to bathe the bed in light.

Hunter pushed his fingers farther into Paige's pussy and smiled in a way that made her wish her hands weren't bound in restraints. If she had been free, she would have pushed him away.

Austin stepped into the room and closed the door. The sound of the lock engaging drew a ragged breath from Paige, but when the overhead light blinked on, she got a good look at his expression. It wasn't one of interest, but one of disgust and barely contained anger directed at Hunter in April's body.

"Are you going to kill her, too?" Austin asked with such venom that Paige shrank into the mattress, his finger pointed in her direction.

Hunter just grinned and shook his head. "But the whore I'm wearing probably won't see the sunrise," he said, continuing to stroke Paige in a way that moved her toward another orgasm, and she shifted, either trying to avoid his touch or the embarrassment of coming in front of Austin, especially with the glare he was sporting.

"Stop fingering her," Austin snapped.

"But she likes it," Hunter said, using April's seductive purr. "And you like to watch, don't you?"

Austin pressed his lips together and his hands slowly clenched before his harsh stare met Paige's. "And you're just going to let him... her... whatever," he growled.

Paige lifted her wrist, showing him the hospital restraint and shrugged, but she didn't dare speak, not with the testosterone fest that was going on between the two of them. If she asked Hunter to stop, he might get mad, and she did not know what he would do to Austin. Hell, the crazed look in his eyes even left her with doubts about her own safety.

"Did he tell you he murdered a fraternity full of guys?" he asked, and Hunter's hand stilled.

"Murdered?" Paige whispered. The word sounded foreign, and her eyes widened.

"Yeah, he had a fucking orgy with the fraternity until Max came in. It was like watching a god damned porn flick turn into the chainsaw massacre."

Paige blinked and her body chilled as her gaze met Hunter's green eyes peering out of April's face. No words formed, and his haughty grin left her voice locked in her throat.

"She isn't very happy with me at all," he said, pointing to his chest. "But then, can you blame her? Fucking the fraternity wasn't nearly enough of a payback for what they did to you. Even Max's little tirade wasn't enough."

"Hunter," Paige gasped.

"Seeing him choke on his own blood, though, that was more than enough. The rest of them, well, their feeble screams and pleas for mercy, were just icing on the cake."

"You... killed them?" She blinked, staring into the eyes of the person she had promised her life to, the one who, while he was alive, had a heart bigger than anyone she knew. The man she agreed to marry wouldn't have dreamed of taking a life, even in self-defense, but what she saw in the ghost's gaze ran a ribbon of fear around her heart, squeezing out any loyalty she had to the man. His ghost was pure evil. A spiteful killer.

When he reached out to touch her, she cringed, knotting her shoulders into a hunch. His hand stopped and the wintry smile faded. If she had freedom of movement, she would have been across the room as far away from him as humanly possible.

April's lips thinned and her eyes narrowed, spitting green rays like deadly blades in her direction. "You wanted them to pay," his voice came from April's mouth.

"I wanted them to go to jail for what they did, not for you to take matters into your own hands," Paige snapped at the insinuation in his voice.

"That isn't good enough for me," he said and climbed off the bed, grabbing the jeans on the floor and slipping them on. "They killed me. They deserve an eternity in hell for destroying everything dear to me." He stormed past Austin, unlocking the door, and marched out before Austin could intercede.

Paige stared at the door as it closed, and then her gaze moved to Austin's. He ran a shaking hand through his hair and crossed, covering her up with the sheet before he took a seat in the chair next to the bed.

"You're not..." she started, and the way his glare jumped to her shut her up.

"No. I'd kind of like to see tomorrow."

"He wouldn't..."

One of Austin's eyebrows rose in a silent challenge.

She really didn't know what he would do, and despite their rocky start, she wanted nothing bad to happen to Austin.

Paige dropped her head on the pillow and stared at the ceiling, letting the silence settle. When he stood, she turned toward him.

"Where are you going?"

"I need some sleep," he said, and she studied the dark circles under his eyes before giving him a nod. "I've got the afternoon shift tomorrow," he added.

"Will you help me stop him?" she asked, dreading the answer based on the way he tensed up.

"I don't have the foggiest idea of how to stop a ghost," he said with a sigh.

Paige exhaled. "I might have an idea."

Austin met her gaze. Dread and intrigue played in his eyes. "You can tell me about it tomorrow."

Paige didn't stop him when he left. She had to think this through carefully. If her idea backfired, she could be the one with her soul left in limbo.

Magick
Chapter 8

AUSTIN HIT THE BED and dropped into the dream almost immediately. The shower scene played in slow motion, the way she felt, the sound of her ragged breath. It all seemed so surreal.

"You want her?"

The strange voice whispered in his ear, and he shivered, distracted. His gaze returned to her shimmering skin, the ecstasy etched into her features, and his soul stirred.

"Do you want her?" the voice asked again, this time louder, closer.

"Yes," he whispered, his fingers ran down her slick abdomen.

"Allow me in and you can own her," the voice echoed.

He blinked, meeting her heated gaze. He wanted her, but owning her didn't feel right.

"Say yes, and I'll give you everything you desire."

Her mouth moved, forming the words, but the voice didn't match her usual seductive purr and his brain wasn't the one in control at the moment.

He whispered a soft 'yes' and then his mind was shrouded in darkness. The blackness overriding his senses caused him to cry out, but he was now locked in the dark prison of his mind. His eyes blinked open, and he watched in horror as his hand opened and closed in front of his eyes.

"I've learned a great deal since the first time I possessed you," his voice whispered in the dark, layered with Hunter's.

Austin shivered, trying to take his body back, but he had no experience in how to excise a ghost. His thoughts turned to Paige for a moment before he thought better of revealing their last conversation.

"You're not going to make me kill anyone, are you?" he forced the words out and Hunter laughed.

"No. My vengeance is complete. Now all I want is Paige," he chuckled. "And since you like to watch, I'll be a nice guy and give you a front-row seat."

"Get out," Austin hissed, but it seemed he couldn't buck Hunter from his form.

"Don't be such a spoilsport. Isn't she what you want?"

Austin pressed his lips together in contemplation. The fact he could still control some of his bodily functions was a plus, and Hunter's offer was tempting, but deep down, he wanted to win her over on his own, not use her dead fiancé to pad his chances.

"I figured out how to stay in a body even when the owner doesn't want me there," Hunter's voice echoed in his head. "The only way to get rid of me is to eat a bullet."

Austin stared at the ceiling through the eyes he now shared with a psychopath. "Is that what you did to Paige's friend?"

"Friend? I would hardly consider April a friend."

"Is that what you did?" Austin asked through clenched teeth.

"As soon as I made her confess to all her wrongdoings in a superb suicide note, yes. She blew her brains out all over that room."

"You pulled the trigger." Austin didn't pose it as a question, just a statement that dropped his heart into this stomach.

All he received in response was an evil chuckle.

"Get some sleep," Hunter said and despite the adrenaline running through Austin's form, his eyes closed, and he fell into the black.

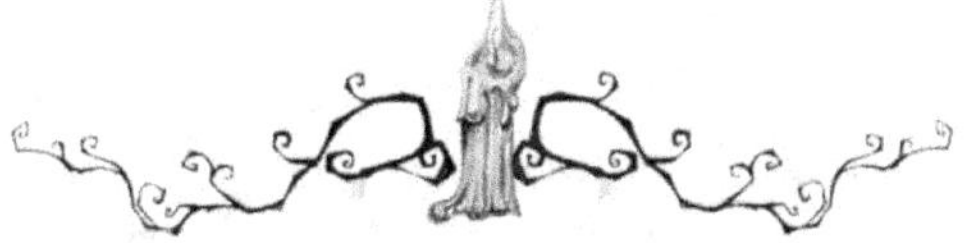

THE ALARM SHOCKED AUSTIN awake, and he slammed his hand on the snooze. Before his eyelids closed again, the bizarre dream ballooned into the forefront of his mind, and he let out a little laugh.

"Rise and shine!" Hunter's voice boomed in his head and Austin grabbed his ears, rolling his face into the pillow before he lost all control over his body.

Horror wrapped around his mind as Hunter animated his form, crossing to the bathroom to do normal things a live person would do. Take a piss, brush his teeth, and shower away the stink from the prior day. When he got a glimpse in the mirror, his eyes were not gray. They were the same green that April's eyes had been the day before.

"You're my bitch," Hunter said to his reflection and stretched his lips into a grin.

"Fuck you," Austin tried to say, but nothing came out of his mouth. The idea of living with this ghost in control for the rest of his life scared the shit out of him. He had to figure out a way to get this prick out of his skin and he tried to send a glare at his reflection, but he had no control over anything anymore.

Hunter dressed in Austin's work scrubs and grabbed the car keys along with his work badge. When he slid into the car, he glanced into the rearview mirror.

"Time to break my baby out of that hospital," he said and winked.

Austin huffed. He needed the job, and if he allowed Hunter to break her out of there, not only would he be unemployed, he might end up in jail. He sat back in his mind, stewing, as Hunter called the shots.

Hunter walked through the halls as if he owned them and he headed straight for Paige's room. When he swung the door open, Paige turned from her spot in front of the window and

Dr. Schaeffer sat in the chair with his ever-present clipboard.

"Oh, sorry," he said and met Paige's stare. Her face paled for a moment, and she blinked before regaining her composure. Her eyes were bloodshot, like she had been crying, and Austin's heart squeezed a little at the hurt in her gaze. She turned back towards the world outside and Hunter backed out of the room.

As the door clicked closed, the tightness in Austin's chest loosened. Paige was no longer bound to the bed, which was a very positive sign, despite the sorrow in her eyes.

"I need to work," Austin whispered, and Hunter huffed, letting him have partial control. The fact that Hunter could shift control so easily sent a chill up Austin's spine. Hunter let him do his rounds and when he came back to Paige's room, all control stopped and Hunter was now in charge.

He slid into the room.

Paige sat on the bed with a laptop computer, her hair tucked behind her ears as she typed at a pace Austin hadn't seen since his college days. Halfway across the room, Paige put her hand up as if she was stopping traffic.

When her gaze left the screen and met Hunter's, he stopped. Austin actually felt the jarring shock rattle through his form at her glare.

"I don't want to talk to you right now," she said. Her voice was soft but firm, echoing the hostility present in her eyes.

"But, Paige..."

"No. You killed a shitload of people. I don't care what you think your reasoning is, it is dead wrong. Not one of them deserved what you did."

She turned away, refocusing on her computer screen, and Hunter remained glued to the spot, unsure of what to say or do. He honestly believed that what he had done was just, and before the anger burned through the disbelief, Austin whispered, "Let me try."

The shift was subtle, but feeling returned to his skin. Hunter was still present in his mind, just relegated to the back seat for the moment.

"Paige?"

This time, when her glare met his, it softened.

"Why did you let him in?" she asked, the pain of her question painted in the creases around her eyes.

Austin shrugged. "He tricked me into saying yes during a dream, and I can't shake him."

Her features hardened. "He's still there?"

Austin nodded and his own fear mingled with Hunter's, creating a burn in his stomach. "Yeah," he said, acknowledging her question verbally, as well as with the head bob. "He seems to have mastered hanging on," Austin added and sent a crooked smile in her direction. "We could test that theory..." He trailed off and his eyebrows rose with hope.

His attempt at humor failed, and her stark stare just made him shift his feet and want to retreat into his fantasy world. Within a blink, he lost control and Hunter took full possession of all his faculties.

Hunter crossed his arms. "Don't be such a judgmental bitch."

Her laugh echoed off the walls, and she dumped the laptop onto the mattress and climbed out of the bed. The moment she stepped in line with his toes, Hunter narrowed his eyes with suspicion.

Her hands planted on his chest and shoved.

Hunter was not prepared for the physical display, or the angry glare that accompanied it. He stumbled a few steps before regaining his balance and was towering over her with just one menacing step. While Austin cringed, Paige did not. She had no clue of the venom brewing inside his body.

He reached for her, and she batted his hand away.

Hunter wrapped his hands around her upper arms and lifted, bringing her to eye level before turning and slamming her back to the wall. With his eyes less than an inch from hers, he growled, "You do not want to piss me off."

Paige's widening eyes showed the shock she must have felt. The rest of her expression remained deadpan, like this was a normal occurrence. Austin hated the ghost inhabiting his body.

"Let me go," she said through clenched teeth.

Instead, the bastard stepped closer, pressing his body against her, trapping her in place. "No."

"Hunter, I don't want this. You aren't the same person I agreed to marry."

His teeth ground together for a moment. "I am the same person." The words came out in a harsh snarl.

"No. You are bitter and nasty and... and..." She stumbled on words as she stared into his eyes. "And not my Hunter," she added in a whisper.

His grip on her arms loosened, and he set her down on the ground, but he didn't give her any breathing room.

"I am what they made me," he said just as softly, and his hand cupped her cheek. The fire in Austin's veins cooled and for the first time since Hunter possessed him, he actually believed he would do Paige no harm.

"They didn't make you a murderer."

"Yes. They did. What they did to me and then to you..." He stepped back, allowing both of them to breathe.

"It was a stupid college prank that went drastically wrong. They didn't set out to kill you."

He laughed and ran a hand through his hair. "Well, they didn't exactly want to have a fucking tea party, either."

"They wanted an orgy, not a massacre."

They stared at each other, the space between them widening into a gap Austin didn't think they could ever breach again.

"They got both," Hunter mumbled, keeping her gaze.

"Yeah. About that. What were you thinking, screwing the whole fraternity?"

"You did it."

"I was drugged."

"I was curious."

Her eyebrows arched. "Curious?"

"I wanted to know what it felt like for a woman." His shoulders rose and fell in a half-hearted shrug, and Paige crossed her arms.

"I could have told you what it's like," she snapped.

"There's no way you could accurately describe it. At least, not in any meaningful way that a guy would get." He stepped closer. "It also helped me understand exactly what gets a girl going." He flashed a grin.

"Fuck you," Paige said and stepped back, right into the hospital bed.

"Is that an invitation?"

"Get out!" She pointed at the door.

Hunter stared at her and then turned and stormed out of the room. Austin tried not to smile at his epic failure, but Hunter caught the underlying glee and issued a growl of derision.

"What the fuck are you so happy about?" he muttered under his breath.

Austin didn't say a word, letting his mind drift to a place where Hunter couldn't reach him.

Magick
Chapter 9

PAIGE STARED AT THE door and slumped against the bed. The conversation with Dr. Schaeffer this morning circled in her head. His explanation that her roommate had admitted to everything Paige was accused of before taking her life, along with his heartfelt apology, had left her hollow.

April's suicide note exonerated her completely of any wrongdoing in Hunter's death, as such, she was free to go at any time, but considering the tragedy that surrounded her right now, the doctor indicated she was more than welcome to stay another day or two.

Dr. Schaeffer said his door was always open and while he had been less than supportive when he thought she was bat-shit crazy, he seemed to have softened, and showed genuine concern for her mental well-being. Even the way he unlatched her from the bed had been done with a humbleness born of being wrong, which was something Paige guessed didn't happen very often to the good doctor.

Paige turned her attention to the outside world, wondering just how fast she would be locked back up if she told him what was really going on. Instead, she had mentioned that April had snuck in the previous day to see her, and she hadn't been very receptive to her at all.

When the doctor had told her the suicide wasn't her fault, she had just given him a cursory glance before returning her gaze to the fall day outside.

"I think it might be a good idea for me to stay and talk this out," Paige had said after a few minutes of strained silence. "I need to get my head straight before I venture out there." She nodded outside and glanced in his direction.

"I can make sure that happens," Dr. Schaeffer said. "I can arrange for you to keep this room until the end of the week, but after that, I'm afraid you can't stay. I'll also arrange for you to get a badge that will allow you to come and go, if you would like."

His offer forced her to blink away the sudden swell of hot tears and she just nodded, pressing her lips together to keep her emotions in check.

That was when Hunter burst into the room, wearing Austin's body. The shock of seeing him occupying the man she had sent after him was almost too much after everything that had happened last night.

She sighed and dropped her gaze to the laptop Dr. Schaeffer had loaned her. Her curriculum was displayed along with a succession of incompletes. She'd have to bust her ass to get back all the lost time, that was, if the school would even allow her to step back into her degree program after all that had happened.

She closed the browser in disgust. School was the least of her worries.

Hunter was a more pressing issue. One that would require her full attention. The longer he held on, the more volatile he would get, and there was no telling what he would do to Austin. Pirating his body for a brief screw was one thing, pirating his life was a completely different story. One she could not live with.

"I have to do something," she said to the empty room and bit her lip. Her gaze landed back on the computer, and she sighed, typing out the commands to a website she hadn't visited in years.

In the search, she typed 'banishment spell.' The details of what she would need were simple, as were the words to send Hunter on to where ever he belonged. Her mind swirled with doubt. If someone had told her a week ago that she would banish Hunter from her life forever, she would have laughed and told them they were crazy. But that Hunter was gone, and she had no choice. She sent herself a note with the instructions and closed out of the website before powering down the computer.

She tucked it away in the nightstand and glanced out at the twilight descending, feeling every bit of the darkness as it crept into her room.

Magick
Chapter 10

AUSTIN SAT IN HIS car in the parking lot, staring up at her window as the night drew darker. Hunter had stewed under his skin for the rest of his shift, but at least he had let Austin take over, instead of sabotaging his job. He let him finish his shift and even allowed him to go home, eat and wash up before he took control again.

"If I can't have her..." Hunter started.

"I'm not hurting her," Austin interrupted, feeling the burn of anger ignite his skin.

Green eyes shifted from the building to the rearview mirror.

"If she doesn't want you, I'll just have to trash this meat suit and find someone that she does want."

"Good riddance." Austin tried to glare back at the reflection, but his stark stare never altered, even with the low chuckle coming from his throat.

"Let me be perfectly clear. Once I'm in a body and have attached the way I have with you, the only way I'm getting out is if you die."

A chill settled far into Austin's bones and his image actually shivered before a tiny smile found its way to his lips.

"But I thought…"

"You thought because I lost the connection when I came, that this time would be no different?" Hunter laughed. "That was my first attempt, and all things considered, it turned out to be a good thing I hadn't figured out how to latch on, otherwise you would be six feet under after going on a murderous rampage."

Horror filled every cell in Austin, and it made Hunter smile. His eyes moved back to the room just as the light went out.

"I suggest you get her to forgive me, otherwise I'll have to find someone else to win her over."

"You're going to give me control?" Austin asked. His voice filled the car and another glance at the gray eyes staring back at him confirmed the question. He ran a hand through his hair and stepped out of the car, heading into the building.

Austin bypassed having to sign himself in with a wave to Veronica, the night nurse staffing the desk. He headed to the stairwell and stopped as the door latched behind him. Drawing a shaky breath, he took the stairs two at a time until he reached the third floor.

His mind was a complete blank in what he could say to sway Paige. He loathed the spirit inside him and couldn't comprehend forgiving him for his heinous deeds.

But he also hadn't been engaged to the shit.

He stopped in front of her door and glanced down the hall, making sure it was clear before slipping inside the room. Instead of going to the bed, he took a seat in the chair and put his face in his hands with an audible sigh.

"I told you I didn't want to see you," Paige said in the dark.

"It's Austin, not Hunter," Austin said and leaned back in the chair, peering through the darkness at the barely visible bump pattern on the bed. Sheets shuffled and then the bedside lamp turned on.

Paige met his gaze with a deep crease between her eyes.

"He's in here, but he's letting me do the talking." He shrugged and glanced down at his hands. With a sarcastic laugh, he said, "If I can't convince you to forgive him, I guess I'm a dead man." When she said nothing, he glanced at her.

Her shocked features transitioned to irritation and her lips pressed into a thin line as she propped up on her elbow.

Austin's gaze dropped from hers, running down the front of her to her semi-exposed breast before following the line of her under the sheet. He turned away, gritting his teeth against the sudden swell of dirty thoughts parading through his head. Laughter erupted from him, and he leaned back in the chair, studying the ceiling.

"Here I am, basically a walking dead man, and all I can think of is how you'd feel wrapped around me." He tilted his head to look at her. "And those aren't Hunter's thoughts, either."

Blush crept into her cheeks, and she sighed, slipping out of the bed and crossing to stand in front of him.

"I can't seem to forgive him for what he did to Max and April, but I don't want him to hurt you."

Austin gave her a sad smile and a shrug. "I'm just as much of a jackass as he is, so why do you even give a shit?"

She leaned on the arms of the chair. "You're not as much of an ass as you think you are." She allowed a hint of a smile before turning serious again. "But if he hurts you, he'll lose me for good. Right now, I'm angry, and disappointed, and I really don't want to discuss any of this until I get a decent night's sleep."

Austin cupped her cheek, running his thumb over her lips before meeting her warm stare. "I just need one thing from you," he said, and before she could ask what he wanted, he leaned forward, covering her sweet lips with his.

The kiss burned in the way he thought it might, consuming thought and delivering a delicious thrill. Her lips parted, but he wasn't sure if it was shock or consent. Either way, he explored her mouth and danced with her tongue.

His fingers laced in her hair, drawing her closer, deepening the kiss, and his free hand wrapped around her waist, pulling her into his lap. The sudden weight melting into him seemed to snap the spell, and she pulled away with wide eyes.

They stared at each other and Paige searched his face.

"That was... you?"

Austin couldn't help the grin that surfaced. Her awed tone fanned his ego, despite the shifting burn of Hunter's aggravation.

"You already know what I can do in bed," he said, letting his voice get low in that tone his ex-girlfriends always called his 'sexy-as-sin' voice.

"I know what you can do with your toys," she clarified, and her teasing nature made his cock jump. "I just didn't know you could kiss like that."

"I don't think Hunter likes the way this conversation is going," he whispered and sent a wink in her direction. As a matter-of-fact, Austin could feel the boil in his blood, to the point it was difficult to ignore.

"If he shows his face, he won't ever get my forgiveness," Paige said, leaning away from Austin to level a dead-serious glare.

Austin's smile faded, and he dropped his gaze to the hand planted firmly on his chest. The engagement ring still adorned her finger, and he slid her off his lap.

Paige crossed to the door and flipped the lock, preventing anyone from entering the room without the jangle of keys to give them a heads up. When she returned to the spot in front of him and crossed her arms, he met her gaze.

"I just need some time," she said with a sigh.

"Okay..." Austin drew out the word and leaned back in the chair.

"Tell him I'll meet him somewhere tomorrow night around this time."

Austin raised his eyebrows. "You can leave?"

"Yes. I'm free to come and go as I please, and I have this room through the weekend."

"You say that like this is a hotel?"

"Dr. Schaffer thought I might need some help sorting out everything that has happened, and for once, I agree with him."

Hunter whispered in Austin's mind, "Ask her to meet where I proposed."

"Hunter wants to meet where he proposed."

Paige huffed and turned toward the window, her arms dropping to her sides as she considered the request.

"How about somewhere a little more neutral, like the orchard glen?"

Austin stared at her profile, and his heart sank. She was going to forgive the murdering ghost. The thought sent a rash of angry goose flesh across his skin, and he shifted in the chair, crossing his arms like that would shield him from any further disappointment.

"Fine," he muttered, and she turned her gaze back to him.

"What's with the attitude?"

Austin clamped his lips shut and Hunter chuckled inside him, taunting him with her affections. Hunter made it perfectly clear that Paige was his and always would be.

"I just can't believe..." he started and trailed off, shaking his head and looking away. He'd only known her for a short time compared to Hunter, and he had no claim on her at all, so the sudden letdown left him confused and wondering if Hunter's feelings were seeping into his blood.

She stepped closer and her hand clamped around his chin, forcing him to meet her gaze.

"Isn't it in your best interest for me to forgive him?"

Austin rolled his eyes and tried to pull his chin from her grip, but she slid back onto his lap, shocking him into silent submission.

"Well?"

Just the proximity of her muddled his brain, and his only response was a one-shouldered shrug. Torn wasn't an accurate enough description. He felt shredded by the fact she was willing to forgive the little shit, and yet, the alternative was unthinkable.

"What happens to me?" He couldn't help the question, especially since it had been nagging him since he woke with Hunter in possession of his body. "You forgive him and he takes over for good, right?" He shrugged again. "I'm dead either way."

The reality of the situation set in and when her hand caressed his cheek, he locked gazes with her. The sorrow in her eyes tightened his throat, and he forced himself to swallow. She closed the distance and gave him a gentle kiss. Austin didn't want a pity kiss and tried to pull away, but she followed, pinning his cheeks between her palms.

"Paige," he whispered under her insistent lips.

She pulled far enough away for him to focus on her face. What he saw there was more than pity. Desire painted her cheeks pink, and the way her eyes dipped to his lips and back made him throw caution to the wind. If this was a walking death sentence, he was going to take full advantage of whatever Paige was offering before he stepped into that death chamber.

Austin pulled her close, delivering a steam-filled kiss, and his heart knocked on the walls of his chest when she exhibited the same fervor flooding his veins. The kiss broke, and she trailed a hot line of kisses down his neck while her fingers fumbled with the buttons on his oxford shirt.

He divided his hands between her chest and the inside of her thighs, and all he wanted was her naked and riding him into oblivion. She pushed off his lap and the sudden cooling of air between them sent a delicious shiver up his spine, especially when her kisses trailed down his chest and she dropped to her knees between his legs.

Her fingers expertly undid his belt, and he reached for her, but the warning glare she shot him made him second guess that move, so he settled on gripping the arms of the chair. With each click of his zipper, his breath became more ragged with anticipation.

"Oh, fuck," he whispered when her lips slid over the sensitive skin at the tip of his cock. When she slid him into her mouth, he leaned his head back, letting a low, growling groan of satisfaction fill the room.

Hunter's tirade in his head just made this a bigger slice of heaven and it fueled the thoughts of what he wanted to do to her tonight. The energy spiraled inward until it pooled in his abdomen, building and filling his lungs with harsh pants and a litany of praise that tumbled over her, driving her mouth to a frantic pace.

Austin's entire body went rigid with the power of the orgasm, and instead of holding her head in place while he filled her mouth with cum, he gripped the chair arms and squeezed his eyes closed. She never stopped sucking until the aftershocks subsided and Austin pushed her away.

She wiped her lips with the back of her hand and sent a shy grin his way.

"My turn," he said, pulling on energy reserves he didn't realize he had. In one swift motion, he picked her up from her perch on the floor and laid her out on the bed, tearing at her undergarments with the frantic need driving him.

"Austin?"

The question in her voice stopped him, and he raised his gaze to hers. "Yeah," he asked with a complete lack of breath.

"I just wanted to make sure," she said.

Austin allowed a grin to form. "I'm sure he'll make me pay one way or another for this, but I really don't give a damn right now," he said and didn't wait for a response.

His mouth found the same spot over her clit, and she moaned as he played with her, teasing her with his tongue until her fists balled up in the sheets and her pussy dripped with the juices of multiple orgasms.

Austin pulled away and kissed his way up her body until he met her lips and then he pushed up on his hands, staring into her eyes, waiting for her permission to go any farther.

"I want you to make love to me," Paige whispered. "Austin," she added, staring at him in a way that made Hunter scream in his head.

Austin smiled and slid inside her slowly, enjoying the feel of her; after a few strokes, he pulled out despite her whine of protest. When he shifted her and stretched out on the mattress on his back, she immediately understood without him saying a word.

He wanted her to have the control. He wanted her to set the pace, and he wanted her to be the one making love to him.

With each gentle sway of her hips and soft moans announcing her pleasure, Hunter's curses increased. His promises of pain fell empty because this heaven was worth anything Hunter could dish out.

Paige sped up her gyrations, bringing him to the brink. Her orgasm squeezed around him, milking him into his own. The intensity of it blinded him and shut off his ability to draw a breath. It took him half a dozen heartbeats to draw air into his lungs and a couple more for his vision to refocus.

"Holy shit," he whispered, and Paige let out a laugh, collapsing on top of him like a pliant rag doll. She didn't uncouple from him. Instead, she just lay on his chest with her head tucked under his chin.

It wasn't until her trembling got worse that he reached up and tilted her chin in his direction. Tears painted her cheeks and dripped onto his skin, creating a level of horror that was akin to when he realized he was forever stuck sharing his head with a ghost.

"I'm sorry," he started and went to move her off.

"No," she said and pushed him back in place.

"You're not... mad?"

She shook her head, and he settled back into the pillow.

"Then why are you crying?"

"This was my way of saying goodbye," she whispered and nuzzled back into his chest.

Austin stared at the ceiling, processing her words, still unsure of whether he should be happy or horrified. Instead of dealing with the flow of emotion from her or those within himself, he just ran his fingers over her back and through her hair, focusing on only the physical sensation of having her in his arms.

Hunter was quiet now as well, but Austin knew he was still there. He could feel his malignant form twisting in his mind just as much as her goodbye twisted his gut.

Magick
Chapter 11

PAIGE STAYED ON HIS chest, listening to his breathing and relaxing under the caress of his fingertips. Her mind raced. She hadn't meant to go this far with Austin. Hell, she thought nothing would happen when she turned on the light. It wasn't until he delivered that damned sizzling kiss that all thought stopped.

That kiss fried all logical thought, and she cursed her lack of self-restraint.

He shifted under her, and she lifted her head, meeting his tired gaze and she couldn't help but notice the light blue flecks that speckled his gray irises. She had never had cause to study his eyes before and now that she was; it was like getting lost in a thin layer of fog in the Caribbean.

"I should go."

She knew he should, especially if Hunter got pissed enough to take him over, and she was really testing the limits of sanity at this point.

She nodded and rolled onto her back, allowing him to get out of the narrow bed.

Austin dressed slowly with his back to her, and Paige studied each remaining exposed body part until he was completely covered, and a rash of disappointment flashed over her. When he sat in the chair to tie his work boots, Paige wrapped herself in the covers to ward off the chill that settled over the room.

With his head still tilted toward the floor, he said, "I guess this is it." His voice held such a defeated quality that Paige's heart squeezed under the pressure.

"Austin," she whispered, and he turned towards her, resting his elbows on his knees. "I never wanted this to happen to you."

His lips formed a sarcastic smile. "I'm sure you wished worse on me after that first night, and I really wouldn't have blamed you."

Paige bit her lip, stopping her plans from tumbling out and alerting Hunter. If he knew she was planning to banish him, he would never show tomorrow night. He had to think there was a possibility of reconciliation.

"Well, you said yes to Hunter then, too."

His smile faded, as did the gleam in his eyes, and he stood, giving her a nod before he headed towards the door.

"Make sure he knows about the orchard," Paige said when Austin reached toward the lock. His hand paused, and he sent a hurtful glare over his shoulder.

"He knows."

With that, Austin left her alone with only the slam of the door as a goodbye. She prayed he would forgive her for the farce. She prayed everything went according to plan; otherwise, she'd be subject to the wrath of an angry ghost.

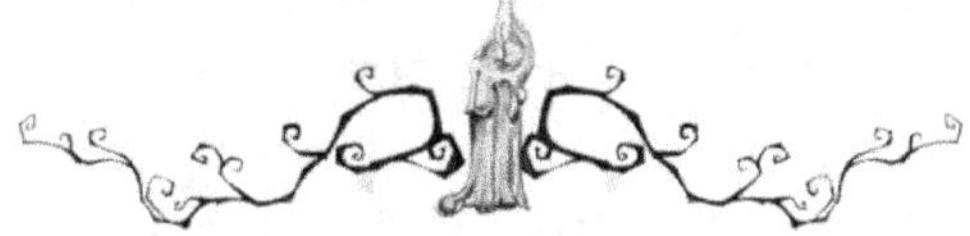

PAIGE WOKE TO THE early morning sunshine and stretched her aching muscles. The trip to the private bathroom was a heavenly relief from the last few days of waiting for a bedpan. She splashed water on her face before brushing the sleep from her mouth and then studied her reflection in the mirror.

Her face seemed thinner, and she wondered just how much weight she'd lost while she was in the hospital. She had been fed three meals a day, but her appetite hadn't been that robust. What she really wanted was a burger and fries, and she let out a soft chuckle at where her mind had wandered.

The knock on the door caught her attention, and she pulled the light hospital bathrobe around her and stepped back in the room in time to see a nurse stick her head through the door.

"Good morning, Miss Turner," she said with a welcoming smile. "This was dropped off at the desk for you a little while ago." She placed a small overnight bag on the chair. "It's clothing and some toiletries that Mr. Shelton thought you might need, now that you are not formally under the hospital's care."

Paige cocked her head. "Mr. Shelton?"

"Austin."

Paige felt the heat rise in her cheeks and offered an awkward smile in return. He had never told her his last name and the thought that he went to all that trouble, after seeing how upset he was last night, layered on the burn of guilt.

"He seems to be quite fond of you."

"He's very easy to talk to," Paige said. "He was one of the few people here who didn't make me feel crazy." The honesty in her statement struck a chord, and while he may have initially thought she was bat-shit crazy, he never made her feel that way.

The nurse dropped her gaze and gave her a nod before she shuffled out of the room.

Paige closed her eyes and hung her head. She didn't mean to make the nurse feel bad. Instead of following her, she approached the bag and opened it, finding a clean pair of underwear, a bra and jeans, a camisole, and a nice sweater. Her thick socks and sneakers were also packed in the bag. The side pocket contained deodorant, a toothbrush, and toothpaste, along with her hairbrush.

An envelope sat neatly on the pile of clothes. Her name was scrawled in handwriting she recognized. It hadn't been Austin who brought the bag for her. This was Hunter's doing, and she pressed her lips together before she sighed and unsealed the envelope, pulling out the note written in Hunter's messy script.

Paige,

I can't say I'm pleased by what transpired last night, but I guess I deserved that after the mess I've made of things. I'm sorry, but if I hadn't done

Paige closed the note and sat on the corner of the bed, digesting the words before she slid the letter into the inside pocket and zipped it closed. Guilt flooded every fiber, creating an unpleasant filth she needed to rinse off. Unfortunately, the bathroom here only had a toilet and a sink, and that wouldn't help her feel clean.

And she desperately needed to feel clean after her duplicity.

She stepped out into the hallway with the bag in her hand and the cheap hospital slippers adorning her feet and approached the nurse's desk.

"Excuse me?" she asked tentatively.

The nurse who delivered the bag looked up from typing her notes and gave her a soft smile.

"What can I help you with, Miss Turner?"

"I haven't had a shower in a few days. Is that possible?"

She picked up the phone and punched in a few numbers. "Dr. Schaeffer, Miss Turner is requesting a shower and I am not sure if I should take her to the patient showers or…" she paused, listening to the voice on the other end, her finger still poised in the 'give me a minute' pose. "That seems much more appropriate, given the circumstances." She gave a nod and hung up the phone.

The nurse stood and stepped out from behind the counter. "Dr. Schaeffer thinks the staff facilities would be more appropriate than the patient showers. The showers for us are a little more private," she said and smiled over her shoulder. "Plus, I think there is a shelf that has a couple of options for shampoo and soap for you to choose from in the locker room."

"Thank you." Paige thought about the showers Austin had taken her to and the locker room she waited for him in afterwards. She hadn't noticed any shelving or options in the locker room that night, but she hadn't been concentrating on much of her surroundings. Instead, she had been marveling over how incredibly satiated and clean she felt, even after such mind-blowing and kinky sex.

"The men have a community shower, but ours are more like the ones you have in the college dorms." The nurse said and swiped her access key, opening a door to reveal the long familiar hallway Austin had rolled her down that night. There were two doors at the end of the hallway. One for the women's locker room, and the other for the men's.

"When you come out, you can press the buzzer," she said, pointing to the intercom to the right of the hallway entry as we passed it. "I'll come get you and take you back to your room."

"Thank you." Paige gave her a nod and headed toward the women's locker room.

"There is a stack of towels to the right of the showers," the nurse called before she disappeared back into the belly of the hospital.

Paige found an array of shampoo and conditioners and body wash, and headed toward the back section of the locker room. The showers were indeed like those in the school dorms, with the small double cube, one with a bench for her bag, and one housing the shower with a thin fabric curtain to contain the spray.

She stripped out of the hospital garb and dialed on the warm water. Stepping under the stream, Paige exhaled, enjoying the lavender-vanilla scent of the body wash she chose. Lavender was a good choice; the calming effects would help later when her anxiety ratcheted up.

The spell was specific, and almost everything she needed to banish the ghost was in her room at the sorority house. While Hunter had said it wasn't recommended that she go there, she had to in order to free Austin from a lifetime under Hunter's sadistic, ghostly rule.

Her mind drifted to Austin. She wanted to believe last night was all him, and not Hunter's emotions running amok in his system. Last night had been nothing she could have ever foreseen. It wasn't a kinky wild fuck, like the other night in the shower. Austin took his time. He was slow and gentle, and god help her, he elicited something deep within her that she had thought was lost to her the moment Hunter died.

Austin proved she still could experience a tender moment with a man other than Hunter. Paige had no idea if anything would develop with him once Hunter was expelled, but the realization that love could exist in a world where Hunter didn't, gave her hope.

She remained under the spray until her fingertips formed waterlogged wrinkles. With a quick twist of the knob, the stream dissipated and Paige opened the curtain before drying off with the hospital issued towel. Her clothing slid onto her skin like velvet compared to the scratchy cotton of the hospital johnny, and she welcomed the feel of denim and lace.

She stepped out of the stall with her hair wrapped in a towel and only her camisole and jeans on. In the locker room, she took a seat on the bench and finished getting dressed. After towel drying her hair, she ran the brush through her long locks as a hint of lavender wafted around her. The simple act of showering and getting dressed gave her the feeling of royalty after being a prisoner in her own bed for the last week.

She dumped both the towel and her discarded hospital clothes into the laundry bin and headed towards the door at the end of the hallway. Her sneakers squeaked with each step, making her slow to a casual canter instead of the rushing pseudo-run she had adopted. She pressed the intercom.

"I'm on my way," the nurse said in a tone that Paige categorized as chipper.

The door popped open a few minutes later, and the nurse waved her through.

"Dr. Schaeffer wanted you to stop by his office," she said in that same singsong voice.

"Okay," Paige said, although she had no idea where the doctor's office was. The nurse soon rectified that, stopping before an open door, and directing Paige inside.

Dr. Schaeffer let her settle in the chair before he adjusted his glasses and leaned back in his chair.

"How are you feeling today?"

"Cleaner," Paige said, and heat painted her cheeks red. "I got some rest, too." She shifted in the chair. "I wanted to take a ride out to the sorority and pack up my things, if that is okay?"

His eyebrows rose in shock.

"My car is there, and my keys are in my room."

"The room you shared with April Carlton?"

"Yes, sir." Paige kept his gaze and pressed her lips together in a sad smile.

"I'm not sure you can do that yet."

Her smile faltered. If he didn't let her go, tonight would be a disaster.

"My mother's music box is in the room, too. It's the only thing I have of hers," Paige said. "At least let me get that, and maybe another change of clothes?"

He chewed on the corner of his mouth and rifled through the papers on his desk. Paige adopted that pleading look that neither Hunter nor Austin could deny; the doctor exhaled in a huff.

"Fine," he conceded. "I will drive you there, but you should only grab the items you need until we receive word that it is okay for you to either move back in or move your things out."

Paige nodded. "Thank you," she said with a measure of relief, and he studied her closer.

"Don't you plan on returning to school?" he asked after a moment.

"Yes, but I think I've had enough of sorority life." She really couldn't see moving back there, especially into her old room, and she doubted any of the other girls would trade now. The constant reminder of April's betrayal and the circumstances of her death would be too much for her to deal with. Besides, she wasn't sure what kind of reception she'd get from the rest of the sorority.

"Aren't you close to the other girls in the sorority?"

Paige glanced out the window and then down at her hands. "Not really. I spent most of my time with Hunter," she said and met his gaze. "I mean, we did sorority things together, but beyond April, I just haven't..." She trailed off with a shrug. "I was either studying or with Hunter, unless I had to represent the sorority somewhere."

"So, you're a lone wolf type?" he asked, but it was soft and not meant as a putdown.

"I guess. Ever since my parents and little sister died, I've kept everyone at arm's length."

"Except Hunter?"

She picked at a hangnail and nodded. A lump in her throat formed at the same time as the conclusion that everyone she loves dies, and she glanced up at the doctor. "I guess I'm cursed that way."

"What way?" he asked and leaned forward on his desk.

"Losing those I care about."

His head cocked. "So, your solution is to close yourself off from the world?"

She hadn't even made a conscious decision to do that, but it made logical sense. "Well, if I don't let people get close, I won't have to go through the pain of losing them." Even as the words tumbled out, she knew how futile a plan that was and how disappointed her parents would be with her.

"That's no way to live." It was his only comment, and he sighed, glancing at the clock. "I have about an hour before my day begins in earnest. Did you want to run that errand now?"

"Sure," she agreed, happy to be getting it done early.

Keys jingled, and he pulled open a drawer, sliding the clutch she had brought to the Halloween party across the desk.

"I imagine you might need that."

She pulled it the rest of the way across the desk and unzipped the bag, afraid they might have left a syringe in it, but only her school ID and room keys were inside. She closed her eyes with relief and when she opened them, Dr. Schaeffer stood and slid on his jacket.

"The police took the needle," he said.

"It wasn't mine," she snapped, the reaction automatic, and Dr. Schaeffer gave her a nod. "I'm sorry; I guess the whole thing still has me on the defensive."

"I can't blame you for that. I wasn't exactly accepting of your story. If your roommate hadn't gone off the deep end, we would still be operating based on the presented facts. It makes me wonder if it had been premeditated. I can't imagine the flawless job of framing you coming out of a panic situation."

Paige chuckled as they walked out of the sanitarium. "Max was at his best under high pressure," she mumbled, but there was a level of coercion that made his words hit home and it also gave some credence to Hunter's vengeance.

"Max wouldn't have set out to kill his best friend," she said, after they slid into the doctor's car. She met his gaze and repeated what she had said to Hunter the other day. "They may have planned the orgy, but they certainly didn't plan on someone dying."

They drove in silence for a while before Paige asked a question that had been bothering her. "What time did they place the nine-one-one call?"

"It was a little after five."

"In the morning?" she gawked.

"Yes."

"I blacked out at a little after ten."

"The coroner said your fiancé died between one and three." He drove with little direction from her. "That was the only inconsistency in their otherwise flawless plan, and they said they panicked and didn't know what to do." He glanced at her just before he pulled to a stop in front of the sorority and threw the car in park.

"By the time they called the cops, whatever they gave me was out of my system," Paige said and reached for the door.

"Yes, and you had already had your psychotic break."

She gave him a shy smile. "Can you blame me?" His wry smile met her, and Paige took that as her exit cue. "Thank you for the ride," she added and stepped out of the car.

"Would you like me to wait until you've gathered what you need?"

Even though he posed it as a question, she got the distinct feeling that there was something more behind it. Austin's words regarding the condition of the room crept into her mind, and she nodded. The thought of having someone outside gave her the extra strength she needed to face the aftermath of her roommate's death.

"Thank you," she said and closed the door. She paused, staring up at the sorority house with dread lacing its way through her bones. With a deep breath, Paige trudged toward whatever nightmare lay in waiting.

Magick
Chapter 12

PAIGE SLIPPED HER KEY in the door to her old room, wincing as the scraping sound filled the quiet house. The click of the lock announced her presence, but no one came to welcome her. She pushed the door open and slid inside. The first thing that struck her was the underlying scent of iron, and the dim light didn't help. It only fueled her imagination.

She reached for the light switch and the bright fluorescents roared to life, making her squint against the sudden flood. Paige's gaze locked on the stained mattress and rust-colored splatter that painted the wall behind April's bed. Comprehension was slow, but when it finally sank in, her hand clamped over her mouth, and she almost spun on her heel and ran out of the room.

The fact she had to fumble with the doorknob gave her just enough time to get a grip on the flee instinct, and she stood staring at the pristine white door, trying to catch her breath.

Without turning toward the blood-soaked mattress, she shuffled to her desk to the right of the door and opened the bottom drawer. The box of candles and spices was still tucked in the back of the drawer, along with the jewelry box Paige had told the doctor about. She reached for one of the empty book bags hanging on the hook on the side of her closet.

The box of candles and spices fit snugly next to the jewelry box and, keeping her back toward the devastation on the other side of the room, she opened the middle drawer and picked up her pocketbook, slinging it over her shoulder. Her gaze dropped to the small photo booklet sitting under where her purse had been. The album contained all her favorite pictures of Hunter, along with some personal mementos, like a small clip of hair from the time he finally gave in and cut off his unruly locks into a more adult looking fashion, concert tickets, and anything Paige deemed worthy of remembrance. Paige picked it up and flipped to the page with Hunter's hair taped in the middle, along with the before and after photos. With a sigh, she snapped the book closed and dropped it into the bag. The pictures and his hair would play a key role in the success of the banishment spell.

Her car keys were still in the top drawer, and she slid those in the front pocket of her jeans before standing and gripping the edge of the chair, hoping to find some strength in the cheap wood. Her bureau was behind her in the direct line of sight of the bloodstains.

She almost chickened out, but she needed clothing for the next couple of days, and with a deep breath, she turned, focusing on the bureau at the foot of her bed, but the knowledge of what transpired on the other side of the room kept pulling her eyes in that direction. She resisted the urge and opened the drawers, throwing underwear, socks, shirts and jeans into the bag.

The last item was in her closet, and she swung the door open, reaching for her warm coat hanging in the corner. The reflection caught her eye, and she froze in place at the vision of April, propped on the edge of the bed, watching her every move. Her heart skipped in her chest, and her throat closed around her windpipe. Air whistled in and out of her mouth, and she forced herself to pull her coat off the hanger and hugged it to her chest as she blinked at her roommate.

"Don't forget your boots," April said, her voice soft and frail, like a swirl of fog.

Paige dropped her gaze to her favorite scuffed up cowgirl boots and snatched them off the floor, dropping them in the overstuffed bag before turning away from the reflection and closing the closet door. The chill bit at her skin and she gripped the handle of the bag along with her coat like both were a buffer that would protect her from the ghost in the room.

She turned, bracing herself for an assault of some manner, but April was no longer visible, and the chill slipped away.

"I'm sorry," she whispered and didn't wait for a reply. Paige bolted out of the room, slipping under the tape and shutting the door with a loud bang. She let the flight reflex take hold and bolted out of the sorority, skidding to a stop at the bottom of the stairs to catch her breath.

The ding of an open car door caught her attention, and she looked up to see Dr. Schaeffer standing with the driver's side door open behind him. She sent a shaky wave toward him and pulled her keys out of her pocket, dangling them and nodding her head toward the parking lot next door.

"Stop by my office when you get back, okay?" he said. Even with the questioning lilt at the end of his sentence, she knew it wasn't a question, and she nodded before heading to her car.

She dropped her bag on the passenger seat and propped the coat over it before leaning back in the seat and running trembling hands through her hair. The keys rattled in her shaking hands as she tried to slip the ignition key in. The third try was the charm, and she turned the engine over; slipping her little Prius into gear, she pulled out of the parking lot just as some lights in the house came on.

Paige didn't wait. She pulled out, taking the one-way road that took her by the fraternity house. Slowing, she pulled to a stop at the curb and stared up at the monstrosity where everything dear in her life had been destroyed. She blinked away the lewd visions that had formed in her mind and refocused on the road, heading toward the sanitarium and the safety of her room.

After storing her clothing in the small closet in her room, she glanced around the room for a more secure place to store her spell box and the photo album. Paige had no idea if Austin was scheduled to work, but if he came in and saw the box, Hunter would know she was up to something. She thought about where she stowed the computer, but the nightstand had no compartment, which left the bed and the chair. If someone bent down enough, they would see the floor under the bed. The chair, at least, had a flap, and she stowed the box and album in the small space under the chair, biting her lip in angst as she stood back to study her handiwork.

With only the music box left in the bag, she stored that on the floor of the closet, next to the foldable wheelchair and the bag Austin had brought her the other day.

With her goodies stowed away, Paige stepped out of her room and gave the nurse a reassuring smile before heading down toward Dr. Schaeffer's office. His door was still open and a quick glance at the clock told her he had another ten minutes before he would have to start his rounds.

He looked up from his computer and nodded towards the chair.

Paige took a seat. "Thank you for driving me there."

"You looked a little frazzled when you came out."

She laughed. *Understatement of the year*, but she kept that thought firmly behind her lips. "I guess I didn't expect there still to be so much blood," she said, and his eyebrows rose. "The room hasn't been cleaned yet," she added. "I mean, the sheets are gone, but the mattress still has bloodstains and there is still some splatter on the walls." She had no idea why she kept talking, but the release of nervous energy left her trembling in the chair.

Concern bloomed in his eyes, and he stood, coming around to her side of the desk. He crouched next to her, covering her hand with his.

The pinch in her upper arm along with the physical contact of the doctor's hand turned off the ramble that tumbled from her lips and she met his gaze, pressing her lips together as calm settled into her muscles. Mist covered her eyes, and she blinked the sudden burn of tears away.

"Paige, your roommate's death was not your fault."

His simple statement drew more heat to her eyes and tears blurred her vision before brimming and tracing hot lines down her cheeks. Paige tried to smile, but nothing he said could wipe away the guilt. She hadn't been able to stop Hunter's rampage. Paige couldn't imagine how horrible the fraternity looked if her bedroom was that bad.

A nurse appeared at the doorway and the doctor gave her a nod before bringing his eyes back to Paige.

"I am going to have Nurse Patty bring you back to your room. The sedative I just gave you should take the edge off, okay?"

Paige slowly shook her head. "I didn't want drugs, sir," she said, and whatever he had slipped her wrapped its control over the shudders racking her form, quelling them. "Isn't it normal to freak out a little in the aftermath of a suicide?" she asked, meeting his gaze.

"Yes, but you were exhibiting signs of shock."

She blinked rapidly, absorbing his words and noticing the physical sensations of her breath coming in fast pants and the tacky sweat that layered her skin along with the pounding in her chest and temples. Paige forced a long, shaky breath and formed a small smile on her lips for the doctor's benefit.

"I wish you hadn't done that," she said after she harnessed her breathing. "I was going to use the time today to look for a place to live."

He stood and gave her a nod. "You'll have the chance to do that in a little while, but for now, I think you need a little rest."

Paige got to her feet and took a step towards the door. Nurse Patty crossed the distance and took her elbow to help steady her. Humbled by the help, Paige gave her a more genuine smile than she could muster for the doctor and let her lead her back to the room.

As soon as the door closed, she did a quick check under the chair, sighing with relief at the sight of her stash. She had more than enough time to put together her hex bag and write the spell on the back of the page with the pictures and hair. It was still early, and a nap would help the shakes that had reappeared as soon as she collapsed on the bed.

Exhaustion consumed her, pummeling her muscles into submission, and her eyelids dropped closed before her brain could argue.

Magick
Chapter 13

NIGHTMARES STRANGLED HER. EACH one entailing the imagined brutality entwined with the decadence of Halloween, and Paige woke with a scream on her lips and sweat soaked into her shirt. The nurse stood in the doorway, balancing a tray on her arm.

"Are you okay?" Nurse Patty asked.

Paige rubbed her eyes, slowing her breathing before she gave a quick nod. "Yeah. Just a bad dream."

Nurse Patty deposited a tray on the nightstand. "I thought you would like something to eat."

"Thank you." Paige covered a yawn and glanced at the clock. Her eyes widened. "It's really five-thirty?" Her gaze snapped to the nurse.

"Yes." She snatched Paige's wrist and glanced at her watch, checking Paige's pulse. "Are you feeling better?" she asked after she let go.

"Still a little groggy, but…" she started, and a yawn interrupted. "Otherwise, I'm okay." Mounting panic said otherwise, and she took a deep breath, focusing on the tray of food. As soon as the nurse took off the plate warmer, Paige's mouth watered despite herself. A cheeseburger sat on the plate, along with a dozen tater-tots, and a tossed salad sat to the side. It was all she could do to keep from devouring it like a half-starved maniac. She smiled and pulled the tray onto her lap, ignoring the dampness of the clothing encasing her. "Thank you," she said, offering a genuine smile and Nurse Patty returned it, crossing to the door with a satisfied nod.

Paige didn't hesitate, and the meal tasted as delicious as it looked. Instead of using the thick paper napkin that accompanied the meal, she licked her fingers and placed the tray back on the nightstand, slipping out of bed. A quick look under the chair steadied her nerves, and she resumed her path to the bathroom. After a quick washing of her hands and using the small washcloth to clean the sweat off, she changed into something dry. Feeling much fresher and more focused, Paige pulled out the box and photo album and settled into place on the bed.

She booted up the computer and spread the napkin out before she pulled the lid off the modified shoebox. The box of matches went into her shirt pocket. She couldn't forget that, otherwise the entire ritual would be moot. The hex bag, along with the picture, needed to burn as she spoke the incantation.

The ingredients were a simple mixture of spices, wax shavings from three different scented candles, and the last item the ingredients called for resided in her photo album. Paige peeled the sticky page back and plucked the clump of hair from its place, dropping it inside the napkin as she recited the first part of the spell that would protect her from the ghost's wrath.

She twisted the contents into the center of the napkin, securing it with a small rubber band before she dropped it into her pocketbook. She looked through the photos until she came upon one that had Hunter with Max in a headlock and April on his back. All three of them were laughing, and Paige paused, wondering if the spell could help April move on as well.

Without another thought, she turned the photo over and scribed the rest of the spell on the back, praying she would have time to speak the words and torch both the photo and the hex bag before Hunter could stop her. She folded the photo into quarters and pulled out two more items from the box. A silver candy bowl went into her nearly empty pocketbook alongside the hex bag, and she placed the picture in the center of the bowl. The last item was a small bottle of lighter fluid that she shook to make sure it wasn't empty before she stowed it away in her pocketbook.

She slid the photo album into the box and replaced it under the chair. Her wallet, keys and matches went into the outside pocket of her purse and then she zipped it up, hiding the contents of the spell, before stowing the bag behind her pillow.

She settled back on the bed with her laptop propped on her lap and started the search for apartments. Twenty minutes and three prospects later, the door opened, and she glanced up with held breath. She exhaled and smiled at the sight of Dr. Schaeffer.

"You look much better than the last time we spoke," he said and took a seat.

"Well, I guess a sedative and eight hours of rest will do that to a girl."

"Do you want to talk about what happened earlier?"

Paige's smile faded. "No, not really."

"You said something about seeing a ghost."

She stared at him and made her eyebrows arch in shock. "I wasn't as prepared for the condition of the room as I thought," she said, stalling to come up with some logical answer. She didn't remember telling him about April's ghost and wondered what else she rambled on about in his office. "I almost turned and ran when I first saw the bloodstains, so I can say with certainty that I was really freaked out."

Dr. Schaeffer gave her a nod. "And now that you've had some rest, what do you think happened?"

"I must have imagined seeing her reflection in my closet mirror. When I turned, no one was there." She looked down at the listings on the computer and then closed the laptop. "That's why I was so freaked out when you saw me, and driving by the fraternity house didn't help."

He seemed satisfied with her answer because he stood and gave her a nod.

"I was planning on driving by a couple of the listings tonight to see the neighborhoods and I was going to stop and grab an ice cream. Is that okay?"

Dr. Schaeffer hesitated, and Paige felt her heart plummet. Tonight was the last night of the waning crescent moon, and she had to recite the spell before the new moon, otherwise she would never be able to banish Hunter. It had to be done within the same cycle of the moon as the possession otherwise; the melding of souls in one body became permanent.

"I need to do this, Dr. Schaeffer, because I cannot go back to live at the sorority house." She didn't leave any leeway in her tone, and after a sigh, he nodded.

"I've put you on my schedule for eight tomorrow morning and we can discuss what the next steps are."

"Okay," Paige said and smiled. Relief swept through her, lightening her load. Now all she had to do was hope Hunter showed up, and that she didn't screw this up.

Magick
Chapter 14

PAIGE CHECKED HER WATCH again and peered into the darkness, trying to see anything breeching the wood line. She stood under the sliver of light provided by the crescent moon, biting her lip and shifting from foot to foot. There was only one path into the glen, and she waited with the silver bowl behind her on a knotted stump they had once used as a mini picnic table.

She nervously flicked the match in her fingers, blinking her eyes, letting them adjust to the darkness surrounding her. She didn't see him at first, but then a solid figure formed, and she jerked at the shock of him already halfway across the distance.

"Paige?" His voice echoed off the trees.

Instead of answering, she turned and struck the match, whispering the remaining words of the spell. She dropped the wooden match and the hex bag, and the picture soaked in lighter fluid burst into flames.

The pounding of her heart could almost be heard on the slight breeze, and she attempted to steel her nerves with a few cleansing breaths, but it was no use. The banishment spell had already been uttered, and a microburst formed overhead, sending small cyclones around the perimeter of the wooded glen, blocking both of them inside the strike zone.

"What have you done?"

Dread accosted her as his voice pulled her attention away from the brewing storm and she turned, meeting his fiery green gaze. Lightning crackled, reflecting against his eyes as he stepped closer and grabbed her shoulders.

"What have you done?" This time, he spat the words between his clenched teeth.

"I needed to make things right," Paige whispered over the building electricity.

"What the fuck do you mean by that?" he yelled, his voice rumbling like thunder.

"I'm so sorry, baby, but you have to move on and let this man have his life back."

Lightning bloomed in a blinding strike, and she flew backwards, beyond the makeshift altar, and landed hard on the ground. White light drowned her senses and the knocking on her chest stilled for what seemed an eternity.

She wheezed and arched into the deep inhale. Pain flared, and then dropped to a dull throb as she blinked her vision back from the edge of blind. Everything blurred when she moved her head, and her eyelids clenched against the unwanted spin.

A groan came from the edge of the woods and Paige forced herself into a sitting position, holding her head and praying the spell worked. Austin's form lay prone and motionless, and her heart jump-started, sending her into action.

Her legs wobbled under her as she attempted to stand. Before she knew it, she was on her knees on the cold ground, and the world swam in front of her eyes.

"Please let him be okay," she whispered, and crawled toward him. The frozen ground bit at her palms, but she shuffled along until she reached him. Paige laid her head on his chest and held her breath, listening for the faint thump of his heartbeat through the flannel shirt.

Fear dried all the spit in her mouth at the silence, and she reached a trembling hand toward his throat, pressing her index and middle finger into the soft flesh under his jaw, searching for a pulse with her frozen hands.

His involuntary shiver and the turn of his head into her hand sent her soul soaring.

"Your hand is freezing," he whispered as his eyes blinked open.

Paige stared into Austin's gray irises, and her hand covered her mouth. Her vision wobbled under the sudden sheen of hot tears.

She glanced back at the wood stump and the fire inside the silver dish flickered, fading into obscurity. The sudden onslaught of weather cleared as fast as a category five hurricane peeling the siding off a dilapidated beach house; Austin stared at the swirling sky, and then at her, blinking in the darkness.

"Whatever the hell you did," he started and paused, just holding her gaze for a moment before continuing. "It worked. I don't feel him inside anymore." Austin pushed himself into a sitting position. His gaze traveled from her to the blackened earth in the center of the clearing.

"We were hit by lightning, weren't we?" he asked after a few minutes of silence. His hand traveled to his chest and then dropped to her knees.

Paige nodded, unable to speak, and she buried her face in her hands before the sob that had been caught in her throat escaped. "I'm so sorry," she said through her splayed fingers.

Austin's warm and trembling arms pulled her to him, and he just held on tight, as if letting go of her might unleash the hell they just contained. His soft coo made her chest hitch, and she wrapped her arms around him, using his shoulder to soak up the river of tears.

Magick
Chapter 15

AUSTIN FOLLOWED HER BACK from the orchard, and under the harsh fluorescents in her room, she had a minute to study him. He looked like hell with dark rings around his eyes and pale skin broken only by blotchy red cheeks. His gray-blue eyes shimmered a few times, but he blinked the wetness away, offering her a macabre smile.

"Thank you," he said, once she was tucked safely under the sheets.

Paige nodded and offered her own forced smile. He leaned over and planted a soft kiss on her forehead before turning to leave. A rash of disappointment spread over her, and she sighed.

"You're leaving?"

He stopped at the door with his back towards her and his chin dropped to his chest. When he finally glanced over his shoulder at her, Paige bit her bottom lip. Austin's eyes were filled with unshed tears.

"I thought…" he whispered and shook his head, turning away from her.

"You thought I'd let him get away with stealing your life?"

He let out a soft laugh and nodded, his back still to her.

"Austin," she whispered, and he turned, scowling, as tears tracked down his face. He didn't speak, just met her gaze and swiped at his cheeks as if his tears were annoying gnats.

"How did you know what to do?" he asked after a few minutes.

"I'm a little rusty, but I used to be into magick," she said, and his eyebrows arched. "I knew what Wiccan spell I was looking for, so it was pretty easy to find." She waved at the laptop on the nightstand.

"And you just happened to have eye-of-newt sitting around?"

His cocked eyebrow pulled a genuine smile to the surface and Paige's cheeks filled with heat. She didn't correct him; instead, she just lifted a shoulder.

"Well, I'm glad you did." This time, when he smiled, it was more natural. He turned and let himself out of the room.

Paige stared after him until the door latched closed. With a sigh, she slipped out of bed and retrieved the box from under the chair, stowing it in the closet with the rest of her things. Her attention dropped to the engagement ring still adorning her finger, and she peeled it off, dropping it in her empty pocketbook.

Sadness encompassed her, and she pulled the pictures out and climbed into bed with the book. Slowly, she flipped the pages, letting the tears flow as she mourned Hunter and her friends. The amount of death and destruction her close world had suffered over the last week finally hit and she closed the book, dropping it to the floor before she hugged her pillow and let her body purge the sorrow.

Paige cried herself to sleep.

DR. SCHAEFFER SHUFFED THE paperwork on his desk while she sat in the chair, staring out the window. She hadn't seen Austin in two days and hadn't had any luck finding an apartment. Even knowing that she sent Hunter to wherever he belonged, she still couldn't stomach the thought of going back to the sorority.

Forms slid in her direction, along with a pen, and Paige leaned forward, signing every line that Dr. Schaeffer pointed to. Her release papers were more complex because of the original criminal assessment. Even though it all proved false, Dr. Schaeffer had to make sure the paperwork was completed. It was a matter of minutes before she would be without a bed for the night and she tried to smile as she slid the papers back, but the fear of the unknown kept it from forming.

A knock at the door pulled their attention.

Austin leaned on the doorframe and his gaze locked with hers. He wasn't in his scrubs, as he would have been had he been on the clock.

"Good," Dr. Schaeffer started. "You're here just in time to help her with her things," he added as he stacked the papers in the folder and closed it. He stood and stretched out his hand. "If you ever need to talk, call me and we can schedule a session."

"Thank you, Dr. Schaeffer," Paige said, standing and accepting the handshake.

She stepped out of the office, giving Austin a sideways glare.

"Where have you been?" she asked, surprised at the irritation crawling across her skin.

"I had a couple of days off," he said and continued to walk, his manner as aloof as it had been when she first met him.

His attitude rubbed her wrong, and she threw the door closed after she crossed the threshold of the room. Austin had to jump to the side in order to avoid being hit. He crossed his arms and tilted his head, studying her in a way that made her stomach clench.

"Stop staring at me," Paige spun towards him.

"Why are you mad at me?" he asked, his voice carried a huff along with the question.

She opened her mouth, but had no words to explain the sudden flush of aggravation. He raised his eyebrows, waiting, and Paige pressed her lips closed, opting to turn and finish stowing away what little she had in the bag he had brought her.

"Have you found a place yet?" he asked.

Paige shook her head. "No."

"Well, you could move into my room," he said.

Paige blinked and turned toward him. "Are you asking me to move in with you?"

His cheeks reddened and he let out a nervous laugh, shuffling his feet before he shook his head. "That didn't come out quite right. I moved into a one-bedroom apartment in the same building and my old roommate is looking for someone to rent my old room," he said, still staring at the floor.

She didn't know what to say and when his eyes traveled from the floor to hers, he added a small shrug and a smirk that she couldn't quite read. She remained silent as she stared at the mischief now twinkling in his eyes.

"I didn't know that was an option," he muttered, and his hands found their way into his pockets.

Paige let out a nervous laugh, trying to assess the flurry filling her. The swirl of emotions caught her off guard and she turned back to the bags instead of responding to either comment.

His hands cupped her shoulders and turned her around. When she wouldn't meet his gaze, he hooked his index finger under her chin, tilting her face until she was forced to meet his questioning stare.

"I wasn't avoiding you," he started and inhaled, bringing his gaze to the ceiling and then back to her. "Not really," he admitted and added a soft smile. "Besides moving my shit out of the apartment, I had to figure out where my head was."

She bit her lower lip to keep it from trembling.

"I needed to know if the things I felt were mine and not some weird transference of Hunter's."

"And?" Paige whispered.

"I'm here, aren't I?"

It wasn't really an answer, and she rolled her eyes. Twirling out of his grip, she gathered the last of the items from the closet before addressing him. "Were you serious about your old apartment?"

He nodded.

"Isn't your roommate the one with the toys?" she asked, and his face turned the color of Valentine's roses.

"Uh, yeah." He shifted, staring into her eyes as dimples appeared in his cheeks. His smirk faded. "Can I ask you a question?"

She stopped packing and leaned on the bed. "Sure."

His mouth formed words several times, and each time his gaze dropped to the floor. "Shit, this is harder than I thought it would be."

"Just ask," she sighed.

"Was it all Hunter for you?" When his gaze finally met hers, she saw the hope scribed in his blue-gray irises.

She slowly shook her head and Austin stepped closer, his hands clasping her cheeks as he leaned in, delivering the same type of kiss he had the other night and her knees wobbled under it. When he pulled away, the sparkle in his eyes echoed the spark igniting in her heart.

"Just for the record, as much as I want to explore whatever this is, I wasn't ready to ask you to move in with me," he said and reached for the bag on the bed, hauling it over his shoulder while he waited for her to gather the rest of her things.

Relief swept through her, and she was sure it bled through in her smile. "I'm not ready for that either, but a nice dinner isn't out of the question."

The End

Continue Paige and Austin's story with Black Magick.

Black Magick
Chapter 1

WHAT THE HELL ARE we doing here?" Austin Shelton asked as Paige shut off the ignition in front of a Tarot and Crystal Readings shop in Chinatown.

Paige Turner stepped out of the car and ducked down to meet his questioning gaze. With a snap of her head, her long dark hair shifted out of her face, revealing the crystal blue eyes that always melted through his frustration.

"I need to get a few things. You can wait here if you'd like." She flashed a smile and closed the door on any further conversation.

Austin glanced at his watch and sighed, turning his attention to the front of the cheesy psychic shop. Although he knew her magic practices had saved his ass in the past, right now, he had less than thirty minutes to get across the city to Cornell, and if he was late, he could kiss his chances at getting in to his first choice of medical schools goodbye. He had a backup plan just in case, and that interview wasn't until the end of the day at Columbia.

The fact Paige was dicking around at a psychic's place of business set the burn in his already twitchy stomach on overdrive. Another glance at his watch and he reached for the door. All he had to do was swing the metal open, and she came trotting back out with a smile and a little bag in her hand.

He took a deep breath, trying to calm his nerves, but they were as untamed as a toddler's hair. She slid into the driver's seat and handed the bag to him.

"For luck," she said in that breathless tone that stalled his brain.

Austin blinked and glanced in the bag at the small crystal that connected two strands of silver.

"What am I supposed to do with this?"

She gave him a cursory glance before she pulled out into the thick city traffic, navigating the streets like a veteran cab driver. It both impressed and terrified him.

"It's a necklace. You should wear it to the interview."

He rolled his eyes and glanced out the window. Despite their recent past, he still didn't know if he could put stock in her psychic mojo, but he sighed and fished the necklace out of the bag. It wasn't gaudy, but it wasn't very masculine, either. He slipped it over his head and tucked it under his dress shirt, forcing a thank you from his lips.

Paige navigated the car into a parking spot across the street from the administrative offices of Cornell. Austin glanced at the signs on the side just to make sure the parking spot was legitimate and then gave her a forced smile and a nod before he reached for the car door. Nerves still clenched his muscles.

Paige climbed out of the car and came around to the passenger side. She stepped onto the sidewalk next to him while he closed the car door and took a deep breath.

"You got this," she said, pulling his attention away from the building, and the conviction in her voice almost had him believing her.

Austin tried on a smile and leaned forward, placing a gentle kiss on her cheek. "Thanks. Are you just going to hang in the car?"

Paige hitched her thumb over her shoulder, and he glanced up at the Starbucks sign across the street.

"I'll be over there nursing a Cafe Mocha and finishing up my paper." Paige gave her laptop bag a pat. "Just relax and be yourself," she added, and gave his hand a squeeze before she turned, heading towards her destination.

Austin waited until she was safely inside the coffee shop before he stepped toward the admissions building. Taking a deep breath, he crossed the street and opened the door to what he hoped was the start of a bright future.

Black Magick
Chapter 2

PAIGE GRABBED A COFFEE, set herself up at the table next to the window, and sat facing the door. She spread her notes out and set up her laptop, getting comfortable for the hour or so she expected Austin to be in his interview.

Every time the bell above the door jingled, her gaze was drawn to the people entering the coffee shop, and then she would get back to her paper. Considering Starbucks was across from the medical school campus, the bell jangled more often than not. Even though the waiting line wrapped around the small shop, the seating was sparsely populated, so Paige didn't feel like she was imposing.

Her fingers flew on the keyboard, and her gaze dropped to the clock in the bottom corner of the screen. It had been over an hour and her paper was almost finished. Her gaze bounced to the door as the bell dinged again, and her hands froze over the keys.

His bright green eyes locked on hers, and he stopped before he got to the counter. The familiar stare penetrated her, and Paige swallowed hard. The moment passed when the new patron moved his gaze away from hers and stepped to the counter.

Paige couldn't pull her eyes away from the stranger. His dark hair fell in soft waves past his shoulders, and his profile was equivalent to a Greek god with a perfectly clear olive complexion and chiseled cheekbones that most girls would swoon over. But it was the eyes that had Paige's gaze glued to the man.

The only time she'd seen eyes that green was when Hunter Garrett had possessed Austin. Her chest tightened when the stranger took the far table at the window and sat facing her. His eyes flashed in her direction, and she dropped her gaze to her computer. Heat filled her cheeks at being caught staring, but a quick glance found him hidden behind an open *Wall Street Journal*.

After a few moments, the corner folded down, and she was caught again. Her heart slammed in her chest, and she barely remembered to press save on her computer before she closed the laptop. In a flurry, she swept her papers together and shoved everything into her computer bag.

Chancing a glance, she caught a smirk on the stranger's face as he watched her flustered behavior. He folded the paper onto the table and leaned back in the chair, studying her with fascination.

She scrambled out of her seat, only to realize the path out the door took her within arm's reach of the stranger. Paige couldn't catch her breath, and a cold fear wrapped around her heart, squeezing at the thoughts rampaging through her head.

Thoughts of banishing Hunter.

What if she had failed?

Her feet moved without permission, and the moment she stepped into reach, his hand wound around her wrist.

"Do I know you?" he asked.

The foreign lilt in his voice should have soothed her, but it just made the fear settle into her bones, creating a dull ache through her entire form.

She shook her head but found she could not tear her eyes from his as they studied her before narrowing just enough for the spit in her mouth to dry. He still gripped her wrist, and the physical contact unsettled her even more than his cautious study of her.

"Are you sure?"

She forced a smile and pulled her wrist out of his grip. "I'm sure," she said and didn't wait for him to speak again. Instead, she bolted out the door with her bag and slammed right into Austin, nearly knocking them both over on the sidewalk.

Austin caught her, steadying her on her feet before she looked up at him.

"You look like you've seen a ghost," he said.

She pulled him towards the car without acknowledging his comment. For both of them, his words were not just the usual cliché. And he pulled her to a stop at the curb behind their car.

"What is wrong?" he asked.

Paige met his gaze, uttering a high-pitched squeak of a laugh.

"Excuse me," a voice from behind them said, and Paige froze. "But you left your pocketbook on the chair where you were sitting."

Austin's brow creased and Paige turned, meeting the stranger's gaze.

"I thought you might need it." He extended the purse to her.

"Thank you," she said and took the offering.

"Are you sure we haven't met before?" he asked, and his head cocked to the side like a curious German Shepherd.

"I'm sure."

Austin put his hands on Paige's shoulders and the stranger raised his gaze from Paige to him. The tightening of Austin's grip told her enough, and she gave the stranger a smile.

"We really have to go," she said and headed to the parking lot. Neither she nor Austin said anything until she was in the city's thick traffic, heading toward the hotel that they'd booked near Columbia.

"Was that... Hunter?" Austin asked, his hands clenched into tight fists.

Paige glanced at his stony profile. He didn't look her way.

"I don't know," she said. "He just asked if we had met before."

Austin huffed and glanced out the passenger window, crossing his arms. "Is that why you were running out of there like the place was on fire?"

Paige pulled into the hotel valet service and put the car in park before she glanced at Austin. "He scared the hell out of me."

Austin swung a deadly glare in her direction. "I thought you banished him."

"I did." Despite her words, doubt colored her voice.

A knock on her window interrupted them and she turned, staring into the dark eyes of the hotel valet.

Black Magick
Chapter 3

AS SOON AS THE hotel door closed behind them and their suitcases were stowed on the luggage racks, Austin took a seat on the end of the bed and stared at her with a sigh.

"If it is him..." His gaze dropped to his hands and Paige stepped closer, tilting his chin up so he would look at her.

"Maybe we freaked out over nothing," she said. "How'd the interview go?"

His lips curved into a smile. "Nice change of subject."

Paige's cheeks flushed with heat. "Well, I'd rather talk about something pleasant instead of Hunter." Just the mention of his name brought a rash of gooseflesh across her arms, and she shivered.

Austin studied her. "The interview went well," he finally said, but he remained stoic. "They said I'd hear before the end of the semester." His hands moved to her waist, pulling her closer. "If it was him..." He licked his lips, keeping his gaze locked with hers. "What does that mean...for us?"

His uneasiness struck Paige as odd, especially since he seemed to have set the pace of their entire relationship. After she was released from the hospital, he had hooked her up with an apartment in the same building he lived in. Despite their sexual escapades while she had been incarcerated, since they left the hospital, he had slowed things down to a crawl.

The past few months had been filled with a flurry of classes, schoolwork, and catching a dinner or a movie whenever their schedules allowed. It was a far cry from the intensity they encountered while Hunter terrorized them.

Austin's sense of humor was truly warped, and it caught her off guard enough to draw a snorting laugh from her. And the man knew his way around a kitchen. Her favorite dates were the ones where he cooked for her, and then they collapsed on his couch for either a movie or a mean game of cards. It was all perfectly civilized.

His quiet confidence was something she found she relied on, so seeing him nervous like he was on the ride into the city today really blew her mind. And the hesitation in his gaze right now shot to her core. Austin didn't show his vulnerable side often, but when he did, it pulled at her heartstrings in a way no other man ever had.

Paige cupped his cheeks and leaned forward, meeting his lips with a tentative kiss. When she pulled away, that hungry spark she remembered from the hospital ignited in his eyes. His arms encircled her, and he delivered the kiss that burned through her like wildfire. He spun her onto the bed next to him without breaking the kiss, and his hand slipped between her legs, rubbing her through her jeans.

He broke the kiss, and his hand stilled, but he didn't move away. Instead, he met her gaze and whispered, "Do you want me, Paige?"

"Yes," she whispered and went to pull him back to her lips.

"Is it just because you saw him today?"

Paige blinked and her mouth fell open in shock. "Austin..."

"I'm serious. You never attempted anything with me over the last few months, and now you're like a she-devil in heat."

"You never even tried to kiss me..." she started and popped her mouth closed. The anger bubbled up inside her, overriding the burn between them. She pushed him away and sat up. "It was like you didn't want me, either. What the hell did you expect?"

Austin rolled onto his back and ran his hands through his hair. "What is it you really want from me?"

"I want the fire back." The words just tumbled out of her mouth before she could stop them.

His eyebrows arched and he laughed. "You want me to fuck you instead of dating you?"

"I want both," she muttered and moved to get off the bed, but his hand on her arm stopped her.

"Why me?"

She turned and met his gaze. "I don't know. You're funny and easy to talk to," she started, and he rolled his eyes. "And when you kiss me like that, you consume me." Surprise registered, and he blinked at her, but before he could speak, she continued. "I could ask you the same thing, you know. Was your attraction to me all driven by Hunter?"

His lips thinned, and he glared at her. "If you think that, you are out of your goddamned mind."

"Then what the hell is our problem?"

They stared at each other, and then Austin broke out in a sarcastic laugh.

"I have no idea," he said after the laughter faded. He stared at her, his expression turning serious as he pulled her back down onto the bed. "All I know is you're the only girl who has ever made me lose my fucking mind."

His kiss crushed her lips, filled with the unleashed passion that had lain dormant for the last few months. Her mind stalled with the intensity of it and the welcomed caress of his hands on her body that shot her into the land of bliss.

It wasn't until the sound of ripping fabric interrupted them that he pulled away from the kiss. Paige pressed her lips together in a smirk.

"Oops," she said as they both stared at the rip in his finely tailored shirt.

"Oops?" His eyebrows rose as his voice challenged her choice of words, but the smile toying with his lips belied his true feelings about the matter. He grabbed two handfuls of her shirt and yanked in opposite directions, grinning when the thin cotton shredded in his grip.

Paige giggled at the raw magnetism pulsing from him, and his salacious grin was just as infectious as the spark he produced in her soul. But it was his stalk up her body with his hands and his mouth that set her on fire. His tongue swiped at her skin between nips, and the low growl of satisfaction in his throat as he nibbled on her ear took her breath away.

The rest of their clothing came off in a flurry, and he worked the magic she had almost forgotten existed. Austin kissed her gently and then trailed butterfly kisses down her neck and chest and her abdomen. His slow progression down her body contrasted with the frantic and animalistic stalk to his lips, and the juxtaposition of it pulled a moan from her even before he settled between her legs.

What Austin did with his tongue, mouth and fingers set her into overdrive. Every memory she had of him between her legs paled compared to this moment. He took his time, making it a slow burn, and every time she was close to an orgasm, he dialed back.

"Please, don't stop," Paige whined when he pulled away again. "Please, I'm so close. So goddamned close."

He smiled at her, and this time, when his tongue flick brought her to the plateau, he didn't stop. The orgasm gripped every muscle in her body. Her fingers dug into his scalp as her wailing gasp filled the room, and a river of wetness flooded from her pussy.

"Fuck me, Austin, please, please..." She squirmed under him as he continued to play with her with his mouth.

His fingers slid inside her slowly, even as her hips gyrated to make him move faster. He pulled his fingers out of her pussy and traced her anus, coating her with her own juices before plunging his finger inside her ass.

"Oh, God," she gasped.

Austin met her gaze and slowly finger fucked her ass. He was gentle enough, so the movement tingled her pleasure centers, and her next orgasm arched her back with the power of it.

When he moved his fingers out of her, she moaned. But by the time she caught her breath, his hard cock slid inside her dripping pussy, filling her with his girth.

"Is that what you want?" he asked, his voice low and sultry in a way she hadn't ever heard. The smile of satisfaction on his lips along with that voice brought her to the brink again.

Paige pulled him to her mouth. She didn't care that his lips were hot with her juices; she just wanted him to kiss her into oblivion.

His heart thundered against her chest, and a low growling groan came from his throat. His hips plunged once more, burying his cock deep inside her, and he pulled away from the kiss.

"Oh, fuck," he groaned, and his eyes clamped shut. Every muscle in his neck tightened with the force of his orgasm, and then the after tremors went through him as he collapsed on top of her.

The air rushed out of Paige's lungs at the weight of him.

"Austin," she barely breathed, and he shifted enough so she could draw in air. It took him a few ragged breaths before he lifted his head from the crook of her neck.

"Holy shit," he said and sent a soft smile in her direction.

"No kidding."

Austin uncoupled and rolled onto his back next to her. Paige debated on whether to roll into the crook of his arm or not. She turned her head, taking in his handsome profile as he studied the ceiling. Eventually, he met her gaze.

"Can I ask you something?" he asked and chewed on his bottom lip in that familiar way he did when he was not in his comfort zone.

Paige nodded and waited for him to speak.

"If I get in..."

"You'll get in," she said, certain of his ability, and he gave her the look that said he wasn't finished. "Sorry," she added at the admonishment in his gaze.

"If I get in to either Cornell or Columbia, will you move here with me next fall?"

Paige stared at him and blinked. "Did you just ask me to move in with you?"

The way his cheeks bloomed red along with the appearance of his dimples was confirmation enough, so when he just shrugged a shoulder, she couldn't help her own smirk.

"You really want to live with me?" she asked, softer than her original question.

"I really don't want to be here without you," he said and turned onto his side, propping his head up on his hand.

"Why?"

He met her gaze and held it, chewing his lip again. The way he formulated serious questions was one of his most endearing qualities. And Paige felt her lips curving into a smile, despite the heaviness in the air between them.

"You haven't really answered my question." He kept her gaze, and Paige's smile faltered.

She rolled, so she faced him, adopting the same position he maintained, and she took his free hand in hers, giving it a squeeze. "I'm not saying no," she started, and his features hardened. She actually felt the emotional wall going up between them.

"But you're not saying yes, either," he muttered, and went to pull his hand out of hers.

Paige tightened her grip, unwilling to let him just end the conversation this way.

"Austin, come on, it's a big decision, and I need to make sure I can finish my degree before I up and run off to New York City with you."

"Do you even give a shit about me?"

She tilted her head and sighed. "You know I do. But you also know I have struggled to finish my degree ever since Halloween. I lost three weeks of school and nearly failed all my classes last semester."

"But you passed. And you're a month and a half away from graduating."

"I applied for graduation, but I haven't heard anything yet. My advisor is looking over my transcripts and will let me know whether I qualify. If not, I may have to take a course or two in the fall."

His eyebrows arched. "Seriously?"

"That's what he said, but he would let me know. If they're available in the summer, I can take them then, but if not..." She sighed and shrugged. "If it wasn't so up in the air, the answer would be easy."

It took him a couple of blinks before her words sank in, and then his rigid features softened. "So, if this wasn't hanging over you, you'd say yes?"

Paige nodded and offered a smile. His gaze moved from hers to the spot over her shoulder and back before he leaned in for a gentle kiss.

"I need to clean up and get ready for my next interview."

"Did you bring a second shirt?" she asked, and his smile disappeared.

He rolled off the bed and picked up the shirt he had been wearing before they started their sexcapades, inspecting the shredded fabric to the right of where most of the buttons remained.

"Shit," he muttered. "My suit jacket won't cover this." He glanced over his shoulder at Paige.

"What other shirts did you bring?"

"Just a sweater."

"The gray one that I love?" she asked. She prayed that was the one because he could get away with that and just the slacks he had on and still look somewhat professional.

"Yeah," he said, refocusing on the tattered shirt in his hand.

"Wear the sweater without the blazer."

He glanced at her. The question written on his face made her raise her eyebrows in a challenge.

"Trust me."

"Well, I'm going to have to, because there's no way I can make it to a store and get to the interview on time." He stood and gathered his clothing before heading to the bathroom.

Paige picked up her scattered clothing and headed into the bathroom as well. Austin was already in the shower, and she pulled the curtain aside. He stopped lathering his hair and met her gaze, moving to give her access to the warm spray.

The only shower they had ever taken together was the one he gave her at the sanitarium, and that crossed her mind as she watched him tilt his head back to rinse the shampoo away. She couldn't help herself. She reached out and ran her fingers down his chest.

A grin formed, revealing the deep dimples she had fallen for more than once, and he ran his hands through his hair one last time before bringing his focus to her. His eyes shimmered with mischief as he stepped closer.

"I can't be late," he said and maneuvered her fully under the spray before he stepped out of the shower.

Paige stood under the water staring at the spot he had just left, expecting him to return, but the sound of the water running in the sink told her that wasn't happening. She didn't know whether to be irritated or impressed by his self-restraint but decided against getting aggravated. She quickly rinsed her body, leaving her hair as dry as she could, and turned off the water.

She took the remaining towel and wrapped it around herself before she pulled the curtain back. Austin glanced from his reflection to her, his eyes drifting over her form while a smile captured his lips. He refocused on his image, combing his hair into place.

"Are you going over to the Museum of Natural History while I'm at the interview?" he asked.

"I'm not sure. It depends if I finish my paper or not," Paige said, and he turned towards her.

"If you do, I'll meet you there, and we can find a nice place for dinner."

"And if I don't?" she asked, stepping closer. She looked up into his gray-blue eyes and grinned.

"Then maybe room service would be better."

He used that tone that made her knees weak, and she stood on her tiptoes, gently kissing him. His freshly brushed breath welcomed her tongue, and his arms wrapped around her, pulling her against his half-clothed form. He smelled delicious, and she deepened the kiss.

Austin's low groan, coupled with him pushing her away, pulled a smile to her lips. She loved the power she held over him and hated to admit it, but he could wield the same type of power over her when he chose.

"You are going to have to hold on to that thought," he said and turned back to the mirror, finishing his minimal preening before pulling on the gray sweater. He stepped back, studying his reflection before he glanced at her. "I hope this passes whatever image the dean of medicine has."

"You look great."

"Thanks." He stepped into the hotel room and gathered his wallet and his leather portfolio case.

"Good luck," Paige said from the bathroom door.

Austin caught a kiss from her before heading out of the hotel room.

Black Magick
Chapter 4

PAIGE SAVED HER WORK and leaned back in the chair, covering a yawn with her hands. She was almost done and really in need of a change of scenery. The morning encounter with the stranger had rattled her, and then the conversation with Austin about moving in with him had thrown her completely.

She thought she knew what she wanted. She thought Austin was just in it for the friendship, especially with how things had been since she left the hospital. It wasn't as if he hadn't kissed her in all that time—he had—and it was always sweet. But it wasn't full of the passion that gripped him today. This afternoon, the man who had opened her to new possibilities had come back into her life.

She chewed on the end of her pen as she stared out the window towards the park, gauging her emotional state. She wasn't sure she could settle for the type of lackluster relationship they had shared for the last few months, but if today was more indicative of the fire between them, she could see being with Austin for the long term.

She stood and dropped her pen next to the computer, deciding it was time to get out of the hotel room before she started over-analyzing their entire relationship. She sent a quick text to Austin and then tucked her phone in the inside pocket of her coat. Paige grabbed her pocketbook and the spare room key before she headed to the Museum of Natural History.

Instead of starting on the first floor and working her way up, she headed directly to the fourth floor and the dinosaur exhibits. She wandered through, reading the plaques and studying the exhibits. After making her way around the fourth floor, she descended the stairs to the third floor, turning to the reptile and amphibian section.

Most of the female patrons seemed to shy away from the snakes and other reptiles, and Paige had to suppress a smile. The special exhibition gallery on the third floor was closed, and she turned to find her way back to the mammal section.

She drew short as the man they had seen this morning blocked her exit. He offered a knowing smirk and herded her into the closed section before her brain could register anything more than shock.

In the dark room, he slammed her against the wall.

"I was wondering just how long it would take before our paths crossed." His voice caressed her with an icy fear.

"Hunter?" Her voice cracked as she uttered his name.

His light chuckle filled the dark. "Miss me, baby?" he answered, but there was no warmth in the statement.

The way he had her pinned to the wall made her heart thunder in her ears, and all the spit in her mouth dried, replaced by tinny fear. Paige forced a swallow, but her tongue stuck to the roof of her mouth. Her lungs squeezed, making her breath wheeze as she fought to draw air into the tight confines.

"I... I banished you," she said, forcing the words between gasps of breath.

"From your boy-toy and the town, but not from existence," he said, his voice low and menacing in her ear.

A shiver traversed her spine, but before it could reach the base of her neck, he bit her ear, drawing a gasp that fell flat on the air. Her brain registered the pain, as well as the lack of an echo, and then understanding of the cushioning on the wall behind her sank in. The room they stood in absorbed sound, making it impossible for anyone to hear her scream.

"I found this poor soul on the brink of suicide, and I made a deal," he continued after releasing her ear. "I'd end his suffering if he would just let me in. The fool believed me."

His dark laugh penetrated every cell in her body, and the only thing that kept her from losing her bladder was the distraction of the hot liquid dripping down the back of her ear, tickling as it slid along her skin.

When he pulled away far enough, his unearthly green eyes shimmered in the dark like evil cat eyes.

"I've been practicing," he said and stepped away.

Paige couldn't move, but she met his gleeful gaze. "How?" she whispered, for fear her voice would shake.

He tapped his temple. "I seem to have brought a little magic back with me."

Dawning horror swept through her. This magic was as black as it got, and she had no idea how to overcome it. Hunter spread his arms wide, and hers mimicked him. He took a dozen steps backwards and her feet followed, moving her forwards into the center of the dark room.

Paige's mind screamed in rebellion, but her body would hear none of her arguments.

"He likes to watch, doesn't he?" Hunter said when he had finished positioning her. He stood close enough for his hot breath to tickle her skin.

"Please don't do this," she said as smooth rope wrapped around each of her wrists, locking her in place.

"You don't find this form appealing?" Hunter waved to the body he was wearing.

She slowly shook her head. While he had chosen a hot package, it was the evil living within that repelled her. Besides, her mind was on Austin and the vulnerability he had shown her today. She had no idea what he would do if he walked in on Hunter having his way with her.

"Bullshit," he snapped and stepped in closer. His hands found her breasts, squeezing them through her thin t-shirt.

She glared at him, and he pulled his hand away, snapping his finger. A spotlight illuminated a bench behind him, and the cuffs dangling from the seat sent a chill through her.

"He made me watch," Hunter growled. This time, when his hands returned, they tore her t-shirt open, leaving her exposed.

The phone in her back pocket buzzed, and Hunter reached around, yanking it from her pants before typing in her passcode. Paige cursed under her breath. She hadn't changed her passcode for over a year, and Hunter knew it as well as his own. He gave her a sideways glare as he typed a message back to Austin, telling him exactly where to go in the museum.

Curtains drew closed, hiding the single bench from her view, and Hunter unbuttoned her jeans leaving them zipped. When a pocketknife appeared in his hands, she tried to jerk back, but she had no control over her physical form. He used the blade to cut through her bra straps, and then he reached behind her with one hand, unlatching her bra. He tossed it into the far corner and pushed the torn t-shirt back so her breasts were in full view.

"You both will pay for what you did to me," he said, his eyes raking over her and chilling her to the core.

Paige drew a breath to scream, and a ball of fabric was stuffed into her mouth, cutting off the scream even before it began. Then Hunter stepped away, disappearing into the blackness surrounding her.

Black Magick
Chapter 5

AUSTIN STOOD ON THE platform waiting for the subway, going over the last hour and a half of being grilled by the dean of medicine. The Columbia interview seemed much more intense than the one at Cornell, but he wasn't sure if it was his lack of comfort in his attire or if it was just his exhaustion finally taking hold. He sighed, hoping he'd impressed at least one of them enough to get an acceptance letter.

His phone buzzed, and he glanced at the text response from Paige. She had taken a break from homework and went to the museum after all. The idea of ravaging her in the hotel room was much more appealing than wandering around The Museum of Natural History. His stomach growled, reminding him that food was the priority, otherwise he wouldn't have the energy for an all-night lovemaking session with Paige.

The subway car squeaked to a stop, pulling him out of his thoughts, and he stepped onto the train. It took another fifteen minutes to reach 81st Street, where he got off, trotted up the steps, and down a block to the entrance of the museum.

He bought a ticket and the moment he was inside; he texted her. The answer came, and he headed toward the third floor, where she said she was. Austin stared at the No Admittance sign on the door and looked down at the text again, confirming this was where she said she was.

He smiled. Maybe she was on the same page as he was since this afternoon's romp in the hotel room. He glanced in both directions before he slid into the room, closing the door as the darkness gathered around him. The click of the lock gave him a start, and when he tried to re-open the door, the knob wouldn't budge.

Austin's internal alarms started just as the slow illumination behind him caught his attention. A single bench lay beneath a soft halo of light.

"Paige?"

"Take a seat," a soft voice purred over the speakers.

It wasn't Paige's voice, and he glanced at the message again, chewing on his bottom lip. She said she had a surprise for him, and curiosity won out. He crossed, trying to see anything beyond in the darkness, but it was impenetrable.

Nerves burned his skin as he lowered himself onto the center of the bench. No sooner had his ass met the metal than cold steel bit into each wrist, locking him in place. Dread pressed on his chest as he tried to pull his wrists free. His phone fell from his grip like it had been yanked out of his hand, and his head snapped up, looking for a sign of who had trapped him in this nightmare.

The light above his head faded to a dull shine, and the ruffle of curtains caught his attention. He stared as a low light illuminated Paige in the center of the stage, bound and half naked. If he hadn't been cuffed to the bench, the idea of screwing around with her while she was in such a compromising position would have turned him on. But the fear in her eyes, along with the rag stuffed into her mouth, dried every ounce of spit in his mouth, replacing it with terror.

A low chuckle filled the amphitheater, and a form stepped out of the shadows behind Paige.

"Hello, Austin."

Recognition set in with the speed of burning fuel. Austin tried to get to his feet, but the handcuffs kept him in place. He let out a roar, yanking at the metal keeping him from protecting Paige.

Hunter's green eyes pierced out of the face of the man they had run into at Starbucks that morning. He grinned over Paige's shoulder.

"Do you know what one of the punishments for witchcraft was in the early days?"

Austin's gaze dropped to Paige's feet as panic gripped every fiber. He only knew of the Salem witch trials when they burned the guilty, but Paige wasn't standing on a bed of wood. A measure of relief flooded his muscles. He shook his head in answer, afraid of what his voice would sound like.

Hunter stepped to the side and yanked a sheet away from a nearby table. The blood froze in Austin's veins. His table of toys in the shower paled in comparison. His toys were for pleasure, but what Hunter had laid out was meant for pain. Austin's gaze shot to Paige. She stared at the array, and all the color in her face drained.

She shook her head, and the chains holding her in place rattled.

"Please, don't hurt her," Austin said, his voice shaking with both fear and anger.

"Oh, I will not be the one who uses these things on her. These are the toys you are going to use on her when I'm finished." He ran his fingers over the sharp sex toys, walking the length of the table until he reached a cat-o'-nine-tails.

Austin met Paige's gaze, staring at the horror visible in her eyes. He imagined he held the same.

"You're out of your fucking mind."

Hunter picked up the whip and stepped behind Paige. "They used to flog the guilty," he said.

Austin attempted to get to his feet, his eyes wide with the adrenaline that pumped in his veins. The whistle of leather through the air ended with Paige's muffled scream.

"Stop!" he yelled before Hunter could strike again.

Hunter paused and stared at him from the edge of the darkness. "Do you want to take her place?"

"Yes," Austin said without hesitation, and the cuffs unlatched.

"Strip off your shirt and then sit down again."

Austin pulled his sweater off, leaving only his light cotton undershirt. When he peeled that off, Paige's brow creased, like something was missing. For a moment, he almost laughed at her concern. She was looking for the necklace she had made him wear that morning, but it was safely tucked in his pocket. Besides, it certainly wasn't bringing him all that good luck she had muttered about.

He lowered himself to the bench, and his arms moved of their own accord, right into the waiting cuffs. A low growl of anger passed through his lips at his inability to control his limbs, and his gaze traveled to the table before movement pulled it back center stage.

If he didn't figure out a way to beat the mental hold Hunter had on him, the bastard was going to make him kill Paige. Truth hit and he locked his gaze on Paige's as Hunter stepped behind him.

"Fifty lashes," he said.

Austin had a moment to wonder if he'd live through this ordeal before the first of the strikes hit, bringing with it burning pain that pulled an unwanted yelp from his lips. Paige screamed behind the rag and pulled at the bindings holding her in place, but Austin clamped his teeth together, staring at her through blurred vision. After that first yelp, he refused to voice anything more than a groan of pain.

The silence seemed to infuriate Hunter more, so each subsequent hit came with more force.

By the time he stopped, Austin's back felt like someone had doused him in gasoline and set him on fire. Warm liquid trailed down his spine, and he didn't know if it was sweat or blood. He pondered how the hell he was able to remain conscious.

Hunter stepped in front of him with the whip dangling at his side, and Austin got a good look at the leather straps. Bile bubbled into the back of his throat at the bits of skin hanging from the straps and the healthy coating of blood.

"Bastard," he whispered and raised his gaze to Hunter's.

Hunter chuckled and dropped the weapon on the floor, and then stepped back onstage and circled behind Paige. Austin met her tear-stained gaze.

"He must really love you," Hunter snarled. He snaked his hands around her, one cupping her breast and the other sliding into the front of her unzipped pants.

Paige cried out behind the rags in her mouth, but she didn't fight him.

Rage filled every fiber of Austin's body, dulling the pain in his back. "Don't you dare touch her," he yelled, but it was an empty threat and they both knew it.

"Oh, I'm going to do more than touch her," Hunter said. "And you're going to sit there and watch, just like you made me watch, and then I'll let you fuck her with your choice of toys."

"You're insane," Austin snarled.

"Maybe so, but you'll get off on it. Just like you're going to get off watching me fuck her."

Austin glared at him, and then his gaze dropped to the movement his hand made in her pants. The fact her hips were moving in the same gentle rhythm made him want to scream. He shifted, pulling at the cuffs, but ended up wincing in pain instead. Fury filled him and he bellowed his anger.

"You motherfucker!"

"Let's give him a show, baby," Hunter said, and slowly drew her pants down to her ankles.

When she stepped out of the fabric, Austin's heart dropped into his stomach. His gaze jumped to hers and the pain reflected there didn't make sense with her movements.

Hunter lifted her leg and secured it in a strap that dangled from her bound wrist. When he did the same with her other leg, Austin snarled. He had positioned her exactly the way Austin had in the shower when he videotaped her. And her pussy was in his direct line of sight.

Hunter pulled the gag out of her mouth. "I want him to hear you moan like the slut we both know you are."

"I hate you," she whispered, but it lacked the conviction Austin expected.

Hunter laughed, and his fingers worked her clit. "You love this, don't you," he whispered in her ear and sent a knowing smile in Austin's direction.

"Yes," she gasped, and her mouth fell open in that familiar habit she had whenever she was horny and enjoying herself.

Austin's chest squeezed with the betrayal, and he searched her eyes for an explanation. The horror that lay in her expression belied the quickening of her breath and the hardening of her nipples.

"This little slut likes to be the center of attention." Hunter worked her nipples as effectively as her clit. "She'll cum like a fucking geyser for me. Does she do that for you?"

"Fuck you," Austin glared, fighting the urge to be turned on by her body.

Especially when the flush started in her neck. The panic in her eyes didn't temper her reaction to what Hunter was doing, and the low halogens highlighted the building wetness on his fingertips. Austin could even smell her heat. His cock twitched at the spectacle, and he silently cursed his lack of self-control. He shifted, focusing on the pain in his back as opposed to the heat filling his cock.

"See, I told you he likes to watch," Hunter said, punctuating his statement by sliding his finger inside her swollen pussy. When he pulled it out, it shined slick. "She's dripping wet now." He chuckled and continued to manipulate her with his fingers.

Austin stared at the slow finger fuck. He couldn't move his gaze away from the juices dripping from Hunter's hand, as if every plunge brought forth an orgasm, but that was just the beginning. His fingers manipulated her clit until she moaned, and her head fell back. Cum sprayed around Hunter's hand fuck, and he sped his motions until another cry ripped from her.

"He's harder than I am," Hunter said, and Paige's gaze dropped to Austin's lap.

Shamed heat filled his cheeks, and when her gaze met his, he knew she was filled with the same mortification he felt. The only thing he could do was lift a single shoulder and wince in response.

"Think I should let him jerk off?"

Paige sent a glare over her shoulder, and for the first time since the curtain opened, Austin truly understood. Paige wasn't in control of her actions beyond the movement of her head, and that glare she sent was so full of hatred that Austin broke out into a cooling set of gooseflesh.

"Do you want to suck him dry before he fucks you into oblivion?"

Her gaze jumped to Austin's and then dropped to his lap before meeting his gaze again. The slight nod was enough.

"Slut," Hunter snarled in her ear, and he pulled his hands away.

The fact she made that annoyed squeak like she didn't want him to stop rubbed the burn in the pit of his stomach even more. The chains holding her lowered her closer to the floor, and Hunter stepped to the side, turning her towards him. She stopped just as her mouth came even with his tented slacks.

"Show me what you want," he said.

She glared up at him and winced.

Austin's fists clenched when she leaned forward and put her mouth around the tip of his covered cock.

Hunter smiled and unzipped, freeing himself so Paige could suck it without the fabric.

"Are you fucking kidding me?" Austin asked.

She hummed as Hunter deep throated her.

"She knows how to blow like a whore, too," he said, glancing in Austin's direction. He remained still while Paige swallowed the length of him before sliding her lips to his tip.

Austin pulled against the cuffs, letting the sharp pain in his back drown the anguish filling his heart. Logically, he knew she wasn't in control, but that didn't lessen the fury at what he was seeing. What pissed him off even more was the hunger that sat alongside his wrath. All of this tickled his voyeuristic tendencies, and he hated the fact this little scenario turned him on.

"Swallow every last inch, bitch," Hunter growled and pushed forward as his hands gripped the sides of her head. "Fuck, yeah," he whispered. He moved his hips faster, fucking her mouth with bravado until he pushed his entire length into her mouth, gagging her while he groaned.

He held her in place, and Austin watched her swallow through the wet gags. After a few more slow thrusts, he stepped back and zipped his pants before turning towards Austin.

The ropes raised her back to the original height, and she hung her head, avoiding Austin's gaze as her chest heaved.

"I hate you," she gasped and glared up at Hunter. This time, her voice carried the conviction it had lacked before.

"Well, baby, that makes us even." He stepped away and waved his hand towards the table of toys. "Pick your poison," he said to Austin.

Austin stared at the array of horns, all of which tapered to sharp points. From rhino to elephant tusks, the thought of sticking one of those inside Paige left his stomach turning. The unlatching of the cuffs startled him, but what followed shocked him even more. His body moved, ignoring the pain each step brought forth until he stood in front of the gruesome tool set.

"I will not hurt her," he said through clenched teeth, and a pain shot through his head like someone planted an axe in his brain.

A shaking hand reached out, finding the thickest horn, caressing the smooth surface of one that would not only pierce her but would stretch her to the ripping point. One that would make her scream until she bled out. He fought against letting his hand close around the hard trunk.

Austin flexed the muscles in his back and sharp pain rippled through every muscle, giving the strength to disobey the silent commands filling his head. With all his might, he turned away from the table empty-handed. He still didn't have full control over his body, but he had successfully defied Hunter's will. His hands clenched into fists as righteous fury filled his bones, giving him more power to resist the horrific images Hunter projected into his head.

"Whatever he makes you do, I want you to know I love you, Austin," Paige said.

Hunter backhanded her, sending her head rocking to the side.

The sound of the slap echoed in Austin's head, and the red mark on her cheek left by Hunter's hand unlocked Austin from whatever hold Hunter had on him. He launched, breaching the distance in a flash. Anger controlled him, and his fist connected with

Hunter's throat before the bastard had a chance to defend himself.

Austin grabbed Hunter's hair and yanked him down, slamming Hunter's face as hard as he could into his knee. The crunch of breaking bones sent a rush of satisfaction through Austin. Hunter went down hard, and Austin turned his attention to Paige, freeing her legs and then her wrists. She collapsed in his arms.

The pain rippled across his back, and he nearly dropped to his knees.

"We have to get out of here before he wakes up," Austin whispered.

Paige regained her footing and found the clothing Hunter had tossed to the side. While she pulled her underwear and pants on, Austin slipped his t-shirt over his head. The scraping of fabric against his raw skin dropped him to a knee, but his shrieking survival instinct pushed him to his feet, grabbing his sweater and cell phone.

"Jesus," Paige's whisper pulled his gaze over his shoulder. She stared at his back and then her gaze moved to his. Horror filled her features, and she took his arm, leading him towards the far side of the dark room.

"You can't go out there like that," Paige said as they reached the far wall, her voice raw and shaking.

Austin reached for the wall, feeling his way in the dark until the egg-crate pattern gave way to smooth metal. "Help me with my sweater," he said and handed it to her. "Just drape it over my shoulders, okay?"

"Okay," she said.

He winced at the weight of the light fabric, but at least it would cover whatever blood was still seeping from his wounds.

Austin ran his hand down the door until it landed on a push bar. He said a little prayer and pushed. The door gave, allowing them to step out onto the opposite side of the floor near the stairwell.

He didn't take another glance over his shoulder. He just dragged her back to the hotel and bolted the door closed before leaning on it to catch his breath. The shakes that had gripped him after crossing half the distance had now taken hold of his entire form like an earthquake had settled in his core. He grabbed the doorframe to get control. It was all he could do to remain standing on his feet.

His stomach clenched, and he nearly dropped to the ground, but the sounds of retching reached through his overwhelmed mind. Paige was leaning over the toilet, vomiting between sobs, and he stumbled to her side, dropping to his knees next to her.

He gently pulled her hair out of the way, letting her purge the vile contents of her stomach into the commode. When she finished and flushed the toilet, he pulled her into his lap and just held tight, unsure of how to react now that the numbness had finally settled in. It took away the raw burn in his stomach and the agony of his flogged back.

He stared into the distance, his eyes not focusing on anything in particular, and Paige curled up in his lap, holding him as tightly as a frightened child. He didn't know how long they sat there like that, and the silence wrapped around them like a comforting blanket.

Anger roiled his stomach as unwanted images played across the space in front of him. Each moment burned into his memory, creating a tornado of emotions. He would never understand how Paige could have loved that fucker. Not with everything he had seen since the first time that bastard had possessed him.

"I'm going to kill him," Austin finally said, disrupting the quiet.

Paige lifted her head from under his chin. "You can't," she said and sniffled.

His jaw tightened, and he nearly dumped her off his lap.

Her hand reached for his cheek, caressing his skin in a touch that thawed the dark chill that overtook him.

"He will kill you if you go after him. He's somehow harnessed black magick."

He leaned into her palm and closed his eyes, dipping his forehead to hers.

"The only place we are safe is back in New Hampshire."

A harsh laugh escaped his chest, and he opened his eyes. "Bullshit. He isn't getting away with what he did. What he almost made me do..." He trailed off and met her gaze.

Her chin trembled. "How did you stop him?"

His eyebrows rose, and he shrugged. "I wasn't going to hurt you."

"I had no control at all. I didn't want him touching me, but I couldn't stop the way he made my body react." Her head dropped to his chest as another sob bubbled up.

"Maybe a part of you wanted it," he said and instantly regretted the words slipping from his lips. Paige yanked herself out of his arms, and she was on her feet and out of the bathroom before he could stop her.

He caught her fumbling with the locks at the door and pressed his hand over hers. She sent a glare in his direction.

"Paige, how come I could resist his commands and you couldn't?" he asked as softly as he could, keeping the accusation from his voice.

"I don't know."

"Are you sure?"

She spun and glared at him. "If you had been wearing the crystal I gave you, none of that would have happened," she snarled in a way that surprised him.

He fell back a step and slipped his hand into his pocket.

"What does this have to do with what happened?" he asked, pulling the crystal out.

Her gaze dropped to the rock swinging from the chain, and her mouth opened a fraction before her hand covered it. When her wide eyes returned to his, a shiver caught him off guard.

All color drained from her cheeks, and she fell against the door, her features falling into that of defeat.

"He shouldn't have been able to control you at all," she whispered behind her hand. "What the hell have I done?"

"Paige," he started, and she dipped her head, looking at the ground instead of him. "This isn't your fault."

"Yes, it is. I didn't do the right spell to banish him, and I can't fight that kind of power." She met his gaze. "And what he did..." She trailed off, going even whiter than before and her arms wrapped around her waist. "I need to feel clean," she muttered and slid by him back into the bathroom.

Austin leaned his forehead against the wall, debating on whether he needed a hospital. The rush of water in the shower pulled his attention away from his own pain. In the bathroom, her clothing was piled on the floor.

All his training in psychology jumped into gear, and he stepped into the room. "Do you want me to help?" he asked just outside the curtain. When she didn't answer, he slid his shoes off and pulled the curtain back, bracing himself for the pain he knew the water would inflict, but her anguish was more important at the moment.

Paige stood with her back to him, and her face buried in her hands. The shake of her shoulders told him enough. He emptied his pockets, dropping his keys, wallet, and phone on the counter along with the crystal before stepping into the shower with his dress pants and t-shirt still on.

She stiffened and shot a glance over her shoulder. Her semi-glare changed as she scanned his clothed form. A crease appeared between her eyes, and she met his gaze.

Without speaking, he picked up the soap and lathered her back, being careful not to rub the shallow welts on her skin. He concentrated on the exquisite burn each drop of water made on his back to keep from getting overwhelmed by the feel of her skin under his hands. The moment he stepped aside to let her rinse, the relief pulled shakes from the core of his soul. Trails of bubbles slid off her back, mingling with thin trails of red before it swirled down the drain.

In some ways, the cleansing of her body reminded him of their first shower at the sanitarium, but this time, her need for feeling clean was psychologically rooted and not a physical need. All he could do was try to patch the damage that bastard did today.

When she turned towards him, he washed her front as gently as he had done her back. She kept her eyes closed, and after he finished, he turned her and lathered her hair, taking his time to hand-comb the suds from root to tip before rinsing it with the same care.

When he was finished, she turned and stepped into his arms. Austin held her, delivering a soft kiss to her forehead.

"We need to get emeralds and black tourmaline," she said after standing in his arms for what seemed like forever.

Begrudgingly, he unwrapped his arms and turned toward the faucet. Her gasp stopped him, and he glanced over his shoulder at her.

"Take off your shirt," she said.

He slowly peeled the fabric off.

More red flowed into the tub and the room spun.

"I think I need to sit down," he said and slowly sank to the floor of the tub.

She turned the water off and threw the shower curtain aside, grabbing a towel before she kneeled down next to him.

"You need a hospital," she said, her voice holding authority.

He met her gaze. "That's the first place he'll look," he answered, knowing she was probably right. But based on what they just lived through, he didn't want to be in a compromising position again, especially in his current condition. "All we need is some antibiotic ointment and bandages."

"Austin, you need stitches in at least a dozen places. I'm calling an ambulance."

He grabbed her wrist when she went to stand. "Do you really think a hospital will deter him? That's what he'll expect, and I sure as shit don't want you anywhere near the kind of sharp equipment they have in a hospital. He wanted you dead today, Paige."

He swallowed the burn of bile and took a deep breath.

"He wanted you dead by my hand."

The reality of how much Hunter hated him was far more than what he carried against Paige. Death was easy compared to the lifetime of guilt he wanted Austin to suffer.

They stared at each other in a stalemate.

"I think I'm going to need help getting to the bed," he said with a sigh, still holding her gaze.

Paige helped him to his feet and stripped off his bloodstained slacks, leaving them in the shower with his shirt. He wrapped a towel around his waist and shuffled to the bed, crawling onto the soft mattress and collapsing on his stomach.

"I'm going to go get something to patch you up," she said as she rummaged through the suitcase. She pulled on clothing before she hand-combed her hair and turned to him.

He sent a tired smile in her direction, clinging to staying awake, to not falling into a state of shock now that the full scope of his wounds was making itself known.

"Paige?" he muttered, and she kneeled by the side of the bed. "You probably should cover me." His teeth had already started the slow chatter as shivers traversed his overly heated skin. The air brushed his wounds like a blowtorch now that his back was exposed.

"Austin, you really need a hospital," she said again, taking his hand in hers.

The last thing he remembered was shaking his head no.

Black Magick
Chapter 6

AUSTIN'S EYES ROLLED BACK, and his head dropped to the mattress. His breathing was shallow and fast, and his hands were cold and clammy, nothing like what they should have been since he just stepped out of a hot shower.

Panic edged in, setting Paige's heart into overdrive. She knew enough about shock from her parents' car accident. She knew if she didn't get him help, he'd die, just like her parents did.

"Austin?" she asked and gently patted his cheeks, praying he would come to. But he didn't react at all. Without stalling any more, she yanked the phone and pressed the button for the front desk.

"Hello. This is Paige Turner in room 508. My boyfriend has been hurt, and I need an ambulance."

"How was he hurt?" the desk clerk asked.

"He's bleeding. Please call nine-one-one. I think he's gone into shock," she said.

"Please stay on the phone."

Paige could hear the clerk speaking with emergency services and then the phone shuffled.

"What is the nature of his injury?"

Paige stared at his back. "He was... flogged."

A beat of silence came over the line. "Excuse me?"

"Some asshole whipped him until his back was a bloody pulp," Paige yelled, losing her composure. "Just get a fucking ambulance here now, before he bleeds out!"

The phone shuffled again; she heard the muffled explanation, and then the desk clerk was back. "The emergency operator said to put a cold compress on the wound until they get here."

"It's his entire back," Paige said, staring at the extent of the damage.

"Soak a towel in cold water and lay it over the wound," the desk clerk said. "The hotel manager is on his way. When the ambulance arrives, I'll bring the technicians up to the room."

"Thank you," Paige said and hung up.

She went into the bathroom and turned on the shower to cold, soaking a towel. She wrung out most of the water and folded it in half, bringing it back into the room before gently laying it across Austin's back.

He started shivering, and Paige grabbed the edges of the comforter and pulled it over his body to keep him warm. Her brain started cataloging things she needed to do, and she shot back into the bathroom. She gathered up their personal items from the sink, dumped them into the small suitcase, and zipped it up with shaking hands.

She dropped Austin's phone, keys, and wallet into her pocketbook and then glanced around the room for her phone. She went back into the bathroom, rummaged through her jean pockets, and came up empty. Neither her phone nor the hotel room key were in her pocket. She shivered.

With her heart pounding in her throat, she went back into the room and double checked the suitcase and her pocketbook. The click of the door opening stiffened her muscles, and she spun towards the sound. Fear burned through her bloodstream and her mouth dried instantly.

An unfamiliar face poked around the door. "Miss Turner?"

Her muscles relaxed. "Yes," she answered and reached for the chair to steady herself.

The hotel manager stepped into the room and crossed to the primary space. He glanced at the lump of covers on the bed. The slow-spreading red stain on the pristine white linens. His gaze snapped to hers.

"He's really hurt," she said, crossing to the side of the bed and taking his hand in hers again. The feel of it settled, the flutter of nerves overcoming her entire form. "I think someone stole the room key," she added as an afterthought. The last thing she wanted was for Hunter to show up and manipulate the staff, or even the medics.

The hotel manager's eyebrows rose, and then he scanned the room, looking for evidence of the crime.

"It didn't happen here," Paige said, and the worry lines in his forehead smoothed. "But I think the person who did this also stole my phone and room key." She glanced at the door. "And I'm terrified he's going to come finish what he started."

The worry lines were back, but before he could respond, the door opened again. This time, a woman opened it, holding the door open for the medical team.

Paige stepped aside and let them get Austin on a gurney while she made sure all their stuff was in the suitcase. When they wheeled him out the door, she followed with their bag and her pocketbook. Every muscle in her body tensed as they stepped out of the hotel, and her scan of the street didn't provide any glimpse of the man in the museum.

She couldn't see him, but she could feel his evil blanketing the area. She took a seat on the bench next to where Austin lay and gave the medic a weak smile. As soon as the vehicle was moving, she closed her eyes, fighting back the sudden burn of tears.

"He's going to make it," the medic said.

Paige opened her eyes, and they landed on his name tag. "Thank you, Sam," she said, reading the embroidered name. "Do you know if the hospital gift shop has anything with black tourmaline?"

He just stared at her like she'd sprung a new head.

The thought of leaving Austin to find what she needed in the city scared her. What if Hunter came looking for her and found Austin unguarded? The thought produced a rash of gooseflesh that rippled up her arms. What if she didn't go and Hunter found her with Austin?

Deep down, Paige knew she didn't have a prayer without the ancient protection of her ancestors. Black tourmaline would cloak them from Hunter's internal eye. Emeralds would turn his evil against him, and anything else she could get her hands on to ward off the evil she would buy, just to keep Austin safe.

Black Magick
Chapter 7

THE STEADY BEEP PENETRATED the darkness, and Austin blinked slowly, letting the shaded light into his reality. The tiled floor came into view, and he stared, groggy and disoriented. Shifting his body sent a river of discomfort over his back, but it was dull and removed from the acute pain he had felt earlier.

"Paige?" His rough whisper overrode the beeping.

When no answer came, the beeping sped up, along with the pounding in his chest. The sudden introduction of panic in his blood wiped the grogginess out of his mind, and the fact he was lying face down on something akin to a massage table entered his thought process.

The shuffle of feet turned his attention to his right, and when white shoes appeared at the edge of his vision, his heart clenched. Hospital. Shit.

"Mr. Anderson, are you awake?"

Confusion clouded his mind, and his gaze darted around, looking for the person the shoes were addressing. Austin picked up his head and turned it towards the voice after doing a quick scan of the machines in front of him.

"Where's my girlfriend?" he asked, his voice tentative, with all the doubts shuffling through his head.

The nurse smiled. "She said she needed to run an errand and hoped to be back before you woke."

His gaze jumped past the nurse, towards the doorway and the hustling hospital staff beyond, before it returned to hers.

"Mr. Anderson, do you know where you are?"

The fact she called him the wrong name registered in his brain, and his brow creased in confusion. A voice in the back of his mind kept his tongue from correcting her.

"You're in the hospital, and you've had close to two hundred stitches in your back. You lost enough blood that you needed a blood transfusion. Now you have an IV line to make sure you are hydrated, and your next dose of pain medicine will be administered in another hour," she explained. "Do you have any questions?"

He attempted to push himself up, but he only succeeded in propping himself up on his elbows before the pain sliced through the fog in his mind. Wincing, he glanced around to get a feel for where he was. It wasn't a private room. Only curtain walls separated him from the next emergency room patient. He gave the nurse a slow shake of his head. While over a dozen questions circled in his mind, he wasn't sure right now was the time to ask any of them.

"When my girlfriend gets back, can you please make sure they let her in?"

"Certainly, Mr. Anderson." She made a note on the file and sent a smile in his direction.

"Um, do you know where my phone is?" he asked before she turned away.

"I'm sorry. I don't. Your girlfriend left your suitcase on the chair." She waved towards the far corner of the makeshift room. "Would you like me to look through it?"

Austin turned his head to the side and stared at their suitcase, wondering where Paige would have packed it. Exhaustion claimed his muscles, and he shook his head, settling back into the bed.

"It's not an emergency," he muttered. The floor blurred and then faded as he slipped back into sleep.

"Please don't make me do this," he pleaded.

"She whipped you to shreds and you want to take pity on her?"

"You did this to me," Austin growled through clenched teeth, glaring at the man standing next to him. His hand tightened around the thick horn, and the man's evil chuckle resonated in the darkness.

"Are you sure about that?"

He stepped to the side and waved his hand, revealing Paige standing behind Austin, whipping him. Every time the lashes hit his back, blood splatters flew into the air. Each biting connection of leather to skin arched his back and clenched his eyes with a grunt of pain. And she smiled an insane grin with each spray of blood.

The vision faded and Austin looked at her bound form. An unjust anger filled him, and he stepped forward, positioning the horn, intending to do as much damage as humanly possible.

Austin gasped. His eyes flew open to the darkened room, and he forced himself to his knees, panting as pain and anguish shuffled through his skin. The heart monitor danced a quick tune, and he forced himself to breathe. Drawing a breath hurt and he let out a gruff groan as cool air caressed his ass. The open johnny hung from his front, and blankets piled on his feet.

The curtain behind him rattled as it opened, and he twisted to take a glance over his shoulder.

"It looks like you are ready for some more medicine," the nurse who had spoken to him earlier said.

"I would rather not," he said and pulled the blanket high enough to hide his bare butt. The nurse met his gaze with a barely concealed smirk.

"You don't have to worry. I've seen a bare ass before."

Austin let a small huff of a laugh escape, and he sighed. "If you have Tylenol, I'll take that, but I really want nothing stronger right now."

She stepped next to him and held his wrist, checking his pulse despite the heart monitor. Then she checked his blood pressure and jotted numbers down on his chart. He remained kneeling on the mattress, unsure of how to get himself into a comfortable position.

"How long have I been out?" he asked and wiped the sleep from his eyes.

She looked at her watch. "A little over two hours."

His gaze bounced to the chair and the suitcase that remained.

"My girlfriend hasn't come back?" Fear gripped him, dulling every other sensation.

"Not that I am aware of," she said, eying him closely. "The police have been waiting to speak with you as well."

He swallowed hard. "Can you check the waiting room for my girlfriend?"

"Sure. Can I send the police in?"

Austin tried to shift and winced.

"Would you like some help?" She stepped closer, but he put his hand up to stop her.

"I can do it," he said through clenched teeth.

He shifted to his side, but his breath had turned into a ragged pant of pain. The back of the bed slowly rose, and he glanced at the nurse with a nod of thanks. The last shift pulled a grunt from his chest, and he slowly eased back against the inclined mattress. The pressure brought the sting of tears to his eyes, and he pressed them closed, counting until his breath came to some semblance of normal.

Sheets shifted and his eyes opened as the nurse pulled the fabric over him, covering him.

"Are you sure I can't give you something stronger than Tylenol?" she asked.

"I would rather not," he whispered.

She gave him a nod and left the room. No sooner had she stepped out of sight than two New York City officers stepped into the room.

"Mr. Anderson," the dark-skinned cop asked as he looked at the tablet in his hand.

"Yes, sir," Austin said, and the lie tasted bitter on his tongue.

"Can you tell us who did this to you?"

Austin's gaze landed on the foot of the bed as he weighed his words. If he told them the ghost of a dead man possessed another and whipped him to shreds, he'd end up in the mental ward. He slowly shook his head.

"It was dark, but you might be able to find some evidence of what happened," he said and looked up. "Third floor special exhibition room of the Museum of Natural History. I was handcuffed to a bench and beaten to shit. If he didn't cover his tracks, the whip should still be there with my blood on it."

They exchanged a glance.

"Are you sure your girlfriend didn't do this to you?"

Austin chuckled under his breath and nodded. "The crazy fuck that did this looked Italian. Dark curly hair, green eyes. He had maybe an inch or two on me in height. Our first encounter with him was at Starbucks across from Cornell this morning, and he freaked my girlfriend out."

The nurse stepped back into the room and crossed to him with two small white cups. One contained the familiar caplets, and the other held water. She handed them to him, and he raised an eyebrow, asking whether she checked the visiting room without the words.

She waited expectantly, and he downed the medicine.

"Well?" he asked as he handed her the cup.

"She hasn't returned, sir," she said.

Cold caressed his cheeks, and his gaze darted to the cops. Fear bloomed in every cell, and he swung his legs over the side of the bed.

"I have to find her," he said and started ripping at the tubes in his arm.

"Mr. Anderson!" The nurse was around the bed and trying to get him back on the mattress before his feet even hit the ground. "If you don't settle down, I'll have to sedate you."

He sent his most chilling glare in her direction. "You don't get it," he growled, fueled by the fire of panic.

"Son, just relax," the officer said, stepping to help the nurse.

"You don't understand, if that freak has her..." His breath locked in his chest, coming in short pulls, like an elephant had sat on his chest. He recognized the panic attack gripping him, but was helpless to stop it.

"You need to rest. Otherwise, you'll rip your stitches out," the nurse said.

He fought against her logic, trying to get to his feet, but the sting of a needle on his backside pulled his head in that direction just in time to see a doctor pulling a needle out of his ass.

"Please," he started, but the medicine worked fast, turning his muscles to jelly. He slumped back into the bedding. A groan escaped as the pain flared. It only lasted a minute and then his eyelids dropped, along with every hint of consciousness.

Black Magick
Chapter 8

AUSTIN WOKE TO A dark room. The silence was the first thing that convinced him he was no longer in the emergency room. He cleared his throat and shifted. Pain flared, shutting off logic for a moment before he realized he was strapped to the bed he lay in.

He coughed, trying to get control over the thumping in his chest. "Hello?" he asked the dark.

His voice hung on the dry air. He attempted to move his arms, but the rattle of metal on a bar left him cold.

He inhaled a deep breath. "Hey!" he belted out at the top of his lungs, ignoring the sting the motion created through his back.

The overhead lights popped on, and he squinted against the brightness. As his vision settled, the door opened, and a bearded doctor stepped into the barren room. The recognition of his surroundings dropped his eyes closed.

"Mr. Anderson," the doctor started.

Austin sighed. He opened his eyes and focused on the doctor. "Why am I in restraints?"

"Do you know where you are?"

"The psych ward," Austin said without skipping a beat. "I work in one back in New Hampshire."

The doctor adjusted his glasses. "You didn't take sedation very well," he said.

Austin's eyebrows rose. The last thing he remembered was the needle coming out of his ass, falling back on the bed, and then everything went black. "What did I do?"

"Besides tearing almost every stitch in your back, you punched the doctor and knocked the nurse over before the officer tazed you."

Austin huffed and closed his eyes. "So, how long have I been out?" he asked.

"We have had you heavily sedated for the past seventy-two hours."

Shock popped his eyes open, and his jaw loosened as he stared at the ceiling, trying to comprehend what that meant. He was terrified to ask the question jumping through his brain like a twenty-two shell ricocheting inside his skull.

"Did she ever come back?" he finally whispered.

"She who?" the doctor asked.

"My girlfriend. The one who was with me at the hotel."

The doctor swiped his finger across the tablet in his hands before he finally shook his head. "There is no notation of a visitor for you."

Austin's eyes squeezed shut. Anguish overrode his senses, and he forced his breathing to remain calm despite the internal alarms. He slowly opened his eyes and met the doctor's gaze.

"Any chance I can use a phone?" he asked.

The doctor glanced at the sheet again. "I will see what I can do, but the police would like to talk to you first," he said and closed the chart.

He nodded and moved his gaze to the ceiling. If he counted the hours he spent in the emergency room, the last time he set eyes on Paige was four days ago. Based on the hospital's continued reference to calling him Mr. Anderson, he guessed he had nothing with him that would identify him otherwise, which meant he was on his own and penniless in New York City.

A plain-clothes officer stepped into the room, his badge hanging open from his blazer pocket. "Mr. Anderson, I'm Detective Connelly." he said, taking a seat on the bench against the wall.

Austin gave him a nod, but something deep down told him to keep his mouth shut.

"You spoke with Officer Petrelli a few days ago, and we followed up on your story at the Museum of Natural History." The detective stopped speaking and leveled a stare that brought a rash of gooseflesh across Austin's skin.

"And?"

"Why don't you tell me?" he asked and crossed his arms.

"Did you find the whip?"

The detective chewed on his lower lip for a moment as he studied Austin. When he nodded, Austin couldn't help the exhale of relief.

"We found the whip and the blood on it matches yours, so that part of your story checks out. Can you tell me about the blood on the stage?"

Austin's gaze darted around the room and then back to the detective. Confusion clouded his mind as he studied his memories. Paige never bled. At least not while they were there together. His hand involuntarily jerked, restrained by the soft fabric, but the metal clanked enough for the detective's forehead to crease.

"She wasn't bleeding when we left," he whispered when his gaze landed back on the cop.

"What did you do with the body?"

Austin's chest hurt. He forced a breath and then a second one as his nightmares surfaced. He shook his head, trying to control the need to panic.

"What body?" he asked after gaining control over the wild beast running amok in his stomach.

"The one that you killed."

His eyes widened, and he shook his head. "I didn't kill anyone," he answered.

"Your fingerprints were on the murder weapon."

"What weapon?" His voice rose an octave higher, following the sudden adrenaline rush pushing his heart to beat a new pattern.

The detective grimaced and opened the attaché case at his feet. When he approached, he turned one of the many photographs towards him.

Austin stared at the bloodied rhino horn, and his entire form shook. The nightmare danced in front of his eyes, and he shook his head.

"I touched it, but I refused to use it on her no matter how much that bastard wanted me to," he said, and his vision blurred. Blinking back the tears, he met Detective Connelly's hard stare. "Can I please use your phone?"

"Why?"

"I need to make sure my girlfriend is okay," he said, his voice shaking in time with the tremors wracking his body.

"Why don't you start from the beginning?"

Austin met his gaze and exhaled. "We came into the city because I had interviews at Cornell and Columbia Medical Schools," he started.

"Who did you speak with at the schools?" Detective Connelly asked.

"The dean of medicine," he said. He closed his eyes and leaned his head back. "And while I was at Cornell, Paige waited for me at the Starbucks across the street. Some guy there freaked her out and followed her when she came out to the car."

"And if I reach out to the dean—"

"They won't be able to confirm," Austin interrupted him and opened his eyes. "Paige signed me in here at the hospital, and she probably thought I'd be safer if she put me under an alias. My real name is Austin Shelton."

The cop stared at him.

"She was still alive when I was admitted, but if she hasn't come back from where ever she went..." Austin cursed the burn in his eyes and his now watery vision. "Please, I need to know."

The detective sighed and glanced at the door before he dropped the pictures back on the bench. When he approached the bed, he pulled the phone out of his pocket. "Normally, I don't stick my ass out for anyone, but either you're a genius of an actor or you're telling the truth."

Austin bit his lower lip and nodded. "I appreciate it. But do me a favor, whatever is said, please don't let whoever is on the line know you are in the room, okay?" he asked, and the detective hesitated. "Her life may depend on it," he added softly. *Not to mention mine*, he thought, but didn't voice it.

The hardness in the detective's face softened a fraction, and he gave a small nod.

Austin rattled the number off and met the detective's dark eyes. He punched the numbers in and pressed the speaker, holding the phone close to Austin's mouth. The phone rang for what seemed like forever, and then a tentative male voice answered.

"Hello?"

"Is Paige there?"

The low chuckle filled the line, and Austin met the detective's gaze.

"We were wondering just how long it would take for you to call, especially since she had your phone when I found her."

"I swear..." Austin growled and pressed his teeth together against the threat, poised to tumble from his mouth.

The low rumble of ancient words came over the line, and Paige screamed in the background. The detective's eyes glazed over, and the phone dropped onto Austin's chest. When the gun came out of his jacket, Austin's blood froze along with his breath.

Paige's pleas came through the line. Her promises to do anything he asked if he would just spare Austin's life burned him more than staring down the barrel of the gun.

Another set of words paused the detective's trigger finger, but by his expression, he now recognized what was happening. All color bled from his face.

"If you hurt her..." Austin huffed as his entire body contracted in anger. The pain that followed nearly ripped a grunt from his throat, but he controlled the sound.

"Please," Paige whispered in the background. "You don't need to hurt him. I will do whatever you want. Just leave him alone, please."

"Paige, you don't need to protect me," he said, his voice soft but firm.

"Are you alone?" Hunter asked.

Austin wasn't sure how to answer that. If he said no and Hunter uttered whatever command he had before, he would be dead in less than a minute. If he said yes, he might still be dead in the same timeframe.

"Yes," he lied.

"Should we test that?"

Austin clenched his teeth, and the detective was able to shake his head. Horror filled his eyes at the lack of control he had over his physical form.

"Go for it," Austin said, playing out the bluff. His heart pounded in his chest and fear squeezed his bladder to the point he was sure he would piss the bed, but his voice remained steady.

"No!" Paige screamed in the background.

The phone clattered to the ground, disconnecting the call and cutting whatever hold Hunter had on the detective.

He stepped back, away from Austin, holstering his gun with a shaking hand. "I almost..."

Austin couldn't help but laugh. Paige was alive and so was he, but he knew there was a time limit on both those things, a limit the shaken detective didn't quite understand.

"What the fuck?" Detective Connelly finally gasped and glanced at Austin.

"Paige said it was black magick." He cracked a sarcastic smile. "You know, a year ago, I would have shit my pants laughing at the thought, but after what I've seen this prick do..." He trailed off and shook his head.

Detective Connelly took the phone off Austin's chest and crossed to the bench, taking a seat. Austin stared at him, waiting for him to speak or dismiss the situation completely.

"I'm not equipped to deal with this," he muttered under his breath. He punched some numbers into the phone and held it to his ear. "Special Agent Williams, it's Detective Connelly."

Austin blinked in surprise.

"Sorry, but I wasn't sure who else to call... I've got a weird one here and..." Detective Connelly turned toward the small window, listening to the person on the other end of the line. "I know you're not active anymore, but..." The detective pinched his nose. "My sister said if

I ever had a weird case, you should be the first person I call. And this is fucking weird.”

Austin moved his gaze to the ceiling, his mind working at figuring out a way to get Paige out of where she was. He had a feeling they were still in New York City. After all, if you want to hide a needle, this was the right haystack for it.

“I can swing by and explain.” The detective ended the call and met Austin’s gaze. “I’m not equipped to deal with this shit, but the guy I just called might be able to help. Let me see if I can get you out of here.”

Austin just nodded, wondering what the hell had just happened. He had never seen a cop do an about face so damned quickly before and especially with someone admitted to the psych ward.

It took a good twenty minutes before the doctor returned to the room, and he quietly unhooked Austin before he spoke.

“You are being released into Detective Connelly’s custody, and I can’t stress enough the care you must take with your back. The dressings need to be changed twice a day, and I would suggest you keep your back as dry as possible. You can safely take a shower, but until the stitches come out, I suggest you don’t lift more than ten pounds.”

“Fourteen days for the stitches, right?” Austin asked as he slowly sat up. He hoped like hell he and Paige were back home by then and Hunter was six feet under. He wanted that prick dead more than he wanted to become a doctor.

“That’s correct.”

A nurse stepped in and placed his suitcase on the bench.

"Would you like some help getting dressed?" she asked.

"No, but thank you," Austin said and slowly got to his feet.

He shuffled across the room and dropped the johnny and hospital issue undergarments on the bench before opening the suitcase. He slid on his only pair of clean underwear, along with the pair of jeans he had packed for their trip home. The undershirt was more of a challenge and putting on his socks and sneakers nearly made him pass out, but he finally had everything set. He stared at the only shirt option he had in the suitcase. He picked up the torn oxford and slipped it on, but he didn't bother buttoning it.

He zipped the suitcase and dropped it to the floor. Pulling the handle out, he rolled it to the door. The handle opened easily, and he stepped out into the hall.

Detective Connolly straightened and gave him a nod. Austin followed him out to the small emergency parking lot where the detective's car sat. The detective took his bag and stowed it in the trunk while Austin slid into the passenger seat. The drive from the hospital to the north side of Central Park took a couple of minutes.

Austin stared at the high-end apartment complex before turning his attention to the detective.

"The FBI pays this well?" he asked.

Detective Connelly let out a little laugh. "Uh, no, not exactly."

The doorman held the door for the two of them before directing them to the elevator. Once in the confines of the lift, the detective pressed the button for the penthouse.

Austin gave the detective a raised eyebrow.

"It was left to him," Detective Connolly said. "He was my sister's partner before she disappeared."

Austin exhaled and looked up at the numbers. "Is that why you're helping me?"

"No, I'm helping you because I had no control over my actions in that room, and I could have killed you. Your girlfriend saved both our lives, and I owe it to her to get her out of whatever you two stepped in."

Austin's face heated, and he dropped his gaze to the ground, feeling humbled by the detective's answer. His hands slid into his pockets.

"I don't know how to stop him," Austin mumbled.

Before Detective Connolly could offer some words of wisdom, the elevator doors slid open, and he stepped out. Austin followed, glancing at the small entry. The detective knocked on the door and waited.

A man with dark hair and eyes that reminded Austin of Paige's opened the door. The thing that threw him was this man couldn't have been much older than he was.

"Hey, Tom, we were looking for your father," Detective Connolly said.

Tom gave him a nod and waved him in, but except for the brief nod in the detective's direction, his gaze remained locked on Austin. The fact he didn't speak unnerved Austin, too.

"Hi, I'm Austin," he said.

Tom gave him a nod before his hands moved in a greeting. It took Austin a moment to realize the man was using sign language. He blinked and picked up the last letter. An M before he glanced up.

Instead of speaking, he signed "Thank you," much to his host's surprise.

"I can hear," he signed. "Just can't talk without a tongue." He offered a small smile and waved Austin farther into the apartment.

Austin stared at his hands and then at his face, wondering if he really understood what the man was saying. He wasn't at the top of his game, but no tongue?

Tom let out a low chuckle and walked away. Austin followed into the living room and his gaze was drawn to the amazing view of the city beyond the room. Temporarily stunned by the cityscape, he slowed to a stop, mesmerized.

A throat cleared, and his gaze bounced to Detective Connolly and an older gentleman with the same dark hair as Tom, but with gray coloring in his temples. But that wasn't what made Austin's mouth drop open. He recognized the fourth man sitting in the overstuffed chair. Paige had gone all gooey-eyed when he came on the television, and he had to admit the guy had a voice that could charm the pants off just about any woman.

"CJ Ryan," Austin said in only a whisper.

The sparkle in the man's eyes was on the border of impish, and he nodded.

"Holy shit," Austin mumbled and glanced around the room again.

CJ met Tom's gaze. "You got this?" he asked, and Tom nodded. "Good, because I've got a show to do," he added, getting to his feet. He crossed to Austin. "My brother can help," he said directly to Austin.

"How," Austin said, not meaning to be rude, but he couldn't fathom how they could possibly help.

"Trust us, we've dealt with worse," CJ said and disappeared out the front door.

"Mark, we've got this," the older gentleman said to Detective Connolly, and both Austin and the detective looked at him.

"No offense, Steve, but I'd really like to bag this psycho," Detective Connolly said.

"Normally, I'd say join the party, but from what you said on the phone, it doesn't sound like something your sister would want me to let you get involved in."

The detective's jaw tightened, and he sent a glare at the older gentleman.

"Do you mind if I sit?" Austin asked before exhaustion dropped him to the ground. He offered a slight shrug, trying to hide the wince that followed.

"Be our guest," Steve said.

Austin took the closest seat. Lowering onto the soft leather was a challenge, and he had to clench his teeth against the discomforting pull of stitches. He glanced up at Detective Connolly.

"The only way to catch Hunter is by using his magic against him," he said and cringed at how that sounded out loud.

"Magic?" A soft Irish lilt pulled his attention to the hallway and the stunning redhead standing in the entrance.

He gave a slow nod. "Yeah."

"Now, I'm going to insist that you let us take care of this," Steve said to Mark.

Austin's gaze moved around the room at the parties still present and fell back on the redhead. His gaze dropped to the unique amulet gracing her neck. He licked his lips as Steve escorted Detective Connolly to the door.

"Hello, I'm Raven," the redhead said and crossed the room, offering her hand.

Austin took it and gave her firm grip a quick shake.

"I'm Tom's wife," she added, sending a smile in Tom's direction.

Austin couldn't help the smile at how much love was in that single look. "Austin," he said after her gaze came back to his. "I'm still not clear how you can help."

They traded another glance before they settled on the couch across from him.

"What kind of magic?" Raven asked.

"Paige said it was black magick," Austin said, wondering what the hell he was doing actually voicing this shit out loud. He glanced behind him, expecting to see the detective, but the front door was cracked and all he could hear were hushed whispers.

"Steve is walking the detective out," Raven said, pulling his gaze back.

"Are you comfortable?" Tom signed.

"I'm fine."

Tom tapped the back of his shoulder and raised an eyebrow, and Austin's jaw dropped for a second time that evening.

"He can read minds," Raven said softly, drawing his attention back.

The door creaked and closed, and Steve crossed into the room, handing the detective's phone to Austin. He sat down at the computer desk on the far side of the room.

"Can you please call them?" he asked when he looked up from the keyboard.

Austin huffed a laugh, and everyone looked at him expectantly. "I don't think that's wise. There are three of you and only one of me, and I'm not in any position to defend myself right now."

Smiles appeared briefly on all three faces.

"It's okay. I highly doubt his magic will affect us."

Austin stared at the phone, unsure of what to do.

"Call," a voice whispered in his mind, and he glanced up, moving his gaze from Steve to Raven and finally to Tom.

The voice in his head wasn't the former two. Tom raised a brow, challenging him.

"If he hurts her..." He trailed off, his gaze bouncing between them.

"I can trace the call if you can keep him on the line for a full minute."

"And if he takes control of you?"

Raven pulled out her necklace, showing the details to Austin. "This protects us," she said.

He stared at it, and then his gaze bounced to hers. "Black tourmaline?"

"No, bloodstone, but black tourmaline is a good, strong repellant, too."

Her accent was almost hypnotic, as was the looping pattern of the Celtic knot.

"We all have them," she added.

"Why?" It seemed like the logical question to ask, and it gave him a minute to gather his wits.

"Black magick isn't the worst thing that exists in this world," she answered, and his flesh broke out in a rash of bumps. "And we are specialists in this kind of thing." She pointed between her and her husband.

Austin glanced at the phone and then over to Steve, hunkered behind the computer, waiting for him to dial. With a deep breath, he tapped his number in instead of Paige's, praying he wasn't putting her in more danger.

"Austin?" Her soft whisper filled his world.

He closed his eyes. "Are you okay?"

Silence filtered between them, and then her sigh squeezed his heart.

"Please don't look for me."

He leaned forward in the seat, unable to digest her words. "Excuse me?"

"Austin..."

"Fuck that, Paige. I'm coming after him whether or not you agree, and this time, I will end him or die trying." He got to his feet, trying to keep his cool while keeping the conversation going. When she didn't speak, he ran his hand through his hair, painfully aware of the eyes watching him. "Is this really you talking?"

"It's me." Her voice was soft and muffled.

"I know this isn't what you want," he said, scanning the cityscape.

"It doesn't matter what I want. He's..."

"He's what?"

The phone shuffled.

"Get away from me," she said, her voice barely registering with the muffle. The crack of skin on skin resounded, and a bang followed.

A video request appeared, and Austin stared at the button with dread. He swiped the controls and waited, holding his breath. It took a moment, but then the wobble of the phone being moved took over the screen and Hunter's face appeared.

A succession of ancient words tumbled from his lips, and his eyes glowed green. A sick twist clenched Austin's gut, almost doubling him over, but he grabbed the edge of the couch to catch his breath.

"Son of a bitch," he breathed, glaring at the laughter spewing from the screen.

The patter of feet heading down the hall gave him enough of a diversion to fight the pain ripping his insides apart.

"I'm going to kill you," he said through clenched teeth.

"Save that anger for your lovely whore," he said, and the phone flipped.

Paige kept her head dipped, her hair hiding her face, and she was naked with thick chains around her wrists and ankles.

"Look at him," Hunter demanded, but Paige shook her head. When his hand reached into the picture, yanking her head back, all pain left Austin, replaced by a fury too big for his body to contain. The discoloration of her cheek and swollen eye fueled his anger, but it was the dried blood on her lip that pushed him over the edge.

The snap of fingers next to him, followed by the chains unlatching and tumbling to the ground on the screen, stunned both Paige and him. She stared at him like the camera was broadcasting on her end as well. The spell broke when she launched at Hunter.

Her feral growl shattered all of Austin's reserves, but all he could do was stare in silence and horror as a group of men came from the shadows, intercepting her before she could get her hands on Hunter.

The camera turned away from the scene.

"I will save a piece for you," Hunter said just before Paige screamed.

The call cut and Austin stared at the screen, waiting for the picture to return, for it to show Paige was okay. Only silence responded.

Austin turned his gaze to the closest person, and Tom's hard blue eyes stared out the window, the muscles in his jaw tight, and his fists clenched. He glanced at his wife and pulled his arm out of her grasp.

"You can't make that jump. I haven't felt that kind of evil since..." Raven trailed off and glanced at Steve before returning her gaze to her husband. "Since I was possessed."

Austin's gaze jumped to hers. "You were possessed by a ghost?"

"No. A demon."

Black Magick
Chapter 9

EVERY MUSCLE IN HER body hurt.

He stood over her like a god, taking pity on his subject.

"I don't know where the hell you got that phone or how you got out of those chains, but next time you decide to disobey me, I'll beat you unconscious." He pushed the hair out of her face. "By the time I'm done with you, he will not want what's left," he added, cupping her chin and forcing her to look at him.

"Fuck you," Paige whispered.

"Is that an invitation?"

Just the thought repulsed her, and she turned her head away. His little group had already done enough damage. When he thought she was sporting enough bruises from their punches, he turned them from an angry pack delivering an ass-whooping to a frenzied group of horny gang bangers with just a few ancient words. They pounded her until each man had their turn at whatever orifice they chose.

Hunter watched every decadent act without a hint of compassion, like she was a stranger starring in a twisted porn flick.

"Get away from me," she whispered, but she couldn't stop him, not with her arms splayed wide.

He stepped closer. "What are you going to do about it?"

She went to lift her knee, but the chain anchoring her foot to the floor stopped her. She screamed in frustration. "What the hell happened to you, Hunter?"

A bitter smile found his lips, but it never reached his icy eyes. "You."

"How do you figure?" she snapped, refusing to let him see the damage he had already caused. While every fiber in her body feared Hunter was right, that Austin would no longer want her after what Hunter had done, she would not give him the satisfaction of seeing just how crushed she was inside.

"I loved you, and you threw me away, banished me from your life."

"You murdered innocent people," she said.

His hand grasped her neck, pulling her close.

"They deserved to die," he growled in her face. "And so do you."

"Then kill me yourself, you gutless bastard," she replied with an equal amount of venom.

The flash in his eyes and the pressure on her throat as he squeezed tighter created a web of panicked heat that spread through her like a shot of alcohol. She tried to pull her arms in to defend herself, but that only rattled the chains.

His grip remained tight enough for her breath to wheeze and her head to get light. Hunter's free hand traced her skin, slowly toying with her until he found a sensitive bruise, and then he poked. Her wheeze froze. Pain radiated from the bruised rib and her eyes filled with tears.

"You should not fuck with me right now, because you just might get exactly what you wish for." He stepped away, staring at her like he'd swallowed something bitter. Then he turned, leaving her alone in the barren room, chained, bruised, and naked, just waiting for the next time he decided he needed entertainment.

Black Magick
Chapter 10

"DEMONS EXIST?" THE THOUGHT of something more evil than Hunter existing in this world dried the spit in Austin's mouth. Nods confirmed it, and he closed his eyes, slowly formulating a swirl of questions. The one that popped to the forefront of his mind was the one that controlled his tongue.

"Why are you helping me? You haven't even asked what happened," Austin said as he stared at the three of them.

Tom tapped his temple. "Mind reader, remember?" he signed. "And I have no tolerance for that kind of animal." Tom nodded towards the phone in Austin's hands.

"I've got a location," Steve said from behind the computer. The printer whirred to life, and he came around with an address to hand to Tom.

Austin intercepted, plucking it out of both their hands.

He stared at the address and folded the paper, tucking it away until he could catch a cab.

"Let's go," Raven said, and both Tom and Steve stopped in their tracks.

"You aren't going," Tom signed.

She huffed a laugh. "Who do you think has a better chance of counteracting the magic?" she asked.

Tom pulled out his medallion and stared her down without words.

"I'm going," she said.

The fire in her eyes almost pulled a smile from Austin, but the reality of the situation kept it at bay.

"You both can't go," Steve said, blocking the exit. "If shit goes down..." His hands landed on his waist, and he stared at the ground.

Austin watched the standoff between the three of them. Tom's hands flew as he articulated his argument in sign language, and Raven crossed her arms and raised her eyebrows in a way that was vaguely familiar. It took a couple of blinks before it hit him. Raven's *you-are-so-full-of-bullshit* look was the same as Paige's.

"Wouldn't three of us have a better chance at this than just two of us?" he asked, silencing the building argument.

"They have a daughter, and if something happens to both of them, she will be an orphan," Steve said.

"We can handle this," Raven said, glaring in Steve's direction. "If it were CJ..."

"I would still give him the same advice now that he's a father," Steve answered.

"Bu," Tom said out loud, and even Austin caught the full enunciation of *'bullshit'* behind his inarticulate response.

"Look, you guys can argue all night, but I'm going after my girl," Austin said and started for the door. He had the address and the pendant Raven had slipped him while he was on the phone. He had thought the anger stopped the bone crushing pain, but it was actually the amulet. Now that he had that in his arsenal, he was sure he could wipe the floor with Hunter.

"Wa..." Tom said.

His full command of 'wait' halted Austin in place. It was almost like the power Hunter had over him in the museum. He couldn't move forward.

His gaze shot over his shoulder at the small group. "What the fuck?" he asked, still frozen to the spot.

"Just give me a minute," a voice said in Austin's head, and Tom put up his finger before his hands began again.

"But..." Raven started.

Tom's hand formed a stop sign, and both Raven and Steve remained quiet.

"Stay here," he signed and stepped towards the door.

Whatever held Austin in place released him, and he joined Tom by the elevator.

"You need me to counteract the spell," Raven said from the doorway.

Tom leveled the kind of look that chilled Austin, and Raven's reaction made him take a closer look at the man next to him. She dropped her gaze to the ground with a sigh and then turned, closing the front door in submission. As soon as they were in the elevator, Austin pointed towards the doors.

Tom nodded. "Yes, I can do a hell of a lot more than just read minds." His mouth never moved, but his hands echoed the words resounding in Austin's head. Tom met his gaze. "And I can do more damage than my wife can," he added. The corners of his mouth turned into a smile that left Austin cold.

"Did you use magic to stop me back there?"

The slow shake of his head sent another wave of chills through Austin.

"How..." he started, but couldn't quite figure out the proper articulation of his question.

"I'm not your average man," he signed, and his voice echoed in Austin's head. "The mind reading and projecting thoughts are just parlor tricks compared to the other talents I possess."

"You know, less than a year ago, none of this shit existed," Austin started. "I was clueless, and a part of me wishes I was still clueless."

Tom's smile faded, and he offered a nod. "I've always known ghosts exist, but I really never considered them dangerous. As far as this shit..." He tapped his temple before continuing, "My brother has always been... special, so the existence of a... supercharged human is normal for me."

The elevator opened to the lobby, and they crossed to the front door, stepping out into the brisk spring evening. Tom waved a cab down, and they slid into the back.

"Normal, huh?" Austin said after he rattled off the address. He glanced out at the passing scenery as they headed downtown. "I feel like I just stepped into a bad horror movie." He sighed and focused on a plan of attack.

"We'll have to scope it out before we go in," Tom said in his head.

He turned his attention to Tom and went to speak.

"Think it, don't say it. This is our best chance at a surprise attack." Tom's blue eyes reflected the passing lights.

Austin gave him a nod.

"If I knew where your girlfriend was, I could do a clean sweep of the building, but I don't want to risk turning her into dust by accident."

Austin's eyebrows rose.

"I can annihilate at will."

Austin narrowed his eyes. What this guy just revealed was a little too farfetched, and he wondered if Tom really had it all together or if he was just fucking with him for fun.

Tom broke out in a grin and looked out the window. "I'm not fucking with you. What I possess is what most people think nightmares are made of," he said and slid his gaze to Austin. "And while I wish it was all just a nightmare, it's as real as us sitting in this cab."

"So demons, magic, ghosts, and freak-level psychics exist. Next you'll tell me vampires and werewolves exist, too," Austin thought and stared Tom down. The slow fade of his smile left Austin as uncomfortable as he had ever been. The half-hearted shrug that followed left his core hollow and roiling.

"Are you telling me..." he said aloud and caught himself before he said too much. If he truly had that kind of weapon at his side, he would do well not to piss him off. He sighed and considered his next question carefully. "What *doesn't* exist?" he finally thought.

Tom stared out the window, and Austin thought maybe he hadn't heard him. But the minute that thought popped into the forefront of his mind, Tom glanced at him and signed, "I heard you."

"And?"

Tom curled his hands like he was losing an internal debate, but he kept eye contact. "I've never met a werewolf," he finally signed.

"So..." Austin started out loud and filled in the gaps in his mind. He shivered and caught his grimace in the reflection of the window. "Why tell me this?" he said with his hands.

Tom stared at his rudimentary sign language. "I have no idea," he signed back. "I usually don't start yapping about all this shit," he continued, offering a shrug. "I guess I'm tired enough to talk. Especially after the last few months." He wiped his face and shook his head as if he were clearing the cobwebs.

The cab slowed to a stop in front of an abandoned warehouse, and Tom peeled cash from his money clip and handed it to the driver before they got out and stood street side. They both stared at the dark building before Austin pulled out the sheet of paper again. The address matched, and he handed the paper to Tom just to make sure. The hardness in the muscles of his companion's jaw made him fold the paper and put it away.

"They're in there, aren't they?" Austin said, and even though his voice was soft, it echoed off the brick and metal structure.

Tom nodded. "I can't tell if Hunter is in there, but I can tell there are a lot of people guarding entry to a room with orders to kill on sight." He closed his eyes and hung his head, putting his hands on his hips as he did so.

Austin read the physical cues. "Are we going to have to... you know... hurt them?"

Tom nodded without opening his eyes. "Ya," he said aloud, his voice holding enough trepidation to keep Austin quiet.

He didn't have to ask how he felt about it. It was clear he didn't want to harm anyone. Austin only wanted to pummel one person, and he really didn't care who else he would have to take down to do it. Tom turned towards him.

"Ever kill anyone?" he asked in sign language and inside his head.

Austin shook his head. "No."

"It's not easy, and it haunts you for a very long time," he said. "Even when it is warranted as self-defense."

Austin dropped his gaze to the pavement and nodded, feeling tiny compared to the man next to him. He had witnessed murder, and the person responsible was inside the building. Until today, killing had never entered his thoughts, but what this man had in mind for Paige just wasn't something he could let loose on this world.

"If you're not willing to do what it takes to get to my girlfriend, why did you come?"

Tom pressed his lips together, sending a glare in his direction. "I came to make sure you didn't get killed trying to rescue her."

"Fine. Let's get this game going," he said and stepped toward the building. Tom's hand landed on his shoulder, stopping him. He pointed to a broken window instead of the door.

"Less attention. They expect you to come through the front door."

"They are expecting me?"

He nodded. "That's what is worrying me. Well, that and the murderous rage inside you."

Austin stopped in front of the window. "Like you wouldn't do the same for your wife," he said, meeting Tom's gaze.

"I have."

His admission sent a shockwave through Austin, and even without an explanation, he believed Tom.

"And you're right, I would do it again if I had to. But I'm equipped to take on multiple attackers, even without the supercharge. I'm a third-degree black belt in jujitsu. Both my brother and I teach that as well as karate, so I'm not without skills. You are. A psychology degree will not get you very far in there. You can't talk your way out of this one."

His brutal honesty got a rise out of Austin, but it wasn't because he was full of shit. It was because he was so right it hurt. He stepped aside and waved Tom toward the broken window, inviting him to go first.

Tom ducked through the hole, and the darkness swallowed him. Austin took a deep breath and followed.

Black Magick
Chapter 11

PAIGE'S KNEES SCREAMED ALMOST as much as her shoulders. All she wanted to do was curl up in a ball and sleep for the next ten years. Hunter promised her a long life of misery, but she had the distinct impression that was just a farce. She also knew Austin wouldn't just sit around and leave her at Hunter's mercy, and he was betting on that.

The men who had accosted her had drifted back into the shadows like mindless sentries, but Hunter crossed the room to stand in front of her. He crouched down and lifted her chin, studying her swollen features with a critical eye.

"I hate you," Paige whispered, issuing a deadly glare.

He didn't speak; he just stared until the silence encompassed the room.

Paige wanted to shift under his gaze, but she didn't even have the strength to yank her chin from his grasp.

"I've dreamed of this for months," he said, his voice no louder than a whisper. "But outside of screwing with you at the museum, this has not satisfied my need for revenge. You banished me."

His eyes flashed with enough anger to layer another set of chills over her already freezing form. His fingers dug into her cheeks, and she kept her teeth clenched against the pain and fear ripping her insides to shreds.

"You will scream for mercy before I am done with you."

"Promises, promises," she uttered. She wondered just when she had lost her mind, but it had the desired effect.

Hunter blinked and dropped his hand, sitting back on his haunches.

The door on the far side of the room creaked, and Paige's gaze moved from Hunter to the tall man stepping into the room. Even from this distance, his blue eyes radiated in the darkness like beacons. His gaze locked with hers, and she almost heard the "shhh" as his finger covered his lips.

Unfortunately, Hunter turned toward where her eyes had been drawn. He stood and turned, crossing his arms as the stranger halted after another step into the room. Austin stepped next to the stranger, and Paige's heart sank.

Hunter uttered the same ancient words he had before. But the stranger's brow knit, and his hands moved. Austin focused on the movement and shrugged.

"You brought a deaf mute as backup?"

Austin chuckled and nodded. "I figured it was safer than being at your mercy." His gaze moved beyond Hunter and landed on her. His wince at her condition was visible to both Hunter and her.

Hunter just laughed.

"Kill the deaf mute," Hunter ordered. "And bring that idiot over here," he added.

The men hidden in the shadows moved into view. Every man in the room carried a sharp object from knives to axes.

Austin's jaw dropped open. The first traces of fear filled his eyes as they locked with Paige's.

Two large men hauled him toward Paige but stopped halfway across the floor where he was turned to witness his friend's death.

The stranger assessed the threat surrounding him before he traded a glance with Austin. The complete absence of fear in his eyes shocked Paige, but there was remorse. He sent a nonchalant half-shrug like this outcome had been expected. As the men got closer, the stranger shifted his stance into one that was vaguely familiar.

Hunter's laugh rang out, pulling the stranger's gaze his way. There was something hard reflected in his blue eyes, something that made Paige swallow the hope that flared.

Austin struggled to escape from the grip the men had on him, but it was useless. He was not equipped with the rugged muscles that tensed under the stranger's shirt. Paige couldn't place where she had seen that look before, and she just stared.

The first clod lunged, and the man parried, knocking the blade from the attacker. He threw him into the line that had closed in behind him.

In one move, he took out three attackers, but he didn't have time to recover before an axe swung. He jumped out of the way, but the blade left a clean slice in his shirt. He fought valiantly, with only a scratch here and there. Until the entire group attacked as one.

The man fell in the middle of the mêlée, and a couple of the weapons appeared bloody before they plunged in again.

"You bastard," Austin whispered, still struggling while the men holding him turned him in Hunter's direction.

The roar that came from the center of the attack zone snapped all their gazes, and every attacker fell like a blast had gone off in the center of the group. Everyone was out cold, and standing undamaged in the center of them was the stranger. He gave Hunter a tilt of his head, and then his gaze landed on Austin.

He snapped his fingers, and the two men holding Austin fell in an unconscious pile as well.

Hunter remained stunned and blinking as Austin's fist connected with his face, knocking him down. Hunter got his bearings quicker than Paige could have foreseen, and he was on his feet and behind Paige before any of them took a step.

Cold steel pressed on her throat.

"Don't you dare," Austin said.

"I'll do whatever the fuck I please," Hunter growled, but the knife flew out of his hand, clattering on the floor as the stranger approached.

His glare was intimidating and hauntingly familiar.

"What the fuck are you?" Hunter asked with his hand still balled in Paige's hair.

"Your worst fucking nightmare."

Paige heard the words as clear as day in her head, but the words from his mouth were just a jumble of non-articulate sounds. The venom that came with the words, along with the righteous anger in his eyes, tripped her memory, and she recoiled as much as possible in the chains.

His hand pushed out like a stop sign, and Hunter's grip on her disappeared just before the thud. The man's gaze dropped to hers, and he waved his hand like he was knocking a gnat out of the way. The chains holding her in place disintegrated.

Austin caught her before she face-planted on the ground.

"He's mine," Austin growled, and the man turned his hard glare in his direction.

"Not yet," he signed and said at the same time. He walked over to the table of dark toys and scanned the horrifying contents before reaching out and picking up a simple pair of scissors.

When Austin went to set her down, Paige grabbed hold of him, keeping him in place.

"Don't become him," she said, her voice cracking with panic.

His murderous gaze softened. He slowly scanned the bruises traversing her skin, and his expression turned cold like his heart turned to ice. "He has to pay," Austin said in a tone she had never heard from him.

The high-pitched scream pulled their attention to Hunter, and all she could see were his hands gripping air at his sides. The man stepped away, tossing the bloody scissors to the side, along with the fleshy stub of a tongue. He turned and walked away, but Hunter's scream turned into a growl and he launched through the air. A quick sidestep and Hunter landed face down. The man didn't even glance at where Hunter fell. Instead, he approached Austin and Paige, unbuttoning his dress shirt as he crossed the distance.

He stopped in front of them and peeled the silk off his back, handing it to Paige.

"Thank you," Paige whispered as Austin helped her slip into the fabric, covering up her naked and bruised form.

The man turned his head toward Hunter in time to catch a flying blade an inch from his face. The air rippled, and a burst hit Hunter, tossing him like a rag doll into the far wall. Then the man pulled a phone out of his pocket and tapped a few keys before taking a seat next to Paige and Austin.

"If he wakes up before the cops get here, you can knock his ass out," he signed. Blood dripped from the hand that had caught the knife.

Austin gave him a simple nod.

"Who are you?" Paige whispered.

He extended his uninjured hand. "Tom Ryan," he said when she tentatively accepted the handshake. His voice in her head was clear, unlike the words tumbling from his mouth. "Jackass over there won't be able to control anyone ever again. It's kind of hard to cast a spell without a tongue."

Paige stared in confusion and then looked at Austin. "How come you weren't affected by his spell?"

Both men pulled out elaborate medallions from under their shirts.

"His wife knew how to counteract his spells," Austin said.

"Is that... bloodstone?" Paige asked, mesmerized by the ancient stone symbols hanging from simple silver chains. The Celtic knots made her gaze bounce to Tom's.

He nodded.

She blinked a few times at his sheepish smile, and then the familiarity clicked once again.

"You starred in a movie," Paige whispered reverently.

"No." He shook his head, but the wry smile remained. "Can't act without a tongue." He opened his mouth, showing the stub.

"I swear, you look exactly like the actor in..." She trailed off, searching her memory for the title of the horror movie.

He chuckled, glancing toward Hunter before signing. "I get that from time to time," he said and kept his gaze glued on Hunter. A crease appeared between his eyes, and he scanned the unconscious bodies littering the floor.

"This isn't over yet."

Black Magick
Chapter 12

AUSTIN STARED AT HIM, dumbfounded by the signed words echoing in his head.

"What do you mean it's not over?" he asked and glanced at Paige. Her eyes were full of the physical pain racking her form, along with an exhaustion that was as palpable as the anger flooding his veins. Every time he looked at her, at the bruises and dullness of her once vibrant eyes, his fury nearly overrode all senses. Austin pressed his lips together, pulling her closer in a protective reflex, but her wince made him relax his grip.

Opposite needs yanked at him. On one hand, he wanted to rip Hunter to pieces just to satisfy the growing beast in the center of his being. His need to be there, to protect Paige from what was coming next, to be her rock, overrode the murderous rage.

He glanced around the room, searching for the danger reflected in Tom's tense features. Tom tapped out a number and set his phone on speaker before handing it to Austin. Even before the cellphone hit his palm, Raven's Irish brogue came over the line.

"Tell her I need that counteractive spell," he signed as some men he knocked out started stirring. "They are still programmed to kill me. Knocking them out didn't erase the command."

Austin relayed the message as Tom took to his feet. With three distinct piles of unconscious bodies scattered across the room, his gaze jumped from Hunter to the group that tried to kill him. His greatest threats were the weapons still within reach of those men.

"What's he doing?" Raven asked as silence dragged over the line.

"Um, I don't know. He's just standing there assessing things," Austin said. Tom's hands moved again, signing, while Austin translated. "He said when they wake, they'll go on the attack again unless you can counteract it."

"And he can't make the asshole who cast the spell rescind it?"

Austin gave a sharp laugh—Paige did, too— and he cleared his throat, meeting Tom's gaze for a moment. Tom glanced at Hunter and then back at Austin with a quick shake of his head.

"Uh. No."

"He didn't kill him, did he?"

Tom's eyes rolled, and he signed, "Does she have a spell or not?"

"Uh, no, he didn't. I think you might want to get a move on with the spell," he said, his focus pulled to the shuffle to their right.

A couple of the men were climbing to their hands and knees. When their eyes focused on

Tom, the kill command clicked in every wrathful feature on their faces.

"Come on, Raven, they're coming for me, and I really don't want to hurt them again," Tom signed, and Austin translated.

Tom shuffled away from them, and Austin sighed with relief. Being in the kill zone wasn't something he relished, and by the looks of these zombie-like men, that's exactly where this was headed. Paige couldn't move quickly in her condition, so Austin said a little prayer.

"Who are these people?" Paige asked, pulling the shirt tighter around her as she pressed herself closer to Austin.

"I'm not sure, but at least they're on our side," he said, meeting her wide eyes before glancing at the oncoming attackers.

"Sweetie, we'll explain as soon as we get you out of this mess," Raven said through the phone line. Then the most lyrical words rang through the room, creating a silver mist that flowed from ceiling to floor, cleansing the space with an ethereal shine.

Austin stared at the shimmer and glanced up at Tom. The tension in his face had relaxed, and he offered a nod.

"That should do the trick," Raven said over the speakerphone.

"Ov oo," Tom said aloud.

"I love you, too. Detective Connelly is on the way. I trust you can keep that maniac in line until the police arrive?"

"Ya," he answered and took the phone, ending the call.

The men standing in the center of the room blinked a few times before they looked down at the weapons in their hands. Metal clanked on the floor, and the horror of their misdeeds passed over their features. Hands slowly rose to cover their mouths, and their gazes transferred to Paige's. Remorse lived in their irises. Their muttered apologies were muffled by their hands.

Paige gave them a nod, accepting it for what it was, but Austin glared at them.

"You have the audacity to stand there and apologize for beating her and god knows what else? Where the fuck was your restraint?" he snarled at them.

"They had no control," Paige said.

Anger overrode logic, and he peeled her off and stood, taking a step towards the two men with his fists so tight they throbbed. Tom's hand clamped down on his shoulder, stopping him from doing anything he would regret.

He glared over his shoulder anyway, and his eyes widened. Without thinking, he threw himself in front of Paige. Pain ripped through his upper right chest as the blade sank into his flesh.

The blade meant to kill Paige.

Before Hunter could launch another knife, the room shook and the floor actually rippled at the power rolling from Tom. All metal in the vicinity between where Tom stood, and the concentrated area around Hunter shattered into dust.

The men in the center of the room turned and ran like they had seen the faces of a thousand ghosts.

Austin's gaze turned to Paige, and he offered her what he hoped was a smile. He couldn't hear a thing above the high-pitched ringing in his ears and both his chest and back felt like an angry bear attacked him.

"I guess this just isn't my week," he whispered.

Her hysterical laugh, along with the far away shouts of officers filling the room, followed him into the black.

Black Magick
Chapter 13

HE TRIED TO SWALLOW, but his tongue stuck to the roof of his mouth. His eyelids fluttered against the heavy pull to close, leaving him with the soothing sounds of a steady beeping. The sharp smell of antiseptic made his nose crinkle, and he tried to turn his head. The motion woke the pain, and he inhaled, opening his eyes to the sterile hospital room.

"Paige?" he asked in nothing more than a croak.

A chair to his right scraped on the floor, and an unfamiliar face stepped into view. It took him a moment to place the man. With recognition came the flood of memories.

"Your girlfriend is just down the hall," he said, but his lips didn't move at all.

Austin tried to speak, but his tongue kept scraping across the roof of his mouth like he had inhaled a handful of granite dust. Without having to ask, Tom handed him a cup of water with a straw.

The cool liquid felt like the richest chocolate sauce as it moistened his mouth and throat. He licked his lips and handed the cup back.

"How is she?"

Tom pulled the chair closer. "She's got a few broken ribs, some contusions, and a slew of bruises. She developed a mild case of pneumonia from the way she was bound, but the doctors feel she will fully recover from her physical injuries. There's nothing that is permanent. But her mental state... well, she's a mess," he signed.

Austin was thankful that he also projected the words, because in his drugged state, he was having difficulty following the conversation via sign language.

"Can I see her?"

"You haven't been given the go ahead to get up yet."

Austin stared at him for a moment and then pushed himself into a sitting position. The room spun, and he gripped the edge of the bed, closing his eyes while he counted breaths. When the spinning stopped, he blinked his eyes, focusing on the floor tiles.

"Can you get me a wheelchair?" he asked, still staring at the floor.

Tom passed through the door.

Austin glanced up at the IV and muttered under his breath. It was on the bed frame, not a mobile device.

I got it covered. Tom's thought invaded his mind, and a moment later, he appeared with a wheelchair that had a t-bar for the intravenous bag. He helped Austin into the chair and got the bag all set before he wheeled him out of the room.

Just down the hall must be a local expression because it seemed like a network of mazes and even included an elevator ride to a higher floor.

As they approached the door, Austin said, "You've got to be kidding me."

The clearly marked No Admittance sign graced the doors. Austin had seen that sign so many times in the past, but this time it made no sense.

Tom stopped and stepped into view. "She killed Hunter," he signed slowly, opting not to follow up with the audible in his mind.

Austin stared up at Tom, blinking as the words sunk in. "How?"

Tom blew out a stream of air. "When you passed out, she freaked. I don't know where she found the strength, but as the police were escorting him out, she took the knife he had thrown at you and launched it before anyone could stop her."

Austin's head lowered, and he took a deep breath. "I want to see her," he said.

Tom knocked on the door, and it took a moment before an orderly opened it.

Austin looked up as Tom positioned himself behind the chair. "I need to see Paige Turner," he said.

The orderly looked from Austin to Tom and back before swinging the door wide so they could enter. "This way," the orderly said.

Entry to a psych ward was never that easy. Austin glanced over his shoulder at Tom. He actually winked and smirked at Austin before refocusing on the orderly.

"Where do you think you're going?" a nurse stepped into view, blocking their path.

"I need to see Paige," Austin said, staring her down, hoping Tom could work his silent magic again.

Her eyes moved beyond him, and just by the way she was studying the space, he knew Tom was signing. Her eyebrows arched and her gaze traveled back to Austin's. "Mr. Shelton?" she asked.

Austin nodded.

The nurse sighed and glanced over her shoulder before returning her gaze to his. "I rarely bend the rules, but in this case, I think seeing you will help Miss. Turner." She turned toward a bank of rooms beyond her.

Tom pushed the chair, following the nurse.

She unlocked a door, and Tom rolled him into the dimly lit room. Paige stared out the small window, and Austin's gaze landed on the restraints holding her in place. An intravenous line ran from her arm, and the heart monitor kept the steady beat.

"Paige?" he said and reached for her hand. It wasn't until his skin touched hers that her glazed eyes turned in his direction. He glanced at the nurse. "What the fuck did you give her?"

"Clozapine," the nurse answered.

"An antipsychotic?"

"She wouldn't calm down."

Austin glared at her and turned back to Paige. She stared right through him.

"Paige?" he asked again and squeezed her hand. This time her eyes seemed to focus, and she blinked like she was just waking from a nightmare.

"Austin?" she said in the slow drawl of a heavily medicated person.

"Yeah, baby, it's me."

She glanced at the wheelchair and his poorly fitted hospital johnny, her gaze traveling from the IV in his arm to the bag hanging from the bar and then to Tom standing behind him. When she finally found his face again, he smiled.

"I hear you're a hell of a shot with a knife," Austin said.

She huffed a laugh and started coughing. Despite the drugs, pain traveled over her features, and she whimpered and fell back into the pillow. "I hurt."

"I'm sorry it took me so long to find you," Austin said, and when she turned back to him, she became a blur behind the building tears. He hung his head, resting his forehead on her hand as all the fear and pain he felt the last few days purged.

"Call me when you're ready to go back to your room," Tom's voice echoed, and the click of the door left Auston alone with Paige.

"I killed him," she said with no emotion at all.

"Good," Austin whispered and sniffled as he met her gaze.

Tears filled her eyes and slowly tracked down her face. "I couldn't..." She stopped and took a breath. "I thought..." Again, she trailed off, and the bed vibrated with her silent sobs.

Austin untied her wrist and forced himself to his feet before he took a seat on the edge of her bed, holding her hand to his chest. Her gaze dropped and her fingers moved across the medallion that lay against his skin before returning to his.

He placed his hand against her chest, lightly enough so he didn't hurt her, and smiled at the shape of the same insignia below her shirt. Tom had made sure they were both safe. Even if it was against hospital policy, he wasn't taking any chances after what had occurred.

Her hand followed to his, and she pulled the necklace out from under her shirt, studying it before she tucked it away again.

"I don't know when they're going to let me out."

"You won't be in here long, I promise." He leaned over and untied her other wrist, wincing at the movement.

She sat up slowly with a wince of her own and gently circled her arms around his neck.

They held each other in a loose hug for what seemed like forever until the door opened. Both of them slowly dropped their arms and looked at the doorway. The nurse stood in the entry with her hands on her hips and her lips pressed so tight they were non-existent.

"You unbuckled her?" The question was delivered in an angry screech.

Austin stared her down. "Yes. She isn't a threat. Don't treat her like one, and the next time you decide to give out an antipsychotic to someone, make damned sure you have all the medical facts. She's got pneumonia. Didn't you read the chart?"

"She was just doing her job," Paige whispered, wincing as she lay back on the bed.

"No. She wasn't. If she had read your file, she would never have given you that medicine. It could affect your breathing, especially with pneumonia." He shot a glare in the nurse's direction to find her frantically swiping the screen of her electronic chart. When her face paled, she looked up with saucer-like eyes.

"I've worked in a psych ward for the last five years. I was in New York interviewing at Cornell and Columbia for their medical programs," Austin said. "I know my way around sedatives, and I also know what a mistake costs."

The nurse opened her mouth to speak, and he cocked his head, waiting for the pending argument. Instead, the nurse muttered a soft apology and turned, taking her leave.

Austin waited until the door closed before he turned back to Paige. "I doubt they'll be giving you sedatives like this again. What the hell were you thinking?" he asked as his mind started filtering the questions that had piled up in his stupor.

"I thought you were dead."

Her answer shot the irritation from every limb, and the result was a dizzying exhaustion.

"You won't get rid of me that easily," he said with a smile. "I probably should go back to my room so they can give me a little something for the pain."

"Don't go," she whispered, and her gaze bounced around the room before returning to him.

"Why not?" he asked, but the fear in her eyes gave him pause.

She stared at him. "He's here. I can feel the evil seeping into the air."

His smile faded. "He can't touch you. Not with that necklace."

"But he can taunt me and make it so I can't sleep," she said, her eyes begging him to stay.

Tom stepped into the room, sweeping his gaze from one side to the other, and he offered a shake of his head. Austin's conversation about ghosts popped into the forefront of his mind.

"He isn't here now," Austin said and turned his gaze back to Paige.

"How do you know?" she asked.

"He can see ghosts."

The answer seemed simple enough, and she narrowed her gaze in Tom's direction. He tapped his watch and Austin gave him a nod.

"I have to go, but I'll be back in the morning, and then we'll get you out of here, okay?"

"They aren't going to let me go."

"Yes, they are. You weren't in the right mind..."

"Exactly," she said. "I wasn't and now I'm here again."

"We'll figure it out," he said and shifted to his feet, sliding back into the wheelchair. He sent a smile in her direction.

Tom crossed the room, signing.

"He said he already called his lawyer for us," Austin translated.

"Why?" Paige asked.

Tom's hands continued.

"Because he says he should have roasted that fucker when he had the chance," Austin said.

Silence settled between them, and Paige gave him a nod of thanks before her eyelids slowly closed.

"Love you, Austin," she whispered.

"Love you, too, Paige," he said and squeezed her hand.

Tom rolled him out, and before he rolled off the floor, he made Tom stop at the nurse's station.

"I'm downstairs. If something happens with Paige, please come get me."

"I'm sure she will be just fine. We will keep a close eye on her until the medicine wears off."

"Thank you," he said, and they headed back towards his room.

Black Magick
Chapter 14

PAIGE STARED AT THE ceiling, aware that the crawl on her skin was more from the medication than any precognition. She didn't want to close her eyes. When she closed her eyes, she was no longer safe, and just the thought of it sent her heart rate into a thumping beat.

The dark room did nothing to soothe her fears. If anything, the shadows drilled it farther into her bones. Hunter's presence hung in the air, and just as her eyelids finally slid closed, his low, malignant chuckle filled her ears.

Her eyes flew open to the darkness, and the monitor registered her high-speed heartbeat.

"They won't help you this time." His voice caressed her skin like a dozen finely sharpened knives.

"You can't touch me," she whispered. She prayed both the talisman around her neck and the salt line around the bed that Tom had made before he rolled Austin out of the room would prevent Hunter from hurting her.

The temperature in the room dropped into the frigid zone, and she shivered.

"I brought a friend this time," he said.

Her heart squeezed as the chair slid across the room and jammed under the doorknob, locking her in with the crazed ghost and locking out any chance for help.

"Why won't you just go rot in hell?" Paige said through chattering teeth.

"Because I'm here to drag you there with me." His form materialized in the room, solid enough to see his green eyes glaring in her direction before he shimmered and faded.

The air inside the room swirled like a building tornado, and the light from the hallway faded for a moment. The door handle jiggled but wouldn't open with the way the chair was wedged. The nurse's eyes appeared in the small window, and they widened before she stepped away.

Paige tried to scream over the howling wind, but her voice was drowned by the screeching of equipment sliding across the floor. She glanced down at the salt line, and her heart thundered louder than the wind. Salt grains moved, thinning the line, and once it was breached, she knew Hunter and whomever he brought with him would do unspeakable things.

With each grain that trailed away, her level of fear increased until she found it difficult to draw a breath. The pounding on the door pulled her attention from the dwindling line of protection, and her gaze met Austin's through the glass.

"Help me!"

Even though she knew he couldn't hear over the storm in her room, he nodded and brought a phone to his ear.

Paige's gaze blurred, and she blinked the hot tears from her eyes. The last kernel of salt blew to the side, leaving a breach in her protection. The wind in the room silenced. Only her ragged breathing remained as she stared at Austin's panicked gaze.

A hand wrapped around her throat, pulling her forwards. In the darkness, Hunter's green eyes shimmered.

"I thought about letting them fuck you to death while lover boy watched, but I think it would tear him up more to see you bleed," Hunter's voice whispered in her ear. "And while I promised Max and the boys a good fucking, if they came along, they will have to wait until I'm done with you."

Paige didn't have a chance to speak before Hunter hurled her across the room. The IV in her forearm tore out, leaving a painful gash, and the impact with the wall dazed her. Blood flowed from the cut and the pain from her previous beatings flared, drawing her breath in and locking the air in her chest.

Her gaze darted around the dark as she got to her hands and knees. Austin's yell from the other side of the door sounded distant among the buzzing in her ears. Icy hands gripped her arms and lifted her off her feet, slamming her against the wall with such force, she let out a yelp.

"I want you in agony." His voice pierced her, and then she was flying through the air again.

She hit the side of the bed and sent it crashing into the wall. The snap in her arm was as audible as the scream that came out of her lips. Cradling her broken and bleeding appendage, she tried to crawl into the corner, but icy hands dragged her back to the center of the floor before grasping her hair and pulling her to her knees, facing the door.

Paige's arm throbbed and tears blurred her vision, but she saw enough horror in Austin's eyes to shatter her soul. The pain hadn't reached the blackout level, but she knew Hunter wouldn't let her get to that land of bliss.

The punch to her kidney pulled a scream from her, and she arched away from the pain. The grip on her hair released, and then the sting of a backhand sent her onto the ground again. She caught herself with her broken arm and cried out at the sharp pain radiating all the way to her shoulder. She fell face first into the tile.

Sobbing, she attempted to get to her hands and knees when a foot connected with her side, spinning her onto her back. White spots filled her vision, and a hand clasped her neck, lifting her off the ground before tossing her on the bed. She landed on her stomach across it, but even the soft mattress couldn't absorb the pain of the impact.

"Have at her, boys," Hunter growled.

Hands rolled her onto her back and clawed at the hospital gown wrapped around her. Her attempts to wiggle away were futile. The ripping of fabric was shadowed by the slam of the door against the wall. All movement stopped as two figures stood side by side, backlit by the hall light.

Paige blinked at them and Austin beyond them, along with the panicked night nurse.

"Let her go," the voice in the doorway commanded.

Hunter laughed and his form materialized in the room. "You can't stop us."

Paige got a good look at the two men when they stepped closer. The door slammed behind them, but neither Tom nor the man next to him reacted.

"Hold that thought," the man next to Tom said as he turned his gaze from Hunter to Paige.

White flared around her and she closed her eyes against the brightness while screams filled her ears. She curled onto her side and tried to cover both ears, but her broken arm would not cooperate. When the light faded along with the screams, she blinked her eyes open.

Both Tom and the stranger were engaged in a staring contest with Hunter as he rattled off some ancient hex.

It wasn't until the man next to Tom smirked that recognition set in. CJ Ryan, the famous singer, was standing in her hospital room. He glanced in her direction as the thought barreled through her mind before he returned all his attention to the now solid form of Hunter Garrett.

Every sharp object in the room rose from the floor and aimed in Paige's direction. Hunter smiled in satisfaction as he snapped his fingers and they launched at her. Austin screamed in the background, but neither Tom nor CJ moved.

Paige covered her head, and the flair of white light engulfed the room. The heat from it brushed her skin, and Hunter's angry bellow followed. She squinted into the light and swallowed hard at the sight of the white fire engulfing the ghost. Hunter fought it, but it overwhelmed him until nothing was left but dust. As the light faded, the dust blew in a small swirl before it disappeared altogether.

The door burst open, and Austin was across the room in seconds. Paige met his gaze as tears tumbled from her eyes, leaving hot streaks that pooled in her ears.

The nurse marched into the room and tried to move Austin away, but the glare he leveled in her direction made her hesitate.

"We'll be taking her out of here," CJ said as both he and Tom approached the bed. "For her safety," he added when the nurse sent her sharp stare in his direction.

Paige focused on him and the way he stared down at the nurse.

"You saw the assailant get away and had both Miss Turner and Mr. Shelton moved for their safety," he whispered.

When the nurse blinked, nodded, and shuffled out of the room, CJ turned towards Paige. "Tom, you'll need to carry her. I don't think your friend is in any condition to do that." He turned and walked out of the room.

Tom scooped her into his arms as gently as possible, and she leaned into his solid but soft frame, feeling safe for the first time since they had left home.

Austin smoothed her hair out of her face and glanced up at Tom. "Where are we going?"

"Back to the apartment," CJ said from the doorway. "My wife is a doctor."

Paige closed her eyes, grinding her teeth against the pain. Every step jostled her into the world of agony, and she pressed her lips against the sobs that begged to escape.

When Tom set her down in the car, the pain overwhelmed her, and she let a whine escape. He offered her a sad smile and his eyes reflected the apology without words. Austin slid into the seat next to her. The slam of the trunk shook the car, and then CJ slid behind the wheel.

"You're going to be okay," Austin said as he pulled her against him.

"I'm not so sure," Paige whispered.

"They promised me you'd be okay," he whispered in her ear. "And after what I just witnessed, I think they can make good on that promise."

She glanced at him, but he was staring at the driver with such reverence that she smiled, despite the pain that caused in her cheeks.

Black Magick
Chapter 15

"JESUS, CHRIS, WHAT THE hell were you thinking?" Her voice pierced the cracked door. "We don't even know these people."

"Look, Sarah's brother brought him here, figuring we might be able to help." Steve Williams argued with CJ Ryan's wife in the hallway outside the room.

"I told you it was only a matter of time before this demon spirit came back for them. He was stronger than anything I've felt since..." Raven's Irish brogue trailed off. "Angel fire was our only option to save that girl."

"How many people saw what Chris did?" CJ's wife spat back.

Austin traded a glance with Paige. Her eyes reflected that dull look of extreme pain, and he just wanted it to go away. The discomfort he felt was nothing in comparison, and he forced himself to his feet and crossed to the door, opening it.

"Just the night nurse, Mrs. Ryan," Austin answered, echoing what CJ had just said. "Paige needs help," he added, staring at CJ's wife. "Can you help her or not?"

She studied him and sighed, her eyes softening. "Yes. I can help her," she said with a nod. "You aren't doing too well yourself," she added.

"I'll live," he said and stepped aside, waving her into the room.

Valerie Ryan tucked her hair behind her ears and stepped into the room. She crossed and took a seat on the edge of the bed.

"Who are you people?" Paige whispered.

Valerie smiled at her and glanced over at Austin with a sigh. "This might hurt a bit," she said and leaned forward, placing a simple kiss on Paige's forehead.

Austin stared as Paige gasped, her body arching in the type of pain one only sees in the dying while trying to cling to life. Her eyes rolled back, and she slumped back onto the bed. Austin moved towards her side, but before he reached the bed, sparks surrounded Paige. He stopped a few steps from the bed and stared as the light encompassed her. It seeped into her skin, illuminating her entire form. The bruises stood out against the translucent light until they faded.

Her broken arm moved, bone scraping and resetting. The bloody welt from the torn IV line mended until nothing was left. As the light faded, he stared dumbfounded at Paige. Not a mark was left on her skin.

His gaze bounced to CJ's wife. "Who are you?" he whispered, echoing Paige's last question.

She smiled and stood, crossing to him. "We are made from the blood of angels," she whispered and planted a kiss on his cheek.

Blinding pain ripped through his chest and back, and he stumbled, catching himself on the side of the bed. He sank to his knees, clinging to consciousness by the barest of threads as the welts in his back thatched together. The pain of being whipped was minor compared to the magic flowing through his body, and he panted against the need to drop into the black.

After a few moments, his breathing slowed, and the sharp pain subsided to a dull tingle. He glanced at the crowd gathered in the doorway and then up at Valerie Ryan as he pushed himself to his feet.

"After what I saw, I guess that's as believable as anything else," he said.

"I give you props. Usually that renders folks unconscious," Steve said from the doorway.

Austin chuckled and shrugged, swiping the sweat from his forehead and wiping it on the cloth of his hospital gown. He blinked at his attire.

"You wouldn't happen..."

"To have clothes that might fit?" Steve finished.

"Yeah, I'm afraid there isn't much to salvage from my suitcase." He waved toward the small suitcase in the corner of the room.

"Hang on."

Steve came back a few seconds later with sweats, socks, and a Brooksfield University t-shirt, along with an unopened bag of boxers.

"My wife picked those up last week, and I hadn't gotten around to opening them yet," he said, handing the clothing over and taking leave so Austin could get dressed in peace.

Austin didn't second guess the sizes. He took his new bounty into the adjoining bathroom and untied the hospital gown. When it dropped to the floor, he stared at the bandage on his upper left chest. He peeled the gauze away from his skin and blinked. Not even the slightest of scars was visible. His fingers grazed the spot, and a phantom twinge hit, like the injury was there, somewhere, aching to remind him of the horrors he'd endured.

He turned and stared at the pattern of bandages splayed across his back. With what felt like a contortionist's movements, he peeled each one away to display flawless skin. He dropped everything in the garbage before stepping into the shower to wash away all remnants of his scars. Then he wandered into the quiet living room and stared out over the city.

"Kind of tough to absorb, isn't it?"

He turned and met Steve Williams's gaze.

"Where is everyone?"

"They headed back to the concert now that the danger is gone." He offered a shrug. "Care for a drink?" he asked, waving toward the corner bar.

Austin let out a little laugh and nodded. "The stronger, the better."

Steve poured two scotches and handed one to Austin. He knocked it back like a shot and closed his eyes as the warmth spread through his center. He handed the glass back.

"Brooksfield U?" he asked, pointing to his shirt.

"Yeah, that's where I met my wife." He took a seat. "I'm sure you have more pertinent questions than that," he added.

Austin looked away from the incredible view. "I don't even know where to begin."

Steve huffed a laugh and leaned back.

"Ghosts, psychics, witchcraft, and now blood of angels? All I can say is, what the fuck?"

Steve's laugh caught on and turned into a belted guffaw. Austin felt his lips twitch into a smile in response.

"She will buy it more readily than I." Austin pointed toward the hallway before taking a seat on the plush couch. His hand absently swiped the spot where the knife had cut into his skin. "And I don't know how..." he started and trailed off before meeting Steve's gaze.

Steve leaned forward, resting his elbows on his knees as he placed his glass on the table. "I want to stress how important it is not to let any of this get into the public's hands."

Austin tilted his head. "You think..."

Steve's hand came up in the universal symbol for stop. "I don't know, but I've been protecting those two boys since they were kids, and I'm not stopping now." His gaze hardened a little.

"Look, I've witnessed a ghost kill a fraternity full of guys. That same ghost decided I was his best bet for getting his girlfriend back and tricked me into letting him possess my sorry ass. And that seems almost believable compared to this. Who the hell am I going to tell about this shit without ending up in a padded cell?"

Steve leaned back in his seat, his features relaxing before he raised his glass and took a healthy sip of scotch.

Austin's gaze moved back to the city skyline. "Why us?" He shifted in his seat when his gaze returned to Steve. He noted the tilt of his head.

"Tom said you had a good heart," he finally said.

It was Austin's turn to huff. "I don't think so."

"Where are we?" Paige's soft voice pulled his attention to the hallway where she stood. She had the shredded hospital gown wrapped around herself.

Austin stood and crossed to her. "We're still in Manhattan," he said, and her eyes widened, filling with fear faster than he could blink.

"It's okay, he's gone."

Paige's blue eyes caught his, and her blinking increased as Austin's words settled. "I must have been dreaming…"

He slowly shook his head. "It was all real," he said and tucked a stray hair behind her ear.

"Raven left some clothes that might fit her," Steve said.

Paige stiffened, her gaze shooting from Austin to where Steve sat in the shadows.

"Come on. Let's get you dressed, and then I'll fill you in," he said and led Paige back to the bedroom. "You might want a shower before you dress," he said, his gaze finding the traces of blood still smeared on her skin.

Paige followed his gaze and stared at the bloodstained skin of her arm before her head snapped up to stare at him. She turned and stepped into the brightly lit bathroom and stepped in front of the mirror, ripping the cloth off her body. She stared, much as he had, at her perfectly unblemished skin.

Austin leaned against the doorjamb, waiting for her to meet his gaze. She even turned around to find the whip welts, but there was nothing but soft skin. She turned towards him with wide eyes and spread her arms, asking the question without words.

He offered her a ghost of a smile and a shrug. "I seem to have made the right kind of friends," he said.

She let out a hysterical, high-pitched laugh before her chin trembled.

Austin stepped into the room and pulled her into his arms.

"It's like it never happened," she sobbed. "But I know it did. I know I was beaten and raped by the monster."

He smoothed her hair and whispered, "Shhh" into her ear while she shook in his arms. He kept his eyes open, because if he closed them, all he would see was her flying across the hospital room screaming for him while he remained locked out and helpless. His eyes stung, and he blinked, tightening his grip on her so he wouldn't start shaking right along with her.

She pulled away, looking up at him. Her teary eyes widened, and her soft hand cupped his cheek, her thumb wiping his tears away.

"I couldn't do a damned thing," he said, his voice shaking in a way he hated. But he was as helpless to stop the aftershock as he was of stopping Hunter's ghost.

"But you did. You called in the cavalry."

He huffed and shrugged at the same time.

"I'd just like to know if what I think I saw was real."

"You saw an angel, didn't you?" he asked, because what he saw happen in that room couldn't have been real unless she saw the same thing.

She laughed and blushed a little. "I thought I saw that famous singer that I love, but yeah, he looked like an angel, with wings and all."

"Take a shower. I'll bring the clothes in here, and then we can talk with Mr. Williams." He stepped out of the bathroom, crossed to the pile of clothing on the bureau, and brought it back into the bathroom while Paige rinsed in the shower.

She stepped out a few minutes later and dried off before slipping on the clothing he handed her. As each article was pulled on, another perfectly smooth, unblemished part of her body was covered.

While she didn't sport any injuries on the surface, inside, she was as damaged as he was.

She wrung out her hair and then hand-combed it before meeting his gaze. In her vibrant blue irises, he saw the soul-crushing pain, and he offered what he hoped was a smile, took her hand, and lead her into the living room where Steve still sat. There were now three glasses on the coffee table, each filled halfway with golden scotch.

"I figured you would need a drink." He nodded toward the glasses.

Austin took both glasses and handed one to Paige as they sat on the couch together.

After they each took a sip, Steve leaned forward, extending his hand. "I'm Steve," he said.

Paige shook his hand. "Steve... Williams?" she asked, tilting her head like she did when she was thinking.

He nodded.

"Special Agent Williams?" she asked as her eyes rounded wide.

"Former. Yes." He leaned back in the seat.

Austin glanced at Paige, and she met his gaze. Pure awe cascaded down her face until her mouth popped open. And he knew he was missing something significant.

"You don't remember the news stories?" she whispered.

Austin shrugged, but before he could try to answer, the front door opened, and the rest of the family poured into the apartment.

Paige's eyes widened farther at the first one into the room.

"Oh, my god. I wasn't dreaming," Paige said, and her head whipped back towards Austin. "That's CJ Ryan!" She pointed and her hand shook as much of the rest of her, but it wasn't based on fear. Instead, it was more of the fan girl he knew she was at heart.

Austin grinned and stood.

"I never got a chance to thank you," he said and stuck out his hand.

"Anytime. It's what we do," CJ said, and clasped Austin's hand in a solid handshake.

Austin glanced behind him. "And thank you as well. I don't know what kind of magic you spun, but it saved her life, so you will always have my gratitude."

"As my husband said, it's what we do, so my pleasure," Valerie said in a soft voice, and held a key out to Austin. "We got you a room at the Plaza."

"I...uh...," Austin said, staring at the key.

"And some new clothes," Raven said from behind the group, stepping into the line of sight with Tom.

Tom pulled out a card and handed it to Austin before signing.

"He said we should call them if we run into trouble or if either of us needs to talk. They've all been where we are, so..." Austin translated and then looked at the card. The logo for a paranormal research firm stood out in stark contrast to the handwritten phone number beside the office number.

"Thank you," Paige said, finding her voice.

CJ paused at the entrance to the hallway and turned. "Your parents really named you Paige?" he asked with a smirk.

Paige blushed and nodded.

"Do you have a middle name?"

"No. It's just Paige. Paige Turner," she said, and a smirk found her lips. It found everyone's lips.

CJ Ryan smiled, scribbled something, and then tossed a compact disc to Paige.

Austin glanced at the note. *To the girl whose name will always make me smile. It was a pleasure meeting you, Paige. Next time I'm playing in the city, I'll make sure you and Austin have front row seats. CJ Ryan.*

She glanced up from the signed CD like it was a shiny diamond instead of just a collection of his best music, and then looked at Austin. For whatever it was worth, the words pulled the shine back into her eyes, and Austin smiled, thanking whoever was up above for sparing her.

"Well, I'll just grab our things," Austin said and headed to the room to collect what little they had left.

CJ caught him at the door, his expression dead serious as his eyes penetrated the deepest part of his soul.

"It's going to be a long, hellish road back," he started, but Austin stopped him by raising his hand.

"I know, and it might tear us apart in the end."

CJ's lips twitched into a smile. "Only if you let it. And if you do, he wins."

The shock of his words was like a jolt of electricity, and he jerked a step back. "Why do you even care?"

CJ glanced over his shoulder for a moment before returning his gaze. "I recognize angel blood when I see it. It's one of the few things I'll risk my ass for these days," he said and walked away.

Austin stood frozen to the spot, and then his gaze traveled toward the living room. "Who?" he asked, thinking about the color of Paige's eyes. It seemed to be in the same color palate as both Tom and CJ.

CJ stopped before he stepped into the bedroom at the end of the hall and turned in his direction. "Paige isn't a descendant," he said, reading Austin's mind accurately. "She's just a very talented Wiccan, like my brother's wife."

The suitcase fell out of Austin's grip as he stared at CJ Ryan, the man who wielded angel wings and annihilated the evil hurting Paige. His index finger slowly pointed at his own chest. When CJ smiled and gave a shrug before disappearing, he nearly sat on his ass in shock.

"What the hell does that even mean?" he asked no one in particular.

Black Magick
Chapter 16

AUSTIN STARED OUT THE window of The Plaza Hotel, focusing on nothing as Paige shuffled through the television channels. The news story she stopped on pulled his attention to the television. It was the report of what happened to them, including the so-called attack at the hospital.

When Detective Connolly stepped into the shot to make a statement, Austin took a seat and listened as the facts poured out. The only thing not included was that Paige had killed Hunter. Instead, they catalogued it as a suicide.

Paige turned toward Austin, her eyes wide and her mouth open in the same kind of shock radiating through him.

"Did they?" she asked, pointing toward the window.

"I honestly don't know, Paige. Detective Connolly was so shaken by what happened to him at the hospital that he just might have done that one on his own." He glanced at the television and back at Paige. "Either way, it makes both of us free and clear of any wrongdoing." He added a shrug for emphasis. "So, we're free to go home after we get a decent night's sleep."

"I'm not sure I'll ever sleep again," Paige mumbled.

He slid into bed next to her and pulled her into the nook of his arm. "We will, eventually," he said and kissed her forehead. "Until then, I'll do my best to keep the nightmares away."

She looked up from his chest, and a tear spilled down her cheek. She didn't need to say the words because they reflected as clearly as the sunrise over the city, but when the shaking words whispered between them, he smiled at the ones left unspoken.

"Thank you for not giving up."

"Baby, I could never give up on you," he said and gently planted a kiss on her cheek. "How would you feel if I applied to Dartmouth?"

She blinked at him and shifted onto her elbow. "But your dreams…"

He shut her up with a kiss and then said, "Dartmouth has a decent medical program. Besides, you're there, and if I'm being honest here, you are my real dream."

"Even after all this?"

"Especially after all this," he said and tucked a strand of hair behind her ear.

Paige seemed to curl into herself, and her gaze dropped between them. "You know what they did to me."

"Yes. But you aren't the only one damaged by this," he said softly, and her gaze lifted. "I couldn't stop what happened any more than you could, and that's going to eat away at me. Just the way what they did will tear you apart inside."

"So, why go through that pain?" she asked, and a little part of him died inside.

"We have something here, right?" He wasn't sure he wanted to hear the answer, but her tentative nod sparked his hope. "Do you trust me?"

She blinked at the question, and her chin trembled. "I trust you with my life," she said, and her husky voice cracked, making it sexier than normal. "But I'm not sure I can give you everything you want."

"What is it you think I want?" he asked, using his softest, calmest voice despite the aggravation eating away at his stomach.

She dropped her gaze to his chest, avoiding his eyes. "Sex," she whispered.

His head fell onto the pillow, and he stared at the ceiling, silently counting down from ten in order to make his voice calm and devoid of anger.

"Is that really all you think I want from you?" he asked without looking at her. She didn't answer, and he stifled the urge to growl out a swear word or two. When he finally made himself look at her, the tears were spilling down her cheeks, and she was looking out the window instead of at him. "The past few months I didn't make a move because I needed to know this was more than just the bedroom connection, because God knows we have the sex thing down to a science."

Her head snapped towards him.

"You wanted to know why I didn't touch you? It's because I didn't trust what I was feeling. I had to be sure it wasn't just a sex thing."

She stared at him.

"And I basically asked you to move in with me at the hotel, so that should give you a clue about what's really important to me."

"You still..." She couldn't finish her statement and she sat up, wrapping her arms around her legs.

"If we let this fall to pieces, then that fucker wins, and there is no way I'm going to let that happen. You know why?"

Tears spilled, and she shook her head, still looking out at the city lights.

"Because I fucking love you. That's why."

Her chin trembled, and she buried her face in her hands. Each sob ripped through him, and he sat up, wrapping his arms around her and pulling her into his lap. Her arms snaked around him, and she cried into his shoulder, clinging to him like if she let go, he might disappear like a wisp of smoke.

After what seemed like forever, she picked up her head and met his gaze.

"I'm such a mess," she said, wiping her face.

"Yeah, you are, but I'm not exactly the rock of stability, either."

She uttered a soft laugh and pressed her lips to his. "You're more of a rock than you know." Her breath tickled against his lips, and when she pulled away, she met his gaze.

"I think this, what we have, is worth it," he said.

Her eyebrow cocked. "You think?" she asked with a teasing sniffle.

"Yeah. I think. As long as we're both in the same place."

Her hand caressed his cheek as she stared into his eyes, and he bit his tongue, avoiding asking her the direct question. He wanted her to say it of her own accord, and he was afraid he may have already pushed it too far. When she leaned her forehead against his, he swallowed the disappointment.

"I didn't realize how far gone I was until..." she said and paused, taking a deep breath before continuing, "... until I thought I'd lost you."

He pulled away, and their eyes met. She leaned in, delivering a soft kiss with a spark behind it. He let it morph into more, and their tongues mingled, intimate and tender, tangling in a slow roll that took his breath away. It was the type of kiss that promised more, but he also knew now wasn't the time to explore the boundaries.

He broke the kiss and pulled a slow breath before opening his eyes to hers.

"I am in the same place, Austin, but I'm afraid that might not be enough."

He smiled, cocking his head while he kept her gaze. "I can't promise you it will be easy, but I can promise it will be worth the fight."

The End

Continue Paige and Austin's story with Practical Magick.

Practical Magick
Chapter 1

AUSTIN SHELTON STARED AT the road in front of him, lost in thought. Everything Tom Ryan had said crawled under his skin like a cluster of spiders. Austin still couldn't decipher how much was fact and how much was bullshit; from being a descendant of the archangel Raphael to Tom's lecture telling him to throw away his training and just treat his girlfriend without kid gloves. He glanced at Paige in the passenger seat and sent her a strained smile.

"What's wrong?" she asked, reading his apprehension correctly.

Austin looked away, focusing on driving and trying to put his unease into words. "Are we okay?"

Her silence lasted long enough to pull his attention her way, and her chewing her bottom lip in contemplation set his heart racing. He gulped air and tried to calm the sudden shudder clenching his muscles. He did not want to lose her.

"I don't know," Paige answered. "You seem to want to know everything going on in my head, but have issues sharing what's in yours."

His defensive wall slammed into place, to the point he actually heard those steel doors clanging in his head. Austin forced himself to pry them back open, resetting his reaction, especially after Tom's astute observations. If he closed down now, Tom's little preview of his future would absolutely come true, and he did not want that.

"You could have told me about the angel thing," she said, and turned her gaze from the passing scenery to him.

Austin let out a laugh. "Seriously?" He glanced her way. "That's what you're upset about?"

Her lips thinned, and she turned away.

Austin took a deep breath, hell bent on turning this conversation around. "Sorry," he said. "It's just... I didn't know what to think. We had just been through all that stuff with Hunter's ghost, and I didn't know if CJ's comment was bullshit or if he was just bat-shit crazy."

"The point is, you didn't say a thing." Her hard glare landed on Austin, making him shift in the driver's seat.

"I didn't think it was worth the time to discuss," he mumbled. "I guess maybe I should have mentioned it."

The edges of her lips softened, and she nodded. "So, what do we do now?"

Austin glanced at her and shrugged. "I don't know. How much of what Tom said do you think was true, and how much of it was him being on the cusp of a breakdown?"

Paige offered a half-hearted shrug.

"I know he has some unimaginable powers, but angel descendents? That's just insane."

"We both saw his brother when he took out Hunter. He had wings, so maybe it isn't as farfetched as you think."

Austin sighed. "I can understand ghosts, but the devil?" He shook his head. "I don't accept that concept."

"What if he's right?" she asked with such force it drew Austin's gaze to hers.

"God help us if he's right."

Practical Magick
Chapter 2

AUSTIN SCANNED THE CROWD, searching for Paige in the sea of family and friends attending graduation. When his gaze landed on her, he smiled. Paige nodded, and even from this distance, the pride in his accomplishment shined on her face.

He refocused on the stage, waiting for his name to be called, so he could collect his medical degree. While this was a big milestone, he still had at least four years of psychiatric residency to fulfill before he could apply for his medical license. If he chose child and adolescent psychology, that added another two years onto the docket.

His acceptance in the Dartmouth residency program was a relief, especially since Paige seemed to have settled in with him here in Hanover. Now and then, he thought of Maine, but nothing had happened since he left the Ryans behind a few years back, so he just wrote it all off as crazy talk.

When the dean of medicine called his name, Austin rose and crossed to the stage. A chill hit him in the center of his spine as he climbed the steps. It traveled in a slow creep until his flesh crawled with it, and Austin forced a smile as he took the diploma and shook the Dean's hand.

He waited until he was at the bottom of the steps before he did another sweep of the crowd. Paige was still staring at him, but the slight cock of her head unnerved him more than the chill had. He moved his gaze on, towards the back of the auditorium. A figure stood masked in the shadows, and that chill settled again just as Austin arrived at his seat. He ducked into the sea of graduates, thankful for the standard robes that made them all a carbon copy of each other when seated.

Austin's mouth dried, and he forced a swallow, ingesting what seemed to be the last of his spit. His hand traveled to his chest where the amulet that Tom Ryan gave him still lay, like a talisman warding off evil.

As he sat listening to the dean of medicine drone on, each second ticked by, and apprehension crept into his muscles, tensing them into tight knots. Having Paige half an auditorium away sent his heart into a staccato beat that drew sweat into his tightly clasped fists.

Before he formed a coherent thought, the medical students were asked to rise and recite the Physician's Oath. Austin recited it by memory, just like the other hundred students standing with him. The words calmed his racing heart, and once the oath was spoken, the flutter in his stomach receded.

Everyone was directed to move their tassels, and then the congratulations came over the loudspeaker. Within a split second, the graduating class announcement settled on the crowd, and the graduates' caps flew into the air. Austin turned, catching Paige's eyes, and all the momentary fear he felt on the stage disappeared.

His grin actually made his cheeks ache, and as the graduates dispersed, he walked straight to Paige.

"Stage fright?" she whispered in his ear when his arms wrapped around her.

"I was hoping no one noticed," he said, pulling away and planting a kiss on her lips. He didn't want to worry her about whatever had grabbed his imagination.

"I don't think anyone noticed, but I know you well enough to notice the change in your eyes, even from this distance."

"You ready to go celebrate?" he asked, changing the subject.

Paige lit up, and Austin smiled at her enthusiasm. "Sure."

He escorted her to the car and helped her into the passenger seat. An undeniable chill shifted through his shirt, and he shivered, but refused to let this overshadowing fear rule his actions today. Not with the plans he already had set in motion.

Austin drove to a little restaurant at the edge of town. La Bistro served the best Italian in the region, and he had a private table reserved, along with a bottle of champagne.

He pulled the chair out for Paige and sent a soft smile in her direction. The way she beamed at him warmed him to the core. Only Paige could turn his insides to molten mush, and he prayed tonight would go as he planned.

As soon as the champagne was uncorked and poured, Paige picked up her glass and raised it to him. "Here's to graduating from medical school!"

"Actually, I'd rather toast to us," he said and tapped her glass with his before taking a sip.

"That's sweet," Paige said. "But you're the one who put in all those long hours studying."

He slowly nodded. "But without my favorite study partner, I never would have gotten through it." He set his glass on the table. "This leads me right into my plans for making this night memorable." Austin moved from his seat, taking Paige's glass from her and setting it on the table. With her hand in his, he took a breath and dropped to his knee, ignoring the pounding of his heart in his ears. He couldn't recollect a time he was this nervous, and he reached into his coat pocket, pulling out the little velvet box.

Paige's eyes widened, and he smiled up at her.

"Paige, I really couldn't have gotten to this point without you by my side," he started, and the tables close to theirs became quiet. Austin fought the urge to look around and just concentrated on her wide blue eyes. "And I don't even want to entertain a future where you aren't with me. I want to spend the rest of my days with you. Build a life and a family with you." He swallowed and flipped the box open with his free hand. "Paige, will you do me the honor of becoming my wife?"

Her hand fluttered to her mouth, and every second without an answer pumped his already pounding heart. The sudden nod, along with the whispered "yes," eased his nerves. He grinned, sliding the diamond engagement ring on her left hand.

When she glanced down at her hand, another gasp escaped. The one-carat diamond, set in a rose-gold, tapered channel band, sparkled in the light. Her eyes widened.

"Oh, Austin," she whispered and pulled him to her lips.

The kiss ignited more than the usual hunger, and when their lips parted, Austin considered skipping dinner and heading home for a different kind of dessert. Her stomach rumbled, taking the decision out of his hands, and he climbed to his feet amidst the clapping patrons.

Heat filled his cheeks as he took his chair, and he gave a stiff smile to the other customers before focusing on Paige. His smile transformed into the genuine kind, and she returned it.

"So, what kind of wedding do you want?" he asked as he leaned back in the seat.

Paige stared at the ring before she brought her gaze back to his. "Small, private."

He nodded, happy that she didn't want a big to-do. "We will have to flip a coin to see if Heather will be maid-of-honor or best man."

Paige giggled at Austin's reference to their former roommate and closest friend. "She will probably choose best man because she knows I would pick a hideous bridesmaid dress just to screw with her."

"Maybe I should ask Tom to be my best man," he said with a light chuckle. "After all, it was his ass-kicking words that slapped some sense into me."

Her eyebrows rose. "What did he say to you?"

"He told me to stop treating you like a victim."

"Really?" She leaned back in the seat.

Austin nodded. "Yeah. Basically, he said my schooling was crap, and if I kept treating you like your therapist instead of the man who loves you, I was going to lose you." He reached for the champagne. "It was a hard pill to swallow, but he was right."

"Wise man," she said and sipped her champagne. "But I doubt he'll remember us after all this time. What about Dr. Schaeffer?"

"That might be a better choice, especially since he's been my mentor for years." He smirked at her as the waiter approached.

Dinner flew by, and by the time they got back to the apartment, Austin only had one thing on his mind. Before the locks on the door were all engaged, he had Paige in a lip lock that burned through him like a lightning bolt, and he couldn't get her coat off fast enough. She already had cast his aside and was working on his sports coat and tie.

Breaking the kiss, he gasped. "What the hell are you wearing?"

Paige just laughed and untied the sash. Her coat slipped off her shoulders as easily as if it were a silk scarf. Austin slowly raised his eyebrows at the ease with which she shed her coat, but when she stepped back into his arms, all curiosity regarding her apparel disappeared, along with every stitch of clothing they wore.

Her hands caressed his skin as Austin led her into the bedroom. The kiss continued until they fell onto the soft mattress. He pulled away from her silky lips and stared into her sky-blue eyes, losing himself in their luminosity. Rolling off her, he stretched out next to her, scanning her voluptuous form. His fingers trailed from her pouting lips down the line of her neck, pausing to caress each perfect breast before he moved in to take that same perfection into his mouth. Her sigh fanned the flame burning in his soul. But he wanted to make this last. He wanted to tease her until she was begging for him in her hellishly sexy voice.

He trailed his tongue from her tit down to her belly button, thinking about nothing but the salty tang of her skin. Austin smiled as gooseflesh surged across her stomach.

He gave her a sideways grin. "What exactly would you like tonight?"

"Everything," she said with a soft exhale.

Austin's eyebrow rose. "Define everything." He needed her to qualify her request, especially with their past. They had gone from uber-kinky sex toy and bondage play to plain vanilla after the ordeal with Hunter. They had never quite managed to return to those early days of absolute abandon. He didn't want to make a mistake, or assume the intention in her statement, and he certainly didn't want to do anything to trigger the nightmares for either of them.

Not tonight.

Tonight had to be special.

"I'm not putting boundaries on us tonight," she said, meeting his gaze and her lips cocked into a smile. "You can break out some of your... toys, too." She blushed and averted her gaze.

Austin reached for her, hooking her chin with his finger, forcing her to meet his gaze.

"Is that really what *you* want?" he said, praying she would finally get over her last hang-up. Since Hunter kidnapped her, she had allowed nothing to go near her ass, and the thought of fucking that tight hole, while pleasuring her with a dildo, nearly made him cum on the spot.

"I think it's time I just let it go. You've never hurt me, and I have to trust you not to."

"Baby, you don't have to prove anything to me," he said, closing the distance and placing a soft kiss on her lips.

"Are you telling me it's not what you want?" she asked.

He chuckled. "I'm not going to lie. The thought of making love to every inch of you, of filling your ass, and your pussy, until you can't cum anymore, has me on the verge of exploding like Mount Vesuvius." He took a deep breath. "But I do not want to do anything that will fuck with your head."

"I trust you, Austin."

"I certainly hope so." He gave her a peck on the cheek, rolled to his nightstand, and pulled out the seldom-used dildo and jelly. He had

every intention of taking her to heaven and back
before the clock struck midnight.

Practical Magick
Chapter 3

THE GLEAM IN HIS eyes pulled a nervous smile to Paige's lips. Now that she'd opened the door to more kinky sex, her heart doubled down, sending a tribal beat through her body as the nightmares started clawing at the edges of her consciousness, but she was hell-bent on getting past this hang-up.

Austin wanted a life with her, and this was one of his wishes. He loved her. Besides, they had done all this before, and more importantly, she had liked it. But that was before Hunter got hold of her and had his attack dogs rape and pillage her until even Austin's touch made her wince.

When his lips found her breast, she jerked and his head snapped up, meeting her gaze with wide-eyed shock as if he knew her nerves belied her words.

"I don't need this, honey. I just need you."

She searched his eyes, seeing the sincerity there clouded with his desire. He would just go back to the mundane and vanilla flavor if she said the word. She wanted to be free of her past, and until this moment, she thought the only way to do that was to deny herself the pleasures Hunter had ruined for her.

Austin had been her savior in so many ways, and this was just another way he could secure his place deeper in her heart. Fear was her enemy, and she was done running from Hunter. This was the last roadblock to gaining her entire soul back from that asshole.

"I need this," Paige said. "I need to..."

He stopped her with a kiss fueled with equal amounts of passion and fear. She tasted it on his tongue and felt it in the tremble of his arms. She pulled him to her and deepened the kiss, letting go of the hesitation stripping her of her sense of abandon.

He broke the kiss and met her gaze again before that slow sizzling smile spread over his lips. This time, it didn't create a swirl of nerves in her chest. Instead, it sparked a slow burn in her belly, and the anticipation of his next move caught her breath in her throat.

Every caress of his fingers and swipe of his tongue against her skin tingled, leaving her alternating between a hot sweat and cold shivers. When he settled between her legs, he smiled, revealing those deep dimples she adored just before he dipped his mouth to her already dripping pussy. The bliss he created between her legs brought her over the brink, and she whispered his name, allowing herself to get lost in his touch.

By the time he moved his fingers from her pussy to the ring of her ass, she was too far gone to freak out. The slow pressure of his wet index finger penetrating her anus brought another moan from her lips. Her gaze locked with his, and he flicked her clit with his tongue, bringing her closer to another orgasm.

Her hands balled up in the sheets in anticipation of the rush of energy, and when he pushed a second finger inside her ass, the pressure turned to pure pleasure.

"Austin," she panted. "I want you inside me."

"Not yet," he said, and continued to tease her with the slow stroke of his fingers and the quick flick of his tongue. The combination sent a rush through her, and she arched into it, crying out with the power of the orgasm. Austin chuckled against her clit, but didn't stop. In fact, the pressure increased as he slid the vibrator inside her soaking pussy.

The feel of it, along with his fingers still coaxing her ass, shot her into a different realm, one she hadn't been to since before Hunter stripped her of her sexual abandon. She snaked her hand into Austin's hair and held him in place, enjoying the benefits of his tongue along with the vibrations filling her.

The pressure suddenly disappeared, and she whined at the sudden emptiness, releasing his hair and meeting his almost frantic eyes.

"Roll onto your knees," he said.

Paige didn't hesitate, not with the vibrator still plunged inside her, creating tendrils of pleasure right from her core all the way to her fingers and toes. When the tip of his cock pressed against her ass, she had a moment of panic and almost pulled away, but his arm snaked around her, his fingers finding her overly sensitive clit at the same moment of her doubt.

"Relax," he whispered, but didn't push any farther into her. Instead, he kept steady pressure without breaching her anus.

Paige closed her eyes and hung her head, fighting between her internal demons and the pleasure her body was wrapped in. She glanced over her shoulder, and Austin offered her that soft smile that promised he would never hurt her. She sent a smile back and let the pleasure conquer the fear.

She pushed backwards, letting the tip of his cock slip inside her ass. The pressure almost stopped her, but he slid easily inside once her muscles relaxed and accepted him.

"Oh fuck, Paige," Austin groaned, pulling her towards his groin, filling her.

They moved slowly at first, and Paige let go of the last of her barriers, bringing them to a frenetic pace that produced multiple orgasms from her in a matter of minutes. They came in unison and collapsed, trembling in one mass of arms and legs.

When she finally caught her breath, she turned her head, catching a breathless kiss from Austin. The dildo still vibrated inside her, making them both twitch involuntarily at the sensation. Austin pulled her onto her side, spooning her as he reached between her legs and removed the cause of their continued aftershocks.

"Damn, girl, I think you stopped my heart there for a minute," he said in her ear.

"I don't think I'll be able to walk." Paige laughed and squeezed his arms tighter around her. "Unfortunately, I have to get up," she said, peeling him off her, her body shuddering from the sudden de-coupling.

She gave him a smile over her shoulder as she rolled out of bed and headed to the bathroom to relieve herself. As soon as the toilet flushed, Austin stepped into the bathroom and grabbed for his toothbrush.

"You okay?" he asked as he stepped next to her at the sink.

"Yes. I'm better than okay." She leaned over, kissed his cheek, and reached for the toothpaste to polish her teeth. The ring caught her eye, and she stopped, staring at the diamond. "This really is a beautiful ring," she said. "Thank you."

Austin rinsed his mouth and smiled. "No need to thank me. You deserve the best, and I hope tonight was as perfect for you as it was for me," he said, stepping closer to her.

She stood on her tiptoes and kissed his minty lips. "It was the perfect ending to the perfect evening."

Practical Magick
Chapter 4

THE SUN PEEKED THROUGH the shades, and Paige turned her face away from the bright light, stretching her aching limbs. Austin grunted next to her, and then his arms wrapped around her, pulling her into him. His breath tickled the back of her neck, and she squirmed in his grasp.

"Morning, babe," he mumbled in her ear and planted a kiss on the back of her head.

"Morning." She stretched again, letting out a high-pitched squeal. Rolling, she took in his sleepy eyes and tousled hair. He looked sexier than she imagined Thor did in the morning, and Austin was all hers.

"No nightmares?" he asked, and the sudden concern filling his eyes shot straight to her heart.

"No. None." She smiled, and his face relaxed, smoothing over the worry lines on his forehead. "So, when do you want to get married?" she asked, directing the conversation away from anything negative.

He lifted his shoulder in a shrug as a yawn captured his voice. "We could fly to Vegas today if you want."

"I'm trying to be serious," she said.

"I am being serious. I'm ready to get married."

"I have to at least get a dress," she said and wondered why she was being resistant to the idea. Las Vegas would provide the small private ceremony she craved, but the idea of leaving the safety of this town didn't settle well. They hadn't been attacked or haunted since they set foot back in Hanover, and she set the original protection spell to keep them out of harm. Paige didn't want to tempt fate.

"I was hoping to marry you before I start my residency," he said with a pout.

Despite the nerves jumbling in her stomach, she nodded. "I'd like that. But Las Vegas?"

"There is more to do out there than just gamble." He raised his eyebrow. "Besides, I've already booked the trip." He reached into his drawer and fanned a couple of airline tickets at her with a grin.

She balked. "What about my job?"

"Already taken care of."

She had no more valid arguments, and she rolled onto her back, staring at the ceiling.

"What's the matter?" Austin propped up on his elbow, staring down at her.

"The protection spell won't work outside of Hanover." She met his gaze.

His smile faded, and his gaze dropped to the tickets before returning to hers. "We can't hide in this town forever."

She swallowed hard and nodded, even though every cell in her body screamed against the idea. She wanted to marry Austin, but leaving their safety net brought forth a thousand doubts. "What if he comes back?"

Austin closed his eyes for a moment, and the expression that crossed his features unnerved Paige. It was almost murderous. When his eyes opened again, they stared at the tickets in his hands before moving to hers.

"He won't." He delivered the answer with a level of ferocity she had never heard in him before, and his conviction impacted her enough for her to nod.

"Okay."

The slow grin that formed on his lips pulled a smile from Paige, despite her misgivings. He practically bounced out of the bed in response and had the suitcases on the foot of the bed in a matter of minutes.

Paige didn't move as fast as Austin. She headed into the bathroom to take care of her morning needs and brush her teeth. Before she returned, Austin had already packed his bag and was now working on packing hers.

She leaned against the doorjamb and watched him as he debated which bathing suit to pack. Surprisingly, he opted for the one piece.

She cleared her throat. "The bikini is more comfortable," she said.

He spun in her direction. "I was thinking you might want more cover up and less sunburn," he said, flashing her that awkward smile he wore whenever he miscalculated.

Paige moved to her bureau and started pulling out clothing. "How long are we going for?" she asked, pausing with a handful of underwear.

"Five days, and I've already packed most of your things. You just need to pick out a dress, a pair of sandals, and grab your cowboy boots."

"When did you pack my stuff?" There was no way he had time when she was in the bathroom.

"The other night when I did the laundry," he answered, taking the underwear out of her hand and putting it back in the drawer. "Go pick out a dress."

Paige rolled her eyes and crossed to the closet. "What kind of dress?"

"One for dinner and a show."

She glanced over her shoulder, impressed with his planning, and picked out one of her sexiest dresses along with a pair of sandals.

"Don't forget your boots," Austin added as she turned away from the closet.

She grabbed the worn cowboy boots from the back of the closet and brought her clothes over to the neatly packed suitcase. She shuffled through what he'd packed, and he closed the top on her hands.

"I promise, you have everything you need," he said and glanced at his watch. "We don't have much time before we have to haul it to the airport." He zipped the bags. "And I know you want to take a shower."

"Austin?" she asked, and he turned back towards her. "Thank you."

He grinned and grabbed her hand, pulling her into the bathroom. They stripped and stepped into the warm shower, cleaning off the remnants of last night before dressing in comfortable clothes for the flight.

Practical Magick
Chapter 5

THE PLANE RIDE WAS smooth, and the skies clear all the way from New Hampshire to Las Vegas. When they stepped into the baggage claim, Paige's gaze fell on a man dressed in a tailored suit, and a shiny black hat carrying a sign with Austin's name on it. She elbowed Austin in the side and nodded toward the sign.

Austin grinned. "That's our limo driver."

"Really?" Paige asked with wide eyes.

"Yes. I've had this planned for a while."

"What if I had said no?"

He laughed and reached for one of their bags before it passed on the baggage carousel. "Then I would have had a hell of a time in Vegas on my own."

"You would have come without me?"

Austin straightened, his gaze still locked on the conveyor. "If you turned down my marriage proposal?" He slid a sideways glance at her. "I would have left right from the restaurant."

The candor in his words sent a shiver through her, and she bit her lip, lowering her eyes just as her bag went sailing by on the belt. "Oh," she said and pointed. Austin glanced where she indicated, but the bag had already turned the corner.

"I'll get it the next round."

They waited for her bag to swing back around, and when it did, Austin collected it for her, and then the two of them approached the limo driver.

"I'm Austin Shelton," Austin said and pulled out his wallet, flipping it to show his driver's license.

"Mr. Shelton, welcome to Las Vegas," the driver said and took both their bags from their grips. "I understand we are making a stop on the way to the hotel?"

Austin grinned and nodded. "Yes, sir."

"Where..."

Austin gave Paige a single eyebrow raise that shut her up. This entire weekend would be chock full of surprises, and she would just have to enjoy the ride, whether or not she was comfortable. She hoped he would not spend all their time in the casino, but something told her that Austin wasn't into losing his shirt.

"What are some things you have planned?" she asked after the driver tucked them away in the darkened limousine.

"Don't worry about it. Everything has been taken care of."

"Define everything?" she said. This not knowing what was coming next was very difficult for her, especially with her control issues.

He picked up the remote and pressed a button; closing the divider between the front of the limo, and where they sat. When he turned his attention toward her, his eyes sparkled with mischief. "I promise you will not be disappointed." Austin pushed her down onto the seat, and his mouth covered hers before she could utter a word. The kiss was insistent and demanding, and when he broke it, he stared into her eyes. "You ready to become Mrs. Shelton?"

"I've been ready for the last couple of years," she said, prompting his grin to widen. "But I don't exactly have a dress."

"That is quite the conundrum," he said and tapped his lip as he sat up. He chewed on his lower lip for a moment before lowering the panel dividing the passenger area from the driver.

"Excuse me?"

"Yes, sir," the driver answered, without looking away from the road.

"I believe there might be something we need before we make that stop."

This time, the driver did glance back. "I think you will find the contents of the garment bags hanging behind the back seat to your satisfaction, sir."

Both Austin and Paige turned, taking in the His and Hers bags behind them. The front of the limo had been a focal point for them when they stepped inside the luxury vehicle, and neither of them had taken notice of the bags.

Austin gave a single nod to the driver, and the divider rose, blocking any further interaction. Paige studied his grin before turning and nearly ripping the bag off the hook.

Curiosity got the best of her, and she pulled a tailored wedding dress from the bag.

She gasped as she looked at the stunning Ines Di Santo mermaid-style wedding gown. She glanced back at Austin. "You remembered?"

She had been trolling through the television channels when a wedding dress fashion week show came on, and she had fallen in love with the entire line, but the one in front of her was the one she actually said something to Austin about. He had taken a cursory look at the television before burying his nose back in his medical books.

"Of course I did. That was the one and only time you said you would kill for a dress like that. Fortunately, you don't have to go that far," he said. "I just hope it fits."

She studied the tag. The size was spot on, but she hoped it ran true. Otherwise, she might either swim in the dress or not be able to breathe.

"You can either dress here in the limo or put it on at the chapel. Your choice."

This was insanity at its best, and it only took weighing the options for a split second before she started stripping in the limo.

Austin chuckled. "I really didn't think you'd be able to wait," he said as he unzipped the other bag and unpacked a black tuxedo with a pristine white shirt. The sharp red tie was the only hint of color between the two of them.

Stripped down to her underwear, Paige unzipped the dress, spread it in the small aisle space between the seats, stepped into it, and pulled it up and over her shoulders before attempting to zip it. The angle of the zipper challenged her, and finally she turned to Austin.

"Can you give me a hand?" she asked, steadying herself in the center of the car.

"Raise your arms," Austin said, and she reached her arms up, using the ceiling of the mini-party bus to steady herself as he pinched the top of the dress together and worked the zipper up.

The dress fit like a glove, but it wasn't tight enough to restrict her breathing. She grinned, twirling in a circle in the small space between the bench seats before she spied shoes in the bag. Taking a seat, she strapped on the matching white stiletto sandals, and finally looked up at Austin putting the finishing touches on his tuxedo.

He stowed his wallet in his back pocket, fished another jewelry box out of his coat, and slipped it into his front pocket. "Rings," he said to her inquisitive look.

"You really thought of everything, didn't you?"

He grinned and then snapped his fingers. "Something old," he muttered and rummaged through their toiletry bag. "And blue," he added and handed her an antique sapphire ring. "It was my mother's."

She glanced at the ornate ring, and Austin slipped it on her right hand, fitting it on her middle finger as opposed to her ring finger.

"You forgot borrowed," Paige said, highly amused by the detail Austin put into this.

"Ah! That's where the chapel comes in. You can borrow a bouquet."

Paige took a seat, pulled out her makeup from the toiletry bag, and touched up her face. When she looked at her hair, she sighed. There wasn't much she could do with it at this point, so she drew a comb through it, neatening up the mess from the flight.

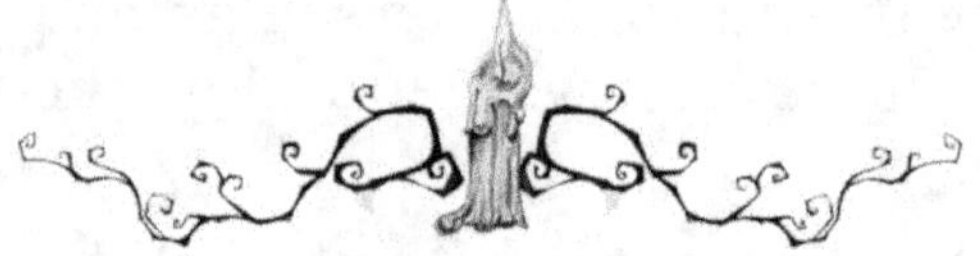

AUSTIN WATCHED HER HIGHLIGHT her eyes and paint her lips, and each swipe of the gloss made him want to lean over and take her right there. The critical eye she gave herself in the mirror was a mystery to him. She was the most beautiful creature on earth, and he counted his blessings.

The car slowed, pulling into the remote desert chapel that boasted the best sunsets in Las Vegas, and from the look of the painted mountains in the distance, he had no doubt their advertising was accurate. The driver laid a red velvet runner from the limousine to that of the chapel.

The door opened a moment later, and Austin stepped out and turned to help Paige. When her hand landed in his, his entire body tingled with the contact. She stepped onto the velvet runner and took in the modest surroundings with a broad smile.

"Somehow, I thought you'd choose a drive through chapel on the strip," she said.

He let out a light chuckle. "You should know me better than that. I want this to be special, not rushed or cheap like it would be in one of

those places." He tucked her hand in the crook
of his arm and led her into the Chapel Under the
Stars.

Inside, a familiar face grinned.

"Heather!" Paige squealed, and broke free
from Austin's grip, running across the distance
to where their friend stood, and gave her a hug.

Austin grinned. It wouldn't be special without
their best friend, and she had dressed the part
of both best man and maid of honor with her
tuxedo top and red satin fit and flare skirt. It
was the perfect combination.

Paige stepped back, noticing the outfit, and
she glanced over her shoulder at Austin. "Did
you tell her to dress like this?"

"Nope," he said. "That was all her idea."

Heather appraised Paige and sent Austin a
nod of approval. "Looks like he didn't miss a
single detail."

"He didn't," Paige said.

She glowed and Austin's cheeks hurt from
the grin plastered on his face, yet he couldn't
wipe it off. His major surprise had been a
sweeping success by the looks of it.

The doors on the opposite side of the entry
swung open, revealing an unobstructed view of
the mountains and the orange and red sun-
streaked sky. Breathtaking was an
understatement.

"Hello, Mr. Shelton. It's wonderful to finally
meet you in person," the minister said as he
crossed from the side of the chapel, offering his
hand.

Austin shook it. "Nice to meet you as well,
Father Kantral," he said and turned to Paige and

Heather. "This is my bride, Paige, and our dearest friend, Heather."

Handshakes were exchanged before Father Kantral sent a text. A moment later, the side door opened, and a woman of Native American descent stepped inside with a large basket of floral arrangements. She approached Paige.

"You have your choice of bouquets," she said.

Paige glanced at Heather for a moment and got a shrug in response. Father Kantral took Austin by the elbow and escorted him to the altar of the open-air chapel where he positioned him on the right, looking out over the mountains.

"What is Heather's last name?" he asked as he pulled a pen out of his pocket.

"Anderson," Austin said.

The minister jotted her name in one of the witness spaces on the marriage certificate before he handed it to Austin. "Is everything in order before we begin?"

Austin scanned the details and nodded, handing it back.

"My wife will act as your second witness, okay?" Father Kantral said with a smile.

"Perfect," Austin said.

The minister gave a nod to the back of the chapel where they had entered, and music filtered from the trusses above.

Austin turned to see the woman who brought the flowers slip around to the side with a video camera in her hand, her focus drifting from him to the door where Heather stepped into the main aisle. She walked as slowly as the natural speed demon could muster and then stopped and stepped to the bride's side of the aisle. Both of them looked back.

Even though they had walked in together, seeing her bathed in the desert sunlight yanked all the air from his lungs. Stunning or breathtaking wasn't even close to an accurate description of Paige at that moment. Angelic came to his mind. He drew in a small breath.

She smiled as she approached with a flowing bouquet of multi-color roses that matched the sunset.

In all his planning, he never thought their wedding would be this perfect, and as she stepped next to him and handed Heather the bouquet, Austin had a moment of intangible fear that this was all the happiness he would be allowed. He swallowed and shook the fear away, putting on a smile and focusing on this moment.

The simple ceremony was over before it began, and when the minister said he could kiss his bride, he didn't hesitate. Holding her close to his chest, he dipped to her lips. The kiss stalled time, possessing everything pure and true in both of them.

Heather clapped and whooped enough to make him think they were amongst a small crowd. The kiss ended, and they went about the business of signing the certificate along with Heather and the minister's wife.

"I need to get back to my conference," Heather said as they waited for the final paperwork in the lobby.

"Thank you for making this perfect," Austin said and caught a hug before relinquishing Heather to his wife.

"I wouldn't have missed it for the world."

"Thank you so much. I couldn't imagine this day without you here," Paige said and gave Heather a squeeze.

"Mr. Shelton?" Father Kantral asked, pulling his attention away from Paige and Heather.

"Yes, sir," Austin replied.

"Your marriage certificate is all set and here is the link and logon information to access your wedding photos and the video." The minister handed Austin the paperwork and offered his hand. "I wish you a long and happy marriage."

"Thank you, sir," Austin said, and pocketed the paperwork. He pulled out an envelope from his inner pocket and handed it to Father Kantral. "I added a little more than what we discussed."

"Thank you. Enjoy your stay here in Las Vegas."

IN THE CONFINES OF the limo, Paige studied her wedding band before she glanced up at Austin. The pop of the champagne cork resounded in the cabin, and he poured a glass for her and then one for him.

"Here's to a long and wonderful life together!" Austin said with a grin.

They tapped glasses, and she took a sip. The bubbles tickled her nose, but the champagne was sweet, not dry, and she finished the glass, licking her lips and holding the cup out for more. "That was really good!"

He took her glass and set it back in the holder. When his gaze returned, there was an animal need blazing in his eyes. That look thrilled her, and she forgot they were in a limousine heading into Sin City.

"So, Mrs. Shelton, what do you want to do next?"

The seductive purr in his voice set her libido on fire, and she pulled him to her lips. Heat filled every cell, and all she wanted was out of the wedding dress and into his arms for another night of unbridled passion. She had no idea how far from Sin City they were, so, instead of waiting for the honeymoon suite, she stripped her underwear and climbed onto his lap, straddling him while her dress draped over his legs.

Paige slowly twirled her hips, grinding against his groin, and he responded, hardening underneath her. His hand slid up her thighs underneath the dress, and he grinned up at her. The adoration reflected in his eyes took her breath away. She sighed when his thumb found her clit, circling it at a leisurely pace that drove her mad.

He shifted under her, and the sound of his zipper, muffled as it was, came in as clear as his soft groan. The pressure of him as he slid inside her wet canal made Paige arch, pushing her thighs farther apart, accepting his girth. They moved in concert, their hips gyrating in slow circles as they made love in the limousine, consecrating their union, and further linking their souls.

Paige slumped into his arms with her heartbeat thumping in her ears. She pressed her mouth to the side of his neck, planting a kiss. The same beat resounding in her chest rushed through his veins, tapping a pleasant melody against her lips. Austin's labored breath matched hers, evening out at the same pace.

"I love you," he whispered in her ear.

Paige pulled away from the crook of his neck and placed a gentle kiss on his lips.

"I love you, too," she said and glanced out the window. The desert still surrounded them. "Where are we going?" she asked, and his gaze followed.

The crease between his eyes deepened, and he shifted her off his lap. After he zipped his pants, he crossed to the window separating the cab from the back of the limousine. Paige slid on her underwear and straightened herself out before Austin knocked on the window.

When nothing happened, he pressed the intercom button.

"Excuse me, but aren't we supposed to be in Las Vegas by now?" Austin asked.

The chuckle that came over the intercom chilled Paige, and she stared at Austin. His gray eyes grew in alarm.

"My boss wants to see you."

The voice that came over the speakers shot fear straight into Paige's core. Austin had never heard Hunter's voice, but she had, and that singsong tone laced with malice set her trembling. She reached for the talisman around her neck, and Austin's gaze snapped from her face to her hand and back.

"What happened to the limo driver who picked us up at the airport?" Austin asked, and his hand went to his chest as well. His gaze never left Paige's.

"Oh, he's here, but I doubt he'd be in any condition to drive." A pause and another chuckle filled the air. "Aren't you going to ask who I am?"

"Hunter." Paige said, loud enough for her voice to be picked up.

"Give that lady a cigar."

Austin released the intercom button and collapsed in the seat facing Paige. "How?"

She just shook her head. They both had seen Hunter's ghost annihilated at the hospital in New York. How he could be driving this vehicle was as much of a mystery to her as it was to Austin.

Paige gripped her bloodstone necklace as if her life depended upon it, and she closed her eyes, muttering a protection incantation for both of them. She knew the protection spell by heart, but unfortunately, she didn't have any of the spices or stones with her to ward off evil.

Austin moved closer, kneeling in front of her. "Baby, we will get out of this," he said and took her hands.

His shaking voice and clammy hands did nothing to slow her erratic heartbeat.

"Who's his boss?" she finally asked.

Austin huffed a laugh. "I think we both know who that is."

She looked up at the impenetrable divider and everything clicked. There was only one being that could pull someone out of hell.

"Lucifer," they both whispered.

Paige dropped her head against the seat, staring at the ceiling. "I knew we shouldn't have left Hanover."

Austin laid his forehead on her hands. His shakes vibrated through her, mingling with her own tremors. All of Hunter's horrifying promises paled compared to Tom Ryan's description of Lucifer.

Paige reached over and fished through her pocketbook, pulling out both her wallet and cell phone. She shuffled through the faded business cards and pulled out the one for Ryan-Andreas Paranormal Investigation Agency. The handwritten phone number was barely legible, but she punched the numbers into the cell.

That three-tone announcement blared in her ear, followed by the automated voice telling her that the number was no longer in service. The initial panic turned into a flood of fear, and she hung up. A moment later, she punched in the office number.

After three rings, a tired female voice answered. "Ryan-O'Keefe Investigations, how can I help you?"

"Is Tom Ryan there?" Paige asked in a hushed voice, praying Hunter didn't overhear her.

"I'm sorry he isn't. May I ask who is calling?"

"Do you have his number? It's kind of an emergency."

A pause met her ear, and a sigh came over the line. "I'm sorry I don't have that information, but perhaps I can help?"

"I need Tom or his brother!" Paige said in a hiss, knowing her lack of calmness wasn't helping the situation.

"I'm sorry, but I can't give that information out. Can I take a message?"

Paige closed her eyes against the sting of tears and bit her lip. "It's Paige. Paige Turner." She sniffled and tried to steady her voice. "It's a matter of life and death, and I need Mr. Ryan unless you can be in two places at once."

A sharp intake of breath followed. "I remember you, Paige. This is Bridget. I'm sorry, but I honestly don't know where Tom is. I can try to get CJ, but I think he's doing a fundraiser tonight."

"Do you know when Tom will be back?"

Silence filled the line. "I'm not sure he'll ever return. He left a few years ago to close the portals."

"Well, he's doing a really shitty job, because a ghost we thought was dead is taking us to Lucifer, and unless there is a portal in the desert outside of Las Vegas that he's about to shut down, we're dead." Paige's voice rose to a pitch she didn't think possible, and her chest constricted under the pressure.

"You're a witch, right?"

"Wiccan," Paige corrected.

"Well, the best advice I can give you is to use that, however you can, while I try to get hold of CJ. May God be with you," Bridget said and disconnected the call.

Paige stared at the phone and then dropped it in her bag, meeting Austin's gaze. She shook her head, unwilling to say there was no hope in a rescue scenario.

They were totally screwed.

Practical Magick
Chapter 6

PAIGE SAT IN THE limo, frozen with fear. Austin glanced at her pocketbook, which actually could be a small carry-on suitcase in and of itself. His mind raced, and he looked around the interior of the limousine, and out the window at the dark desert.

After a moment of his own paralyzing terror, he threw their flight clothing into her bag, along with a few bottles of water. He changed from dress shoes to his sneakers and handed Paige her tennis shoes. They would fare much better in the desert than the stiletto heels she wore.

"What are you doing?" Paige asked as he zipped up her pocketbook, locking the contents inside.

He glanced at the dress she wore and grabbed his discarded tuxedo jacket. "Put this on."

She didn't hesitate, and he sighed, thankful for her compliance. An argument right now could kill their chances. There was only one way out, and it was risky. Jumping from a moving car was always risky.

He hauled her pocketbook over his shoulder and nodded towards the door. Hitting pavement was going to hurt and possibly break things, but all things considered, that option seemed worlds better than having his heart ripped from his chest.

Her eyes widened like they'd just won the jackpot. She moved faster than he expected, and when the car slowed and took a turn, Austin grabbed Paige against his chest, flung the door open and pushed off the edge of the limo. They hit the ground, and he forced his body to roll away from the moving vehicle as he cradled Paige's head to his chest.

When they stopped rolling, she looked up from her position on his chest, and Austin did a quick assessment of his body. The elbow that connected with the ground first was numb, but both his legs seemed to be intact.

"You okay?" he asked.

Paige nodded, climbing to her feet and offered him her hand.

He made the mistake of reaching for it with the numb arm, and it screamed to life. He yanked it back to his chest, fighting the sudden onslaught of nausea and pain. He rolled to his side and pushed up with his good arm. Her pocketbook was a few feet away, and he pointed.

"Grab that and then we need to haul ass before Hunter figures out what the hell just happened."

"Where are we going?"

Austin glanced up the road where the limousine had gone, and the brightening of the taillights set him in motion. Instead of going back the way they came, he turned, grabbed her hand, and darted into the scrub, heading in the opposite direction, praying his calculated decision wouldn't backfire.

Each jogging step sent a sharp pain from his elbow to his shoulder, and he ground his teeth together to keep any vocalization in check. A quick glance back and all he saw were taillights. He didn't ease up until Paige yanked at his arm.

"Rest," she panted.

In the distance, an outcrop of rock sat against the dark landscape, illuminated by the crescent moon.

"When we get there, we can rest," he said, pulling her on with him. They kept running, keeping to the shadows as much as possible. He veered towards the rocks, praying it wasn't an illusion of the desert landscape, and sooner than he expected, they curved around the first rock, sliding to a stop at the nothingness on the other side. The sliver of light the moon cast didn't do the desolate landscape the justice it deserved.

He leaned against the cool rock, tilting his head back while his lungs struggled to pull air in past the burn. Paige collapsed onto the sand, rolling to stare at the stars as she caught her breath.

"Water," he finally said, sliding into a sitting position and tried to ignore his arm, for the moment. He would have to address his injury sooner rather than later, but for now, he needed to wet his parched mouth.

Paige glanced at him and rolled, nearly ripping her purse apart.

"Just a little," he warned as she twisted the cap and brought it to her lips.

She paused at his words and gave a nod before taking a modest sip. Paige handed him the bottle, and he took just enough to coat his mouth. He handed it back, and she secured the cap before sitting up and really looking at him.

"I think that went better than I expected," he said, and she let out a shaky laugh. "Although my elbow is shattered all to hell."

"It would have been worse if we jumped at full speed," she said and crawled next to him, setting her bag on his lap and rummaging through the contents.

When she pulled out an ace bandage, he huffed. "You still have that in there?"

Paige gave him a smile. "I hadn't changed bags for the season, or even for this trip." She reached into the bag and retrieved her phone. The shattered screen drew a sharp breath from both of them. She pressed the side button twice, and the tiny flashlight lit up the space.

Austin grabbed the phone, dousing the light with his hand, and shook his head. Her gaze darted to the direction they came. She took the phone from him and turned off their only actual light.

"I can't wrap your arm if I can't see it."

"That's okay. I just need a sling right now, and we'll figure the rest out when we get back to civilization."

Paige handed him one end of the ace bandage and wrapped the fabric around his neck and down around his arm. It wrapped three times before she took the free end he held and tied the two ends together in a knot. She adjusted the bandage, so the first strip hit just under his elbow, the second in the middle of his arm, and the third just shy of his wrist. It was an impressive field patch job, and he gave her a smile.

"I'm not sure where the hell we are," he said when she settled back. "The chapel was west of the strip, and I wasn't exactly paying attention to anything outside the car." He ran his hand through his hair and looked up at the night sky. When he found The Big Dipper, he followed the line from the edge of the ladle directly to the North Star.

It was farther north and east than he anticipated.

"They took us south." He closed his eyes, trying to remember anything about the geography of Nevada beyond the desert. "And unfortunately, we have to head in the same direction he went. I think we're at least thirty miles from civilization based on how long we were in the car."

"So, it will take us at least a day to get back to Las Vegas?"

"That would be my best guess. Do you have any energy bars still stowed in the bag?"

Paige nodded. "I still have a couple."

"Good. We only have three waters, and I think I got all our clothes from the flight shoved in there, so we have something to help us deal with the sun and heat. But if we're out here more than a day or two, we're screwed." He climbed to his feet and offered her his good hand.

She stood, collecting the bag before they headed towards the North Star. The silence of the desert was very different from a quiet spring night in New Hampshire. At least they had the benefit of the stars, and if they stayed far enough away from the road, they wouldn't be seen.

Each step sent sharp stabs through his elbow. He slowed to a stop, closed his eyes, and willed his stamina to deal with the pain. The alternatives were much worse. He had to keep moving. If not for himself, then for Paige.

"Are you okay?" Her light touch brought the clarity of the situation back.

He glanced at her. "Yeah. Just needed a minute to get my head wrapped around all this," he said, buffering her from his pain. In the darkness, he thought her eyebrow rose at his obvious lie, but then she wrapped her hand in his good one.

"Slow and easy," she said.

"Yes, and try to watch the shadows on the ground in front of us. We don't want to end up stepping off a cliff."

She huffed a laugh and squeezed his hand. "Or step on a rattlesnake."

"Not sure which would be worse right now," he said. "Think your protection spell will work on the desert dangers, or is that only for devils and demons?" He glanced at her profile in the dark and only caught a flash of her white teeth as they started moving again.

"It's only for demons and the devil," she said. "But as long as we don't bother the animals, they won't bother us."

A howl in the distance begged to differ, and her hand clamped harder on his.

Every nerve ending in his body jumped on high alert. Something menacing resounded in that howl and he shivered. "Keep moving," he said and picked up the pace, despite the jarring agony flaring in his arm.

"That didn't sound like a coyote," she muttered under her breath.

"Don't worry about it right now. Let's just put as much distance between us and whatever that is as we can."

"What if we are heading towards it?"

Austin didn't answer. He focused on the ground in front of him as they jogged through the sandy terrain. "Do you know a spell that will protect us from all dangerous creatures?" he asked after a few moments.

"I need more than words to make that happen, and I'm fresh out of potions."

Her sarcasm wasn't lost on him, and neither was her labored breathing. He slowed the pace to a fast walk. Without his coat, the chill of the night desert air seeped right through the dress shirt and deep into his bones. He clamped his teeth against the shivers and silently berated himself. The fifty some degrees back home would feel like a summer day, but somehow being out here with little more than a fading adrenaline rush was not keeping his body temperature up enough to sustain heat.

"Austin," Paige said and pulled to a stop.

"What?"

"You're shivering." She took off his coat and threw it over his shoulders.

"Babe, you can't be out here with just that on." He tried to shuck the coat off, but she wouldn't let him.

"I am fine. I'm not the one who's injured. Besides, I have a shirt in the bag if I need one."

Even in the dark, the blue of Paige's irises sparkled with intensity and resolve under the light of the stars. He conceded, slipping his good arm into the coat. The weight of the fabric lying on his elbow made him jerk at the first touch, but he inhaled, accepting the discomfort as the price he had to pay to be warm.

"Jog or walk?" he asked.

"Walk," she said. "This dress is kind of a hazard. I keep stepping on the front edge when we try to run."

"I guess I didn't think of the practicality of that dress in the event of an escape. But you look stunning in it, even with all the dust and dirt."

"You can see the dirt?"

He let out a soft laugh and glanced at her. "I had a quick look when you flashed the phone light. Just enough to see some serious dirt smudges."

"Damn," she muttered under her breath.

He glanced up at the stars. "This isn't exactly how I pictured our wedding night."

She snorted a laugh and squeezed his hand. "I'm sure."

"I was kind of looking forward to a repeat of last night." A grin formed on his lips as he thought about their wild lovemaking. The reality that he might never get to have that again sobered his mood, and he let a sigh escape. He refocused on the dark landscape.

They continued traveling northeast, keeping the North Star to their left as they walked. When the landscape lightened enough to make out the scrub dotting the horizon, Austin slowed to a stop. Exhaustion pummeled his muscles, and Paige looked every bit as tired as he felt.

"We need to find a shaded place to hunker down for the day," he said, but nothing stood out on the landscape, not even an outcrop of rock or a clump of cacti.

Paige pointed, and his gaze followed her finger. There was something due east toward the road, but from this distance, it could easily be an illusion, but it was their only option. They headed that way. He couldn't gage the distance from the road, but the closer they drew, the more his nerves started riding the rail.

"What is that?" he muttered, squinting to see better.

Paige let out a soft laugh. "It's a billboard."

Austin slowed almost to a stop, and Paige followed his lead, standing next to him while he chewed on his bottom lip. Another glance at their options clinched his decision, and he resumed his pace.

"We need to find shade," he said again, scanning the brightening sky. "It's going to get real hot, real quick," he added. "So, before we get some rest, we need to finish one of those waters."

"I just want to curl up and sleep." Paige yawned.

"Water first, then sleep." Austin forced his feet to continue and his focus to remain on what he prayed was a ground level billboard and not one that was propped on a stand. If it was on the ground, they had more of a chance for shelter from both the sun and any prying eyes. If it wasn't, they may get relief from the sun, but it would leave them totally exposed to anyone traveling on that road.

Another eerie howl filled the air, and Austin traded a glance with Paige before he scanned the ever-lightening landscape. A distinct trail stood out in the sand behind them, and Austin's gaze snapped to the train of Paige's dress.

"Paige?" he asked, and she stopped looking around for the source of the howl and met his gaze. "I think you might need to pick up the dress for this last leg."

She glanced behind her and followed the trail. "Oh, shit," she said and gathered the extra fabric of her skirt into her arms.

With a last exertion of effort, they jogged the last hundred yards into the shadow of the ground level billboard and collapsed under the t-bar frame. The poles would provide a little relief from the sunshine, but they would have to shift to avoid the full sun.

Paige pulled out a water bottle and took a healthy sip before handing it to him. Austin gulped down the liquid, careful not to over drink his share, and handed the quarter-filled bottle back. He carefully stretched onto his back, in what he assessed as the optimal shaded area.

Without his permission, his eyelids closed and
darkness engulfed him.

Practical Magick
Chapter 7

PAIGE DOZED, BUT JERKED awake every time her head bobbed. Austin needed rest, especially with his broken arm. She hadn't got a good look at it, but the fact he was still in the tuxedo jacket and shivering in the sweltering heat said more than she cared to know. Whatever he had done to himself, his body was fighting back something fierce.

She glanced at the sigils she made in the sand around him, inspecting them for any break in the spell. Satisfied that he would remain invisible to Lucifer and Hunter, she curled up in the shade, using her pocketbook as a pillow, and watched Austin sleep.

He looked so peaceful, even with the sheen of sweat speckling his forehead. He shifted, and his face scrunched, ruining the serene image. His eyes blinked open, and he stared above him like he didn't know where he was. When his gaze fell on her, creases appeared in his forehead.

"How long have I been out?" he asked.

Paige shrugged. "Half the day?"

His eyebrows formed perfect arches, and he blinked in rapid succession. Slowly, he sat up and cleared his throat. "Water?"

Paige reached into her bag. A sudden sting exploded on the back of her hand, and she yanked it out of the bag with a yelp. A scorpion crawled out of the confines, skittered across the sand, and disappeared under the billboard.

Her hand burned, and she held it to her chest, squeezing her eyes closed as the pain spread from the sting zone and tingled up her forearm.

"Paige?" Austin asked; and his voice held enough concern for her to open her eyes.

Her skin throbbed, and she glanced down at her hand. The thing looked like she'd slid her hand into an oven mitt. The angry red swell spread just as quickly as the burning sensation. Her chest constricted, making it difficult to draw air, and her gaze snapped back to Austin's.

Austin rolled onto his hands and knees and hobbled over with care not to fall on his broken arm. His face paled with the motion, but his eyes never left hers.

"Breathe," he said softly, and stopped right in front of her. He sat back on his knees and cupped her cheek.

His hand was as hot as the air, and the panic filtering through her was replaced by a bloom of worry. She lifted her good hand to his forehead and pulled it away just as fast. Dumping the contents of the pocketbook, she grabbed for the water and nearly shoved it into his chest.

"Drink," she wheezed.

He took the bottle from her outstretched hand, unscrewed the cap, and tipped it to his lips. When he pulled it away and offered it to her, she shook her head. Her breathing was already labored, and she couldn't afford to hold her breath long enough to drink.

"You are running a fever," she said through each wheeze.

"And you're reacting to the scorpion bite. Drink."

He held the bottle out, and despite the fatigue layering his eyes, determination sparked stronger. She gave in, took a small sip, and passed it back to him. They went back and forth, sipping water until Austin drank the last drop.

Paige's arm tingled, but her breathing had normalized enough so her panic didn't rekindle. Her hand was still swollen and red, but the puffiness tapered off a couple of inches past her wrist. It still throbbed, but it wasn't hurting like it had been after initially being stung.

"Take off your coat. I want to take a look at your arm," she said.

Austin shrugged the coat off, and as the dark fabric fell away from the make-shift sling, Paige stifled a gasp at the rust-red splotches on the fabric of his shirt, along with the unnatural angle of his arm. He looked down and uttered an unusual laugh.

"It's a good thing I'm going for psychiatry and not surgery," he said, but his face colored into the green zone.

"Austin, you need a hospital. Now," Paige said.

His eyebrows rose. "In case you hadn't noticed, we're in the middle of the desert."

"But..."

He held up his good hand, stopping her. "We don't have a choice. My arm will get fixed, eventually."

"You've got a fever," she said.

"That sometimes happens with broken bones."

"I need to get you some help," she said and climbed to her feet. "You just stay here."

"Paige, the last time we were in danger and split up, the shit hit the fan. I can deal with this until *we* get back to civilization."

She bit her lip and scanned the horizon. The heat of the day shimmered, and she weighed her options. Worry nipped at the edges of her skin, but he was right. The last time they separated, Hunter almost got his wish for revenge. If she left and the devil found Austin, she would find a corpse when she returned.

Their options were limited. Trying to reach help in the brutal desert sun would backfire, just as surely as separating would, and there was no guarantee that a car would stop for them if they kept to the sparsely traveled road. She slowly lowered back onto the sand, her dress billowing around her before it settled.

"Did you want to change out of that?" He waved at her soiled wedding dress.

She smoothed the fabric over her abdomen. "It's actually cooler than my sweats would be," she said with a little shrug.

His lips twitched into a smile. "You still are a beautiful bride."

Paige let out a laugh, looked down at the silky fabric marred with dirt and sweat, and then back at Austin. "Sweetie, I think you must be hallucinating."

"Maybe." His smile turned goofy. "But you're still beautiful to me."

Paige rolled her eyes. "Get some more rest. I imagine we will have a long walk tonight."

"You need some sleep, too."

"After finding that scorpion in my purse, I don't think so," she said, eyeing the shady spot where the critter had disappeared.

The rumble of a diesel engine caught their attention, and Paige was up on her feet and heading towards the road before the thought of danger resounded in her mind. The sight of the eighteen-wheeler cruising in her direction sparked hope, and she waved her arms like a madwoman.

The downshifting of the vehicle made the tires squeal and dirt kick up as the brakes locked, bringing the monster vehicle to a stop within a few feet of where Paige stood. The driver rolled the window down and leaned on the door.

"You look a little lost, young lady," he drawled with the perfect Texas accent.

Paige let out a little laugh. "You could say that. Any chance my husband and I can catch a ride?"

His amicable expression turned guarded.

"He's behind the billboard in the shade. He's got a broken arm and we really could use the help," she added. She didn't dare break eye contact for fear the driver might change his mind and take off.

He scanned the horizon and then gave a
small nod.

"Austin," Paige yelled.

He stepped out from the shade, holding her
pocketbook and his coat. He gave the driver a
small nod of appreciation, and they crossed to
the passenger side of the rig.

Paige climbed up first and then took both the
coat and her purse from Austin while he climbed
into the truck and closed the door.

"Thank you," Paige said, turning to the driver.

"Did you two get lost on the way to a chapel?"
he said in that Texan drawl.

"On the way home from one," Austin said.
"And things just went to hell from there." He
offered a sickly smile. "I'm Austin and this is my
wife, Paige," he added as he tilted his head back
onto the headrest.

Paige glanced at his profile before turning
back to the driver with an equally awkward
smile. The driver had at least ten years on them,
and he had kind eyes. Her protective instincts
were already on high with Austin, but her senses
were not screaming danger, so her muscles
relaxed.

"Rob Townsend," he said and offered his
hand to Paige.

She shook it, and then he shifted the truck
into gear.

"I'm guessing the nearest hospital is in
order?"

"As long as it's in Las Vegas," Austin said.

"That's the closest one, son," Rob said.

Quiet filtered through the cab as they headed away from the dangers of the desert and into civilization.

Practical Magick
Chapter 8

ROB PULLED TO A stop on the main road, just short of the emergency entrance driveway of Sunrise Hospital.

"Here we are," he said and put the vehicle in neutral.

"Thank you for your help," Austin said and offered his right hand to the driver. After a quick handshake, he turned to the door and took a deep breath, preparing himself for the drop from the door to the ground.

He pushed the door open and clamped his teeth together. The drop took a mere second, but the impact that ran through his arm and the agony that flared almost dropped him to his knees. Paige landed next to him and then reached into the truck for her purse and his coat.

"Thank you." She closed the door and turned to Austin. "Think you can make it?"

"I can make it," he assured her, but even he wasn't convinced. Each step made his entire form throb. The only thing that sidetracked his mind from the pain was the growling of his stomach. Paige's was equally obnoxious, and he gave her a sideways look.

"You still have those protein bars?"

"Yeah, but I'm not sure you should eat right now," she said.

His stomach said otherwise, and chose that moment to make it known, but he saw her point. His arm would require surgery and he wished like hell that Valerie Ryan was in the vicinity. With one magical kiss, she could heal his arm in minutes, not months.

Instead of commenting, he glanced at her still swollen hand. "You should get that checked while we're here, too."

"You need the medical attention first," she insisted as they stepped inside to emergency room chaos. "Besides, I'm not leaving your side."

Her gaze haunted him, and he nodded. Neither of them wanted a repeat of New York, especially since this time there was no savior to step in and clean up their mess. He took a seat at the check-in desk and closed his eyes, breathing a few deep breaths before he opened his eyes and focused on the registration clerk. She was still typing away and hadn't looked up at them yet.

Austin cleared his throat, and without missing a keystroke, the clerk said, "I'll be right with you, sir."

"My husband's arm is broken," Paige said.

Austin sent a glare over his shoulder at her. "My wife was stung by a scorpion."

The registration clerk turned to the printer, pulled the latest printout, and put it in a folder and into a rack before she turned towards Austin and Paige. She scanned their soiled wedding clothes and blinked.

"Not exactly the wedding night either of us imagined," Austin said.

The clerk raised an eyebrow. "Name and insurance card?"

"Austin Shelton and my wife, Paige," he said, waving towards her. He dug his wallet out and flipped it open. He pulled out a couple of cards stuck in the holders, laid them on the desk, and shuffled through them until he found his insurance card. He handed it to the clerk and glanced at Paige. "Do you mind putting those back?"

She reached over his shoulder and picked up the cards, but not before the clerk saw her red and swollen hand. She had more dexterity than he did and slid the cards back into the wallet.

Austin smiled at her and then returned his attention to the clerk. "We want to be treated together if possible. We've had a hell of a night, and considering what happened, we both would rather not be separated."

"Can you tell me what the issue is?"

"Compound fracture of my left arm. I'm pretty sure my medial is shattered, and I think my ulna is the one that punctured my skin." He gave her an awkward shrug.

"When did this happen?"

Austin glanced at Paige. "Probably around eight or nine last night?"

Paige nodded.

The clerk glared at them. "And you waited this long to come to the emergency room?"

"We were stuck in the desert with a broken cell phone, so yeah. This was the fastest we could get here," Paige snapped back.

The wheeze in her breath made him look closer at her. "I think my wife is having a reaction." He stood and put his good fingers to her throat. The rapid pulse and labored breathing set his panic button on high. "She got stung by a scorpion about an hour ago." He turned to the clerk. "She needs an antivenin."

The clerk looked up. "Sir, we need to finish checking you in."

"I just graduated from medical school, so I'm not just your average Joe off the street," he said. "I am sure we can finish registering while she gets looked at." Irritation flushed his skin, and he had to take a breath to calm himself. It wasn't this woman's fault. She was just following a script, but with how fast Paige's heart was racing, she was at risk of going into cardiac arrest.

"Sir..."

"Neither of us has had anything to eat since before our flight out here yesterday, and we've had about twenty ounces of liquid in the same timeframe. As if that isn't enough, add walking all night through the desert, and that just adds to the risk. She hasn't had enough food or water to counteract the scorpion venom. So, get off your ass and get a nurse over here before my wife has a heart attack." His voice echoed over the din, turning heads in their direction.

"Austin, I'm okay," Paige said, but her breathing and unhealthy pallor said otherwise.

A nurse stepped to the counter. "Can I help you?"

"My wife is having a reaction from a scorpion bite," Austin said.

"I'm not the one with a compound fracture," Paige said, sending a glare in his direction.

The nurse glanced between Paige and Austin before her gaze dropped to his arm. That seemed to clinch it. She nodded, waved us around the counter to an exam room, and turned to Austin.

"Her first, please," he said, nodding towards Paige. "My arm isn't going anywhere, but her heart is racing, and her breathing isn't right."

The nurse paused and then rerouted to where Paige sat to take her pulse. After a moment, a crease appeared between her eyes, and she took Paige's temperature. She stepped out for a moment and returned with a doctor.

"She was stung by a scorpion," Austin said before the nurse could. His anxiety over Paige's deteriorating condition made his chest pound.

"I'm Dr. Sanchez," the doctor said to Paige as he inspected the wound on Paige's hand. "We are going to give you a shot to help counteract the venom in your system, okay?"

"That probably would be a good idea," Paige answered, her breath more labored, like it had been in the desert right after the sting.

The nurse produced a syringe and administered a shot to Paige's upper arm of the stung hand.

"That should loosen your chest in a few minutes." The doctor turned from Paige towards

Austin. "I normally don't appreciate a patient making a scene in my ER, but in this case, I'll give you a pass. We'll monitor her for the next few hours, but barring any unforeseen complications, I believe she'll be fine." He crossed the short distance to stand in front of Austin. "Now, let's look at that arm."

Austin, with help from the nurse, attempted to strip the makeshift sling. Paige stepped next to him to help peel his shirt off, revealing the true extent of his compound fracture. The movement, along with the sudden lack of support, made the room tilt. Austin took a deep breath and blinked the spin away just in time to see Paige sway. The color of her face slapped his focus into sharp clarity, and he reached out with his good arm to steady her before she face-planted in a dead faint.

His touch yanked her gaze away from his arm, and when her eyes met his, he said, "Why don't you sit this one out?"

"That's not such a bad idea," Paige said, and the nurse helped her to the chair.

Each slow movement of his arm threatened to pull him back into that sickening spin that made his stomach roll. Somehow, he found the strength to keep control and not succumb to the pain or the perpetual souring of his stomach.

"Let's get you down to x-ray to see exactly what we are working with," the doctor said.

Austin gave a nod, although he wasn't sure if the acid in his belly would remain on lockdown for any prolonged movement without a sling.

"Nadia, can you please get Mr. Shelton a wheelchair for the trip down to the x-ray department?" Dr. Sanchez said to the nurse, and she gave a nod, disappearing into the hall.

Paige stood when the nurse returned with a chair.

"The doctor wants you to rest," the nurse said.

"I'd like her with me," Austin said, trading a glance with his wife. Despite the knowledge that Paige should rest, he didn't want her out of his sight, especially with Hunter on the loose, along with something much worse. Any separation, no matter how minute, made them vulnerable.

The x-ray technician took Austin into the room and slid a film onto the table before waving at the chair.

Austin sat, glanced at Paige, and offered what he hoped was a reassuring smile before the technician moved his arm into place under the x-ray machine. His teeth involuntarily clenched at the movement, and he closed his eyes, willing himself to deal with it.

"I know it's tough, but you just have to hold it there for a minute," he said, and stepped away.

Austin forced a slow breath as the machine whirred. The light switched off, and the technician returned, bringing the wheelchair in with him.

"You're good to head back to the exam room, and the doctor will be right with you."

Austin pulled his arm against his body and shifted into the wheelchair. Without prompting, Paige stepped behind him.

"I got you, honey," she said, and while her voice lacked strength, it was no longer labored.

Austin just nodded without looking up at her. The pain became an animal in its own league, and he had to concentrate on breathing to keep it from overwhelming him. Even his vision had tunneled.

"You okay?" Paige whispered in his ear.

Breathe, his mind commanded. He obeyed, ignoring her question until she parked him in the exam room next to the empty chair. When she stepped in front of him and crouched down, he met her gaze.

"Austin?"

"I'm okay. Just trying not to throw up."

She rubbed his leg and nodded, taking the seat next to him.

Dr. Sanchez stepped into the room after a long couple of minutes, and Austin raised his gaze to the light screen where the doctor clipped the x-ray. The film showed him just how extreme the break was, and Austin closed his eyes. He knew what came next, and there was no way he was going to allow the hospital to put him under.

"I'm going to have to take you to surgery to set your arm," the doctor said as he looked at the x-rays.

"No."

The doctor turned towards him. "This is a complicated break."

Austin stared him down. "Just give me a local and set it here." Austin said through clenched teeth. "Or a regional if you have to. I do not want to be put under."

"You don't seem to understand. This isn't something that can be done with a little twist of your arm and a splint. This is going to require at least half a dozen pins...”

Austin held up his good hand, stopping the doctor from any further explanation. “I can see what is needed, but I would prefer my doctor back home do the surgery. No offense.” Surgery meant being separated from Paige, and he had no intention of letting that happen.

“Sir, I strongly suggest you let us fix this for you now. Any further delay could lead to permanent loss of dexterity and increase the possibility of infection.”

“I respectfully decline surgery, but thank you for your concern. Now, can we get this bone back into my skin, patch the cut, and put me into something I can travel with?” His voice sounded so much stronger than he felt.

Dr. Sanchez’s eyebrows rose, and he pursed his lips for a moment, irritation clearly displayed in the creases of his forehead, but he finally nodded. “Fine,” he said and stepped out of the room.

“Are you sure?” Paige whispered.

He turned to her. “Do you really want to be separated right now?” The question popped out, framed in sarcasm, and she shook her head. “Neither do I. We can take a detour when we land.”

Her eyes widened. “Really?”

“Yeah,” he said and ran his good hand through his hair. “I’m no longer sure we are safe anywhere,” he added, meeting her beautiful blue eyes. “And I’d rather be near the big guns, if you know what I mean.”

Before she could answer, the doctor stepped back into the room with a nurse and an orderly.

Dread wrapped around Austin's midsection. Knowing what was coming didn't help him at all, and even though the nurse produced three syringes, the knot still bloomed in his chest.

It'll only take a few minutes at most, so suck it up. He admonished the shake that started in his good hand and the fear that nearly closed his throat. He clamped down on the armrest of the chair, forcing a brave face.

The nurse moved the chair into the center of the room next to the exam table and set the brakes.

"Are you sure I can't convince you to let us fix your arm with a surgical procedure?" the doctor asked.

Austin moved to the exam table at the prompting of the nurse. "Yes. Positive. If you want me to sign a form, I will." He leaned into the inclined back of the table.

"As soon as we set the arm and clean out the wound, I will have you sign a refusal of further care form." Dr. Sanchez nodded to the nurse.

She stepped forward and administered the shots in his arm above and below the wound.

It didn't take long for the tingling sensation to take hold and the pain to dull to a soft throb. The relief from the agony left him feeling like all his bones had turned to jelly. It wasn't until the orderly stabilized his upper arm and the doctor stepped into position that he tensed.

He locked gazes with Paige. "You probably don't want to watch this."

"I'll be fine. Do you want me to hold your good hand?"

Austin shook his head. If he held her hand, he would probably break it. "I'm fine," he lied and punctuated it with a reassuring smile.

Saline dripped from his arm as the doctor cleaned the surface. When he set the saline-soaked gauze onto the tray the nurse held, Austin looked away. The orderly's grip on Austin's upper arm tightened. Pressure gave way to a jolt that nearly ripped a yelp from his mouth, but he clamped down, refusing to give in to the sudden and blinding pain.

He forced breaths through his nose, and the shifting and grinding of his bones came close to catapulting the contents of his stomach onto the floor, but he held on with grim determination. Hot liquid drizzled on his semi-numb skin, pulling his gaze back to the procedure. Blood flowed from the open wound, but it wasn't flowing at the rate a severed artery would. Austin breathed a sigh of relief as the doctor's grip loosened.

Dr. Sanchez slipped a splint on Austin's forearm, stabilizing it before he tended to Austin's open wound.

Relief flooded Austin, and he took long, slow breaths. He closed his eyes and leaned his head back on the pillow; the crinkle of the sterile pillowcase filling his ears. The doctor packed his wound with antibiotic beads and covered it with surgical tape before positioning his arm for a more secure brace.

Practical Magick
Chapter 9

PAIGE WAITED UNTIL THEY secured Austin's arm in a cast and gave him a more appropriately fitted sling before she stepped to his side, taking his good hand.

"When was your last tetanus shot?" Dr. Sanchez asked after he finished.

"Four years ago," they said in unison, and traded glances.

Paige still couldn't believe Hunter was back. It all seemed like a wild nightmare, and she wondered when the hell she was going to wake up. From the moment they stepped off the plane, her nerves had been jumping. The wedding muted the jumbled sirens in the pit of her stomach, but they remained like a fog over the ocean before a storm rolled in. She kept thinking about their last happy moment—making love to Austin in the limousine. And Hunter was there, watching. Just the thought sent a shiver through her, and Austin caught her tremble out of the corner of his eye, tilting his head at her in response.

"You have eight hours before those beads fully dissolve, and I would suggest you not wait that long. I trust that gives you enough time to get home and see your doctor?" Dr. Sanchez asked while the nurse handed Austin a refusal of treatment form to sign.

"That should be enough time. I'll need the x-ray." Austin nodded towards the light panel where the film still hung. "And you wouldn't happen to have a hospital shirt I can use?" he asked, looking at the tuxedo shirt they had to cut off him.

"Yes, I can get you one," the nurse said as the doctor slid the film into a paper slip and handed it to Austin.

"Make sure he gets that checked out as soon as you land," the doctor said to Paige before he stepped out of the exam room.

The nurse returned with a blue scrub shirt. "It's a large," she said and approached Austin. "I can help you with this if you'd like."

"That would probably be wise," Austin said, and the nurse unclasped his sling. "Can we take this undershirt off, too? It's kind of ripe," he added and met Paige's gaze.

She released his hand and helped him peel the damp undershirt from his back. He was right—the fabric held that sick sweat quality that nearly gagged her as she dropped it on the chair next to his destroyed dress shirt. With that out of the way, both the nurse and Paige helped him get the hospital shirt over his cast and the rest of the way over his sculpted chest. She sighed as his skin disappeared under the clean shirt and met his gaze while the nurse refit the sling around his neck.

"Thank you," Austin said to the nurse.

"You're welcome," she replied and reached into her pocket, pulling out a small sample prescription bottle. She opened it and handed one pill to Austin. "You'll need to take one every four to six hours to manage the pain." She retrieved a glass of water and held both the sample and the water out for Austin.

"Paige can take that." He nodded towards the bottle, and the nurse handed it off to Paige.

She dropped it in her pocketbook on top of their flight clothes with a sigh. Her dress was starting to chafe, and she wanted nothing more than the comfortable sweats and t-shirt stowed in her bag.

"Is there anything else you need?" the nurse asked.

"No. I think we are good," Paige said for the both of them.

"When you're ready, we have both of your release papers at the counter."

"Thanks," Austin said.

The minute the door closed, Paige turned to Austin. "I need to change. Did you want to put on your jeans, too?"

"Yeah, but I'm going to need some help."

"Can you unzip me first," Paige said and turned her back to him so he could help with her dress.

"I really wish we had the chance to do this at the hotel," he mumbled, echoing her silent sentiments, and she glanced over her shoulder, meeting his gaze. He gave her an endearing smile and a half-hearted shrug.

"Well, when you're better, I'll put a dress on just so you can take it off."

His dimples deepened.

She shed the dress from her shoulders, and it dropped to the floor. A small squeeze of disappointment struck her as she glanced at the dirt-stained dress. None of this was how she imagined their wedding night, but the relief of being alive overshadowed all other emotions. While a shower would have felt like a dream at the moment, comfortable clothes came a close second, and they were the only choice she had. Paige changed into the sweats and t-shirt, thankful that Austin had the forethought to shove their clothes into her purse before they jumped from the car. Without his quick thinking, she would have ruined her feet in stilettos and had nothing to change into.

Once fully dressed, she slipped her sneakers back on and turned to Austin.

He stood with his wallet in his good hand and his pants around his ankles, and that little crease of concentration deepened between his eyes.

She stepped around the table and had to suppress a smile as he tried, and failed, to remove his high-top sneakers to get the dress pants off.

"Sit down before you fall," she said, and he glanced up at her. His goofy smile returned, and she wondered just how fast that pain medicine worked on an empty stomach. He looked like he was sporting a serious buzz.

He leaned on the exam table and waved to his feet. "I can't seem to get these things off." He lifted one of his feet towards her, but it only went as far as the width of his pants, producing a small giggle from him.

Paige smiled in amusement. "That pain medicine works fast."

"Yup," he said with a grin, confirming her suspicion.

"We need to get some food into you," she said, more to herself than him, and set his jeans aside before she crouched down to help. Pushing the pants up, she found the laces and untied them, taking off his right sneaker and then his left, before helping with the pants. She shook his jeans, making sure they were free of critters, and then held them under each leg, shimmying the fabric up over each foot before pulling the belt loops until the jeans sat comfortably around his waist.

"Tuck yourself in while I get your shoes on," she said, and he leaned forward, catching a kiss.

His soft and warm lips stalled her, and she had to force herself to step back. The time bomb was ticking, and if they didn't get out of town as soon as they could, it would blow, and that would be the end of their future.

She dropped and busied herself with his shoes, and once they were on and tied, she stood and dumped her purse on the exam table.

"What are you doing?" Austin asked.

"I need to make sure there aren't any more of those things hiding in here, and I want to make sure we have the car keys so we can get home from the airport."

Thankfully, nothing but sand and the usual crap she carried remained in the purse. She wiped the empty purse with his discarded dress shirt before wiping and returning her wallet, make-up, hairbrush, pens, snacks, and the last water into the now clean confines.

"The keys aren't here," she said and looked up at him.

He stared at the contents of her purse and patted the pockets of the jeans. When his gaze landed on the pants on the floor, she swept them up, checking each pocket.

"Check the jacket," he said, nodding towards the tuxedo jacket draped over the corner chair.

She crossed and picked up the jacket. The weight of the thing gave her hope, and she turned, pulling the keys out of the inside pocket like she had just performed a world class magic trick.

"Don't forget the paperwork. We'll need that when we get home."

She shuffled through the pockets, dropping the keys and papers into her purse, along with Austin's money clip. "For a second there, I really thought we were screwed," she said and looked at the dress still crumpled on the floor, along with the tuxedo pants. "And I don't think the dress will fit in my bag."

"Maybe they'll have something we can carry the wedding clothes in," he said and stepped to the door.

Paige gathered the pants, jacket, and her dress, draping them over her arm before she followed Austin to the desk. Her breathing had normalized, and the swelling in her hand had gone down to almost normal. Although the area around the scorpion sting was still red, she had little to no lasting effects from her reaction since they administered the antivenin.

Austin signed every form they put in front of him and then took the pile of clothing from Paige when it was her turn.

"Do you have a bag we can put our clothes in?" Austin asked the desk clerk.

She glanced at the clothes draped over his good arm, and her hard gaze softened at the sight of the dirty wedding dress. "Yes. As soon as your wife finishes signing the paperwork, I'll get you one."

Twenty minutes later, they stepped outside, and the evening chill hit.

"We need to get to the airport," Austin said.

"Should we call a cab?" she asked.

His drugged gaze found hers before he slowly shook his head. "We should call Heather and see if she can come get us."

Paige's eyes widened, and her nerves settled at the thought of their trusted friend helping instead of an unknown stranger. They stepped back inside the emergency room. At the desk, it took a moment for the receptionist to acknowledge them.

"Do you have a pay phone I can use? I need to call for a ride," Austin said and offered a tired smile.

"Phones are around the corner that way," she said, pointing to their right, away from the exam rooms.

Paige and Austin found the pay phone and fed one of their credit cards into the slot. Austin dialed by memory, impressing Paige. She wouldn't know anyone's number off the top of her head. After all, wasn't that what the phone programming was for? He leaned against the wall with the phone to his ear.

"Um, is Heather there?" he asked.

The peaceful expression morphed into outright horror, and his gaze dropped to Paige's.

"I understand," he said with a voice laced with ice. He turned and hung up, stepping away from the phone like it was on fire.

"Austin?"

"He has her," he said, his voice barely a whisper.

"Hunter?"

Austin let out a small laugh. "No. Heather could deal with Hunter."

The heat ran out of her cheeks and fingers, leaving her cold. "Lucifer?" she whispered.

He nodded and took her hand with his good one, pulling her out of the hospital. At the end of the driveway, he turned in the opposite direction they had come in. The pace he was walking made her almost have to jog to keep from stumbling.

"What did he say?"

"My life for hers," he said.

Paige stopped, yanking him with her. As much as she loved Heather, she couldn't conceive of sacrificing Austin. "I can't let you do what you're thinking."

"Paige—" he started.

"No! I am not letting you do that, because Lucifer will kill all of us. There is no dealing with the devil. Look what he did to Tom's wife. Do you want to watch while he does that to me? Or worse, watch while Hunter does whatever the hell he has in store for me?"

Austin's face scrunched in anger. "What the hell would you have me do? Run away like a fucking coward?"

"If it means staying alive, yes." She didn't want to sacrifice a friend, but she knew what Hunter was capable of. Austin hadn't been there when he made those men abuse her. He hadn't seen the sick joy Hunter got from others degrading and beating her.

"I don't want to die. But I cannot sacrifice someone else to save my ass. It's not in my DNA. And you can't be anywhere near here, so I'm putting you on a plane, and I'll deal with this."

"Bullshit! If you are going on a suicide mission, I'm following you."

"No."

"You have no say in whether I stay or go. If you go, I go. Which means you'll end up sacrificing me, too." Paige yanked her hand from his. "So, choose."

He stared at her with his mouth popped open in shock. The turmoil of her words worked its way into his eyes, coating them with tears. Guilt bit at every cell inside of Paige, but she held her ground.

"Til death do us part," she added softly, when a tear escaped from the corner of his eye.

"Jesus Christ, Paige," he hissed, glaring at her.

"You have nothing at your disposal. You aren't special like the Ryans. You don't have a chance in hell of walking out of there alive if you go alone." Hot tears choked her voice, and she dropped her gaze. "It's a lose-lose situation."

He closed his eyes and dipped his chin to his chest. "What about your magic? Can that help?"

Paige's skin tingled with self-doubt. "I had no strength against Hunter's black magic back in New York."

He opened his eyes and stared at her. "If I asked you to try, what would you need?"

"I only know practical magic. Things that can keep us hidden and safe, not how to battle the devil. Black magic is his domain."

Austin's gaze darted around and then landed back on her. "What about voodoo, or shit like that?"

"Austin, be serious," she said, hating the sharp tone in her voice. He was desperate and she could see it in the bounce of his eyes and the sweat now speckling his brow.

"I can't just let this happen. I have to try." He attempted to cross his arms, but the cast prohibited it, and he finally shoved his free hand in his pocket.

"How?"

"I don't know. And we have to think on the move, because we have exactly one hour to show up at her hotel."

Paige glanced around at the sparsely populated desert surrounding them. The famous Las Vegas strip was nowhere in view. "How far are we from the city proper?"

"Again, I don't know," he snapped and turned, trudging in the same direction he had started. "I don't even know how to get a damned cab."

Paige caught up with him after a few steps. Her mind flooded with spells that might help, but they weren't what she needed. If her phone worked, at least she could find local herb shops, if they existed, and gather the right ingredients. Banishing Hunter had required a great deal of focus, along with his DNA. She doubted the same could be said for the devil.

Entertaining the use of black magic wasn't an option. Dealing in the dark arts meant selling her soul to the devil himself, and that was courting disaster. She wasn't sure Austin understood that, and she was too tired to explain the delicacies of black magic and the dangers if it turned on you. Even dealing in hexes and curses crossed into the gray area between white and black magic. Besides, she didn't know any spell that would banish Lucifer.

If Lucifer got hold of Austin, that was one more angel descendant gone. One more lost soul to power the devil up for the ultimate battle against Tom and CJ Ryan.

She stopped and grabbed his arm.

"If you go, Lucifer will kill you. You're just another angel offspring for him to use to get stronger. You'll be aiding his cause."

He halted. "I still can't sacrifice Heather."

"But you'd willingly sacrifice me and the rest of the world?"

He closed his eyes and turned away. Paige's chest squeezed. If they didn't make it there in an hour, it was a lost cause anyhow. While she hated herself for thinking that way, she had to admit, that was the loophole.

"You know he gave you an impossible task, right?"

Austin started walking again, and Paige stood in place, trying to figure a way out of this mess without losing her husband or her closest friend. Heather's death warrant had already been signed, but Austin's hadn't. She stared after him, her mind racing over every chance they had. Then a thought occurred to her, and she bolted, catching up to him quickly.

"Are Raphael and Lucifer related?" she asked, trying to remember any Christian lore she could.

"I guess. Why?"

"How?"

"I think they're brothers," he said, glancing at her and slowing his pace.

"We might just have what I need to create a hex that could give us an edge."

"What's that?"

"Angel blood."

Austin halted and stared at her. "You want... my blood?"

"I would only need a little, but yeah. I think I just might be able to create some sort of diversion. But it won't last more than a minute or two, if it works at all."

"What else do you need?"

"I'm not sure. I wish I had a working cell phone," she said.

It was a risky proposition, but one she would gladly try if it meant saving her husband. She could create a spell that would theoretically freeze someone momentarily, but she wasn't sure she could target it the way she would need

to. If things went awry, it would mean the end
for all of them.

Practical Magick
Chapter 10

AUSTIN STOOD IMPATIENTLY NEAR the door of the Whole Foods market while Paige grabbed the items she thought she would need. Her idea was as ludicrous as him barreling into the devil's lair to rescue Heather, but it was the only option. If he walked away without trying, he could never live with himself.

Tom's haunting words kept coming back to him. He was ill-prepared to deal with any confrontations, despite the meager green belt in jujitsu he had achieved since they left York. And now, with a severely compromised arm, he had very little chance of putting up a fight.

He'd never wanted to feel helpless again after what happened in New York, but here he relived that nightmare all over again. Anger burned through his nerves, jolting his heart into a rapid beat. Another glance at the clock and his patience nearly evaporated.

They were still outside the edge of town, but at least now they could make out the strip in the distance. Thankfully, someone had taken pity on them and given them a ride to the Whole Foods market just south of the strip.

Even with the ride, Austin had as much faith in reaching Heather on time as he had in Paige's cockamamie spell, but it was their last hope. However, if they didn't reach the Bellagio in the next half hour, all Paige's preparations would be in vain.

"Paige, you need to move faster," he said under his breath.

She glanced his way. Her eyes were filled with doubt, and he sent a reassuring smile in her direction. She turned back to her task, and with a few spices and a soda in her basket, she headed to the checkout counter.

Austin exhaled a breath. After a few moments, her purchases were bagged, and she headed to where he stood.

"I'm sorry. I wasn't sure which spices were the right ones to do the spell in my head."

"What happens if it's wrong?" he asked and pushed the door open, letting her lead the way. The chill of the desert night gripped them, and the medication meant to last for hours seemed only to be taking the worst of the edge off now.

"It could do the opposite of what the spell intends," she said.

Austin shivered at the thought. If he stepped into the room and froze, he wondered if he would feel the devil yanking his heart from his chest. They started toward the city as Paige handed him a bottle of ginger ale.

"Drink half of that, okay?"

He did as she asked and handed the bottle back to her, letting out a loud burp.

Paige pulled a bay leaf out of the spice container and shoved it into the bottle, muttering some incantation that Austin couldn't make out. She followed by emptying the cinnamon spice into the ginger ale. The soda fizzled but didn't overflow. Black pepper and sea salt followed.

As she emptied the thyme into the bottle, she glanced at him, and they stopped next to a rock wall. She set the bottle on the rocks and took his uninjured hand. Flipping open the small pocketknife she'd bought, she sliced the pad of his middle finger.

"Shit," he hissed, but didn't pull away from her grip.

"The gods have heard my prayer and stand behind me, adding their might to mine. From this point forward, they will allow me to stop time. Time is mine to command until my task is done."

As the drops of Austin's blood hit the soda mixture, it sizzled, and they traded a glance. Paige did the same to her finger and added a drop of her blood as well before capping the bottle. She opened the small plastic first aid container and wrapped the cut on his finger in a band-aid. Before she bandaged her cut, she drew a bloody pentacle on the plastic bottle. As soon as she finished covering her cut, she handed him the potion and dumped all the garbage into a garbage can sitting at the nearest corner. She pulled out a piece of paper and pen from her pocketbook and scribbled words on the sheet before she handed it to him.

Austin held the note, so he caught the streetlight. "Time…"

"Shush, not now," Paige cut him off and hauled her pocketbook over her shoulder. "We need to say that when we get there."

Austin studied the simple words. "This is it?"

"Yes. Sometimes the simple spells are the most powerful," she said and picked up the garment bag the hospital had given them.

Austin studied the sludgy mixture as they began walking towards the strip's bright lights. He glanced at her. "What do I do with this?"

"When we get there, you need to shake it and then throw it into the middle of the room as we say that incantation. If this works, everyone else but us will freeze. That includes Heather, so you may have to haul her over your shoulder to get her out of there." Paige offered him a shrug.

"That might prove to be a little difficult," Austin said and sighed. "But if it's what we have to do, I'll do it. While I'm getting Heather, you need to find her purse, or wallet, or whatever the girl carries her license around in, because we are going directly to the airport. I'm not letting my guard down until we are in York, Maine. Got it?"

Paige slowed down. "York?"

"I need my arm fixed, and then we need to find a place to stay because I'm not sure anywhere else on this planet is as safe as that town is."

"What about our stuff?"

"We'll get it, eventually."

Paige said nothing else, but Austin didn't take it as a sign of unhappiness. He glanced at her as they walked, and her brow was furrowed, her stare cast down to the ground. Her lips moved, and a hush filled the surrounding air. She glanced sideways, catching his eye, but kept on mumbling the strange words.

The strip seemed closer now. He could actually see the Mandalay Bay driveway as they headed north on the boulevard. His legs moved faster, calculating the distance. Twenty more minutes would be enough to cover the mile and a half to their destination, but they would have to haul ass, and even then, they would cut it close.

He wasn't sure if exhaustion was playing tricks on his mind, but the closer they got to the city, the more Paige seemed to shine. It was almost as if the boundless energy of Las Vegas was pooling in the center of her petite being, absorbed through some odd metamorphosis.

The bottle in his hand vibrated, and he glanced down. Mesmerized by the swirling liquid inside, the yank on his shirt pulled his attention just in time for him to avoid a collision with a utility pole.

Paige let out a small laugh and met his gaze before nodding to her left. He turned, taking in the famous Bellagio fountain. Shock skittered through him like an army of red ants. The last hotel he remembered passing was the Mandalay Bay. They traveled a mile and a half in what seemed like a blink.

He glanced at Paige, and the glow was still there, surrounding her like a complex aura.

"It's time," she said, and they crossed the road, heading for the lobby entrance.

His entire body vibrated the closer they got to the building, and by the time they stepped through the doors, his nerves matched the swirl in the bottle he held.

"Do you know what room?"

"Yeah. She's on the sixteenth floor of the south tower. Room 1666." He actually shivered as the words tumbled from his mouth. "It has a view of the fountain," he added as they headed toward the bank of elevators on their left.

They got lucky and stepped into an empty elevator, and Paige pressed the button for the sixteenth floor. As soon as the doors closed, she turned to Austin.

"The minute we step into the room, pitch that thing as close to the middle of the room as you can. I suggest shaking it a little as we walk to the door. And the minute it leaves your hand, recite the spell."

Austin glanced at the paper crumpled around the cap of the bottle and tried to smooth it out to read the words. Retaining the spell seemed almost as impossible as beating Lucifer, but he made himself silently repeat the words.

Time stand still. I order you. No minutes pass until I'm through doing what I have to do. Time stand still, I order you.

The mantra replayed as the floor counter ticked. When the elevator stopped, his mind went blank, and panic filtered into his muscles, locking him in place. Paige took his elbow and gently led him out of the elevator before the doors closed. Her touch restarted his brain, and his lips moved with the silent words.

He glanced at her as they stopped in front of the door. Her eyes held the same fear pummeling his muscles.

"I love you," he said and started shaking the bottle.

"I love you, too," she replied and knocked on the door.

Time slowed to a crawl, and Austin was acutely aware of the pounding of his heart, the adrenaline fueling it with octane, accompanied by the shaking of his breath. The spell looped in his head, and the moment the door swung open, everything stopped.

Austin stared into Hunter's amused eyes, and fury beyond his control filled his already jacked bloodstream.

Before he could react, Paige stepped between them. "He who came unbidden to wreak havoc upon this world, I say enough." Her growling shout yanked his focus away from the bastard hell bent on killing them both.

A wave of light exploded from Paige, knocking Hunter across the room like a rag doll in a hurricane. Without him blocking the door, Austin got a view of the room—of Lucifer holding a knife to Heather's throat. He pitched the bottle in his hand, and his voice bellowed with the same ferocity as Paige's had.

The bottle exploded on impact, and a strange fog rolled across the floor. Paige's voice joined in with his, and he darted towards his friend even as Lucifer started the deadly drag of the blade across her neck. All motion, including the knife biting into her flesh, stopped. Austin's brain calculated her chances of survival as he smacked Lucifer's hand away, sending the knife clattering across the floor. No blood escaped from the shallow wound.

Austin chanced a glare in Lucifer's direction and caught the building rage in his nearly black eyes. Demons flanked the chair like frozen sentries, and Austin focused on Heather. Paige slid next to him, still chanting the spell, and she flipped open the pocketknife, tearing through the bonds holding Heather to the chair.

Austin leaned forward and jammed his shoulder into Heather's stomach before he wrapped his good arm around her waist and hauled her up. He turned in time to see Paige swipe Heather's purse off the desk. The fog surrounding them flowed into the hallway, thickening and dulling sound.

Paige's mouth formed the word *run.*

He followed her fast footsteps down the hall to the elevator bank. She stabbed her finger into the down button. The numbers moved in slow motion and Austin's chest burned from the exertion of holding Heather and the strain of waiting for the damned elevators.

His adrenaline jumped as he glanced the way they came. Shadows crossed the fog, and his gaze darted, looking for a staircase. The moment he spied the exit sign, the elevator doors opened, swallowing a trail of fog along with both Paige and him.

The doors closed, and he shifted, leaning against the wall and getting the full view of the elevator. They were not alone, but the other couple didn't move. Their eyes remained glued to the floor counter, and he couldn't detect even the motion of breathing.

"Did we freeze the entire hotel?" he asked, turning to Paige, who had the same wide-eyed gaze he guessed he sported.

"I don't know. And I'm not sure how long that will hold Lucifer. I don't know about you, but one look at his face scared the crap out of me," she said.

He huffed a laugh. "He was aware of what was happening. I am hoping it holds him long enough for us to be in the air on our way home."

The doors to the lobby opened and they, along with the fog, spilled out, but it seemed lighter than it had in the enclosed space. Movement in the lobby slowed to a crawl, but it didn't freeze. By the time they reached the front door, Heather let out a small moan.

A couple climbed out of a cab, and before they closed the door, Austin slid inside and Paige followed. He dropped Heather onto the seat, and her head landed on Paige's lap.

The driver glanced in the rearview mirror.

"I'm off duty," he said.

"Please, sir, we need to get to the airport as fast as possible," Paige said, her glance bouncing between the front seat and the hotel.

"I'm sorry," the driver stated.

"Drive," Austin growled. He'd had enough crap for the day and getting into an off-service cab would not stop him from getting out of town. "Or your guts will be painting the dashboard."

Paige's head snapped in his direction. "Please, just drive," she whispered.

The driver's gaze jumped from Austin's to hers and back. He put the car in gear and pulled away from the hotel lobby.

Heather's eyes opened the minute they pulled off the property and onto the road. Her breath sucked in and then huffed in almost a pant, and she popped into a sitting position. Austin kept his focus on the driver, even with Heather's wheezing breath and trembling form sitting next to him.

"How?" Her shaking voice finally interrupted the silence.

"I'll explain later. All you need to know is we got you out. But we aren't safe yet," Austin said without looking away from the rearview mirror.

The driver met his gaze, and a crease formed between his eyes.

Heather's arms ensnared Austin in a hug. "Thank you," she said through a sob.

"Don't thank me, thank my wife. She provided the diversion."

Heather's arms retreated, but Austin knew if he lost eye contact with the driver, he would lose his chance of escape. There were more questions in the eyes periodically glancing back at him in the mirror than he had answers for.

"I'm sorry I had to force my hand," Austin said to the driver. "I'm not usually a violent man," he added and gave a sideways glance at both Heather and Paige. "But my friend was in danger, and this is the only way I knew how to get her far away from the bastards that kidnapped her before they figured out she was gone." He met the driver's stare. "You just happened to be at the right place at the right time."

"Is what he said true? Someone kidnapped you?" the driver asked Heather.

She let out a shaky laugh. "I guess you could call it that. They had no intention of letting me leave there alive," she said.

His eyes hardened in a way that made Austin flinch, and then his gaze jumped to Austin's. The cab driver gave him a nod. "Son, you can put your weapon away. This ride's on me."

"Thank you, but I don't really have a gun," Austin said.

The driver raised an eyebrow in his direction and let out a little laugh, but he kept on driving.

Austin relaxed, resting his head on the back of the seat a second before he glanced at Heather and Paige. His gaze dropped to the slow trickle of blood flowing from the cut on Heather's neck. "Do you have that little first aid kit, Paige?"

Paige took the hint and had Heather face her while she put a bandage on the cut.

"Your ex is a twisted fuck," Heather whispered.

Austin chuckled at Heather's choice of words. "You have no idea."

"Oh, yes, I do. He got off on telling me exactly how he was going to kill her," she said, hooking her thumb towards Paige.

The cab pulled to a stop next to the airport departure gates, interrupting the conversation at just the right time. Austin wasn't sure the cab driver would be able to stomach any more of the conversation, especially if Heather started talking about Lucifer himself.

She had been in their hands for twenty-four hours. He knew all too well what kind of damage Hunter could do in that timeframe and highly doubted Lucifer would intervene.

He pulled out his wallet and shuffled a twenty out of the billfold as the girls climbed out onto the curb. The cab driver put his hand up, refusing the money.

"I'm grateful you helped us, even if it was under duress, so please consider this my way of saying thank you."

The driver took the cash, and Austin crawled out the passenger side and stepped onto the curb with the girls.

"What are you two into?" Heather asked after the cab pulled away.

Austin corralled them into the airport, where each of them changed their flights to the one taking off within the next hour. With only their pocketbooks, the bag with Paige's wedding dress, and his tuxedo as carry-on items, they were through the security gates in minutes.

They arrived at the gate just as the beginning boarding call was announced. It wasn't until they'd collapsed in their assigned seats that anyone spoke.

"Seriously, what the hell are you two into?" Heather whispered from the aisle seat.

Austin turned his head towards her. "We aren't *into* anything, Heather."

"Then what the hell was that all about?" she hissed. "And I thought your ex was dead?" she added, glancing at Paige.

"Hunter Garrett died five years ago," Paige said.

"Then who the hell was in that room?"

"The devil and Hunter's ghost," Austin said just loud enough for Heather to pick up. "The same ghost that nearly killed both of us in New York."

"Excuse me?" Heather gasped. "Are you telling me those men weren't real?"

Austin glared at her. "They were very real and very dangerous. I still do not know how we pulled this off. Hell, we still could be gutted by Lucifer, so I'm not letting my guard down until we are somewhere safe."

Paige remained silent between them. Her lips moved in that silent chant he had become accustomed to, and he closed his eyes, leaning his head back against the headrest. Whatever spell she was creating kept them safe, and after the power he witnessed in that hotel room, his doubt of her magic had all but disappeared.

"We'll get you up to speed on exactly what's going on when we get home. Okay? It's complicated, and I'd rather not discuss this in public." He opened his eyes and glanced over Paige's head. Heather met his gaze and nodded.

Paige laced her fingers between his and squeezed as the plane taxied. He squeezed back, keeping his attention out the window as they sped up and lifted off the ground. His arm throbbed, and all he wanted to do was close his eyes and sleep. But the fear that the bottom would drop out on him if he let his guard down kept his eyes open and focused on the dark shadows of the landscape below.

Practical Magick
Chapter 11

THE BUMP OF WHEELS on the ground jerked Austin awake. He blinked and shifted, prompting a sudden dose of pain from his arm. Paige's head rested on his good shoulder, and he shrugged, moving her enough to wake her as well. Heather was already awake, but her eyes reflected the same exhaustion he felt.

Paige let out a small whine and stretched in the seat, reaching her arms over her head and arching her back. Both Austin and Heather looked at her in appreciation and smiled at her lithe form. Austin caught Heather's leer and cleared his throat. Her gaze rose to his, and a flush of red painted her cheeks. She offered him a shrug and looked away.

Happy to be on the ground in New Hampshire, he let her less-than-casual inspection of his wife go.

"Can I bother you two for a ride home? I had gotten a ride to the airport with one of my co-workers," Heather said and sighed as she shuffled through her purse. "And can I use one of your phones? I think mine is still back in the hotel room."

"We need to pick up new ones as well. Ours broke when we jumped out of the limousine," Paige said.

Heather slowed her pace, glancing at the two of them like they had lost their minds.

"Austin, what the hell is going on? Her ex-boyfriend's boss said he needed your blood. Why?"

Austin kept walking, aware of the crowd still around them and the lack of safe ground beneath his feet. "Wait until we get to the car." He pulled Paige along with him, and eventually Heather came back into his peripheral vision. The parking garage level their car was on seemed unusually abandoned, and while Heather continued to shoot questions his way, he ignored her. His concentration was otherwise preoccupied with the alarms raging in his stomach. He lifted his finger to his lips and gave Heather a sideways glance.

That did the trick. Her mouth popped closed, and he almost audibly sighed with relief. Paige slowed her pace, her gaze scanning the lack of movement as well. Eerie silence pressed on them, and her grip on his arm tightened.

"You have our keys?" he asked in barely a whisper.

She nodded and tried not to jangle them as she raised them within sight. A white fog rolled across the concrete towards them, and what walked out of the shadows sent raw, burning fear through him.

Hunter spread his arms and grinned. "You really thought that pathetic spell of yours could stop me?"

"What the fuck?" Heather whispered.

Paige stopped, and so did Austin. She trembled against him, and he wrapped his good arm around her, bringing her closer. Heather stepped nearer as the shadows surrounding them came to life. There had to be at least a dozen beings surrounding them.

The lights started flickering and at the same time, Paige's breathing became ragged.

"Actually, I expected you," Paige said, and Austin snapped his gaze her way. She twirled her finger at the garage surrounding them. "How do you think you got here?"

Hunter's smug smile faltered. Austin couldn't tell if she was bluffing or not, but her trembling had increased.

"You?" Hunter asked.

"Silence!" she bellowed and pulled the pentacle out of her shirt, stepping in front of Austin. "You are grounded to earth that seals and binds. Fire scorches your energy, burning away what used to be. The cruel winds gust, tearing away your mortal form. Water rages, eroding your bonds to your master. The elements are mine to command, and destroy your power they must."

A howling wind ripped through the parking garage, and Austin moved closer to Paige.

"The mother has heard my prayer, and the gods stand behind me, adding their might to mine." Paige's head tilted back, and her arms straightened by her sides with her palms facing

Hunter. "To you, who came unbidden to wreak havoc upon this world, I say: enough!"

The blast that flowed through him pulled the air from his lungs. His gaze jumped to where Hunter's ghost stood, engulfed in what looked like a tornado of fire. Screams pierced the swirling wind, and he covered his right ear with his palm, trying to shield his other with his shoulder. But it wasn't enough to drown out the cries of the dying demons and ghosts surrounding them.

Paige swayed, drawing his attention. Before he could react, Heather stepped in faster, catching Paige as she dropped. Her eyes were half-open and only the whites showed.

Austin grabbed the keys off the ground.

"Can you carry her?" he asked Heather.

She nodded and stood with Paige in her arms.

Circumventing a now blazing Hunter, Austin led Heather to the car and held the back passenger door for his friend. Heather nearly dived into the backseat with Paige, and Austin hustled to the driver's seat. He didn't bother buckling himself in, he just shot through the empty spot adjoining his, away from the nightmare in the garage.

"Is she okay?" he asked, unable to look in the rearview mirror for fear that Hunter or one of the other demon ghosts would look back at him. The garage exit loomed ahead, and he concentrated on getting the hell out of there.

"She's breathing," Heather said, her voice carrying the nearly hysterical quality of someone on the verge of a breakdown. "What the fuck, Austin?"

"Lucifer wants my blood because apparently I'm a descendant of Raphael." He chanced a glance in the mirror now that they were out of the garage, and Heather's blank stare met his. "The archangel," he added when she didn't respond.

They drove in silence. When he veered east onto Route 101 instead of staying on Interstate 93 north, Heather said, "Where are you going?"

"The only safe place I know," he said. "How is Paige?" He caught the shake of Heather's head in the rearview mirror as they passed another streetlight.

"She's pale, and she hasn't come out of it yet."

"Shit," he muttered and pressed harder on the gas pedal.

"She's breathing, Austin. And her pulse is strong enough for me to detect, so I don't think you should panic."

He gave her a quick glance and concentrated on driving. They had less than one hour to their safe haven. Whatever Paige had done in the garage had drained everything out of her, and that worried him. What if it did more than just push her past the point of exhaustion? Just the thought sent a jolt through him, and the car swerved in response.

"Should I be driving?" Heather asked after a moment.

Austin glanced at her in the rearview mirror and shook his head. "I'm okay. The pain is keeping me pretty damned sharp right now."

"If you're a descendant of an archangel, what is Paige?"

"A damned talented wiccan." He stared at the dark road. The streetlights were scarce on this stretch, and all he saw in the backseat was Heather's outline.

"Austin?" Paige's weak voice cut through the dark.

"Yeah, babe?" he answered while his heart rammed in his throat.

"Did I…"

"You stopped them all. God knows how, but you did."

"Are we safe?"

"Not yet. But we're heading that way."

"I don't think I'm capable of doing that again," she mumbled, and her voice trailed off into a fading exhale.

"Oh, shit, she's convulsing!" Heather gasped.

Austin swerved into the breakdown lane and threw the car in park before hitting the overhead lights. "Turn her on her side and hold her head still if you can," he barked as he twisted in the seat to get a view of Paige. Her entire body was rigid, and her eyes had rolled back.

Heather turned her on her side. "What's happening?"

"She's having a seizure," he said, trying to keep his voice calm now that Paige was on her side. The convulsions faded, and thankfully, she didn't vomit. "Grab the tuxedo coat out of the bag on the floor and cover her, okay?"

Heather nodded and followed his direction.

"Just keep her calm. She likes it when I play
with her hair, so try that, and keep her on her
side in case she gets sick."

Heather's chin quivered, and her eyes filled
with tears. In all the years that he'd known her,
he had never seen her cry, but now tears
breached her lashes, slid down her cheeks, and
fell onto Paige's forehead.

"She'll be okay," he said to calm his friend.
"I'm going directly to the hospital when we get to
where we are going. Okay?"

Heather nodded and bit her lip, her hand
tracing Paige's cheek before combing through
Paige's dark locks.

Austin turned, banging his arm on the
steering wheel. He flipped the light off before
Heather had time to see him flinch. His stomach
rolled, but he caught it before it decided to
forcefully expel its contents. He swallowed, took
a deep breath, and pulled back onto the road.
This time, when he pushed the pedal to the
floor, Heather made no comment.

Practical Magick
Chapter 12

AUSTIN PULLED INTO THE York hospital emergency entrance a half hour later with his heartbeat thundering in his ears. Paige hadn't regained consciousness.

"I'll be right back," he said to Heather and climbed out of the car. If he had been anywhere else, he wouldn't have left Paige alone, but the minute they crossed into York, all his anxiety evaporated.

The emergency room was blessedly slow for the middle of the night, and he crossed to the registration desk.

"I need some help to get my wife inside. She had a seizure about half an hour ago and hasn't regained consciousness."

The clerk nodded. "Hey Ron, we need a gurney in the emergency bay!" she yelled over her shoulder.

A moment later, a large orderly came through the doors with a gurney. Austin followed him to the car and helped get her onto the gurney. He

closed the car door, and both he and Heather
followed the orderly inside into an exam room.
The desk clerk came in with a tablet in her
hand.

"Is Dr. Ryan on call?" Austin asked.

The clerk, whose nametag read Kitty, shook
her head. "No, I'm sorry. She usually doesn't
work in the emergency room."

Austin chewed his lip for a moment. "Is there
any way you could get in touch with her for us?
We're friends of the family and would feel a
whole lot better if she knew we were here."

She studied Austin, and her gaze dropped to
his arm before it traveled to Heather and the
patch job Paige had done on her neck. "Why
don't we start with your license and medical
cards, and I'll see what I can do."

Austin pulled out his wallet and flipped it
open. After a failed attempt to get his license
out, he just handed her his wallet. He was just
too damned tired to struggle with it. "It's in
there, along with our medical cards."

Kitty left the room, and Austin crossed to
Paige, giving Heather a tight smile. Worry soured
his growling stomach and he brushed the hair
away from Paige's face. He moved the pads of his
fingers to her throat, searching out her artery to
get a beat on her condition. When they settled
over the carotid on the right side, he closed his
eyes, clenching his teeth at the faint pulse.

"What's wrong?"

He had forgotten Heather was in the room. "I
don't know. Her heartbeat should be stronger
than it is. And I can't exactly explain to the
nurse that my wife spent all her energy to kill a

group of demons and ghosts." He ran his hand through his hair, then slid into the nearest chair. "I don't even have a clue of what to do for her. An IV? Hydrate her? I don't know."

"What about you? Are you okay?"

"I don't know. My arm will need to be looked at. They only packed it with eight hours' worth of antibiotics."

Her eyebrows rose.

"Compound fracture," he said to her unasked question. "You should have that cut looked at, too," he added, pointing to the bandage on her neck.

She gave a little laugh. "Aren't we the lovely trio? You, with your heritage and broken arm. Her, with her freaky magic and mystery coma. And me, with a surface wound that was meant to be a killing blow."

Her eyes filled with tears, and for the first time, he studied her. Her hands shook as she tried to steady them, and he left Paige's side. Stepping in front of where Heather sat, he crouched in front of her.

"I'm sorry you got caught in the middle of this," he said.

"I wish I really understood what *this* is," she said, adding finger quotes around the word this.

He gave her a hug, and she reluctantly wrapped her arms around him, accepting his comfort. "It's as fucked up as you think it is. Things I never entertained to be real are." He pulled away and wiped the tears from her cheeks. "I thought it was just ghosts, and when the Ryans told me what I was, and who was hunting people like me, I wrote them off as not having a full deck." He gave her a shrug. "Even after our experiences with Hunter, I still had that grain of doubt. Paige believed them, and I think she's been practicing. Powering up, so to speak."

"She freaked me out just as much as seeing her ex in the garage." Heather let out a strained laugh.

"Yeah, well, I've been freaked out ever since I met Paige." He grinned. "And not just for the obvious reasons." He squeezed Heather's hands and stood. "I'm trusting you with information that can't go anywhere. I'm not the only angel descendent. The Ryans are as well, and they seemed to have gotten an extra dose of angel magic."

"What do you mean by that?" she asked and sniffled, wiping the tears from her face.

"Let's just leave it at they are special, and that's why both Paige and I feel safe in this town."

Austin glanced over at his unconscious wife and then looked up at the clock. A little over a half hour had passed since the clerk brought them into the exam room. Too much time had passed, in his experience. Usually, a nurse would have at least checked in by this time.

"I think I'm going to see what's taking so long," he said and turned towards the door. Before he could reach for the knob, the door swung open, and an exhausted-looking woman who looked vaguely familiar stood on the other side of the door. Right behind her stood a face much more recognizable, and from Heather's gasp, she recognized him as well. CJ Ryan smiled in response.

"I didn't mean to get you out of bed," Austin said, glancing between Dr. Ryan and her husband.

"Yeah, well, we figured if one or both of you were here, there was a good chance you both would be banged all to hell. Especially after Bridget's call the other night," CJ said and looked past Austin to where Paige was stretched out on the exam table.

Dr. Ryan closed the door and waved at Austin's cast. "How bad is your arm?"

Austin glanced around for the garment bag and sighed. It was still in the car in the loading bay, if it hadn't been towed yet. "Compound fracture. I would venture to guess the antibiotic beads they put in the wound are probably all dissolved by now."

She gave a curt nod and lifted Paige's wrist. "What happened to Paige?"

"She did a spell that toasted Hunter and some demons and then passed out. She only regained consciousness for a few minutes in the car and then had a seizure."

Both CJ and the doctor stared at Austin.

"I thought we got rid of Hunter in New York," CJ said.

"Apparently, if you go to hell, Lucifer can resurrect you if he wants to."

Their eyebrows arched.

"You went against Lucifer, and all you got was a broken arm?" CJ asked.

Austin laughed. "I broke my arm jumping from a moving limousine," he said and snapped his fingers. "Which reminds me, Paige was stung by a scorpion and given antivenin at the hospital in Las Vegas. Could this be some sort of reaction?" He waited for a response and when none came, he continued, "We would have flown out earlier, but when I called Heather for a lift to the airport, Lucifer had her."

Now both gazes moved from his face to Heather's.

"He used her to lure me back to the hotel. I guess he's got to be pretty hard up for angel blood," Austin added.

CJ and Dr. Ryan let out identical, high-pitched laughs.

"He's been slaughtering our bloodlines. Since Tom went to close the portals, it's gotten worse," CJ said. "How the hell did you get her out of there alive?"

Austin pointed to Paige. "A time freeze spell."

"That actually worked?" Dr. Ryan asked.

"Yeah. It was pretty freaky."

"Is that why I don't remember anything?" Heather asked.

"Probably," Austin said. "I haven't eaten anything of substance since breakfast the day we flew out here. Do you think you can find the cafeteria and grab me a sandwich, Heather?" He caught CJ's twitch of a smile at his subterfuge to get Heather out of the room.

"I can show you where the cafeteria is," CJ said.

Heather's eyes nearly popped out of her head at the invitation from the rockstar. "Really?" she whispered. She stood on shaky legs and stepped out in the hall, her eyes glued to CJ's profile.

CJ turned back to Austin, gave him a wink, and closed the door behind them.

"I guess my wife isn't the only one to have the fan-girl thing going on," Austin said to Dr. Ryan.

She glanced at the door, and a small smile formed on her lips. "Your friend usually isn't interested in men," she said and sighed. "What exactly are you hoping for here?"

Austin looked at the floor, and heat filled his cheeks. He just assumed she would be more than willing to heal them with the power she held. As a matter of fact, he thought he wouldn't even need to ask. Suddenly, he understood what kind of nightmare she would be living if everyone knew what she was capable of. He forced himself to meet her gaze, and he pulled in a sharp inhale at the scrutiny with which she studied him.

"I guess I made an assumption," he said, feeling much smaller than the six-foot frame he sported.

She rolled her eyes and shook her head. "You assumed I'd fix both of you just because you came?"

"I did, and I apologize for my brazen assumption. However, if you aren't willing to use whatever magic you have, then I need your medical expertise. I need Paige assessed, and she probably needs hydration at the very minimum. She's only had a protein bar during the last forty-eight hours, and the amount of energy she expended casting that spell was beyond any human capabilities I've ever seen. It must have tapped everything she had to cause the seizure and drop her into what I'm assuming is a coma. As far as I'm concerned, I need surgery to fix my arm," he said, relying on everything he learned in medical school, as well as the advice of the doctor in Las Vegas. "Can you help us?"

She huffed and opened Paige's eyelids, flashing her light to get a reaction. "Let's get her hooked up to an IV and then we can discuss options."

Austin gave her a nod, despite the disappointment scratching under his skin. He stepped back to let her take over.

"You just finished medical school. Consider this the beginning of your residency. I expect you to help," she said, shocking him.

"That's going to be a little difficult, don't you think?" he said, raising the cast and wincing.

She raised an eyebrow. "When a patient needs you, you suck it up," she said, and suddenly Austin felt like he had been transported back into medical school. "You'll find everything we need in the drawers behind you."

Austin turned and searched through the drawers, pulling out gloves, a catheter, sterile gauze and alcohol pads, along with a bag of saline. He placed the items on the tray in the corner and rolled it across the room to Dr. Ryan's side.

"I got you everything you need, but I don't have the dexterity to actually insert the catheter," he said as he locked the tray in place.

The minute he stopped next to her, she leaned over and planted a kiss on the shoulder of his injured arm. The pain was immediate, and he nearly dropped to his knees. He stumbled back, falling into the seat behind him.

"Fuck," he whispered, leaning over in a ball and holding his arm to his chest. It burned like he had stepped into a flamethrower.

"By the way, congratulations on both the degree and the wedding," she said in a softer tone.

He glanced up through a sheen of tears, forcing himself to breathe. His brain had a hard time wrapping around what she was doing, but then it became clear when she hung the IV line on the t-bar over the bed and inserted the end into the catheter she had placed in Paige's arm.

"Your wife will be fine." She leaned over and planted a kiss on Paige's forehead before turning to him. "Never assume that I'm willing or even capable of making whatever ails you go away, understand?" she added, sending a glare his way.

"Why the IV?" he choked out, staring as sparkles of light danced around Paige and settled into her skin.

"She's dehydrated. So are you. But you seem to be handling it better than she is." She retrieved an identical set of items from the drawers, hung the second bag on the t-bar, and pointed to the spot next to the bed. "Bring your chair over here, please."

It wasn't framed as a request, and he pushed the chair, inch by inch, to the spot she pointed to, because he wasn't sure he could stand with the agony writhing in his bones. The fact he was still conscious was a marvel.

Austin didn't even feel the needle going in, but when the cool liquid slid into his veins, he shivered. He met her stare. "Thank you."

Dr. Ryan pulled up the small rolling chair and parked in front of him. "There are two reasons I helped you. First, my husband said I should. I don't always listen to Chris, but he said you're one of us, and our numbers are dwindling faster than either of us cares to admit. Neither Chris nor I really understand what that means. Which brings me to the second reason. Your wife seems to have some of the same skills my sister-in-law had, and honestly, it's saved my life a couple of times. It wouldn't hurt to have a witch on our side when Lucifer decides to come for us."

"She's a wiccan," Austin said through chattering teeth.

Dr. Ryan nodded and crossed to the door. "Can someone grab me a couple of warm blankets?" she called into the hallway. Within a blink, the orderly who had helped bring Paige in appeared with two blankets. Dr. Ryan took one and then pointed the orderly toward Paige.

She wrapped the warm blanket around Austin's shoulders, and the heat from the fabric saturated through him, counteracting the cold saline mixing in his veins. As soon as the orderly left the room, Dr. Ryan crossed to the cabinet, pulled out a cast saw, rolled the table in front of the chair, and patted the metal.

His entire arm throbbed, but he raised it, laying it on the table as she instructed. She started cutting through the fiberglass.

"You said Tom was closing the portals?" Austin asked, while the fog of pain slowly abated.

She nodded as she turned off the saw and set it on the counter behind her.

"Did Hannah go with him?" he asked. He couldn't conceive of bringing a child along on such a dangerous task.

She stopped and stared at him, her eyes wide, and the sudden sheen of tears covering her pretty calico eyes knotted his stomach.

"Hannah passed away a few years ago, right before Tom left."

He closed his eyes and leaned his head back against the wall. There wasn't anything he could say to alleviate the awkwardness that now persisted between them.

"I'm sorry," he said when the fabric scissors slid onto his skin. He opened his eyes and concentrated on her cutting off the fabric wrap that had been under the cast.

She ripped the tape that had covered his wound, revealing nothing but unblemished skin. He flexed his fist and opened it before he met her gaze.

"I'm not sure I could keep that kind of gift under wraps," he said.

"I'm not God. I do the best I can with my medical skills and rarely create a miracle. It's hard to know who should be saved or not, and if I save someone, I always wonder if I've interfered with the grand plan and altered all our fates."

He slowly leaned back in the seat, grasping the magnitude of her powers. While he initially had seen them as a gift, they could soon become a burden, a curse of epic proportion.

"Believe me, when I first got this, I saw all the possibilities you see, and then reality slammed home." She shrugged. "If I shared this with the world, I would be hunted by more than just mankind. And who knows? I could end up imprisoned by some ungodly entity and only allowed to help those whom they deemed worthy."

"You would never know peace," Austin said, and she nodded.

"I have made the choice to use it, but too many miracles in one place, related to one doctor, raises eyebrows."

"I'm sorry," he whispered.

"This isn't a miracle." She rolled her eyes at him. "It's just a little immune boost," she added, and for the first time since she came in, her lips actually toyed with a smile. "So, just relax and stop feeling like a shit-heel."

Practical Magick
Chapter 13

PAIGE MOANED AND SHIVERED as the cold penetrated every cell. Her eyes flew open, and a white ceiling filled her view. Panic gripped her, and she turned her head to the left. When she gazed at an empty hospital room, she whipped her head in the other direction, and all her angst disappeared.

Austin's head leaned against the wall, and his mouth had fallen open. A blanket hung precariously over one shoulder, and a soft snore filled the room. A tube ran from his arm to nearly empty matching IV bags.

She relaxed back onto the hospital bed. "Austin?" she whispered.

He jerked with a start, his eyes darting around the room before they landed on her. Then he smiled, slid the chair closer, and leaned on the bed with both arms. "Hey," he whispered.

She reached for his arm, pulling it closer as she sat up. There wasn't a scratch on it.

"Either we died, and this is heaven, or we're in York," she said.

"Who said York couldn't be heaven?" he asked and squeezed her hand.

She glanced up at the bags, pointing.

"We were both dehydrated. Dr. Ryan thought we needed it, and I'm thinking she was right, because I feel one hundred percent better."

"And Heather?" Paige looked around again, just to make sure she hadn't missed their friend.

"I thought she should have those cuts looked at," he said. "Besides, I'm not sure how to explain my lack of injury." He lifted his healed arm and shrugged.

"After everything else she's seen today, do you think it matters?"

He let out a huff of a laugh. "You're probably right. Besides, she's too busy drooling over CJ Ryan." He rolled his eyes.

Her heart skipped a beat. "He's here?"

Austin raised an eyebrow at her. "Really?"

Heat filled her face, and she looked down so her hair covered her view. "Sorry, honey, but his voice is like a myriad of angels." She shrugged.

He pushed the hair away, catching her gaze. "I guess, since you saved all our asses, I should give you a pass," he said, and his dimples played hide-and-seek before they finally formed with a genuine smile. "How are you feeling?"

"Okay. I'm just a little hungry."

"Heather brought some food earlier, but I kind of scarfed it all down." His cheeks turned red with the admission. "And CJ offered Tom's house if we wanted it. He said he'd figure out the rent once he got a message through to his brother."

Paige stared at him. "Just how long have I been out?"

"Only a couple of hours, but as soon as Heather came back, I asked about a place to stay. I'm not all that gung ho about going back to Hanover, but if you'd like to, we can."

"What about your residency?" While she wanted nothing more than to stay in this safe haven, she couldn't let him give up his dream of becoming a doctor.

"Dr. Ryan said she'd pull some strings and see if she can get me into the program up in Portland through Maine Medical Center and Tufts University." He chewed on his bottom lip like he wasn't sure of the decision.

"Is this what you want?"

He laughed and leaned back in the chair. "I want to be safe." He glanced at the door before meeting her gaze. "That's all I want. For both of us to be safe."

"Okay," she said. "As long as you can transfer your residency." She could find a job anywhere, and if Dr. Ryan could pull the strings to make it happen, then it all would work out.

He studied her. "How the hell did you pull off that spell?"

She sighed and shrugged. "I gave it everything I had and tried to absorb as much energy as I could. I had a feeling we were in for some catastrophe when we got on the ground, especially after the glare Lucifer gave us. He wasn't going to let us get away with spoiling his plans if he could help it, but I don't think he knew what I was capable of."

"I think you got rid of Hunter this time."

"I wouldn't bet my life on that right now." She turned away, glancing out the window and wondering if the magic she launched really was strong enough to protect them from Hunter and his wrath. After all, the devil resurrected him once. Who was to say he wouldn't do it again?

"I should probably book us a hotel room tonight," he said, and yawned. "We can head back home tomorrow and figure out moving arrangements."

"I just want a shower and some clean clothes."

The door swung open, and Heather stepped in, followed by Dr. Ryan.

"I see the patient is finally awake," she said, glancing at the chart in her hand before she looked up at Paige with a smile. "Your friend here needed a couple of stitches, but other than that, she's good to go."

"I'm feeling much better now," Paige said. "I didn't realize dehydration could cause such issues."

"As I told your husband, some people react better to dehydration than others, so I'd suggest you monitor that for future reference."

"Thank you for coming in the middle of the night. We really appreciate it," Austin said.

"Yes, you certainly didn't need to come, but it means a lot to both of us," Paige said.

"Anytime," Dr. Ryan said and focused on Austin. "Did you want me to make that call?"

"Let me send my application in first," Austin said. "Besides, we might have a little time before the shit hits the fan, right?"

Paige's attention jumped to Austin, and she huffed. Any distance from York was a gamble. Even Austin going to Portland for school was a risk, but at least she could set a protection spell on the car and wherever they ended up living.

She wasn't sure their place near Dartmouth was still protected, either. Hunter knew where Austin lived. He had been there, and now that he was flesh and bone and not just a spirit, she wasn't at all sure that what she had in place would stop him. The devil made him whole once. Who was to say he wouldn't resurrect and send the fiend after them again? Just the thought of leaving the haven of York without the Ryans' protection filled Paige with dread.

"Honestly, I'm not sure I'd take the gamble," Dr. Ryan said to Austin. "I think your wife may be the more practical one right now."

The minute the doctor's gaze locked with Paige's, she felt like Dr. Ryan could see right into the depths of her soul. It wasn't pleasant to think someone could see all that you were, but this woman could, and it rendered Paige silent.

"So, you're suggesting we just up and leave everything behind?" Austin asked, looking between Paige and Dr. Ryan.

"I'm suggesting you weigh the options— together—and make a decision. If you've pissed off Lucifer, he's not one to wait on enacting his vengeance."

"If they want to get their stuff, I'll take a ride with them," CJ Ryan said from the open doorway.

Dr. Ryan spun on her heels and sent him a glare.

"That's not necessary," Paige said, interrupting what looked like a primer for an argument.

"We could always do that time freeze thing and pack up a moving truck," Austin joked.

Paige glanced at him and chewed the inside of her lip, contemplating his idea. It might be worth trying, and it wouldn't drain her the way the water, wind, and fire spell did.

Heather stepped into the room and stared at CJ. "Did I hear you might be escorting us home?"

Paige let out a laugh at their friend's brazen study of him. It was like he'd suddenly made her straight. When Heather's gaze jumped to Dr. Ryan, she had the same level of hunger in her gaze that she had looking at CJ, and Paige guessed she was plotting ways to get the three of them in some sort of compromising position.

Paige traded a barely concealed smile with Austin.

"I think Paige is right. We'll be just fine," he said, and Paige wondered if it was his valiant attempt to avoid subjecting either of the Ryans to Heather's twisted desires.

"CJ made reservations for you at The York Harbor Inn, so you two can get some rest," Dr. Ryan said to Paige and Austin and then turned towards Heather. "There's a room there for you as well," she added, and Paige noted the hint of blush building in the doctor's cheeks. "I'll have you two out of here in a few minutes."

The doctor and CJ stepped out of the room, but the hushed voices drifted in from the hallway. The tone was not happy, and Paige exchanged a glance with Austin before they both focused on Heather.

"You certainly know how to clear a room," Austin said and crossed his arms.

A nurse knocked on the door before Heather could come back with some crude response. "Hi, I'm Lydia. Dr. Ryan said you two should be all set." She headed to Austin's side, where she undid the IV tube, removed the catheter, and replaced it with a band-aid. She moved to Paige next, giving her a warm smile. "I heard you had quite the desert adventure."

Shock skittered over Paige, and she recoiled.

"Your friend said you two got lost in the desert on your wedding night." She nodded towards Heather as she removed the catheter from her hand and covered the entry point with a band-aid.

Paige let out a laugh. "Yeah, it wasn't quite what we had planned."

Heather just grinned, like she had added a lot of juicy details to the story she'd spun.

"Well, I think the accommodations the Ryans got you might make up for it," she said, and turned to leave. "Take your time. Your release papers are already at the front desk."

"Thank you," Austin said.

Austin came to the side of the bed and took Paige's hand, helping her out before he pulled her into his arms. He held her longer than normal, and when she pulled away, she caught the sheen in his eyes, as if all the events of the last forty-eight hours had just hit him. She had yet to feel the full force of the impact. He trembled, and she pressed her lips to his, hoping the touch would steady him.

"I love you," he whispered.

"You can get all sappy and shit at the hotel," Heather said, interrupting their moment.

Paige caught the spark in Austin's eyes just under the unshed tears, and he smiled at her before taking a breath and collecting himself.

"Let's go get some rest," he said and took her hand.

"That seems like the best plan I've heard all day," Paige said.

They headed out of the hospital room. Austin thanked the desk clerk for calling the Ryans for him, and they all signed their release papers.

"Oh, wait," the clerk said, as they turned away. She held out a set of keys. "We moved the car. If you turn right when you leave, you'll see it in a parking spot straight ahead."

"Thanks," Austin said and took the keys.

Practical Magick
Chapter 14

THEY SAID GOODNIGHT TO Heather in the lobby and headed to the room that had been reserved for them. Austin opened the door and escorted Paige inside. The nurse hadn't been kidding when she said it would make up for the desert. The suite had a large Jacuzzi tub overlooking a view of the harbor. Bathrobes and slippers were set up on the end of the bed, and a bottle of champagne and chocolate-covered strawberries sat on a plate along with a single rose.

Paige stripped her clothes right where she stood and stepped to the side of the tub, turning on the faucet. Austin bypassed the champagne and grabbed the tray of strawberries, bringing them to where Paige stood waiting for the water to heat. She looked at the offering and then up at him with a tired smile.

"I'm not sure which I want first. Food or a bath."

"Why not both?" He took one strawberry off the plate and held it out for her. She bit into it and closed her eyes, murmuring her approval. Just her eyes at half-mast and the red strawberry juice on her lips were enough to light his fire. He set the platter down on the counter and took her face between his hands, placing another kiss on her supple lips.

He worked on taking his clothing off as well and had to break the lingering kiss to pull the hospital scrub top off. Paige took a moment to pour some exotic oils into the water. A pleasant lavender scent drifted from the bath, and they both stepped into the water. She settled between his legs, leaning her back against him, and reached out to turn the jets on low.

The pulse on his lower back was as pleasant as her nuzzling his lap, and he was torn between settling into a relaxing spa experience or taking advantage of the moment and making love to his wife. She melted into him with a satisfied sigh, and her lack of any sexual advances told him it was the spa experience tonight. With the choice made, he turned the jets on a higher setting and let the pulse of the water massage his muscles. He fed her strawberries between wiping the dust and grime from her shoulders and washing her hair.

The water was a filthy gray when they finally stepped out.

"I think we should probably rinse off in the shower," Paige said and took his hand.

Austin let her lead him into the bathroom, and they stepped in the shower where she returned the favor, soaping him up as tenderly

as he had cleaned her in the tub. He closed his
eyes, letting out a soft groan of contentment.
She lingered on his cock, coaxing it with long
slow strokes of her soapy hands, and he opened
his eyes, meeting her relaxed gaze.

Her hint of a smile shot a dose of adrenaline
through him, enough to kick start his energy
reserves, and he pulled her into his arms,
planting a kiss that communicated everything in
his soul. Paige responded to his touch like a
blooming flower reaches for the sun.

He pushed her against the back wall of the
shower stall, picked her up, and wrapped her
legs around his waist. The kiss turned almost
feral in its intensity, and he slipped inside her
with all the impatience of a teenager. Her nails
dug into his shoulders, and they both moaned at
the connection.

Austin plunged his full length inside her, and
she arched, squeezing her legs around him. They
moved in frantic thrusts, creating such friction
between them that the water seemed to steam
on contact with their skin. The thought of
moving this to the bed crossed his mind, but the
need to make love to her, to connect,
overwhelmed him and kept his hips moving with
such bravado that she gasped each time he filled
her.

The clean wetness of her kept him pumping,
his hands gripping her ass like this was the end
of their time together instead of the beginning.
The kiss transcended, taking him to a different
level of awareness. Her pants mingled with his
own, and he finally pulled away from her mouth
to stare into her blue eyes. Strands of wet hair

were pasted to her cheeks, and the sexy moan that escaped her supple lips made his muscles clench in anticipation of her climax. He held onto his own, wanting her to come first, but her stunning beauty just about undid him.

"Oh. My. God," she nearly shouted. Then her muscles clenched, and her eyes rolled back with the force of her orgasm, clenching her pussy around him, and bringing him sailing over the edge.

He pulled her close, squeezing his eyes at the blinding release, groaning her name under the warm spray of the shower. His legs trembled with the weight, and he pressed his forehead against the wall, unwilling to let her go.

"I love you, Paige," he whispered.

"I love you, too," she answered in that breathless quality that made his mind stall.

He finally let her slide to her feet and stepped back under the water, cradling her against his chest. This complete and overwhelming connection with her was one he never wanted to go without. After a few minutes of contentment just standing under the hot spray, he released her and shut the water off.

"I don't know whether to be sorry for dragging you to Las Vegas or not," he said, and offered her one of the plush towels with a smile. "If I hadn't, you wouldn't be my wife, and I'm not at all sorry for that."

"The wedding was beautiful," she said, cupping his cheek before hiding her voluptuous body with the towel. "I think we both had hopes of what our wedding night would be like, but unfortunately, none of it happened. But I wouldn't trade our wedding itself for anything. You planned it perfectly, right down to the location and having Heather there. I couldn't have asked for a more perfect place to say our vows."

He leaned over and captured a kiss. "No regrets?"

"No. But I'm curious. What else did you have planned for us out there?"

He smiled. "Horseback riding, a hot-air balloon ride, a desert camping trip, stuff like that. I also had a nice dinner and Cirque du Soleil tickets planned."

"Seems we had our desert experience." She yawned.

"Yeah, not the experience I planned, though." He dried off, led her into the bedroom, and crawled under the covers to spoon her. Austin wrapped his arms around her, pulling her closer as he nuzzled her neck.

"If you want to stay here, we will," he whispered in her ear.

She squeezed him tighter and turned enough to catch a kiss. "Thank you," she said in her sleepy voice and shifted closer.

Her breathing transitioned into a soft snore, and he kissed her shoulder before drifting off to sleep with her body wrapped in his.

Practical Magick
Chapter 15

AUSTIN STOOD ON THE deck of Tom Ryan's house, overlooking the ocean, while Paige directed the moving company. Heather had taken CJ up on his offer for a town car ride home the next day, but Austin had pulled her aside before she left to ask her to find a moving company that would not only pack everything in their apartment and haul it to York but also bring Paige's car. It took her a few days, but she came through.

They went from the honeymoon suite at the York Harbor Inn to an air mattress on the floor of the master bedroom in Tom Ryan's house. CJ hadn't been kidding about letting them rent this place, and it was everything both Paige and he had dreamed of in a home.

"He really said we could rent to own?" Austin asked CJ.

"Yes," CJ said, and pulled out the paperwork. "I've got the terms right here. Take your time. If you want to hire a lawyer to look them over, that is always smart, but it's a damned good deal."

Austin took a cursory glance at the document, and his gaze zeroed in on the closing price for the home. "This has to be a mistake," he said, pointing at the ridiculously low figure. "He is selling this to us for two hundred thousand dollars? Isn't this worth millions?" He shuffled through the papers again. "And there's no interest factored into the payment schedule."

"Those were the terms my brother asked for," CJ said with a shrug.

Austin glanced out at the small yard leading to the bluff over-looking the Atlantic Ocean. Then he turned back to CJ, still not believing what was in the papers. "Is this a joke?"

CJ shook his head. "No. Tom figures you will have enough to pay in medical school bills, and you probably could use the break, especially with how expensive houses in York are. He isn't planning on coming home anytime soon, either, so he thinks you'd be the perfect couple to live happily ever after here."

"I'm not a charity case," Austin said, feeling more of that than anything else at the moment.

"Never said you were. Tom doesn't need the money, Austin. We're rich on an absolutely obscene level, so if I were you, I'd take the deal."

Austin folded the papers and hesitated, glancing at the house again. Paige loved the place, but he didn't feel right about getting it for a song.

"Look, it's a deal because he can do that for the two of you. He said if you balked, I should tell you to consider it a wedding gift," CJ said.

Austin rolled his eyes, torn between wanting the place and his pride. "I feel like I'm going to owe your family for eternity. First your wife actually gets me transferred to the Tuft's program, and now this?" He shook his head, waving at the house. "How am I ever going to pay you back?"

CJ smiled. "By keeping the bloodline going."

Austin glanced at Paige through the glass. "Once it's safe to have kids, I can do that."

CJ's smile faded, and he gave a nod. "Welcome to York," he said and took his leave.

Austin glanced at the papers again before stepping inside the house. He crossed to Paige just as the last box was brought inside, and she gave a tip to the movers before seeing them out.

"What did CJ want?"

"Rental agreement," he said, holding the papers out to her.

As she scanned the documents, her cheeks turned the rosy color of excitement.

"Is this for real?" she asked, and Austin smiled. "Seriously?"

"Yeah, babe, this is ours in ten years, based on the payments outlined in the back. They are a little more than the rent we paid in Hanover, but I think we can do it," he said.

Paige launched into his arms, and he couldn't help but grin.

Austin would do anything to keep Paige safe, and if she was happy as well, that just made the choice to move to York seem eons better than any alternative out there. He was finally seeing the dark clouds that had hovered over their future thin down to the point the sun just might shine through.

"I love you, girl, but we have some serious unpacking to do, and then I suggest we christen every room in the house. What do you say?"

She grinned and whispered in that sexy, breathlessly husky voice of hers, "Why wait to unpack?"

The End

If you enjoyed this book, please consider leaving a review!

ABOUT J.E. TAYLOR

J.E. Taylor is a USA Today bestselling author, a publisher, an editor, a manuscript formatter, a mother, a wife, a business analyst, and a Supernatural fangirl. Not necessarily in that order. She first sat down to seriously write in February of 2007 after her daughter asked:

"Mom, if you could do anything, what would you do?"
From that moment on, she hasn't looked back.

Besides being co-owner of Novel Concept Publishing, Ms. Taylor also moonlights as a Senior Editor of Allegory E-zine, an online venue for Science Fiction, Fantasy and Horror, and co-host of the popular YouTube talk show Spilling Ink.

She lives in New Hampshire with her husband and during the summer months enjoys her weekends on the shore in southern Maine.

Visit her at www.jetaylor75.com to check out her other titles and sign up for her newsletter for early previews of her upcoming books, release announcements, and special opportunities for free swag!